SEDITION

ROAD TO THE BREAKING
BOOK 3

CHRIS BENNETT

Sedition is a work of historical fiction. Apart from well-documented actual people, events, and places that figure in the narrative, all names, characters, places, and incidents are the products of the author's imagination, or are used fictitiously. Any resemblance to current events, places, or living persons, is entirely coincidental.

Sedition

ISBN: 978-1-7331079-7-6 (Trade Paperback)
ISBN: 978-1-7331079-8-3 (eBook)

Publisher's Cataloging-In-Publication Data
(Prepared by The Donohue Group, Inc.)

Names: Bennett, Chris (Chris Arthur), 1959- author.
Title: Sedition / Chris Bennett.
Description: [North Bend, Washington] : [CPB Publishing, LLC], [2021] | Series: Road to the breaking ; book 3
Identifiers: ISBN 9781733107976 (trade paperback) | ISBN 9781733107983 (ebook)
Subjects: LCSH: United States. Army--Officers--History--19th century--Fiction. | United States--History--Civil War, 1861-1865--Fiction. | Sedition--Virginia--Fiction. | Underground Railroad--Fiction. | Man-woman relationships--Fiction. | LCGFT: Historical fiction.
Classification: LCC PS3602.E66446 S44 2021 (print) | LCC PS3602.E66446 (ebook) | DDC 813/.6--dc23

To sign up for a
no-spam newsletter
about
Road to the Breaking
and
exclusive free bonus material
see details at the end of this book.

Sedition [si-dish-uhn] noun:
1. Incitement of discontent or rebellion against a government, 2. any action, especially in speech or writing, promoting such discontent or rebellion, 3. rebellious disorder.

DEDICATION

To
my sister
Leslie (Bennett) Johns,
Nathan Chambers'
biggest fan!

Contents

"All is not as it seems.
Trust not your eyes,
but rather your heart."

– Evelyn Hanson

Chapter 1. Righteous Revelations

"We wish peace,
but we wish the peace of justice,
the peace of righteousness.
We wish it because we think it is right
and not because we are afraid."
– Theodore Roosevelt

Wednesday August 15, 1860 - Greenbrier County, Virginia:

It was getting late, nearly time to turn in for bed, and the regular monthly meeting was winding down. The dimly lit cabin hosted the Elders of Mountain Meadows Farm. The group had been meeting unbeknownst to the white masters at least since Old Toby was a boy, and likely longer. Of course, he wasn't a member then, and at the time was only vaguely aware there was such a thing.

In the meeting he went by his African name, Ganda, as was the custom. The other four members, likewise, addressed each other as Mimba, whose slave name was Peggy, Mussu (Titus), Camba (Naomie), and Juba (Betsy).

As usual, they'd had little to talk about this evening. They had briefly discussed the amazing events surrounding the big wedding, but since there was nothing to do or decide concerning it, that discussion quickly died out. Over the years they had met to discuss what to do about the latest severe beating—usually nothing—or to smuggle out a runaway from some other farm— this happened once every few years or so. Otherwise, it was more of a formality; a tradition kept alive to give the slaves on the farm a sense someone was at least attempting to look out for their interests, as futile as that might be.

Ganda was ready to start the process of ending the meeting when the door opened unexpectedly. Everyone froze.

They'd always feared the white overseers might discover the meeting and break in on it. So they had practiced — *ad nauseam* — what to do and say in such an event.

But they immediately relaxed. The person in the doorway was female and had a dark face, though they couldn't make out who she was in the dim light.

"We ain't yet finished our meeting," Ganda scolded, "please come back in about … oh, a half hour or so …"

They held the meeting in a different cabin each time, and they had a regular system in place to tell the normal cabin residents when the proceedings were over. But, like with anything else, there were always those who hadn't paid attention. So it was not unheard of for people to return to their cabins early and disrupt the meeting.

It surprised Ganda that the intruder didn't immediately apologize and retreat from the room. Instead, the woman came in, removed the rough shawl wrapped around her neck and stepped up to the table.

Ganda suppressed a gasp of surprise. She was the last person he expected to see here.

"Megs! What're you doing here?"

"You're not welcome here. Get yourself outta this place 'fore we throws you out!" Mimba hissed.

But Megs seemed undeterred. "My name is 'Odah.' And though I ain't much strong, I'll fight with all my strength anyone who tries to make me leave 'fore I've had my say." She scowled at those seated.

Her statement was so shocking and unexpected, none of them could think of how to answer it.

"I know the things y'all say 'bout us slaves that works the house. You call us 'house whores,' or 'master's pets,' or 'slavers' spies,' or … well, a whole lot o' other unkind things I don't care to repeat. I been putting up with such lies and nonsense for more'n forty years now, and ain't once complained. But *today* I'll have my say … and you'll listen, and then … well, then we'll see what happens."

2

Ganda looked around at the others. No one seemed to know what to do. So he looked back at Megs and said, "Well … all right, go ahead'n have your say."

She grabbed an extra chair, pulled it up close to the table, and sat.

"I came to this farm when I was just a teary-eyed tot, chained by the ankle in a slaver's wagon. I was terrible sad and afraid, and missing my Momma and Daddy in a painful, aching sort o' way. But the women in the cabins took me in and comforted me and treated me like one o' their own children. So I stopped crying and moping and started helping fix the meals and take care o' the babies as I'd done back at the other farm. But one day an overseer comes into the cabin, looks around, grabs me by the arm, and takes me up to the Big House. The head maid takes one look at me and says, 'She'll do—just leave her off here, and I'll start teaching her up.' That night they set me up a pallet of straw covered by a wool blanket in a small storage room back o' the kitchen, with three other girls. I never went back to the cabins. They taught me to make a bed, and wash laundry, and do a hundred other things that needs doing 'round the Big House. I worked hard, and did what I was told, as my Momma had taught me to do.

"But one day, a few weeks after I moved to the Big House, they sent me and two others outside to fetch something. I saw a couple of the women from the cabins—the same who'd comforted me when I was alone and afraid. And you know what them, kindly, and righteous outside the Big House slaves said to me? *Nothin'!* Just exactly *nothin'!* They wouldn't say hello, nor ask after how I was doing, no sir. They just scowls, and turns their eyes, and walks away. I was only a little girl knowing nothing of such doings. It hurt to have them treat me so, when I ain't never done nobody no harm.

"And now, as for being a whore—I ain't never been in a man's bed before, neither white nor black for that matter. Which is, I'm guessing, more'n a lot o' the women who lives in the cabins can say. And in fact, in all the years o' being in the Big House I only know'd o' one time the master took one o' the slaves to bed, and she was from the cabins, *not* from the Big House. For years it burned me to keep knowing that to myself, and especially not to tell Miss Abbey, who has always trusted me. But I knew it'd just hurt her feelings, and likely get that cabin woman into trouble, so I bit my tongue and stayed quiet.

"And … speaking on being a *spy* … as us house slaves is supposed to be, according to you *holier than thou* cabin slaves. I know all about the thing y'all call 'The Way.' Have know'd of it for years, and ain't never once told any white man about it. And I've know'd of the runaways from other farms you've helped hide and send on their way north. In fact, I'd say there ain't hardly nothin' goes on 'round this farm I don't know something 'bout. But I ain't never told anything of such to the white folks. Some kind of spy I am!

"Now, if this don't convince y'all how *wrong* y'all been all these years, let me tell you one more thing. Miss Abbey and I have come to be close … very close, almost as sisters, if such a thing is possible when one is a slave to the other. I'm not ashamed to say it. Miss Abbey's a kindly woman, who was born into her life same as we were born into ours. She's had little enough say about anything to do with slavery.

"In fact, we have been so close over the years, Miss Abbey has offered me my freedom on three different occasions. But do y'all know what I told her, all three times?"

She paused and looked around the group. But it was a rhetorical question, and she didn't expect an answer.

"I told her I would only accept my freedom when I was *the last slave on this farm.*"

This statement perplexed the Elders who gazed at her with blank looks. Finally, Ganda spoke, "You mean to say … you wanted her to sell off all the others first? But why? That don't make no sense, Megs—er, sorry, I mean *Odah*."

"No, no … that ain't what I meant by it! *Damn!* I gotta spell it out?! What I meant by *the last slave* was … I wouldn't accept my freedom unless all o' y'all others was freed *first*. That's what it means!

"And the last time she asked me, she practically begged me with tears in her eyes, and still I said 'no.' So she said if I ever

4

changed my mind all's I had to do was tell her, and she'd free me that very day.

"So that's the kind of 'house whore' I've been!"

Then she sat back, folded her arms across her chest, and scowled at them.

There was a long silence, until Juba said, "*Damn ...*" and shook her head slowly from side to side, looking down at the table. She looked up and met eyes with Megs. "Now I am sore ashamed o' anything bad I ever said or thought or heard ... about y'all that's in the Big House. I feel just flat ashamed is all I can say ..."

"That goes for me to," Nimba said quietly, and the others nodded their agreement.

And Ganda said, "Odah ... hearing what you done said, I am ... well, yes, embarrassed and ashamed, as Juba said. But also ... well, I feel a bit like old Moses, when he done climbed up that big ol' hill and heard the voice o' God speaking. Not meaning to compare you to God, mind. It's just ... well, now I feel a duty to go spread the word among the people. Of how wrong we been about y'all, all these years, and how ... well, how downright honorable and admirable you been, Odah.

"I ain't never heard o' nobody turning down a chance for their freedom even once, not to speak o' three times! Nope, never did hear o' any such thing in all my years. And ... I reckon I owe you a proper apology, as do we all. But also ... a big ol' thanks ... so *thank you*, Odah! Thank you most kindly, from way down in the bottom of my old heart."

The others nodded, and said, "Yes, thank you, Odah ... thank you, God bless you," and so on until Megs' scowl turned to a smile.

"Oh ... it ain't such a *grand* thing. I just thought y'all should know, us in the house ... well ... we're still slaves too. And we still be on *your* side, despite the things that's been said of us over the years."

And then Ganda reached across the table and grasped Megs' hands in his and gave them a firm shake and a squeeze and smiled at her. Both now had tears in their eyes.

5

But when he let go, Megs surprised the group again, when she announced, "I thank you very kindly for your words. They mean a great deal to me … more than you know. But, that ain't why I came here. I only said *those* things so's you'd understand who I *really* am. So's you'd agree to listen to what I actually came here to say."

"Well, I can't even guess what you could say to top *that*, Odah, but speak away. I reckon you done earned the right."

"Thank you, Ganda. What I came to say is this; before he returned from out west, all the slaves, both in the cabins *and* in the house, feared the Captain would prove hisself some kind o' bloodthirsty monster. But now, after all these months, he has proved to be nothing of the sort. Instead, he's been a Godsend to us all. He has said he gonna free us all, when the time is ready. And to prove the truth of his word, he done made life better for us starting on the first day he was here. Think on it … things we now take as normal, *he* done for us. The Sabbath day off every week, and then on account o' that, a celebration every Saturday night out on the lawn with a fire, and dancing and whatnot. And his men done repaired all the holes in the cabins, so when it blow or rain y'all can still be warm and dry. And he stopped the beatings and sent nasty old Sickles down the road. He also done sold off all them vicious hounds, that the old master'd got to hunt down runaways. And he done give us the day off for celebrating the American country's birthday—and the Captain's. Without even saying nothing he's made the food better, the clothing better, and the bedding. And I ain't even mentioned the great, wonderful … unbelievably grand, honest-to-God church wedding! Made me wish I was young again so's I could o' been one o' them brides …" she sighed a heavy sigh.

"Who ever heard of a master doing even half them things? And … he ain't never asked for *nothing* in return!"

She paused and again, looking around the table. There were nods—clearly, they agreed with what she was saying.

"But ever since what happened with … well, when Miss Evelyn left this farm … the Captain has been a different man:

downcast and sorrowful-like. But even so, still kindly and respectful o' us kind.

"Well ... I for one, mean to *help* him. To do everything I can to help him feel better ... to be *happy* again. If it's in my power to do."

"All right ... we'd not disagree 'bout that, Odah. But what are we all gonna do 'bout the Captain's sadness?"

"Before I answer that, Ganda, I wants to prove to y'all I understand exactly what 'The Way' means. I'm gonna tell y'all what I know of it.

"It's likely been around as long as they's been slaves, maybe even back in the times of the Bible. Anyway, you could call it 'The Way to Be a Slave,' or 'The Way to Survive Slavery,' or 'The Way to Pay Back the Master,' or some such. But here at Mountain Meadows, we's just called it 'The Way' since ... well, since Ganda was a boy at least. Likely longer.

"It means to never do as good as you can. Never work as hard as the master would like. Don't do any *extra* work to help the master. But more than that. It means, leave every tenth weed un-hoed. 'Accidentally' chop off the good crops, break the unripe cotton branch, cut the horses' tack. Or ... any number of a hundred different things to hurt the master without him knowing it.

"And ... it also means to act a part, like one o' them actors in a play. To pretend to be slow of mind. To misunderstand what the master wants, make him doubt you can do more, 'cause you're too stupid. That you can't possibly understand how to do difficult, or complicated things, so's he has to do them his self or have one o' the overseers do it. And so on, and so on. How am I doin' so far?"

"Okay, okay, yes ... you understands it, there can be no doubt. And we're mighty beholdin' to you for not telling the old master about it. But why you been talking 'bout 'The Way' anyhow? It weren't never meant to hurt the house slaves."

"Well, that's good, cause since I been head maid, I ain't never put up with any such nonsense! What y'all don't seem to get about it is ... it hurts the person doing it as much or more than it hurt the master. If'n a man can't never take no pride in what he do ... then he got nothing to take any pride in doing! I reckon if this is the life we're stuck with, then *by God* we should still do our best. Not for the master's sake, but for our *own* sake—our own self-respect. Else we really are good for nothing, like them wicked slavers say. We're just proving 'em right, which I don't *never* want to do. I'd rather show 'em they're wrong for enslaving us and treating us as animals. Why you reckon Miss Abbey wants to free me? 'Cause she seen I was a real, intelligent, capable human being, not some kind o' trained animal ... and it shamed her soul.

"So to answer your question ... I came here to talk about 'The Way' 'cause ... *it must stop* ... it must stop *now!*"

ഇറ്റ

Tuesday August 7, 1860 - Richmond, Virginia:

After the carriage pulled up in front of their tiny house, Evelyn had to take quick advantage of a short window of opportunity. She'd have to smuggle Violet out while the driver was busy helping carry in a load of goods for Miss Harriet.

From where she stood right outside the carriage door, she reached up under the seat of the carriage and gently nudged what appeared to be a bundle of clothing.

"Come Violet. We must hurry," she said in a quiet but urgent tone.

"Yes, miss," came the answer. The girl scrambled out from under the seat, and slipped out the carriage door, feet first.

Evelyn took her by the hand and hurried her around the side of the house and into the back yard. Fortunately, it was getting on to evening. The shadows were long in the yard, making it difficult to see what they were doing from one of the neighboring houses, should someone happen to be looking.

They had a small woodshed up next to the house. So Evelyn made for that, opened the door, and urged Violet to enter.

"But it's ... dark in there, miss ..."

"Sorry, but I can think of nowhere else to hide you. Thankfully the shed is mostly empty this time of year, so you'll have plenty of room. I've hauled plenty of wood from there, so I know they built it tightly. I've never seen any rats in it.

"Once Miss Harriet goes to bed I will come with food and something to drink and will bring a candle for some light. In the meantime, please find a place to sit, and be quiet and still. Later we'll figure out what to do next."

"All right ... and ... thank you, Miss Evelyn. You done saved my life, I know that for sure."

"Well ... we'll see about that. But I will do what I can. Goodbye for now ... I will see you later."

Several hours later, Violet heard a movement in the yard outside the woodshed door. Though it was dark outside, there was a moon out, so she could see the door opening, and the outline of a person standing in the doorway.

"It's me, Violet."

The door shut quickly.

"Give me a moment ..."

Violet heard a rustling sound, then a sharp scratch, followed by a burst of light that quickly withered to a gentle glow. Evelyn held the match up to a candle she held in a metal candle holder, the kind with a loop one could hook a finger through to carry it around the house. The candle provided a cheery glow that lit the inside of the tiny woodshed, so Violet could see it for the first time. In the dark she had worked hard not to let her imagination get the best of her. Miss Evelyn had said there were no rats. But ... in her imagination she could come up with even worse things. Now with the candle's illumination, she saw it was a simple, relatively clean room made of wood. She sighed involuntarily once she had a look around. Not so scary after all!

Evelyn sat next to Violet on the wood floor, and laid out a cloth bundle, which she quickly unwrapped. It contained a piece of meat, a few slices of cheese, and several slices of bread. She'd also brought a full water bottle with a cork in the top.

"Eat Violet. You must be starved ... God knows the last time you had a meal ..."

"It was at first sun-up, ma'am. Thank you very kindly ... this is ... better'n I usually have all day!"

9

"You're welcome. Please … eat!"

Violet needed no further encouragement. Seeing and smelling the food made her stomach growl. She'd been too anxious about the loneliness and the dark unknown earlier to even think about food. But now that it was in front of her …

Evelyn sat and watched Violet eat. She figured the girl was only fourteen or fifteen—much younger than herself, though in many ways Evelyn still saw herself as a young girl. She found she enjoyed watching the girl eat … there was something satisfying about it she couldn't quite put her finger on. Then her mind started working on the problem of what to do with Violet. She couldn't stay in the woodshed forever. Even a full day in it would be tiresome beyond reason. But … what to do?

Fortunately for Evelyn, Violet had already been contemplating a solution to the problem.

Between bites, Violet said, "Miss Evelyn … when I was on the farm … one of the old women told me about … about a *special* place. She swored me to secrecy on it. But … well, seein's how you're tryin' to help me an' all … I reckon it'd be all right to tell you."

"Tell me what? What special place?"

"A place to go if we ever needed to get away … to run away. She called it a *railroad station* … only she said it ain't got no trains. I … don't rightly know what it means, Miss Evelyn."

"Railroad station … with no trains …?"

Evelyn contemplated this for a few moments, trying to recall any rumors she'd ever heard regarding runaway slaves. She remembered someone talking about something called …

"The Underground Railroad!"

"What, miss?"

"That's what it means … 'a rail station with no trains.' There are white folks in the South who don't agree with slavery, and they help runaway slaves get to the North, or Canada. They move them from place to place in secret, so the slavers won't catch them. They have a system … well, from what I understand, houses and buildings all over the place. And they move your people from one to another, until they've reached a Northern place where there's

10

no slavery. They call it the 'Underground Railroad,' and refer to everything about it in railway terms: conductors, rail stations, passengers, tracks, and so on."

Violet nodded, "Yes'm, I do recall hearing o' such a thing once, now's you mentions it."

"Violet, did the old woman tell you where this 'rail station' might be?"

"Yes ma'am. If'n I can remember it … at the time it didn't seem all that important. I had no mind to run away before … before … well … the master done what he done."

"Yes, I understand. Please relax, and try to recall what she told you. See if you can remember it."

"All right," Violet leaned back against the wall of the shed and closed her eyes. She sat that way for several minutes, so long Evelyn feared she may have nodded off. But then she opened her eyes and said "Jackson Street. She said a blue house on Jackson Street, across from a red house. Go around back, and knock on the door three times hard, pause a few seconds, then knock two times more softly …"

Evelyn thought for a moment. "Jackson Street is only … four or five blocks from here! But it'll be dark in a few minutes. Hmm … in the dark a red house or a blue house looks the same as a green house."

"Yes, ma'am."

"Well … I'm afraid you must spend the night in this shed, and all the long day tomorrow, until Miss Harriet is in bed again. In the meantime, I must go for a little walk. And see if I can find this blue house, across from a red house, on Jackson Street. Pray to God nobody's repainted their house since she told you that!"

Violet smiled, "Yes, ma'am! And don't you worry, now I've seen the inside with a little light, I can see this-here shed's a right-fine little room. I've slept in much worse."

"Yes … I'm sure you have. And I'm sorry that's true. Maybe someday you will sleep in a place a whole lot better!"

"Thank you, ma'am. That'd be right-fine, that would."

"And, Violet, you can stop calling me ma'am. Just call me Evelyn."

11

"Yes, Miss Evelyn."

"I should get back inside the house now, in case Miss Harriet awakes and notices I'm gone. I'll come in the morning with more food and drink—enough to last the long day. Then I'll have my little walk, and ... we'll see what we can see."

Chapter 2. Commitment to the Cause

*"There's no abiding success
without commitment."*
– Tony Robbins

Wednesday August 15, 1860 - Greenbrier County, Virginia:

Nathan sat in the library, sipping slowly on a glass of whiskey. He was reading the summary of a plan Tom and William had put together on the most recent studies of various types of "artificial" fertilizer. How each had been developed, its current supply and availability, the expected increase in crop yields, and of course, the cost. They had broken out each according to its potential effect by crop, and by region, the expected increase in production and profits. They'd also noted various assumptions about weather, expected prices, and shipping costs.

It was meticulously researched, well organized, and rationally presented. It also managed to be fascinating and engrossing, despite a subject matter most people would consider dull in the extreme. As such, it was exactly what he'd expected of a report researched and written by Tom Clark and William Jenkins.

And yet, despite all that, Nathan found his mind wandering. He was having trouble focusing on the document. He realized, despite his best efforts, he was still suffering through the doldrums. Thankfully, he'd not suffered any further bouts of excessive drinking since his forced sobering—courtesy of Tom and Jim, and several buckets of cold water. But he still couldn't muster up much enthusiasm for anything.

He knew the sudden departure of Evelyn had hit him harder than he'd thought possible. Harder than anything had ever hit him in his adult life. Surprisingly, even harder than the violent deaths of several people he had loved and felt extremely close to.

What was it about her? No matter how many times he went over it in his mind, he could not puzzle it out. In the end, she was just ... *Evelyn*. She was ... *special* ... in a way he could not quite

13

put his finger on or explain to anyone. Without him realizing it at the time, she'd worked her way deep into his heart in a manner no one else had ever done. Then, her sudden, unexpected, and unexplained departure had shaken him like nothing ever before. He'd watched people killed violently, and he had committed acts of extreme violence himself, but afterward had felt the same. Sad maybe; ashamed, yes, but still essentially the same person. And he'd always resumed his normal life in short order. But this time, something was different. As if the world had changed ... or *he* had changed. He no longer felt confident in his own happiness.

As he contemplated these dark thoughts for the thousandth time, there was a knock at the library door. It was getting late in the evening, and he had been thinking of turning in for the night, so he was not expecting anyone.

"Yes?"

Megs poked her head in the door, "Captain, may I come speak with you ... on an important matter?"

"Yes ... yes, of course, Megs. Come in."

He set Tom's paper on the side table and sat up straighter in his chair. To his surprise, Megs entered followed by five field slaves, none of whom had ever been in the house before, to his knowledge. Despite his surprise, he remembered his manners, and rose to his feet.

"*Oh!* Please do come in. Welcome ... Toby, Titus, Naomie, Betsy, Peggy," he named each as he looked them in the eye, ushering them politely into the room. Megs had planned ahead, it seemed; the two men carried small chairs with them, apparently from the kitchen, so there'd be enough seats in the library for all.

"Please, do be seated."

When all were seated, he looked at Megs with curiosity, then around the room at the others.

"To what do I owe this unexpected pleasure, ladies and gentlemen?"

"Captain ... in this group, Toby speaks for the rest of us," Megs answered, nodding her head toward the old gentleman.

"All right, Megs. Toby ... what can I do for *you*, sir?"

14

"Well, Captain ... I want to apologize for interrupting you at such a late hour. But Megs here ... well, she done convinced us we needed to speak with you, sir. And once she did, we decided we shouldn't wait another day on it. I hope once you hear what we have to say, you'll agree, sir."

"It is quite all right, Toby. You aren't disturbing me ... I was just doing a little reading before heading off to bed. Please ... do feel free to say what's on your mind."

"Thank you, sir. First off, I want to make the *proper* introductions."

"But Toby, I already know—"

"Please ... bear with me, sir ... I know you knows the names o' everyone here ... you done already amazed everyone on how quickly you knew who everyone was. The old master, in all his years, never did what you done in a week. But no ... what I'm speaking of is ... *different* ..."

Nathan raised an eyebrow, a look of curiosity on his face, but said nothing.

"My name is Ganda ... this is Mimba, Mussu, Camba, and Juba," then finally gesturing toward Megs, he said, "and this is Odah."

Nathan said nothing, gazing at Toby wide-eyed. Out of habit he reached in his pocket, took out a cigar, and stuck it in his mouth, though he had no intention of lighting it.

He looked around at each for another minute, then said, "I am *honored* ... truly. I've heard of such before, of course. I hear on some farms it's common practice for slaves to refer to each other by their African names, even in front of the whites. But my father never approved—even forbade the practice of having such names. So my congratulations to you on preserving these names in secret, and ... my thanks for trusting me enough to tell them to me. I am *truly* touched and honored by that."

"Thank you, Captain. We're very happy you feel that way about it. It is ... very joyful for us to hear you say that. But we ain't come here just to tell you our African names. It was just ... a way of starting, maybe. A way of letting you know we trust you and ... we mean to tell you things important to us that have been secret

15

for a long time—too long, now it seems, if you were to ask your Megs ... our *Odah*."

She nodded at Toby and smiled as he looked over at her.

Nathan looked back and forth between them. His curiosity was now piqued, but he stayed quiet, assuming Toby would continue at his own pace.

Then Toby turned and gave the others in the group a nod, to which they each nodded in response. He held out his right hand balled up in a fist, with the fingers facing down. Each of the others did likewise. Nathan looked at Toby with a curious expression but said nothing.

Then Toby turned his hand over, so the fingers were facing upward, and opened his hand. The others did the same. Each held something brown-colored in their hand. He leaned closer to Toby to have a better look. The thing was only a couple of inches long, but had a familiar look. It appeared to be made of well-aged and oiled leather—multiple strands woven together as one might do with a ... "A whip. That's a piece cut from a bull whip, isn't it?"

Toby nodded in answer and smiled.

Nathan's eyes widened as it suddenly came to him, "The whip I chopped into pieces ... the day Sickles tried to whip Rosa. But ... how, and ... *why?* I recall scooping up those pieces and throwing them as far as I could out into the fields."

"Yes, that you did, Captain. And at first no one paid it no mind. Then sometime the next day somebody showed up carrying a piece o' that old whip he'd found on the ground in the field. Pretty soon others had picked up pieces and were carrying them. Then ... well it suddenly became important to the people to ... well ... to find all them pieces. They even brought them all together in a room one day and pieced the whole thing back together to make sure they was all there. A few was still missing, so folks scoured the ground until they'd found them all."

"Well, I'm impressed with your determination ... but that still doesn't answer the *why* of it. It's now just pieces of chopped up leather ... no good for anything I can think of."

Toby was quiet for a few moments, gazing at the thing in his hand, as if searching for the right answer. "Captain, you recall the

Bible story of when the Christ got powerful angry at them money changers, and scattered coins all across the temple steps?"

"Of course, it's described in John chapter two, verses thirteen through sixteen."

"Yes, sir ... if you says it, I'll believe it. Anyway, imagine sir, what it'd be worth today if you held in your hand even the smallest and most worthless o' them coins that was tossed on the ground by the Christ his self."

Nathan thought about this for a moment, then in a voice filled with awe, said, "Why ... it'd be worth a king's ransom!"

"Yes sir, I reckon so. Now ... to the people these pieces o' whip is like them coins. Not much value in themselves ... but they's a symbol, sir. A symbol o' the day you put a stop to the beatings. A symbol of your promise to set us all free one day. Not to be blasphemous and say you're like the Christ or nothing, sir, but think on it; years and years from now, when all the people on this farm have been free for almost longer than they can remember, they'll be able to show their grandchildren a piece of that whip. And they'll remember the start o' when the bad days came to an end, after which the people was set free."

"Well I ... I don't know quite what to say about that ... I can understand the feelings, but ... it was just an old whip, after all. But if it means that much to you, then ... well, once again I'm *honored*, and thank you for that."

Again Toby became quiet and seemed to be deep in thought. Finally, he said, "Captain, please forgive us. But we must now ask you to promise never to repeat a word o' what we's about to say to another white man."

Nathan looked at him for a moment, as if thinking about how to respond. He sucked on the unlit cigar. Then he pulled it from his mouth.

"Before I agree, let me ask you ... might anyone be harmed if I fail to tell them these things you are about to tell me? If so, then I don't think I can in good conscience agree, despite my current *considerable* curiosity."

"Well, sir ... I reckon not knowing this thing might harm a *slaver*. But not in the physical way, not in the ... Nat Turner sort o'

17

way, if you take my meaning. We know of no such matters as would do anyone an injury, sir."

Nathan looked at Toby for another moment, then over at Megs. Then he looked around the room, making silent eye contact with each of the others, wordlessly holding each in his intense gaze for several seconds. He suddenly stood from his chair and walked over to the side of the room, where shelves were lined with dozens of books. But he did not reach up for any of these. On its own stand, below the others lay a great, leather-bound book. It was open to the middle, with a red ribbon marking the page. Nathan lifted it carefully from its stand and closed the cover. He turned back toward the group.

"This is the Chambers' family Bible. My grandfather brought it to Mountain Meadows more than fifty years ago, and it *never* leaves this room. In the back pages are written all the great momentous events in the family history: births, marriages, and deaths of all the family members—most recently my father, Jacob Chambers. This book not only contains the Holy Bible of God, and the Gospels of our Lord and Savior Jesus Christ, it is also sacred and valuable beyond price to my family. I would give away a wagonload of gold before I would part with this book."

He carried the book back to his chair, and sat down, the great book in his lap.

"I swear on this most sacred and holy book, that whatever you tell me in this room, will never leave my lips, nor be written down by me, so long as I live. Unless you tell me at some future time it is all right to do so. This I swear in the name of the Father, Son, and Holy Spirit."

Toby gazed at him open mouthed.

"Well, sir … I expect that's about as serious a promise as I ever heard-tell of."

He chuckled, "To be honest, I'd o' believed you, sir, if'n you'd just said 'yes.' But I thank you kindly for takin' this so serious-like. It is a serious matter to us, so … so I reckon the things you've said are proper to the occasion, and for that I thank you again, sir."

18

Toby proceeded to tell Nathan all about "The Way"—the history of its beginnings, not only at Mountain Meadows, but throughout the South, and its current manifestations and specific examples—without naming any names.

Nathan sat back in his seat, a look of amazement on his face.

Toby paused in his narrative, and looked at Nathan, as if to gauge his reaction.

"Good for y'all ... good for you ..." Nathan finally said. "That was a righteous action, and a well-executed campaign. I like to think I'd have done likewise in your place.

"But I'm also very sorry you've been forced into this situation. I have to believe it was also harmful to your people ... to their *self-respect*. Never being able to do a job as well as you knew you could do it. Unable to take pride in what you were doing, except ... well, I guess taking pride in sabotaging the slavers.

"*Damn* ... it's another sad part of this whole tragic tale we've been living. One more reason to put an end to the whole, miserable business."

He noticed Megs exchanging a look with Toby, and nodding, as if she agreed with what he'd just said.

"Thank you for being understanding, sir. But I suppose you must guess by now we decided to tell you this thing on account o' we decided to stop doing it on this farm. So long as you're our master, and so long as you honestly mean to free us all ... when the time is right."

"Oh, well thank you very kindly for that! I greatly appreciate you telling me about it, and for agreeing to stop the practice. And, yes, I honestly intend to set y'all free, just as soon as we've set this farm on a track where it can sustain us all without free labor. And when y'all feel confident enough to go out into the world and be free without worrying about starving to death in the process. That I also swear on this great book."

"Well, sir, it goes beyond just stopping 'The Way.' You see, our Odah here is ... well, she can be very *convincing*, it turns out. We don't mean to just stop *harming* you sir ... we're fixin' to start *helping* you do what you's setting out to do.

"Though we like your Sergeant Jim plenty well—he being a very kindly and polite gentleman, despite him being some kind o' powerful-hard man-killer when he was out West, from what we hear. Well, I know you done put him in charge o' farmin' after ol' Sickles was run off, but he ain't no kind o' farmer is all I'm gettin' at.

"And, not to sound all high-and-mighty and whatnot, but there ain't nothing to be know'd about tobacco or cotton that your old Toby don't know. And now I'm offering to run your harvest for you sir, such that it just might be the best harvest that's ever been on this-here farm."

Nathan sat up straight in his seat. "You would do that, Toby ... er, *Ganda*, I should say? I would be terribly grateful."

"I would ... and you may still call me Toby, Captain. Yes, I will do it ... but not for *you* sir, for *us!* The better the harvest is—and maybe next year's as well—the sooner we be free."

"Amen to that, Toby. *Amen to that!*" Nathan answered as he jumped from his seat. He immediately shook the men's hands, and kissed the hands of the women, which made them smile, and giggle in response. No man, white or black, had ever before done such a thing to any of them.

"You will *not* regret this meeting tonight, nor your decisions. This I swear ... not just on the sacred book, *but on my very life!* You will *never* regret this. Thank you, thank you, *thank you!*"

Nathan's heart swelled. There was still goodness and light in the world. There was still hope, after all. And though he still hurt over Evelyn, he could feel a stout breeze fill his sails, puffing them full out, moving his ship forward with a sudden lurch! *Hallelujah!* he thought; his doldrums had finally come to an end!

༄༅ ༄༅ ༄༅ ༄༅ ༄༅ ༄༅

"Hey, Tony ... hold up a second ..." Ned called out just as Tony was to step up into his cabin to see what was to be had for dinner. He was tired from a long day in the fields, hoeing and weeding, and didn't feel much like talking.

But he knew he was just about Ned's only friend, so he stopped and waited anyway. His other cabinmates pushed past him and in through the open doorway.

"What is it, Ned?" Tony asked as Ned stepped up to the wooden platform that served as both patio and step for the one-room cabin.

"You hear 'bout what them Elders done said?"

"No … been out hoein' all day, and them weeds don't like to talk much," Tony answered, too tired to attempt a friendly response.

Ned nodded in acknowledgment of Tony's half-hearted attempt at humor but didn't go so far as to smile or laugh.

"They's tellin' the folks to stop doin' 'The Way.' Startin' in today."

"What?!" Tony asked, suddenly feeling more alert and less tired. "I can't hardly believe it … we been doin' things that way from back before my daddy was born."

"Yeah, but no mo'. And there's worse … they say we all's gonna start helpin' the Captain run things … they even say old Toby's fixin' to take over doin' ol' Sickles' work."

Tony just stared at Ned, mouth agape. Then he slowly shook his head, "Well … looks like Captain done got his wish. One fancy weddin' and now all the folks wants to just kiss his feet as he walks."

"Not me," Ned said, adopting the usual cold look he used when speaking of the white masters. "Captain's still a slaver … and we's still slaves. Ain't nothin' changin' that."

Tony couldn't disagree and could think of nothing to add, so he nodded his head, turned, and entered the cabin.

༄ဢၸၥႜႛၸၥႜၸၥ႞ႜ

Evelyn came at morning's first light, once again bringing food and drink—more this time than the previous night, as it would need to last all day.

"If it gets hot, you may open the door a crack, but don't make it too obvious. By mid-afternoon shade will cover the lawn, so it will cool back down a bit. If you need to … well, you know …

21

relieve yourself ... there's a bucket there in the corner. You should not leave this shed for any reason. The neighbors, or Miss Harriet might see you. I am going now to find this famous blue house. I will return tonight after Miss Harriet goes to bed."

"Thank you, Miss Evelyn."

Evelyn left, closing the door softly behind her.

Violet leaned back against the shed wall to contemplate all that had happened in the last few days. The more she thought on it, the harder it was to reconcile her earlier thoughts about white women with Miss Evelyn. In her experience, high society white women treated everyone, even other white people, as lesser beings. And they certainly wouldn't lower themselves to help someone in need, especially a runaway slave. And yet ... Violet knew enough about the laws to know what Miss Evelyn was doing was illegal. She was risking not just the anger of other white folks, but actual imprisonment, and for what? For a young, black, slave girl she didn't even know! It made no sense.

And the way she took charge and seemed to know exactly what to do ... it just didn't fit. Most white women seemed ... unable to do anything for themselves, as far as Violet had seen. Without their men, or their slaves, they were practically helpless. And Miss Evelyn was the most beautiful woman Violet had *ever* seen, white or black. A woman like *that* could have ... well, pretty much anyone, or anything! Why would she risk it all for her? It was a puzzle, and Violet could not figure it out. But she was grateful and said a silent prayer thanking God and Jesus for sending Miss Evelyn to help save her.

It was a long, hot day in the woodshed, and one of the loneliest Violet could recall. Whatever faults it had—and they were too numerous to count—the one thing one never experienced back on the farm was being lonesome. There were always too many people around. Always the master, the missus, or the overseers watching, making sure no one was slacking in their labors. And during dinner time there was always a crowd of exhausted and hungry field slaves, elbowing each other to get their share, then trying to find a place to sit down to eat. Then a night of fitful sleep, trying to ignore the chorus of snores, in a cabin too crowded for comfort. No, loneliness was never in it, she decided. This was a new experience, and she wasn't sure she liked it. She eagerly awaited Miss Evelyn's return, hopefully with good news about the blue house.

Finally, as the sun was setting, the door opened and a figure slipped in, closing the door behind. Once again, a match was struck, and a candle was lit.

"Good evening, Violet."

"Good evening, Miss Evelyn. Did you find it? Did you find the blue house, on Jackson Street?"

Evelyn had an odd look on her face when she answered, "Yes … yes … I walked the whole length of Jackson Street. There are twelve blue houses, and four red ones, of various shades. But there is only one place where there is a blue house directly across from a red one. The red house sits next to the Lutheran Church on the corner of Fifth Street."

Violet smiled and covered her mouth to suppress a squeal of joy. But she noticed Miss Evelyn didn't share her excitement for some reason. She had a thoughtful and serious look.

"What is it, Miss Evelyn? I can see they's something botherin' you."

"Violet … close your eyes and think back. Try to remember exactly what the old woman told you about this place. Are you sure she said, 'go to a *blue* house across from a *red* one'? Or … is it possible she said, 'go to a *red* house across from a *blue* one'?"

Violet looked at Evelyn, and her eyes widened. "*Oh!* Oh … I … I thought she said *blue*, but … now you ask … I … I don't know. It could be I got it backwards. Why, Miss Evelyn? Why do you ask?"

Evelyn sighed, sat, and leaned back against the wall. "Because … when I look at the blue house … it doesn't seem right. It sits side by side with its neighbors. They keep their gardens neatly trimmed, with no large bushes or trees in front. And there's a low fence around the backyard. Anyone trying to knock on the back door would be easily seen walking up to the house and going through the gate to the backyard. And even once in the backyard they'd be in plain view of the neighbors to the sides, and in back.

23

It seems to me … this would *not* be a good place for the … 'railway station' you spoke of."

"Oh! Well, then … maybe it is *not* the right place after all. Maybe as you feared … someone done painted their house a different color …"

"Could be. But … the reason I asked you the question was that the *red* house sits next to a church, is overgrown with bushes in the front, and has no fence. A narrow dirt trail leads to the backyard and … the backyard runs up against a wooded ravine, rather than more houses. To me, this seems a better place for this kind of … *business*. But if we get it wrong, it would look very suspicious and might be disastrous. Take your time and think back … see if you can remember anything else … maybe the old woman mentioned the church?"

Violet closed her eyes and tried to remember. But … at the time it hadn't seemed important, and now …

"I'm sorry, Miss Evelyn … I just ain't sure. It's been too long. Oh … what you reckon we should do now?"

Evelyn was quiet and thoughtful for a moment.

"Come, gather your things and let's go. When we get there, we will decide what to do. You can't stay here forever, and I can think of nothing else to do."

"Well, Miss Evelyn … I ain't got no *things* to gather …" Violet said and smiled with a shrug.

"Oh! Yes, of course. Sorry … a polite habit. Let's go straightaway, shall we?"

"Yes, Miss Evelyn."

An hour later it was fully dark, but there was a bright, full moon, and scattered lights from the windows of houses illuminated the road. They stood on the street in the place Evelyn had recounted. On the south side of the road was the neat little house Evelyn had described as the blue one, though now the color was indistinguishable in the dark. Directly across on the north side of Jackson Street was another house. It was larger and was set back further from the road. Looking to the left of it, Violet saw there was a big church, and in between were many bushes, which had a haphazard and overgrown look. A narrow trail led into the bushes, presumably heading into the backyard of the house.

"Well, what do you think?"

"I sees what you meant earlier, Miss Evelyn. This'n looks much more like what one would want for … *secret* kind o' business. The other'n … not so much."

"Yes, the more I think on it, the more the one by the church seems right. For one, the church would be rarely occupied, and it's even possible the church is helping with the endeavor. But … if we're wrong …"

"Yes'm, it could be *very* bad. What should we do?"

Evelyn thought about it for a moment, then said, "Well, we certainly can't go to the back door, not knowing for sure if it's the right place. It would be pretty difficult to explain why we're there. Here's what we'll do …"

A few minutes later, Violet crouched down behind a bush. She was close enough to the front door to be able to hear what was said, but in the darkness, no one would see her.

After looking to make sure she was satisfied with Violet's hiding place, Evelyn strode boldly up the stone steps to the front door and knocked. She knocked hard three times, then two times more softly after a pause, though the instructions had been to do so on the *back* door. She thought it might give whoever was inside the idea she was in the know about the "railway station." It couldn't hurt, in any case.

After a few moments, the door opened a crack, and light streamed out from a handheld lamp.

"Yes? Oh! How can I help you miss?" a man asked, opening the door wider. He was tall and lean, with round glasses. He had dark brown hair graying at the sides, and he immediately reminded Evelyn of an older, taller version of Nathan's man, William.

"Excuse me, sir, I am … very sorry to disturb you at this late hour. But … well, I am looking for a certain … *train station* … and someone told me it was somewhere hereabouts."

"Oh! Well, you are quite off course, miss. You must head left, southeast that is, on Jackson Street here, then turn right on Sixth

Street, and go four blocks to Broad Street. The train depot will be on your left. You can't miss it."

"Oh my ... I guess I *am* a bit strayed. But tell me about this station, if you would. The person who told me of it said it was ... of a *red* color, across from a *blue* building. And surprisingly this station has no trains, and one must always enter by the back entrance, and knock three times, then two more times after a pause."

The man didn't immediately answer, but the expression on his face changed, suddenly becoming more serious.

"Tell me, miss ... who was it told you such a strange tale?"

"It was ... a young woman of my acquaintance who is ... wanting to travel. In fact she is currently in desperate need of a new home ..."

"And this young woman ... where is she?"

"I have left her back by the street, until I made sure of our location."

He looked her up and down, then said, "Come around to the back door, with your friend. Even though it's dark, the front door may be seen from the road, and from some of the neighbors' houses."

"Thank you, sir. We shall be there in a moment."

Evelyn collected Violet and they were soon at the back door of the red house.

"So you was right, Miss Evelyn ... it *was* the red house!"

"Yes, so it would seem."

The back door had steps leading down to the basement level, so they took the steps down to the landing. Evelyn stepped up to the door, wondering if she should knock three times, as Violet had originally been instructed. But as she raised her fist to knock, the door opened, and the man who'd greeted her at the front door, ushered them in.

When they had entered the house, it was clear they were in the basement. But the room was clean and well-lit by lamps set on high shelves on the walls. The man closed the door, turned to them and said, "You may call me Bill."

"My name is Evelyn Hanson, and this is ..."

"No … don't tell me … I don't want to hear her *real* name … no offense, miss. If I don't know, no one can make me tell it. And as for you, Miss Hanson; I appreciate the trust you've placed in me by telling me your *real* name, but that should be the last time you say it in this house."

"Oh! Do you really think that's necessary?"

"Yes, it is. In fact, at the risk of sounding overly suspicious, I must ask you to wait here while I have a few words with … your *friend* here. I must be sure of who you are before we speak further."

Violet looked over at Evelyn, who nodded, "It's all right … tell him whatever he wants to know. I'll be right here waiting for you."

"Yes, ma'am."

The man who called himself "Bill," turned and escorted Violet to another door, which he opened and led her through, closing it behind them.

Evelyn looked around, and finding a wooden bench against one wall, stepped over and sat. She let out a deep sigh and tried to relax. She realized her heart had been pounding much harder than the small amount of walking warranted. In the last two days she had done things she would never before have imagined doing. And though it was more stressful and frightening than anything she had ever done before, she found herself feeling good about it. Something told her it was … the *right* thing to do, despite what the law, and most people, might say. She remembered Nathan saying once, he'd rather do the *right* thing than the *normal* thing. She now knew, at a very personal level, what he'd meant by it. And … she noticed she had not heard that strange, questioning voice whispering in the back of her mind the past two days. What did *that* mean?

After ten minutes that seemed more like an hour, the door opened again, and Bill and Violet came back in. Evelyn looked Violet in the eyes, to makes sure all was well, and saw that it was. Clearly Bill had not said or done anything to frighten or upset her.

"Well, Bill?"

"I'm sorry, Miss Evelyn, but it was necessary to confirm your story. I am now convinced you're here for no other reason than to help this unfortunate young lady. In this ... 'business' ... I'm in, you can't be too careful. There are men working for the government who have no other job than to hunt for me, and others like me. And many of these men would rather murder me quietly than risk putting me on public trial. There I'd be able to speak out against the evils of slavery in front of all the newspapers, some of which even sympathize with our cause."

"Oh my. I never realized what you do is so ... dangerous! Of course, I knew y'all risked imprisonment, but murder? Surely not?!"

"I'm afraid so, Miss Evelyn. At least two of my associates have met their end that way. Believe it. Speaking of ... I must follow my own rules, and no longer refer to you by your real name. Do you have a pet name, or nickname, known only to a few friends you might go by? I find that's better to use than a made-up name. It's much easier to explain a slip-up that way, or if someone you actually know hears someone call you by that name. Or vice versa."

Evelyn thought a moment, then said, "Yes ... you may call me Eve. Only a few of my closest girl friends have ever called me that."

"Very well then, Miss Eve it is."

"And as for you, young lady," he said, turning toward Violet, "do you have an African name?"

"No sir."

"All right ... my next question, if you'd have said 'yes,' would have been, 'did your white masters know your African name?' Whatever else happens, you must not tell me, or anyone else, your *real* name. Do you understand? It is best your real name stops here, so they have no way to track you down. So ... I will give you a *traveling* name ... which you shall use until you feel comfortable with ... well, wherever you end up. I prefer to use African names, for the same reason I have told Miss Eve to use a nickname; in case there's a slip-up, it won't surprise white people if a black person also goes by an African name.

28

"Over here I have a book where I write down any African names I hear. I will read off the female ones, and you pick out one you like. All right?"

"Yes, sir."

He stepped over to a shelf built into the wall on one side of the room. There he picked up a ledger-type book and opened it. He thumbed through several pages, before stopping, presumably on the list of female names.

"Okay ... so just say 'stop' if you hear one you think you might like. I will repeat it again and pause, that you might think it over. All right?"

"Yes, sir."

"These are not in any special order, just how I wrote them down. Auba, Camba, Jugg, Bucko, Otta, Agua, Beneba, Cuba, Abba, Phibba ..."

"Stop ... go back ... three names, please sir."

"Hmm ... Cuba?"

"Yes ... Cuba ... I likes the sound o' that."

"Very well, *Miss Cuba* it is. Welcome to ... the first stop on the road to freedom. I wish you luck, and that you find the dream you seek."

"Thank you, sir."

"Come ... both of you ... I will show you ... the *others.*"

He opened the door at the back of the room, and this time Evelyn passed through with them. It was a long, dimly lit hallway which seemingly led the whole length of the house to a set of stairs leading up to the house above. Evelyn initially assumed they would go up those stairs, but just past halfway down the hallway Bill stopped. He turned to his left and reached up high to a small indentation in the wall. He seemed to pull down, and Evelyn heard a quiet, clicking sound. From what appeared to be a solid wall, a door opened silently outward. Bill pulled the door open and waved them to enter.

They entered a surprisingly large room, which had a table, several chairs scattered about, and a row of eight or ten sleeping pallets. Evelyn gazed around the room in amazement. A person might pass through the basement with no idea this even existed.

She realized that was exactly the point; if the "wrong" people came to this house, they might search through the basement and never find this hiding place.

And, the room was *not* empty. It currently held a half-dozen men, four women, and three small children. All were perfectly quiet as Bill, Evelyn, and Violet stepped into the room. "It's all right, everyone ... this is Miss Eve ... and her friend, Miss Cuba, who will be joining your 'train.'"

The people in the room stood up and came to greet them, smiling, and giving out their own traveling names, all of which sounded strange and foreign to Evelyn, clearly African names such as those Bill had just been reading. Though the people smiled, and looked happy, Evelyn sensed a tension under the surface. These were people who knew they were in grave danger, that quiet and secrecy were their best defense against those who would hunt them down and put them back in chains. There was no laughter, nor boisterous talking. Even the young children seemed to sense the need for quiet. The apparent discipline of the group impressed Evelyn.

"Now, Miss Eve, it is time to bid farewell to your friend, Miss Cuba. But take heart, she shall be in good hands. And with good fortune, and the help of many more virtuous people such as yourself, she shall soon find a new home in the house of freedom."

"Thank, you, Bill. Will you please give us a moment?"

"Yes, certainly. I will step back into the hallway. When you're ready to leave, just knock."

Evelyn and Violet stepped over toward one of the walls and sat on a bench.

"Well ... I guess this is goodbye, Viol ... oh! *Cuba*, I should say."

Violet smiled at Miss Evelyn's near slip. "Oh, Miss *Eve* ... how can I ever thank you for what you've done for me? I ... I really can't think of why you did it. But I know for sure—if I live to be a hundred years old—I shall never forget you. And I shall always be grateful. If ... if I get out of this alive, it will all be thanks to you." She had tears in her eyes, and Evelyn started to tear up as well. She leaned over and gave Violet a hug, which she returned with affection.

"No ... no, don't feel you owe me anything. You may not believe this now, but ... you have also done a great deal for me. Maybe even, you have saved *me* as well. My dear friend, Mr. Chamb ... oh, I should say ... a *dear gentleman friend* of mine, would say ... *God* brought us together for a reason—to help each other, and maybe others as well. Goodbye, my dear. I truly hope we meet again one day in a happier place, but if not, know I will always think of you, as well. As long as I live, I will never, ever forget you. This I too know for sure."

And now Evelyn's tears were also flowing, and the two embraced for one last time. Then Evelyn stood, waved goodbye, turned, and walked back to the hidden door. She knocked, and a moment later the door opened, and she stepped out into the hallway.

She followed Bill up the stairs to the main part of the house. He ushered her to a seat at the kitchen table.

"Coffee?"

"Oh, yes, please. That would be splendid. Thank you."

A few minutes later, they sat across from each other, blowing on steaming hot cups of coffee.

"It is a fine thing you've done for that young girl, Miss Eve."

"Thank you, Bill ... I assume that's not your real name?"

"Actually, it is. I am Bill Johnson. Dr. Bill Johnson ... a dentist by trade, for my day job."

"Oh! I thought you had a rule against using real names in this house."

"Well, in front of our ... *guests* ... I only use 'Bill.' But ... well, after all, this is my actual place of residence, and I even treat patients here occasionally, for various dental problems. So it would be unreasonable to pretend being someone else!"

"Yes ... I suppose so. But doesn't that put you in great danger?"

"Yes, it does. In fact, I have resolved myself that they *will* catch me one day. But, well, I guess I don't have to tell *you* ... sometimes a person must follow their conscience, regardless of the dangers.

31

"When I was just an ordinary dentist, and knew nothing of this whole business, a white man came and knocked on my door one night. He said he had a slave who was suffering terribly from a festering tooth. I agreed to treat him. But somehow, during the course of the treatment, it slipped out he was a runaway, and not the actual property of the man who'd brought him. The white man begged me not to tell, and I agreed. I thought that was the end of it. Then another man came a couple of weeks later and asked if I would be willing to treat other such 'slaves' in need of dental care. Soon they approached me to help them in other ways. Well, as you can see, it has led to this ..."

"Good for you, sir. I'm very impressed with your sense of honor, and your courage."

"Thank you, Miss Eve. I'm happy to hear you feel that way because ..."

"Yes?"

"Well ... in our *business* we're always in desperate need of more volunteers. I'm sure you can understand it's a thankless job of long days, and even longer nights. We are but a drop of water in a great ocean of need."

"Yes ... I would imagine so."

"To be perfectly frank, Miss Eve ... a woman of your *station* ... would be an invaluable asset in many ways."

"Oh ... how so?"

"Well, for starters—forgive my forwardness, but someone of your class, who *looks* like you, would be ... hmm. Well, let's just say you would be absolutely the last person the authorities would suspect of being involved in this kind of business. And ..."

"Yes?"

"Well ... you could be our eyes and ears in the upper crust of society. We need more help and support from the well-to-do to avoid being crushed by the authorities. You could help us recruit other high society members and warn us of any pending action by the government you might hear of. And, aside from all that, we need people who can escort our 'passengers' to safety. Those currently doing it are run ragged, working late nights every day of the week with no respite. Any help you can provide will be greatly appreciated. And it will help those poor souls in the most desperate need of help to obtain the freedom they deserve as fellow human beings."

"You make a persuasive argument, Dr. Johnson."

She sat back in the chair, and sipped on the hot coffee, as she thought about what he was asking of her. Though most people might consider this a monumental decision, she knew ... from a place deep down in her soul ... this was the *right* thing. Something she was *meant* to do ... maybe even something to help define who she was in life. Maybe even ... the answer to the question, *Who am I?*

"Yes! Yes, I will do it."

At first, he looked surprised, shocked even. Then he sat up and clapped his hands. "Oh! That is wonderful news, Miss Eve. Thank you, thank you very kindly! And God bless you."

"Thank you, Dr. Johnson. And God bless you as well, for all that you do."

"Miss Eve ... welcome ... welcome most *sincerely* ... to the *Underground Railroad!*"

ᏍᎤᏍᎤᏋᏟᏋᏟᏍᎤᏍᎤᏋᏟᏟᏍᎤᏍᎤᏋᏟᏋᏟ

An hour later Evelyn was halfway home, walking alone in the dark streets of Richmond. They'd started installing gas streetlamps in the center of town nearly a decade ago, but they hadn't yet extended as far as her home on Jefferson Street. And Jackson Street, where Dr. Johnson lived, was even further out.

But there was plenty of moonlight, and enough light coming from the houses along the road to see by. She'd never been afraid of the dark. It had been one of the many practical things her father had taught her when she was a young child. As long as she kept her wits about her, and paid attention to her surroundings with all her senses, the dark was nothing to fear. But now, she had to admit, she was starting to get a bit nervous. As she crossed the last intersection, she'd noticed a man walking in her direction, approaching the intersection from her left. She thought little of it at the time. But when she got further down the block, she glanced back and saw the man had turned and was now following her. Probably just an innocent coincidence, but ...

Dr. Johnson had offered to walk her home, but he couldn't do it until after the "conductor" had arrived to escort the "passengers" to their next destination. And he had no idea when that would be. But it was usually very late — often past midnight — to ensure there would be the least amount of people out and about or looking out windows. In the end, Evelyn had decided not to wait. There was always a chance Miss Harriet would awaken and possibly notice her absence. A restless stroll in the moonlight might be easily explained away, especially given Evelyn's recent erratic behavior at Mr. Chamber's house. But arriving at three o'clock in the morning was a whole different matter.

So she had chosen to go it alone, but now she was starting to have her doubts about that decision. She tried to act casual and intentionally resisted the urge to quicken her pace. But in a very short distance it became obvious the man would soon overtake her, still several blocks from her house. He was striding along at a determined pace, like a man trying to cover the most possible ground in the least amount of time, without actually running. And his longer legs only added to his advantage.

So she stopped where she was, and turned to face him. Better to meet this unknown man face to face than to have him come up behind her in the dark.

She was not especially afraid; she was tall for a woman, and she knew how to fight — another useful skill her father had taught her, along with the neighborhood boys near the farm where she grew up. She could land a good hard punch and knew how to kick a man in a way that would quickly take the fight out of him. Besides, there were many houses close by, and a good healthy scream would bring plenty of people streaming out to see what the commotion was about.

So she waited calmly as the stranger steadily approached. She could make out very little about him in the dark, but it did now appear his clothing was a dark color, either black or navy blue. And she noticed small hints of gold piping and braiding on the sleeves, and on the man's hat. Some kind of uniform, maybe? A soldier? Or a policeman? That seemed more hopeful, though she didn't really want a policeman to question her, given the errand she'd just completed.

As he came up to her, he slowed and came to a stop at a respectful distance.

"Good evening, miss."

"Good evening, sir."

She saw he was a young man, her own age or even younger— clean shaven, with long dark hair. *Probably not yet old enough to grow a beard*, she decided. And he was definitely wearing a uniform, but not of a soldier.

"Are you a policeman, sir? I turned to see who was following me, not being able to make you out in the dark."

"Oh no, ma'am, not an *actual* police officer, but I hope to be one someday soon. No, ma'am, not an officer, but I do work for the police department ... I am one of the *watchmen*. We walk about the town and keep an eye on things. If we encounter any mischief, we go fetch one of the officers. There are thirty-five of us watchmen, but only eight actual officers, ma'am."

"Hmm ... how interesting ... I never knew that. I thought all policemen were the same. Well, anyway, Mr. ... *Watchman* ..."

"Oh, sorry for my rudeness, ma'am ... I am Watchman Collins ... Jubal Collins. Nice to meet you, ma'am."

"I am ... Miss *Eve*, Watchman Collins. Nice to meet you as well. And were you indeed following me, sir, or was I simply imagining things in the darkness?"

"Oh ... well, not initially, of course ... just making my normal rounds. But when I saw you walking alone after dark, I reckoned the proper thing to do was to follow you—to make sure you got safely to where you were going. Not that anything bad generally happens in this neighborhood—nice, polite, decent folk, for the most part. Unlike some other areas. But, well, better safe than sorry, my Daddy used to always say. Sorry if I frightened you ... it was actually the opposite of my intent, as you can see."

"Yes, I see that *now*."

"Where were you going tonight, anyway, all alone in the dark, if you don't mind my asking?"

"Of course I don't mind, Watchman, given your gallant concern for my safety. I was simply feeling hot and restless and thought a nice walk in the cool evening air might help me get to sleep."

"Oh, yes ma'am. It will do that, I should know. But still, don't you think you ought to have someone come along with you? You, know … just to be on the safe side?"

"Well, my dear mother had already gone to sleep, so I had no one to walk with me."

As she was saying this, a thought seemed to jump unbidden into her head. Her immediate 'role' with the Underground Railroad, as Dr. Johnson had explained it, would be to keep her ears open. To provide him any information she thought would be helpful to the cause: which plantations were actively buying slaves, and which were selling. Which places treated their slaves in a particularly onerous manner, so were ripe for 'intervention.' And … any news about attempts to crack down on the Underground. It occurred to her Watchman Collins, as much as he was a nice, polite young man, was an officer of the 'enemy' in her new role. Any information she could glean about his activities might prove useful.

"But sir … I do find it most reassuring to know you're out here at night keeping watch on things. It makes me feel that much safer walking about."

"Oh … thank you ma'am … just doing my job, as they say."

"Yes … true, but it is a brave and mostly thankless task, is it not? I mean, wandering through the streets night after night all alone, just looking for any trouble or mischief?"

He smiled and looked down at his shoes. She imagined if it were light enough out, she'd probably see him blushing.

"Tell me, good sir … if I were to be out walking alone again some evening, and were feeling … well, a bit uneasy, or … *lonesome* maybe, where might I be able to find you?"

She felt a twinge of guilt for playing him like this, but … Dr. Johnson might be very interested in knowing where the watchman would be … watching … and when.

"Oh … oh … well, I … I ain't supposed to tell anyone my exact route … you know … in case the wrong sort were to find out …"

"Oh, yes … I see. But surely, sir, you don't think *I'm* … the wrong sort?"

She favored him with a dazzling smile, which seemed to have the desired effect.

"Oh *NO* ma'am! Certainly *not!* I didn't mean to imply … oh, no, not *that!*

"I'm sure there'd be no harm in it … if you was to ever have need of me at night … or whatnot.

"So … I start out from the station … the new one, you know … at the corner of 6th and Broad Streets, at exactly 9:00 pm. And I walk north up 6th, and take a right on Clay …"

In the next ten minutes or so Watchman Collins proceeded to tell Evelyn his entire evening route, including approximate times he would be at each intersection. She listened carefully, concentrated, and had him repeat it enough times she could commit it to memory.

"That'll be my route for the next month or so, then they'll change it up again, and I'll go a different way."

"Oh … thank you so much for sharing it with me. I will feel so much safer knowing I can find you if I ever … have *need* of your company."

"Yes, Miss Eve. And I feel better about you walking alone at night knowing you can find me … if need be."

"Well, I'd best be getting home now. And you'd best get on with your route, or you'll be off schedule, if I haven't already caused you to be."

"Oh, that's quite all right, miss. It is my duty to assist citizens in need, even if it changes my schedule somewhat. Shall I walk you to your door?"

"Oh, that won't be necessary, sir. I'm nearly there, and I'm sure I shall have no trouble. Thank you again for your concern. Perhaps we shall meet again … *out here in the dark* …"

"Yes, Miss Eve. Perhaps we shall. Good night, ma'am."

They parted company. She felt a combination of excitement, and guilt, for having convinced him to divulge his route to her.

She decided that was probably the normal feelings one would have in her new role, using her wits, personality—and *looks*, she had to admit—to get people to tell her things they'd typically not tell anyone. And then … use that information against them later.

She would have to reconcile herself to those conflicting emotions if she were going to carry through with this. And she was determined she *would* carry through with it. It was the only thing she'd done, or even thought of doing, in her adult life that felt like it had any purpose or meaning. Except maybe … the time at Mountain Meadows with Nathan … then she shook her head, and with an effort, kept her thoughts from going there. Not now … *not yet* … maybe later …

ᏋᏌᏕᎧᏣᏋᏌᏕᎧᏣᏋᏌᏕᎧᏣᏋᏌᏕᎧᏣᏋᏌ

The entire farm was gathered once again to listen to the Captain speak. But this time it was not a Sunday, nor was it Independence Day. It was an ordinary day, Saturday, September 1, 1860. And they hadn't gathered in front of the manor house, nor seated around the big wooden table across from the cabins.

This was an entirely different kind of gathering, although the participants were the same. The entire population of the farm, black, white, and canine—Harry the Dog being in attendance, as always—was lined up along the road on the edge of a great field of cotton.

The field was a thing of both natural, and man-made beauty, sparkling white in the sun. It had been a golden summer, and the cotton had responded with great enthusiasm. While some years at harvest time the cotton plants barely reached waste-high on a man, this year cotton bolls popped out at eye level and beyond. He'd never been a farmer before and had always considered such things tedious and mundane in the extreme. But this day Nathan gazed out at the field in wonder. He had to admit it was a *glorious* sight.

He took a deep, satisfied breath, then turned to face his audience. The sun had just crested the mountains to the east, and the air still held the cool crispness of the night.

"Good morning, everyone!"

"Good morning, Captain!" was the response from over a hundred voices at once. Nathan laughed. It was a genuine, happy laugh; he was in the midst of a great work, and the leader of a great people, who were following his lead into a better world.

"When I arrived back at Mountain Meadows, nearly three months ago now, I told y'all my plans—to transform this farm into a place that would thrive without slave labor. That would pay a real wage for your labors and ... allow me to set y'all *free*. Now, standing in front of this field today ... if anyone had any doubts about this plan ... *my God! Just look at this field!* Cotton bolls as high as a gelding's eye! Surely God has blessed our endeavors with this bountiful abundance!

"Now ... I know y'all have seen some changes at this farm since my arrival—no work on the Sabbath ... leading to a celebration every Saturday night."

He looked over at Big George, who'd instigated the pre-Sabbath functions, and he smiled. George returned the smile along with a quick chuckle.

"Repaired cabins, better clothes, and better food. But most importantly ... I've stopped the beatings. Since my arrival there've been no lashings, no whippings, no beatings, no kickings ... not even any spittings! Unless you were to accidentally step in front of Sergeant Jim when he's trying to make a point!" he smiled at Jim, who shrugged, and laughed.

"Now I've been led to understand the cotton harvest has traditionally been ... a particularly strenuous time for all concerned. The former owner of this farm was ... a stern task master—hard on the white men he employed, who in turn made it very hard on y'all, who had to pick cotton.

"Let me ask y'all if I have a fair understanding of how it generally went."

He paused and looked around, making eye contact with many of the people before continuing.

"Each man and woman was given a sack with a strap, such as this one here."

He held up a sack made of linen, with a strap at the top that would be looped around one's neck and one shoulder.

"And they were given a large basket like those, over there. Each worker would go down a row of cotton until the sack was full, then would dump it in their own basket. At the end of each day, they weighed the baskets. Each worker was expected to collect 200 pounds of cotton a day."

There were nods of agreement among those in the crowd.

"After the weighing they took the cotton away to the gin and bale press. If anyone fell short of their 200 pounds that day, they'd receive painful lashes with a leather strap — the number of lashes somewhat dependent on how low the weight was, and somewhat dependent upon the mood of the overseer that day. Either way, such lashes were extremely painful ... and, worse maybe ... very degrading."

There were many sullen looks at this statement, but nobody disagreed.

"And to further add to the misery, if anyone collected well *beyond* their 200 pounds, their reward was ... they'd be expected to collect that same amount the next day. Or they'd feel the lash.

"Do I generally have the right of it?"

There were nods of agreement at this, and some very serious looks. Clearly many had unhappily suffered the cotton harvest under the previous regime.

"All right, good. Now ... let me tell you how it's going to be this year.

"There will still be sacks and baskets, and we will still weigh them ... but not to give out lashes. Instead, the person with the highest weight will be paid a silver dollar, right there on the spot. And no punishment if he doesn't do the same the next day.

"And anyone who turns in less than 200 pounds? What will I do to them? *Nothing*. Nothing at all. You see ... Toby has agreed to be the foreman of this harvest ... and he has appointed his own overseers from amongst you. Y'all will supervise the harvest, and you will decide among you how to best encourage those who bring in less than they're capable of. I will leave that to Toby and his overseers. My only requirement is there will be no beatings, and no painful punishments of any kind. I am hopeful everyone will just encourage one another to do their best. The better this harvest is, the more money this farm can make, and the closer we'll be to your freedom.

"And to show I mean what I say, I myself will pick cotton during this harvest. And so will Miss Abbey, and all the other white men on this farm. We will be among the workers, while Toby's overseers will weigh the cotton, and work the gin and press. He has assured me y'all know how this works better'n any o' us white folks, and I, for one, believe him!"

There were now many smiles and laughs at this, including from the white farmhands, and especially from the former soldiers, who nodded their agreement.

"Looking upon this bountiful and magnificent field of cotton, I can't help but call to mind a very particular passage from the Bible. In John, chapter four, verse thirty-five it says, *'Behold, I say unto you, lift up your eyes, and look on the fields; for they are white ... all ready to harvest.'* My *God* ... I believe these words were written especially for us standing here today!

"Let us give praise to Him who made this bountiful cotton harvest possible, by the words of an old, but appropriate hymn ...

> Praise God, from whom all blessings flow.
> Praise Him, all creatures here below.
> Praise Him above, ye heavenly host.
> Praise Father, Son, and Holy Ghost!

"Amen."

"Amen," the people echoed back, with many voices.

"So ... now to initiate *the great cotton harvest, of the year of our Lord eighteen hundred and sixty*, Toby will teach me how to pick a cotton boll. And then I will lead the harvest. But I must warn you ... I mean to earn that dollar today!"

He smiled, and enjoyed the laughter, hooting, and various catcalls and challenges that followed from the young men gathered about, both black and white.

Then Toby stepped forward, picked up a sack, and slung it over his shoulder. Nathan reached down, grabbed a sack, and followed his example. Toby smiled and walked up to the first cotton plant.

"Now, the trick, Captain, is to try'n pull the cotton from the boll without prickin' your fingers. You see, once the cotton boll opens and dries, we take to calling it a cotton *burr*—on account o' it's got four or five hard, sharp spurs on it, like to cut your fingers. And not all the bolls is ripe at the same time, so you want to take care and not break off any branches that ain't yet ripe. We can collect them bolls later. You pick the bolls like so," he reached out with his left hand and plucked the cotton from a large boll that was head high. At almost the same time he extended his right hand and plucked another boll. He gave it a slight twist to free the fluffy white contents from the hard burr. In one continuous movement each hand went smoothly back to the sack, depositing the cotton before repeating the motion again. Toby's hands moved almost too quickly for Nathan to follow.

Nathan shook his head, turned to the crowd watching with anticipation, shrugged and made a comical face. Then he turned, reached out and grabbed the cotton from a boll in front of him with his right hand, giving it a tug. The cotton stuck to the boll just long enough for his hand to pull away, then fell, unceremoniously, to the ground at his feet. He shook his hand and said, "Ow!"

He stuck his wounded fingers in his mouth and sucked on them, while he sheepishly leaned down, and picked up the cotton from the ground with his left hand.

This was met with laughter from the people gathered around.

Nathan smiled good naturedly, then looked over at Toby.

"I see I'm going to have to start out a little slower and work up to it."

"Yes, sir. I do believe that'd be for the best."

Soon Jim, Stan, William, Georgie, and Jamie joined in, trying their own hands at picking the dangerous and obstinate crop. Soon all had bloody fingers, but were smiling, laughing, and poking fun at one another—enjoying the challenge of the new experience. Zeke, Benny, and Joe joined in good-naturedly. And although they'd supervised the picking for many years, and had even participated a few times, they weren't much better at it than the soldiers.

Miss Abbey proved much more proficient. It quickly became clear she had done this before, but Nathan couldn't imagine when or where—surely his daddy wouldn't have allowed it! So, he moved up next to her and asked, as they continued to pick.

"Oh … it was a long time ago … when I was a little girl and living at my folks' farm outside Richmond. I'd get bored of my studies and sneak out of the house during the harvest so I could chit chat with the young black girls my age who were out picking the cotton. Likely I was more mischief than help, joking and laughing, singing songs—anything to pass the time. Fortunately for me the overseers didn't know what to do with me, so they pretended not to notice I was there. Anyway, I did it enough to get fairly good at it, as you have noticed, thank you kindly."

Nathan smiled and shook his head, "You never cease to amaze and impress me, Momma. Makes me wonder what else there is that I don't know about you."

Abbey returned the smile, "A woman must have her secrets …"

As the white folks moved slowly off down the row, to the great amusement of all the black ones, Toby turned to them and called out, "Well, what're y'all waiting for? We got work to do! Let's get to it. We shore can't let one o' them win that silver dollar!"

This triggered a general scamper to collect baskets and bags and get moving down the other rows.

The household slaves, responsible for providing the meals at midday, and again in the evening, were excused from picking. They headed back toward the Big House to start their work. Likewise, the very old, very young, and their immediate caretakers were excused. They too walked back toward the cabins. Otherwise, it was all-hands-on-deck—especially on the first day of picking.

After the first day, a team would split off to start running the cotton gin and bale press. And another would transport the cotton from the fields to the gin. But today, everybody would pick.

Nathan had asked Tom to supervise the weighing and to record the numbers, so he could award the dollar to the winner.

The next harvest day, which would be Monday, Tom would switch with William, after which it would be someone else's turn.

Nathan moved along, working on getting the hang of pulling the cotton loose without further injuring his already bloody fingers. He'd given up trying to pick the cotton with each hand as Toby had done. Instead, he held the boll steady with one hand while he carefully pulled the cotton out with the other. He concentrated on stuffing the results into the sack so it wouldn't fall to the ground. He now had even more sympathy for the field workers than he'd previously had. And the work was not all at a convenient eye level. More than half the time he had to lean down to pluck the cotton from an ankle-high boll. Soon he could feel the effects of that stooping in his lower back. And, though he'd only been at it less than half an hour, sweat was now rolling down him in streams. This was going to be a *very* long day, he decided.

He was now even happier with his decision to start the harvest on a Saturday. Not only did September first seem like a nice, auspicious date, but because tomorrow was the Sabbath, they could all work their hardest during the daylight hours without worrying about getting up early the next day. And, as a bonus, the evening activities would seem even more like a celebration — not just another Saturday night — to commemorate this historic harvest that would start the people of Mountain Meadows on the road to freedom.

It also meant all the weary workers would have a day to recuperate from their first day's exertions, before having to go at it again. This, he knew, would be especially helpful for the new hands, himself included.

He was beginning to really feel the heat of his exertions. So he paused a moment to unbutton his shirt, pulling it back and flapping it to cool himself, though he dare not take it off completely or the hot sun would quickly burn his flesh beet red. He happened to glance through the cotton plant to the next row over. He saw someone staring back at him. From the size and shape it was obviously a woman. She looked familiar, but he couldn't quite make out who it was. He thought it odd she'd be

44

staring at him like that. But he shrugged and went on with his work.

On the other side of the row Rosa quickly turned away. Then she looked around guiltily, hoping no one had witnessed her little indiscretion. To her relief, everyone was focusing on their work, and no one appeared to be looking her way. She turned back to the task at hand, but the sight she had seen was now burned into her mind.

Being a house slave now, she was excused from picking the cotton, but had volunteered anyway once she'd found out the Captain would be picking. She'd intentionally headed down the row opposite him. And she'd worked her way along, trying to stay even with him as he worked on the other side of the plants. For reasons she didn't completely understand, she felt a strong urge to stay near him and she'd hoped to get a glimpse of him as she went down the row.

She'd only wanted to see where he was so she could time her progress to stay more or less even with him. Instead she'd been met with the shocking sight of him unbuttoning and opening up his shirt. The sight of his broad, muscular chest, beaded with sweat, had nearly made her gasp out loud. It was a sight that stirred ... *something* ... inside her she had never before felt and didn't understand. It was different from the sweet, gentle, protective feelings she'd previously felt for him—a *burning* thing ... a thing not easily suppressed or quickly forgotten. That image of him stayed in her mind the rest of the day, and for many days thereafter, especially when she lay down in her bed alone at night.

But for now, there was cotton to pick, and she didn't want to look too foolish doing it. She didn't have the luxury of laughing it off, as the Captain had. She knew there was already plenty of resentment against her because she had moved into the Big House. Though for some reason she couldn't quite understand, that resentment seemed to have eased somewhat in the last few weeks. And the people did seem to appreciate her volunteering to pick the cotton.

She moved further down the row from where she'd seen the Captain. She nearly jumped at the sound of his voice coming from close by the plant she was picking. At first, she flinched, thinking he was calling her out for her earlier spying. Then she realized he wasn't talking to her at all.

"Someone start a song! This is tedious work, as I'm sure y'all know! Who'll start a song that we can all join in, to help pass the time? Sergeant Jim, do you know any good cotton-picking songs?"

"Well, sir … I know plenty o' good drinking songs. And more than a few good whor … uh … that is … *romancing* type songs. But … not any cotton-picking songs, to speak of."

"What about you, George? You're always good for starting a song of a Saturday night!"

Most everyone called him "Big George" on account of his great size and strength—as tall as the Captain but much more muscular. But he preferred to be called George Washington, having taken the name of the first president after the big wedding. He was also a regular singer at the Saturday night bonfire, so Nathan knew he had a good, strong voice and a knack for coming up with songs.

"Yes, sir … I reckon I could start a song, if'n y'all will join in with me."

"That we will, George, that we will. Long as you don't make the words too tricky!"

"No, sir … no fear o' that … don't think I could sing any that was tricky, no how!"

There was a smattering of laughter, and someone called out, "That's the truth!" which triggered more snickering, and laughter.

George smiled and began to sing. He had a fine, clear baritone voice, and projected it well. It was a tune he'd learned at the previous farm he'd worked, but some of the others also knew it. Soon everyone picked up on the chorus and joined in on the "Hallelujahs."

> O come my brethren and sisters too,
> We're goin' to join the heavenly crew.
> To Christ our Savior let us sing,

And make our loud hosannas ring.
O hallelu, O hallelu,
O hallelujah to the Lord,
O hallelu, O hallelu,
O hallelujah to the Lord.

Oh, there's Bill Thomas, I know him well,
He's got to work to keep from hell.
He's got to pray by night and day,
If he wants to go by the narrow way.
O hallelu, O hallelu,
O hallelujah to the Lord,
O hallelu, O hallelu,
O hallelujah to the Lord.

There's Chloe Williams, she makes me mad,
For you see I know she's goin' on bad.
She told me a lie this afternoon,
And the devil will get her very soon.
O hallelu, O hallelu,
O hallelujah to the Lord,
O hallelu, O hallelu,
O hallelujah to the Lord …"

There were many, many more verses … George seemed to have no end of them. Nathan was never sure if he'd memorized them all or was making them up on the spot. Either way, it was a pleasure to listen to, and to sing along with, and it certainly made the working less burdensome.

Nathan smiled as he listened to the sweet sound of the singing, and joined in the chorus with gusto, along with everyone around him. Despite the hard, hot work it was a heady feeling … like they were all in it together, and this was a new beginning … and even better things were coming soon.

Then a thought flashed unbidden into his mind: *Evelyn would've loved this.* He nodded, and surprised himself by saying out loud, "Yes … she would have!"

Dearest Evelyn,

I have started this letter a hundred times, and a hundred times I have torn up the paper and started anew. I cringe to think of the veritable forest I have destroyed in the attempt!

I have finally come to realize my difficulty has been that I truly don't know what to say. Each time I have started out to apologize, beg your forgiveness, and ask you to return to Mountain Meadows that we might try again. But each time I have faltered because I honestly don't know what happened. What caused you to leave.

I will apologize now, for my abruptness. I fall back upon my usual excuse of military training and experience for that. I hope and trust you will forgive me this lifelong, bad habit.

For the sake of the friendship we have shared, and whatever more we have meant to each other, I ask you find it in your heart to tell me why you left, just as things felt, to me at least, so very affectionate and warm. I will go so far as to say I have never felt such feelings before, and if I am not sorely mistaken, you were feeling the same.

Be assured I still hold you in the highest regard and welcome any correspondence you may see fit to send my way.

I am, with great affection, your humble servant,

Nathaniel Chambers

Mountain Meadows Farm, Virginia

P.S. It looks to be an historic harvest. The cotton is eye-high and looks like a field of deep snow. I wish you were here to see it.

Evelyn set the letter down on the bed with a heavy sigh. She had read it a dozen times or more, and each time she teared up before finishing. Her heart ached for the pain she'd caused him. Such a *good* man ... the best she'd ever known ... more than that ... the only man, other than her father, she'd ever truly loved and admired. What *had* happened?

She wished she knew the answer. She couldn't even begin to think of how to answer his letter. How could she explain to another person something she didn't truly understand herself?

Yes ... how can I? Who am I? the tiny voice spoke in the back of her mind.

Oh, Nathan ... how can you ever forgive me? I can't imagine ever loving another man. If you stop loving me ... I think I will surely die. But ... but I can't be with you now ... not yet ... not until ... until what?

Until I know who I am ... the tiny voice answered.

Yes, yes ... always that! she thought, then threw herself down on the pillow, and cried herself to sleep.

⅋ℭ℞Ⅽℬℰℭ℞ℭℬℰ⅋℞ℭℬ

"Evelyn ... Evelyn! Wake up ... it is nearly afternoon. Are you going to sleep the day away?"

She sat up, rubbed the sleep from her eyes, and responded.

"Coming, Momma."

She entered the small living room, and sat in one of the chairs, next to a steaming hot cup of tea Miss Harriet had poured for her.

"Sorry ... I was up late ... had a hard time getting to sleep."

"Reading that letter ... a hundred times, I expect?"

"Yes, ma'am."

"Well?"

"Well, what, Momma?"

"Come, girl ... don't be a ninny! Tell me what he said! Bad enough you wouldn't even open it all yesterday afternoon ... now you have made me wait nearly half the day today to hear about it."

"Oh ... yes, that was ... very thoughtless, and unkind of me. Let me just fetch it from the room. You may read it for yourself if you wish."

"Oh, never mind getting up ... I'll just fetch it myself."

Harriet went into the bedroom, and returned a moment later, letter in hand. She went over to a side table to fetch her reading glasses before sitting back down next to her cup of tea.

After a few minutes she looked up, and said, "This is very encouraging. Surprisingly, he still seems to have good feelings for you."

"Yes ... it would seem so."

"Not that you deserve them, after your notorious behavior."

"Yes, ma'am. I couldn't agree more."

"Dammit, Evelyn! It is hard to be angry with you when you are so ... so damned *agreeable!*"

"Sorry, Momma. It's just I *do* agree with you. My behavior with Mr. Chambers was ... *inexcusable*. He was a perfectly wonderful, beautiful gentleman ... in every way. I really don't know what came over me. I ... have never experienced anything like it before and I ... still don't really understand it."

"Well, that makes two of us, at least. But ... you do seem to be feeling better, yes? You've had a better look about you the last several days, that is until ... well, until this letter arrived yesterday. That seemed to have shaken you a bit, if I'm not mistaken."

"Yes, Momma. Though I should have known it would be coming ... still ... to see *his* own handwriting, and ... to read *his* own words ... it was ... I don't know. It was ... *emotional.*"

"Yes ... I would think so. But, it's good to see there's still hope for the two of you ... if *you* still think so."

"Oh ... yes, Momma ... most certainly *yes!* Nathan is ... well ... he is everything a woman could ask for! There's nothing amiss with him, and most everything that's good, honorable, and ... *desirable*, dare I say?"

"You *may* say it, in front of me ... but nowhere else! But I know what you mean. Mr. Chambers is one of the finest looking gentlemen I have *ever* seen. And, well, has all the other things a man should have. Strength of character, leadership, the courage of his convictions. Though I might not agree with him on all his plans concerning his farm and his slaves—still ... you can't fault

50

the man for making a solid plan and following through with it! If only your father had been able to do that … maybe things might have turned out differently."

"They aren't so very different, you know."

"What? Who aren't?"

"Daddy and Mr. Chambers. They aren't so very different from each other."

"Yes … I suppose … if you think *night* is the same as *day!*"

"Oh, Momma. Will you never forgive Daddy?"

"No … at least not until we're living someplace better'n this dump!"

"It's … not so bad, Momma. There are plenty of folks live in worse."

"Pah! What do I care of *other* folks?! I only care of how you and I are living … and right now that is just one step above beggars!"

"I'm sorry, Momma … truly sorry, for spoiling all your plans. But … if it will make you feel better, I've been thinking … maybe I am ready to go out again."

"Out?"

"Yes … you know … out in society? Out to the balls, and such … I am feeling ready to go out among people again."

"Oh … truly? Well … well, then I will start making inquiries … I may have heard there was some kind of function this Saturday night. I'll look into it."

"Thank you, Momma."

Again Evelyn felt a bit of guilt at her own duplicity. What she hadn't told Miss Harriet was … she was ready to return to society functions, but not to find another potential suitor. She wanted to begin pursuing her new mission: to gather information for Dr. Johnson, and the Underground Railroad.

CHAPTER 3. THE ELECTION OF A PRESIDENT

*"People never lie so much as after a hunt,
during a war, or before an election."*
– Otto von Bismarck

—

*"The outrages which abolition fanaticism
has continued year by year to heap upon the South,
have at length culminated in the election of
Abraham Lincoln and Hannibal Hamlin,
avowed abolitionists, to the presidency and vice presidency
– both bigoted, unscrupulous and cold-blooded enemies
of the peace and equality of the slaveholding states ..."*
– The Semi-Weekly Mississippian, Jackson, Miss.

Friday, Nov. 9, 1860 - Greenbrier County, Virginia:

"Ah, here it is," Tom said. He folded back the third page of the newspaper, preparing to read the summary of the good news they'd already heard via word of mouth the previous day.

Nathan leaned back in his chair and blew a long puff of cigar smoke into the crisp blue sky above the veranda. It was a cool evening, and the sun was about to set, but it was not yet cold enough to drive them indoors. Jim sat in the next chair over, savoring a glass of Bourbon whiskey.

Tuesday, Nov. 6, 1860 - Washington City.

Today Abraham Lincoln of the new Republican Party was elected 16th President of the United States of America with Hannibal Hamlin of Maine as Vice President. The duo received 180 Electoral Votes of the 152 required for victory. The turnout is estimated to be over eighty percent of eligible voters, which would make it the highest in American history, with over four and a half million votes counted.

52

Despite the high turnout, Mr. Lincoln received less than forty percent of the popular vote, with Stephen A. Douglas receiving the next highest of the four candidates at thirty percent.

It is worth noting Lincoln lost every state in which slavery is legal. In fact, Illinois, his home state, is the most southerly state he won, not counting the far-west state of California, which he also won, along with Oregon.

His name did not even appear on the ballot in the southern states of North Carolina, South Carolina, Georgia, Florida, Alabama, Tennessee, Mississippi, Arkansas, Louisiana and Texas, making him the first President not to be on all states' ballots. And he has had the second lowest share of the popular vote among all winning presidential candidates in U.S. history, after John Quincy Adams.

"Well, it was certainly an odd and memorable election," Nathan said.

"True, but I always say, all's well that ends well," Jim added. "Same as on a battlefield; it don't much matter *how* you win, so long as you *do!*"

"Hmm ... I'm not so sure this time," Tom answered with a frown. "There's more."

The reaction to his election among southern states has been swift and vocal, especially in South Carolina. There Governor William Henry Gist has threatened to secede from the United States even before Mr. Lincoln can take office. It has been reported plans are already being made in Charleston to hold a special convention to discuss that very topic.

ജൈയ്യരുള്ള ജൈയ്യരുള്ള ജൈയ്യരുള്ള

Friday, Nov. 9, 1860 - Richmond, Virginia:

"Damn those fools in Charleston, Templeton! They would burn down their own house with themselves inside, just so the flames would disturb their neighbors!"

"Yes, your honor ... so it would seem."

Templeton sat in the governor's office, in the chair opposite his desk. He had a calm, almost relaxed demeanor, in sharp contrast to the other man in the room, who seemed unusually agitated. Governor Letcher did not sit in his chair, as was his normal habit. He paced back and forth behind the desk, occasionally slapping his fist into his open hand to add emphasis to his frustration.

"By God! They've set the whole thing up from the very beginning ... *purposely* ... to get Lincoln elected so they'd have the excuse they needed for the secession. They forced the split in the Democratic party, which practically guaranteed the outcome ... even if the Republicans had nominated a stumbling fool he'd still have been elected. And Lincoln is no fool, by all accounts."

"I can't argue with your reasoning there, sir. Especially in light of the things representative McQueen of South Carolina told us, right here in this office, several months before the election. He practically admitted a conspiracy to take advantage of Lincoln's election for their own purposes."

"Damn it, Templeton. I am simply ... *livid!* Fit to be tied! I heard they were even celebrating the election in Charleston ... fireworks, bonfires ... the whole thing! Not even having the common decency to *pretend* being offended and upset by it! And the worst of it is ... they think to force *my* hand ... to bully me into joining them in this madness. *Me*, the duly elected governor of the great Commonwealth of Virginia! The impertinence! The unmitigated gall! How ... how *dare* they! *Damn* ... and *damn* again! Have I said '*damn*' yet, Templeton?"

"Yes, I believe you may have inadvertently uttered the word, your honor ..."

"*Damn!* There, I've said it again!"

"Yes, sir. And I agree with your sentiments completely, your honor. The whole matter smacks of a very high degree of arrogance and hypocrisy on their part."

"Yes, you're *damned* right it does. Well ... don't just sit there like a bump on a log ... I'm sure you've been considering this, so let's have it. What're we going to do to head off this disaster?"

"Yes ... as you say ... I have been giving the matter considerable thought and attention. If you'll be so kind as to be

54

seated, your honor, I will be very happy to elucidate on the matter."

Letcher glared at him for a moment, then let out a sigh. He resisted a strong urge to chastise the man for presuming to tell *him … the governor or the Commonwealth of Virginia,* when to stand and when to sit. But he knew he was becoming overwrought, and … he also knew he needed Templeton now more than ever, and it wouldn't do to unnecessarily offend the man.

"Very well, Templeton, I will sit and listen to what you've come up with. God knows I could use some *good* news— something to settle my nerves and calm my growing anxiety."

"Thank you, your honor, for humoring me. I find it very … distracting … to discuss important matters when the other person is moving about so. It makes it … difficult to concentrate."

Letcher looked at him, nodded, and waved his hand. "All right then, get on with it."

"Well, sir, the *good news* you are wanting is … I believe there *are* steps we can take to help mitigate the actions of our more impulsive cousins to the south."

"Good, good … let's hear them."

"Yes, sir. The most important thing is for us to seize the initiative. Not to wait and see what others will do, but boldly step up to take the lead on it."

"What? You want me to lead the push for the secession?"

"No … not exactly. What I'm proposing is for you to be seen for the wise, rational, and reasonable leader you are. To acknowledge there has been 'discussion' of secession, and to 'take the bull by the horns,' as they say. To call an early special session of the legislature to discuss the matter, in a serious, formal manner, as befits such a potentially momentous decision. When others see you're treating the issue in a thoughtful, responsible way, it may shame them into doing the same."

"Yes … I like it … a special session … as soon as possible …"

"Yes, sir, but … well, with travel considerations, the holidays, and such, I think … maybe just after the New Year would be the best timing, your honor."

"Yes, yes, the beginning of January … of a new year, and a new direction … I like it. Pray continue …"

"Well, then we steer the legislature toward appointing a commission … or holding a special convention to further discuss the matter."

"Hmm … I see where you're going with this. We make sure the commission, convention, or whatnot, is roughly evenly divided between pro-Union and pro-secession members. That way the discussion will drag out for an extended period of time …"

"Yes, you're getting the gist of it, sir. The longer it takes to come to any conclusion, the more time it buys Mr. Lincoln to prove he's not the devil he's been made out to be. And for you to make sure calmer heads prevail.

"But as for an even split of members, rather than evenly dividing the matter between pro-Union and pro-secession members, it would be best to make sure the vast majority are undecided or neutral. That will ensure no premature voting on the matter. Those who're pro one side or the other will require considerable time to sway the neutral ones."

"Brilliant, Templeton, brilliant! What else?"

Templeton smiled. He and the governor had worked together long enough that Letcher knew when Templeton had more ideas up his sleeve.

"I have in mind the legislature might sponsor, at your prompting, of course, a national peace conference — hosted by us in Washington City. Its mission would be to discuss the concerns of the Southern states: tariffs, the expansion of slavery, the fugitive slave act, etcetera, with each other and any invited Northern representatives. Possibly with Mr. Lincoln present as well. That will place you on the national stage, your honor … at practically the same level as the president. And if all goes well, you'll come out of it as the savior of the nation. And even if not, you'll be lauded for your efforts to maintain the peace."

"Yes … yes, I like it. But I can't be seen as directly leading it … only as its sponsor, otherwise the other governors will be resentful, and think I'm over-reaching."

"Yes, good point, sir. We'll have to come up with a suitable stand-in ... someone you have trust in, but ideally with a reputation beyond the borders of the Commonwealth."

"Yes ... and I know just the man. President Tyler."

"Ah, excellent choice, sir! He certainly has the necessary reputation, being the 10th U.S. President. And, he has been a staunch supporter of your honor, in your present career."

Templeton had already planned on suggesting Tyler but was happy to let Letcher take the credit for the idea. It saved him the trouble of talking the governor into it.

"And I'm thinking ... you should wait a few days before announcing the special session. That will be soon enough to head off anything South Carolina might do, but not so soon as to appear premeditated, or reactive. Yes ... a good week or so after the election should make it look more thoughtful and reasoned."

ಬಿ⊄ಬಿ⊄ಬಿ⊄ಬಿ⊄ಬಿ⊄ಬಿ⊄

Friday, Nov. 16, 1860 - Richmond, Virginia:

> Yesterday, Virginia Governor John Letcher issued a proclamation calling for a special session of the General Assembly to consider, among other matters, the creation of a secession convention. The legislature has been scheduled to convene on January 7, 1861.
>
> – *The Richmond Enquirer, Semi-Weekly Edition*

ಬಿ⊄ಬಿ⊄ಬಿ⊄ಬಿ⊄ಬಿ⊄ಬಿ⊄

Monday, Nov. 19, 1860 - Greenbrier County, Virginia:

"Good afternoon, Captain, sir!"

"Oh, hello there, Toby. Good afternoon to you, as well."

Nathan was in the barn, along with Georgie, checking in on the horses, since the grooms had the week off, along with the field slaves. Toby had poked his head in the barn door to call his greeting.

"Come on in out of the cold, if you wish, Toby."

"Thank ye kindly, sir. I reckon I'll do just that."

He came in and stood next to Nathan as the latter lifted the front hoof of a gelding to inspect the shoe.

"I wanted to thank you kindly, sir, for givin' us'all the whole week off o' doing any field work. We don't hardly rightly know what to be doin' with ourselves."

"Oh … well, I'm sure you'll think of something, Toby!"

The two shared a genuine, friendly smile.

"Yes, sir. I reckon so. I reckon so, at that!"

"Well, Toby, it was my pleasure, and it is greatly deserved, too. That was a right fine harvest. Not just the cotton, which exceeded all expectations, but the tobacco and all the other crops as well. All was done with an efficiency and an enthusiasm that was a genuine heart-warmer to see! And much of it thanks to you, Toby. You're a man of your word, and I am most obliged to you. You can be proud of the job you've done. Thank you, sincerely, sir!"

And Nathan extended his hand, which Toby grasped firmly in answer. He beamed broadly. It occurred to Nathan it was probably the first time in his long life he'd been praised in that regard—or been called "sir" for that matter. Another sorry shame in Nathan's mind. Toby was proving to be extremely intelligent, competent, and capable, despite his advanced age. Though, come to think of it, Nathan had noticed Toby seemed to be walking a little straighter and livelier than he had in the past. Were the increased responsibilities breathing new life into him? Or was he just no longer acting the part of a slave too old to be productive now that he was no longer practicing "The Way"?

"I figure a week of ease and relaxation will do everyone good, myself included. Then we can all start in on wintertime activities, at least until the snow flies. I figure we can harvest some timber for winter firewood. And Mr. Tom has a notion to try our hand at a little simple mining in some of the caves—if we can locate any useful minerals that don't require extensive digging. It seems a good use of our time when there's little to do in the fields. And it could eventually help raise some additional funds.

"I know the old master would rouse you out into the cold just to keep you busy, but I've little taste for nonsense work. We'll all want to find things to keep us from boredom during the long winter, but they should be useful and productive."

"I agrees with you there, Captain. I don't much care for sittin' about all the long winter with nothin' to do. But ... also, these old bones don't like going out for crackin' ice, and shoveling snow, neither."

"I hear you, Toby. I promise you they'll be no work in the cold for no good reason. But ... for this week, we will celebrate the fine harvest, and rest up for the winter work to come."

"Sounds right fine to me, Captain, and I thanks you again, most kindly ... and the others do as well."

"Yes, certainly."

They were quiet for a moment, as Nathan moved from one horse to the next, continuing his inspection.

"Captain ... they's somethin' I'm wanting to ask you about ... actually, the Elders all wants to know ..."

Nathan stopped what he was doing, and turned to look at Toby, giving him his undivided attention this time.

"Yes, Toby? You can ask me anything you please, and I will do my best to answer."

"Yes, sir. Thank you, sir. Well ... we's heard the white folks done elected a new president. Now normally us all pays little attention to such. One president ... well, to be honest sir ... one president seems like all the others to the likes o' us, if you understands me."

"Yes, I expect that's so. And the last several haven't shown much to get excited about, I'll admit."

"Well, this time ... from what we been hearing ... it's a whole other matter. We keeps hearin' o' this *Lincoln* fella. And ... well, sir, we ain't quite sure what to make of it. From hearin' *your* men talk, he seems like a fine and righteous young man. Even a man that don't care for slavin' and might even take it upon hisself to do somethin' 'bout that. Which seems mighty hopeful, to my way o' thinkin', sir."

"Yes, I'd have to agree with you there, Toby."

"But, on the other hand, those of us as have been into town — helpin' gather supplies, offloadin' the harvest, and whatnot —

have heard some o' the other white folks a talkin'. And they make him sound like … like …"

Then Toby laughed, looked at Nathan, and smiled.

"Well, sir, like we all used to think you was gonna be, afore you actually got here!"

He chuckled. Nathan smiled, and shook his head.

"Yes … I understand I was quite the monster … *before* I got here!"

"Yes, sir. That you was. Somethin' fierce! Three-heads, teeth like razors, and breathin' out fire, as I recall! And those were your *nicer* qualities, sir!"

Toby chuckled at his own humor. Nathan smiled.

"Anyway, the white folks seems to think this Lincoln gettin' elected is somethin' like the end o' the world. And they's even talkin' of a war with the folks up North. Well, sir, as you can imagine … we don't know what to make o' all this talk and wanted to hear what *you* think it all means."

"Ah."

Nathan decided he should sit for this one. So he moved over to the side of the stall, found a spot that was relatively clean, and sat down with his back against the boards. Toby came and sat beside him.

"Firstly … from everything I've read and heard, Mr. Lincoln seems like as fine a fellow as God ever saw fit to seat in the president's chair. He seems a Godly man, by all accounts, and makes no secret of his hatred of slavery. So yes … he's no more of a monster than I am."

"Oh, well! That's a blessing to hear! Then this whole election has been a very happy surprise for us'ens!"

"Yes … it would *seem* so …"

"Why do I feel like you's about to say a very loud '*BUT*'?"

"*But* … Mr. Lincoln can't just free the slaves all by himself, even if he wanted to. A president isn't King David, or Caesar … he can't just say a thing and make it so. He's the leader, true … but many, many others must agree with what he wants for it to come to pass, and with *slavery* …"

"Too many folks don't wants it to go away ... 'specially them white folks in this part o' the country?"

"Yes, I'm afraid so. And now they're talking about something they call *secession*. Have you heard of it?"

"No, sir. What does it mean?"

"Well, the word means to split things apart ... in this case, our whole country. Those that don't like Mr. Lincoln, and the things he's saying, are now talking about splitting away from our country, the United States of America."

"Oh ... oh ... and I'm guessin' that'd be a terrible-bad thing to happen?"

"Yes ... I think so ... for several reasons. Firstly, if it were successful, the states that split off will have no reason to *ever* free their slaves, since that'd be the whole reason for splitting off to begin with."

"Oh ... oh, I see. That sounds mighty bad, all right. But you said they was other reasons?"

"Well, yes. Most likely the secession would *not* succeed, because Mr. Lincoln would likely not allow it to happen. I know I wouldn't if I'd just been elected president. Imagine being known for the rest of time as the president who'd lost half the country! Not a very flattering thing to be known for, and I can't imagine any president standing still for it."

"No, I reckon not, sir. So what you figure Mr. Lincoln gonna do 'bout this ... 'cession?"

"Oh ... I think if they go too far ... he'll have to send in soldiers to put a stop to it. And then ... well, then there will most certainly be a war."

"A real shootin' war? Like General Washington fought 'gainst them British fellers? You sayin' them Northern white folks'd fight against the ones round here 'bouts in order for Mr. Lincoln to end slavery?"

"Well, that might not be the initial reason of it, but ... yes, essentially, it would be a war about slavery."

"Hard to believe that all them white folks'd be willin' to risk getting' theyselves kilt just on account o' trying to free us all. That's mighty hard to believe all right."

"Yes … but even so, that may be the case."

"But then, Captain, who you reckon'd win such a war, if it come to it?"

"Oh, the Northerners, there can be no doubt. They have vastly more men, more guns, ships, trains … everything. And they have the factories to make more of anything they need much faster than the South can do it. Oh, the outcome would never be in question, in my mind."

"Well, if that's so … maybe this war'd be a good thing, then? I mean, if Mr. Lincoln win this war, then he frees the slaves straight away, don't he?"

"Yes … likely he would, but …"

"There's that bad word '*BUT*' again …"

"*But* … even though I'm sure the North would win this kind of war—still … likely it would be terrible beyond the dreams of those who would use it to solve their problems. Untold thousands of young men killed, cities destroyed, people without homes or food, and so on.

"You know I fought in the last war, against Mexico. I've seen how terrible a *real* war can be. Most of those fools shooting off their mouths about secession have never been to war and have no idea what they're talking about. They reckon a few brave men march about, fire off their guns, scare off the enemy, and then march back home, the whole thing settled. But real war doesn't work that way. Many fine young men are killed or maimed for life, losing arms, legs, eyes …"

He slowly shook his head as if recalling terrible memories. "And the senseless destruction of the land where wars are fought is … a terrible thing to see.

"Toby, I've known many military men from the North. I can tell you they aren't afraid to fight, and they'll never, ever quit, as long as their president tells them to keep going. And no matter how bravely the Southerners fight, nor how many Northerners they manage to kill, Mr. Lincoln can just keep sending more. And he can keep making more cannons, and rifles, and bullets, and ships and … well, you get the idea.

"In a war like that, it's possible *I* could be killed, and these brave young men I brought with me. This farm might be burned to the ground in the fighting, its fields trampled into the mud. God knows what would happen to y'all during such a thing. Likely either killed or forced to help the slavers fight. No ... nothing good could come of such a war, of that I'm *certain*. Better to end slavery the way we've been planning. To show how it's unnecessary — that a farm can succeed without it. And use our example to shame others into doing the *right* thing. It may take a little longer, but there's no doubt in my mind it *will* succeed. It has already done so in the rest of the world. This is the last civilized country on Earth where there's still slavery, and surely it can't last much longer, war or no war."

"I see what you mean, Captain. So ... then what's to be done about this ... splittin' business?"

"The secession? Well, I've been called over to Richmond by the governor, to talk about just that. I'm hopeful Virginia, at least, will reject this madness. At least I'll do everything in my power, and with my last breath if necessary, to try and make it so."

"Well then, God bless you, and good luck to you, Captain."

"Thank you, Toby. Likely I'll need a healthy portion of both."

☙❧☙❧☙❧☙❧☙❧

"Well, Mr. Sickles ... Bob tells me you have a suggestion for me concerning our troublesome neighbor, and how we can ... even the score ... so to speak."

"Yes, sir, Mr. Walters. I have been thinking on it. And I have come up with ... well, at least the beginnings of a plan, sir."

"Very well, let's hear it."

"Yes, sir. Well, you've heard Governor Letcher has called a special legislative session to consider the matter of ... secession?"

"Yes ... about damned time that useless governor showed some backbone. The entire time this fool Lincoln has been spouting off his mouth, our *beloved* governor has said nothing, done nothing! Yes, about time he stood up and *did* something. But what's that got to do with our disreputable neighbor?"

"Well, as you know, Mr. Chambers is a duly appointed state senator, and as such ..."

"He'll be required to be in attendance ... yes ... I see what you're getting at, Sickles. Because of this special session, we will know *exactly* when he will be away from home. And ... likely he will take several of his soldier boys with him, to stroke his monumental ego ..."

"Yes, sir. That's what I figure. That will leave his farm less defended. And if we plan more carefully this time, and maybe bring along a few more experienced men, we should be able to catch them by surprise. And cause ... well, considerable disruption ..."

"Hmm ... yes ... I like your way of thinking, Sickles ... Bob, what do you think?"

"Yes, sir. I can see there'd be great advantage to carrying out an ... *action* ... while Mr. Chambers is away in Richmond. It'd certainly put the odds better in our favor, if we didn't have to concern ourselves with him personally being there to direct things."

Then Sickles added, "And, sir ... I'm almost certain he'll take his right-hand man Mr. Clark with him. That will likely leave Jim Wiggins in charge ... and I understand you have a particular score to settle with that one."

"Jim ... yes. That arrogant clown. Ruined my new riding boots forcing me to wade the creek. I'll enjoy wiping that smug grin from his face ... with a Bowie knife!"

"But ... sir ... what about the law?" Bob asked. "Are you sure we can count on the sheriff's discretion? Shooting up some furniture, and beating up a few slaves, as we intended last time, is one thing. But riding in and killing his hired men? I'm not sure the law will be able to look the other way on that one."

"Well ... what if there are no white men left alive on the farm? Then who's to testify against us? We'll claim there was a slave uprising, and it was them that murdered all the whites. We just came along to set things right. Nobody'll believe a bunch of frightened darkies; and even if they do, their testimony isn't valid in a Virginia court of law.

"What a lovely homecoming for Mr. Chambers! Imagine him returning to his farm and finding everyone dead except the blacks. And many of them dead as well, though it's unlikely we'll be able to hunt them all down. I'm sure many will flee into the woods the moment they hear gunfire. Perhaps we'll even burn down his house. I'll think on it and decide if it would be better to leave it intact and full of the dead."

Bob looked at Sickles to see his reaction to this last statement. He had an idea to speak with Sickles privately later and try to convince him to help head off this madness. But the look he saw made his heart sink. Sickles had a light in his eyes, and a smile on his face, like he was already seeing the bodies piled in the house. Or the flames climbing high.

Margaret, eavesdropping from her usual place at the top of the stairs, covered her mouth with her hand to prevent an involuntary gasp of shock.

She retreated quickly to her room, tears streaming down her face. She closed the door quietly and sat on the bed. Her heart was pounding, and her head was spinning. Despite everything she knew about her husband, the things she'd just overheard were staggering. It was so unimaginably horrible that Margaret almost couldn't believe what she'd heard with her own ears.

She folded her arms, wrapped them tight around her sides, and shuddered, rocking back and forth. With sheer force of will she held back an explosion of emotion. It was … too terrible to contemplate … just imagining the lovely and gracious Miss Abbey … murdered … all covered in blood—it was … *unthinkable.*

Stay calm, Margaret … stay calm … must think … must think … must come up with a way to warn Mr. Chambers. There's no choice this time. Nothing is more important than this—nothing! Not even my own life. I … must … I must find a way … I must warn Mr. Chambers! Stay calm … and think!

Chapter 4. Storm Clouds on the Horizon

"Take therefore no thought for the morrow:
for the morrow shall take thought for the things of itself.
Sufficient unto the day is the evil thereof."
– Matthew 6:34

Saturday, Dec. 1, 1860 - Greenbrier County, Virginia:

Nathan and Tom clinked glasses and exchanged a smile, the flames from the bonfire shining through the whiskey, giving the contents a golden glow. It was a beautiful, clear evening, with sparkling stars filling the night sky. Though cool, it was not uncomfortably so. And they could feel the heat of the fire even twenty or so feet away where they sat on simple wooden chairs. Jim sat on the other side of Nathan, also sipping a glass of whiskey. Between them and the fire dozens of people danced — an impromptu, unchoreographed production accompanied by a steady drumbeat, and a tune provided by various homemade drums and other instruments.

The only "real" instrument among them was William's violin. And despite his extensive, classical music education, William seemed to enjoy himself—performing the entirely improvised songs that made up the vast majority of the tunes at Mountain Meadows' Saturday night bonfires. His contribution gave any song a depth, beauty, and texture that would otherwise be missing. The lyrics for this song, like many others, were made up on the spot, mostly by Big George, who was the local song lyricist.

"So Tom, you were starting to tell me how we did on the harvest."

"Yes, sir. As you know, your father kept very detailed records, going back … well, I guess since the time he took over the farm from your grandfather, some thirty years ago. Anyway, I looked all that way back, and you'll be happy to know this has been the best harvest *ever* by far, both by volume and price."

"That's wonderful, Tom! Jim, did you hear that? This was the best harvest Mountain Meadows has ever had!"

"You don't say, sir? Well, guess us old soldiers ain't so bad at farmin' after all!" He smiled, raised his glass toward Nathan and Tom, and took another drink. It occurred to Nathan that Jim was likely getting close to his limit. But Jim was always a very pleasant drunk—not the nasty, surly type many men turned into—so he gave it little mind. There were plenty of strong, young men about to help him off to bed, if need be.

"I guess that shows what men can accomplish when they're motivated in a positive manner. And have their own interests at stake, rather than just fear of the whip," Nathan responded, turning back toward Tom.

"Yes, sir. It seems a clear vindication of your approach toward these people, and your plans for the future."

"More than that, Tom ... I believe it also shows ... well, that God is on our side, and agrees with our plans. We as a collective, may have put in a better effort than usual—thanks in large part to our friend Toby—but you have to admit this harvest was amazingly abundant. Well beyond normal. I've heard some years the cotton is no more than knee-high at harvest time. But ... *by God, Tom!* This year some of the bolls were well above my head. Even to the point I had to reach up on my toes to pick them! I've never heard of such a thing."

"Yes, sir. I agree. This was an unusually robust harvest. Well then, here's to being on His good side!"

They shared a smile and raised their glasses, clinking them together once again before taking another sip. Jim leaned forward and clinked glasses with them, though he hadn't been paying attention, so had no idea what they were currently toasting.

Then as Nathan turned back toward Tom to continue their conversation, he heard Jim suddenly laugh, and felt a slap on his arm.

"Look, Captain!"

He turned, and saw Jim pointing toward where the people were dancing around the fire. Tom and Nathan looked to see what had caused Jim's outburst.

Stan was in the middle of the dancers, and was performing some kind of strange, Russian dance. The dance, if you could rightly call it that, involved squatting down almost onto one's heels, hands on hips, or stretched out straight in front. Then the dancer kicked his legs out to the front, one after the other, to the beat of the music, while moving around and trying to remain balanced. Stan performed this seemingly impossible feat with great skill and ease. But he had challenged some of the young black men to do it with him. A half dozen or so were currently hopping about, trying to mimic him, or rolling on the ground where they'd ended up after losing their balance. The rest of the dancers had stopped to watch and were now laughing hysterically at the scene. The groom Cobb was the only one doing a reasonably good job of it, moving in time to the music, more or less, while manfully keeping his balance.

Nathan and Tom shared in the laughter. It finally came down to just Stan and Cobb dancing around each other, while all the others sat on the ground, or stood around them clapping and cheering them on. When the song ended, there was a burst of cheering, hooting, and applause, as Stan embraced Cobb, kissing him on both cheeks.

When the noise died back down a little, Nathan resumed the discussion.

"Tom … you were also starting to tell me why the prices were so excellent this year, despite an abundant harvest all throughout the South. Usually those two things don't go together."

"Yes, sir. Well … that's a double-edged sword, I'm afraid. From what everyone is saying, the prices are staying unusually high, despite the good harvest, on account of … well, sir … the threat of the secession. The cotton buyers, in particular the clothing manufacturers and such, especially in England, are fearful. If the secession happens, and a conflict develops between the North and South, the cotton supply may be threatened. And more than that … if war actually breaks out, the demand for cotton will dramatically increase—both sides needing large quantities of army uniforms, bedding, tents, and many other such items! So they think to lay in a supply of cotton now, for the sake of a possible future shortage combined with a dramatic increase in demand."

"Oh! I see … well, that's not so much to celebrate. Well, let us hope it's not so, and the cotton buyers have spent their funds needlessly."

"Yes, sir. I couldn't agree more."

"Tom … I was thinking we might move up the timeline for freeing the slaves, on account of this unexpectedly fine harvest. But … I suppose we must consider the possibility that everything might go badly, and next year's harvest may be … *compromised*, in some way …"

"Yes, sir. Prudence would suggest we wait and see what happens, before we get too excited about it. If the cotton buyers are right … well … this could be the *last* good harvest for a very, very long time."

"Let's pray not, Tom! Let's pray not!"

"Amen to that, sir! Believe me, I have already prayed on it as much as ever a man can! I've made so many plans for improving the farm, all of which'll be undermined, or outright ruined, if national events turn sour."

"And … changing the subject slightly … what have you learned from looking into the bank accounts, Tom?"

"Well, there is a fairly sizable amount of money distributed among several Richmond banks. But it's not inexhaustible. As you and I've discussed before, we need to get the farm to where it can at least break even, or preferably be slightly profitable without slave labor, before we free them—to ensure its existence long term. To be honest, sir, most of the farm's assets are tied up in the farm itself. For example, Jacob Chambers spent a huge sum four years ago putting in the new cotton gin, its building, and the large bale press. The assets of the farm are in the land, the equipment, the buildings and furnishings, animals, etc. And … well … not to make a big point of it sir, but in the slaves themselves. Given the current situation, with cotton bringing such high prices … you have to figure on average each slave is worth upwards of a thousand dollars. And the strong young males over fifteen hundred each. That's a huge amount of money you're going to ... *write off*, as the accountants would say ... when you free them."

"Yes ... I'm well aware of the economic value of these people. But ... how do you put a price on the freedom of a fellow human being? I would rather free them all and end up a pauper, than keep them as slaves and be the wealthiest man on Earth."

"Yes, I know, sir. It is one of the reasons I came east with you."

Nathan looked Tom in the eye and smiled. "You knew all along what I'd decide to do, didn't you? Even before I knew it myself."

"Yes ... of course, sir! It was always my duty as your aide-de-camp to know what you were going to do, before *you* did! You're a good man, sir. The best I've ever known. I never had any doubt about what you'd decide to do."

"Thank you for that. I'm honored by the faith you continue to place in me. I'll always strive to earn that trust. And, speaking of the money in banks ... have you had time to look into the transfers I asked you about?"

"Yes, sir. I've already made arrangements to transfer the money to the New York bank owned by the family of your friend from the Academy—all the funds from three of the lesser banks, and most of the funds from the largest bank. As you instructed, I've left just enough in Richmond for the expenses of one year running the farm."

"Excellent. Well done. With all this secession talk, I'm nervous about having our family's money tied up in Richmond banks. New York isn't going anywhere, no matter what happens in the South."

"Yes, sir. I think that's a very prudent move."

ℰℐℭℬℰℐℭℬℰℐℭℬℰℐℭℬ

Margaret hurried back to her room from her usual perch above the stairs. Her spying had paid off on several occasions, keeping her informed about her husband's plans. Most of these were mundane farm business and so not particularly interesting. But some were nefarious plots, especially those against Mr. Chambers. This morning she'd been excited to hear Walters planned to saddle the horses and ride out to the edge of Mr. Chambers' property with Bob and Sickles. There they'd reconnoiter the approaches to his property in preparation for their move against him.

This news excited her. It was the first time Walters and his two "lieutenants" would be away from the house at the same time, without going in the carriage. That was critical—everything depended upon Margaret being able to speak with Samuel, Walters' carriage driver.

Walters had told the others to have the horses saddled and at the front door at one o'clock. So she waited until two o'clock to make her move, knowing he'd be gone for three hours at a minimum, and probably longer, to ride all the way to Mr. Chambers' property; and then, presumably, look around and discuss plans, before riding all the way back.

She stepped into the hallway, and saw Minnie sitting in the chair down the hall. The maid appeared to be asleep. The watch on her door, which had been in earnest originally, was now just for show. She'd managed, through threats, blackmail, and a regular system of rewards, to turn all the house slaves to her side. They now only pretended to keep her restrained, a game they all played while Mr. Walters was at home, but quickly abandoned as soon as he departed.

"Minnie! Minnie, wake up! Come here, please."

The woman shook her head, got up and trotted over to Margaret's bedroom door.

"Sorry, Missus ... I guess I ... nodded off a bit, there."

"Never mind that, Minnie. I'm not your master ... I care nothing about that. But I *do* need your help. I need the master's driver Samuel here immediately. I must speak with him while Mr. Walters is away.

"Please send someone to fetch him and have him come here to my room as soon as may be. And remember, Samuel doesn't know anything about our little ... *arrangement*, and he need not know."

"Yes, Missus. I'll have him fetched up to this room straight away."

Minnie left, moving quickly down the front stairs.

Margaret closed the door and walked over to her desk. She opened the top drawer pulling out a stack of papers. All were covered in her own handwriting.

Poems, she thought with a smirk. *Very, very bad poems!*

Quickly thumbing through the stack, she paused, then pulled out one specific page. She set it on the desk and returned the rest to the drawer.

She picked up the paper and read it through. *Awful ... simply awful*, she thought, shaking her head, an ironic smile on her lips. Then she sighed, *no time for anything better*, she shrugged and began folding the paper to a size that would easily fit in the palm of a man's hand. Once she'd finished this task, she moved over to the bed, and sat down to wait for Samuel's arrival.

It was exactly twenty-three minutes by the clock when she heard a soft knocking on her door. She resisted the urge to jump up and immediately pull open the door. She waited for another soft knock, then stood, and slowly walked to the door, opening it only a crack.

"Yes?"

A tall, thin white-haired slave stood in the hallway. "Sorry to disturb you, ma'am. I's Samuel, Missus ... the maids said you was wantin' to speak with me?"

"Yes ... of course, Samuel. Come in," she opened the door wide, and gestured toward a chair set opposite the bed.

He looked at her, then at the chair, as if deciding what he should do. He seemed to make up his mind, stepping into the room, crossing to the chair, and sitting down. He looked up at her expectantly.

She closed the door, came back and sat on the bed.

"Samuel ... thank you for coming. I have something very, very, important to talk with you about."

"Yes, ma'am?"

"But before I do ... I want to tell you ... well, to tell you how sorry I am for the way I treated you the first time we met. When we ... well, you know ... went for a short ride in the carriage, of which no one else need ever know."

He nodded his head but said nothing.

"I was … *desperate* to get away, and to speak with Mr. Chambers. But the master … well, he is … he is a very cruel and evil man, Samuel. He keeps me a prisoner in this room. So I had to go and talk to other folks, even if for only a short while. Do you understand?"

"Yes, ma'am. I expect you's plenty tired o' bein' in this-here room all the time, what with no fresh air and whatnot."

"Yes, thank you for understanding, Samuel. I'm sorry I was stern with you and threatened you. It was really only an act. I want you to understand I never would have harmed you or told the master something to make him angry with you. I hope you'll accept my sincerest apology for frightening you, Samuel."

He stared at her, slack jawed, as if she'd suddenly started speaking in a foreign tongue.

"Ain't no white person never told me sorry for nothin' before ma'am. I … don't rightly know what to say. Except … you ain't treated me half so bad as some others done, and they ain't never said 'sorry.'"

"Well, perhaps they should have, Samuel! Anyway, I wanted you to know I'm not *that* kind of person."

"Yes ma'am … that I can clearly see … now."

"Good … thank you, Samuel. It means a lot to me. Now … I have something terribly important I must ask you to do …"

ᔕᘜᓱᘓᘔᔕᘜᓱᘓᘔᔕᘜᓱᘓᘔ

Sunday, Dec. 2, 1860 - Greenbrier County, Virginia:

The carriage pulled up to the front steps of Mountain Meadows, returning from the morning church service. Harry the Dog trotted past, over onto the grass beside the house, and plopped down, tongue hanging out to one side, panting heavily from his long run. He was a shocking sight to anyone who hadn't seen him before. To say he was extremely large would be an understatement. He was simply gigantic. They guessed by his size, shape, and coloration he was a cross between an English Mastiff and an Irish Wolfhound, but nobody knew for sure. Nor did they know where he'd originally come from, just showing up on the farm one day while Nathan was still off in the Army. But now he'd become permanently attached to Nathan and could not be kept from following him wherever he went, even to church on Sundays, though he always stayed outside any buildings.

Both Nathan and Walters continued to attend church every week, despite their earlier altercation—sitting directly across the aisle from one another, along with five or six of their men. The only difference was, the men on both sides were now armed, including Nathan, who carried his small Colt revolver out of sight in his waistcoat pocket. The reverend said nothing, seemingly pretending not to notice. And now Nathan and Walters no longer greeted each other in the aisle after the service, choosing instead to totally ignore one another.

Nathan opened the carriage door and hopped out, quickly circling around the back to give Miss Abbey a hand out on the other side. Cobb and the other grooms had been used to opening the doors for the old master and Miss Abbey, but the Captain would have none of it. "I'm not an invalid yet!" he'd said with a laugh, after which he informed Cobb he could also very well escort his own mother.

Cobb just smiled, and shook his head, "Whatever you wants to do, Captain. You the boss."

But today as Nathan helped Miss Abbey down, he noticed Cobb coming around the side of the carriage toward him. He had an odd look on his face, as if he had something serious to speak to Nathan about.

"Captain ... may I speak with you a moment, sir? Seems like it might be some kind o' serious matter, else I'd not be bothering you, sir."

"No bother, Cobb! You can speak with me anytime you wish, serious or no."

"I can walk myself inside, Nathan dear ... you stay and talk with Cobb as long as you need."

"Thank you, Momma. I'll be there shortly."

"Well, Captain ... it was a strange sort o' happening. I was over't the church—as you knows full well—just jokin' and

74

hobnobbin' with the other drivers, as we all usually does, now that you've allowed me to do the driving again," he gave Nathan a smile. Nathan had originally forbid Cobb from driving on Sundays, as he considered it work for the slave. But he'd relented after Cobb practically begged him, explaining it was his only chance to visit with his fellow drivers from other farms. He'd been doing it for many years and had developed a number of close friendships.

"Well, sir, old Samuel pulls me to the side, smiles, and says, real quiet like, 'Cobb, I's fixin' to shake your hand now, like we's old pals, which, of course, we are. But when we does, this time I's gonna slip a paper into yer hand. And you gots to take it casual-like, not lookin' down, and just stuff it in yer pocket like you ain't got nothin' at all. You understands me, boy?'

"'Yeah sure, Samuel,' I says, 'but what's it about anyways?'

"Then he held out his hand, smiled, and I shook it, feelin' the paper in my hand. After I slipped it in my pocket, he says, 'Don't rightly know, Cobb. But when I tells you what I'm 'bout to tell you, just keep on smilin' like I's telling a funny story, though … ain't nothin' funny 'bout this one. The Missus says if'n I don't give this slip o' paper into your hand, and if'n you don't give it over to your master … Mr. Chambers, that is … then … well, she says a lot o' good folks, both white and black, is gonna die—awful, and bloody-like. Yeah … like you, I didn't believe it … but them was her words. I weren't gonna do it, on account o' my master is of a terrible-bad temper. But … well, she shamed me into it with them dark words.'

"That's what old Samuel said, sir."

"Folks are gonna *die*, Cobb? You're sure that's what he said?"

"Yes sir, plain as day."

"And you believed him? Sounds a bit of a wild tale to me. Who is this fellow Samuel, anyway?"

"Oh … didn't I say, sir? Samuel—well firstly, he's a fine old gentleman, and I never did know him to lie before. And then— well, sir … he's Mr. Walters' driver."

"Walters ...? Then his mistress is ... *oh my God!* Thank you, Cobb. Thank you! You did rightly taking that note and telling me about it. Do just hand me that piece of paper now, if you please."

Cobb reached into his pocket and pulled out a small slip of paper, tightly folded, handing it over to Nathan. "Here you are sir. I sure do hope ... well, that it ain't true what he said ... or if it is, this-here paper can help put a stop to it."

"Yes ... me too, Cobb. Me too. Thank you."

He turned and went up the steps, two at a time, and strode into the house going directly into the library. There he turned up the lamp burning low on the side table, so he'd have more light for reading. He carefully unfolded the paper and laid it out flat on the table. It was written in a very neat, female hand. And though it was entirely legible, the contents were not at all what he'd expected.

His heart had been pounding as he entered the house, *A letter from Margaret! Beyond all hope she has found a way to send me a message!* he'd thought, with growing excitement and anticipation. But now he felt somewhat deflated. Instead of a letter, he found we was reading ... poetry! He read it through again, as if perhaps he was missing something. But no ... it was clearly an amateurish attempt at poetry. He sat back in his chair perplexed.

Why would Margaret go to all the trouble ... and risk ... just to send him a poem she'd written? And not a particularly *good* one at that ... so bad as to be almost nonsensical. Somehow that almost surprised him more. Margaret had seemed so ... well, *brilliant* didn't seem too strong a term for it! Certainly extremely competent, and clever.

Then he started mulling over that idea in his mind. *Wait a minute! That's it. I'm right, I know it! Margaret would never write an amateurish poem ... if she set her mind to it, she'd make sure it was perfect. That must tell me something ... some clue ... but what?*

He leaped from the chair and poked his head out into the hallway. He saw the maid Sarah down at the far end of the hallway, carrying what appeared to be clean linens, and called out, "Sarah, do you know where Mr. Tom is at the moment?"

"Well, yes, Captain. I believe he's upstairs in the office. I's just goin' up to make the beds. Shall I fetch him for you, sir?"

"Yes, if you please. Thank you, Sarah."

He started back toward his chair, then had another thought and turned back toward the hallway. Poking his head out again, and seeing a figure moving down the hallway, he said, "Oh … Sarah … one more thing …"

But he was surprised when he received a chuckle in return, "Well, I ain't Sarah, sir, far as I know … but how can I help you?"

"Oh … sorry, Megs. I was just talking with Sarah, and so I thought you were still her … or rather … Well, anyway, do you happen to know where Miss Abbey is at the moment?"

"Of course, Captain. I *always* know where Miss Abbey is …" she chuckled, "sometimes even better'n she does!"

"Ha! That I can well believe, Megs … and *so* …?"

"She's out in the flower garden just now, Captain. Shall I send for her?"

"Yes please … and tell her it is … an *urgent* matter."

"Oh! Oh, then I's sorry for making light, Captain. I'll fetch her straightaway."

"It's all right Megs … being an old soldier, I find there's always room for good humor, even under the most trying circumstances."

"Thank you, sir. I shall be but a moment," she turned and hurried off down the hall toward the back door.

Tom was the first to arrive.

"You wished to see me, sir?"

"Yes, Tom. Have a look at this, if you would."

He handed Tom the paper.

Tom read it through quickly, then looked up with a puzzled expression, "Poetry, sir?"

"Yes. What do you think of it?"

"Well … to be perfectly honest … it's … well, not exactly to my taste, sir."

"Come now, Tom … say it plain; it's downright awful!"

"Well, now you've said it, I'll agree. I didn't want to offend, in case you had a different opinion."

"The conundrum, Tom, is … this letter was handed to me by Cobb, who got it from Walters' driver Samuel. And he said it was a matter of life and death this paper get into my hands. *It's from Margaret, Tom!"*

"Margaret? But then …? Why a poem, do you think?"

"Yes, exactly. *Why?* I must admit I was entirely bewildered by it. For a moment I thought perhaps the strain of her incarceration had affected her mind. But then I started considering … from everything I've told you about her can you imagine her writing such horrible stuff?"

"Well, no. So you think it wasn't really from her? Then who?"

"No … that's not what I'm getting at. Think on it, Tom. She risked everything—likely her very life—to get us this message. And she told the courier if he didn't get the message through, good men would die! Well, not knowing who might see the note after it left her hands, she could hardly write *that* out in plain English!"

"Ah … yes … I see. *A cipher!* You think the poem contains a hidden message?"

"Yes, that's what I'm beginning to suspect … ah, here comes Miss Abbey. Let's see what she thinks about it. Hello, Momma. Please come in and take a seat. We have some very interesting news, and something to show you for your opinion."

"Oh, all right, Nathan. Hello, Tom."

"Hello, Miss Abbey."

"The news is … we've received a message from Margaret!"

"Oh?! Oh, how wonderful! How is she? Is everything all right with her?"

"Well, that's the thing we want you to look at. Here's what she sent Momma, and the man who delivered it said it was a matter of life and death."

"Oh my! Let me see …"

She took the paper and leaned over under the lamp on the side table next to her chair. After a moment she looked up, with almost the exact same puzzled expression Tom had shown a few minutes earlier.

Both Nathan and Tom chuckled at her expression.

"Yes, Momma, it seems she has written us … a poem."

"Well … yes … but not a very *good* one, Nathan."

"That's what I said as well, Miss Abbey," Tom said with a grin.

"Momma, to cut right to it, Tom and I are thinking she's hidden some kind of secret message in the poem, in case the paper were to fall into the wrong hands."

"Oh! Yes … that makes sense. If Walters got ahold of it, she'd be in serious jeopardy if he found she'd written us a proper letter. Especially if it was to warn us of some plot of his. But if he were to find a piece of paper she'd written with some poetry on it, he'd probably think little of it. Young women often dabble in poetry, especially ones like her with little enough to occupy their time."

"Yes, my thoughts exactly. True to form, Margaret continues to be quite the clever woman."

"But Nathan … do you know how to read the secret message?"

"No, Momma … not a clue."

"Well, then what good is it, as a warning, if we can't read it?"

But it was Tom who answered.

"Miss Abbey, there are ways to figure these things out. When I was younger, before joining the Army, I used to read about such things. They're called ciphers. I suspect Margaret, being an avid reader, and a … well, *intellectual* type, from what the Captain tells me, must have studied such things also. I used to make them up, and play games with my friends, trying to crack the code, and so forth."

"Oh … well that sounds more hopeful, Tom."

"May I?" he reached out for the paper, and Miss Abbey handed it to him.

"Now, often ciphers are clearly that: just a jumble of mixed-up letters and numbers. Anyone looking at such a missive would know immediately it was a coded message.

"But in this case, she wanted to disguise the fact it even *was* a cipher. That's much trickier to write, because it requires weaving relatively reasonable sounding words in with the actual, secret message. A poem is a good method, because poets aren't expected to adhere to the rules of grammar. And poems are allowed to invoke a feeling, or a mood, rather than being logical and coherent. If that's what this truly is, it's an extremely challenging and difficult task—especially if you don't dare leave any scratched-out notes behind. It requires … well, an uncanny ability to hold a large number of words and numbers in your head at a time, making precise counts of letters, and so on."

"I see. Nathan, did you know about all this?"

"Well, Momma, I'm familiar with the general concepts, but … I've never dealt with this kind of thing before. Tom … do you think you can decipher the message?"

"Well … it can't be too terribly hard, as she'd want to be sure we could eventually figure it out. But it can't be too easy either, or there'd be a risk Walters could unravel it himself."

"Hmm … that's a good point. Walters, despite being a thoroughly reprehensible character, seems extremely intelligent to me. So one must assume anything we could decipher, he could as well. She would know that too …"

"Oh! Yes! That's it, Captain. The *key!*"

"Key?"

"Yes … ciphers generally have a *key* of some kind. Oh, not a literal, metal kind of key you'd use for a door, but rather a special word that's the key to the code. If she wanted us to be able to figure it out, but be sure Walters *never* could, she'd include a key that only *we* would understand!"

"Ah … very good. Very good. But … how do we know what the key is?"

"Well … let's take a look …"

> *A foolish young woman, away from home for the first time, mistook the mother of the son,*
> *She knew nothing of the mighty worlds heart full of hope, never noticed an emblem firm,*
> *But gaily she trundled along seated after that long ride, she never was sure she known,*
> *Nothing bothered her a whit, sitting other ways no sisters dare, rarely at window as I,*
> *She sang a happy song to sound humbly sweet, never knowing how admired a tune nor fond,*
> *All the young pined, never floored by a soaring song as much, shallow rarely the shrew,*
> *And she danced and such, all bright strained in the shiny light o all harsh old azures,*
> *Though tired she was a while was all it necessitated to rise and lead those souls now ,*
> *The chandeliers with light glow all handsome and fine, illumine a world fools take to ,*
> *Tho happily she sang all of almost five feet of her height, never a sound made.*

"Usually the key is in the first part … some clue or riddle, that only we could solve. Of course, it could be hidden anywhere, but

I suspect she'd not want to make it too onerous on us. Let me see here … wait … there's a pattern here … do you notice anything different about the first line?"

"Hmm … it appears to be … yes, it is a different length from the others, except for the last line, which is considerably shorter. She has written the whole thing out so neatly all the lines except the first and last are exactly the same length, the commas neatly line up down the right side, like ducks in a row." Nathan answered.

"Oh, yes, I see what you mean, Nathan. But what does it signify, Tom?"

"Well … I think it means the first line is the key, and the rest of it contains the message. So … the first line says, 'A foolish young woman, away from home for the first time, mistook the mother of the son.'"

"Oh … she must be referring to herself there, Momma, when she came to visit us before … 'a young woman away from home for the first time.'"

"Oh, yes, that must be it, dear."

"But what does the last part mean, do you think? Clearly you are the mother … and I am the son … but … who did she mistake you for, Momma?"

"Well … I don't see how she could have mistaken me for anyone … I introduced myself the moment I met her … even before she introduced herself …"

Miss Abbey was quiet and thoughtful for a moment, thinking back to that meeting. "I told her who I was … and she said she was here to speak with *you*, Nathan … no … *wait!* Wait a minute … she said … oh! Oh! I've got it! She said she wished to speak to Mr. Nathan Chambers … to my *husband!* Nathan, I recall being very flattered, because she thought you were my husband, rather than my son."

"Ah! That must be it, Miss Abbey! Very good—very well done."

"Thank you, Tom … but how does that serve as a … key?"

"Well, likely it points to a single word … let's see … 'mistook the mother of the son …'"

"Husband? She thought I was Miss Abbey's husband … could that be the word?"

"Hmm … no … but I think you're on the right track … you see, it says 'mistook the mother' … not 'mistook the son' … so … she mistook Miss Abbey for …"

"The *wife!* She mistook me for the wife! That must be your key word!"

"Yes … yes, that's surely *it*, Miss Abbey. Well done, again.

"Now … there are many different ways to use the key … some of which get extremely complicated. But we'll stick with our assumption she didn't want to make it too difficult, once we figured out the key. Which, by the way, I can see now Walters would have had almost no chance of ever figuring out, since he wasn't here that day. Even I could never have done it … nor Nathan for that matter. Miss Abbey, Margaret was counting on *you* figuring out the key, and now, I believe you've done it."

"Oh … this is … well, like a puzzle … very exciting!"

"Yes, Momma, but let's not forget the 'life or death' part of the message. It's likely we aren't going to much like what the message says, once we de-cipher it."

"Yes … of course, dear … forgive me, I've been caught up in the curiosity of it and have nearly forgotten the whole point."

While Nathan and Miss Abbey talked, Tom went over the desk by the wall under the library window. He pulled out a sheet of paper, and brought over the ink well, and a pen. Then he dipped the pen in the ink and wrote the word 'WIFE' at the top of the page in large, block letters. He sat and stared at the word for a few moments, as if contemplating what to do with it. Nathan and Miss Abbey watched curiously over his shoulder. He seemed to be counting with his fingers. He stopped and wrote the number 23 under the *W*. Then he wrote 9 under the *I*, 6 under the *F*, and 5 under the *E*.

"The sequence of each of those letters in the alphabet," Nathan stated.

"Exactly, sir. Now … if I'm correct, we start on the second line, and we count out those numbers, in order, and denote each letter that falls on one of those counts. My guess is the spaces between the words should be counted, as they would make the eventual message more readable. But the commas at the end of the line aren't counted, as they would not be useful. Let's try it, shall we.

So Tom started counting off the letters of the second row. First, he counted off 23 letters, representing the *W* in wife.

E.

Then he counted off 9 more for the *I.*

W.

Then 6 for the *F.*

A space.

Then 5 more for the *E.*

T.

Then he started back at the *W* in wife again, counting off 23 letters once more. He was gratified when he counted off the last 5 to get to the *E* in *wife*. It ended on the last letter of the second row.

"Ah! That is a very hopeful sign ... following the pattern of the word *wife*, we have exactly two counts per row."

"Yes, that does seem hopeful," Nathan said.

Tom continued the same on the next line, occasionally rechecking his count before recording the letter. Recognizing all the letters on the remaining rows would line up vertically, like the commas: "ducks in a row." He quickly finished the exercise. When all was complete, he'd written out the following:

> *EW TO MM AFTER N TO R WITH T MURDER ALL*
> *WHITES HAS SICKLES I AM OK LOVE M*

They stared at it a moment, then Miss Abbey said, "Well, I can read some of the words, but it seems all jumbled. Is it still in a code do you think?"

"No, Momma, just highly abbreviated. Otherwise she'd have had to write a *book* to spell everything out! Look here ... *EW* stands for Elijah Walters, and *MM* is clearly Mountain Meadows, which makes the whole meaning plain. Walters is coming to Mountain Meadows after *N*—that'd be me, Nathan, goes to *R*—Richmond, with *T*—for Tom. So putting it all together; when Tom and I go to Richmond for the special session in January, he plans to attack Mountain Meadows and murder all the white people on the farm—so no one can testify against him later, presumably. Likely he plans to burn the whole place to the ground after, to cover his tracks. And … it appears our old friend Sickles is now in his employ, which means he'll have much better information about us than he had last time."

"Oh, my goodness! Surely even *he* … oh, surely *not*, Nathan? He'd not come here to commit mass murder? It is … *unbelievable,* really!"

"Believe it, Momma. You said it yourself, 'he's a very dangerous man.' I've seen a look in the man's eyes. The same as I've seen on many ruthless, bloodthirsty killers out West. Momma, there are a lot more men like *that* than you think … even here where things are supposedly 'civilized.' Don't forget what Margaret told us … she personally witnessed him killing two slaves with his own hand, and she'd heard there'd been others. No, I'm afraid it's *real* all right. But thanks to our friend Margaret, we're forewarned.

"And happily, in the last part of the message Margaret says she's all right … I greatly appreciate hearing that. I've been terribly worried about her these past few months, since there's been no word from her father in response to her letters, nor to my later follow-up letters. So it's a great relief to know she is still well—though I'd still dearly like to come up with a way to get her out of there.

"Tom, let's go talk with Jim about this, so we can start working out our plan of action."

"Yes … very good, sir. So … do you mean to attack him first? A preemptive strike to put an end to his threat?"

Nathan held a scowl on his face but didn't immediately answer. He pulled a cigar from his pocket, stuck it in his mouth, and leaned back in his chair, gazing up at the ceiling.

After a few moments he looked back at Tom. "My heart tells me to do unto him as he would do unto us—but get there first! Load our weapons, saddle up, ride over there, and put Walters and his henchmen to the sword."

He breathed a heavy sigh. "But … my head says we can't do it that way. We will end up looking like the aggressors—like cold-blooded murderers. Though we *believe* Margaret's warning is real, we have no proof. Nothing that would hold up in a court of law.

"No, I fear we must set another trap for him and wait. But this time we must finish the business," he said this with a hard look in his eye that left no doubt as to what he meant by it.

"All right, I can see the logic of it, sir. But … her note says he won't attack until we leave for Richmond? Do you intend to stay home then, and skip the meeting?"

"No! I *must* be at that special session, Tom! The future of Virginia is a stake, and possibly that of the entire nation!"

Tom nodded but said nothing. Miss Abbey gazed at Nathan, a worried expression on her brow. But if she had an opinion on the matter, she kept it to herself. Nathan chewed on the unlit cigar and stared out the window.

"No … I *must* go, Tom. And I must have faith in Jim and the others to defend my home. They're good men, all. Tough, loyal, and trustworthy.

Then he smiled, and shook his head, "And … it's pretty hard to catch Billy by surprise, especially with this much advance warning. Plus, knowing Sickles is there, we can reckon on how he might try to use his inside knowledge to their advantage, and we should be able to counter it. No … I'm confident Walters is once again in for a nasty surprise. But I'm sorry I won't be here to see it this time."

"Yes, sir. That makes two of us, for sure."

Then Nathan turned and met eyes with Miss Abbey, "But I would have you and Megs come with us to Richmond, Momma. I would not risk leaving you here while Walters does what he will. It's too dangerous."

Abbey scowled, "Oh, then will you take *all* the women with you to Richmond? And the children too?"

Nathan leaned back, "Well, no. I can't—"

"Nathan, dear … I appreciate your concern for me, but this is my home. I feel responsible for every living being here. How could I live with myself if I fled to safety while leaving them all in harm's way?

"No, I'll *not* do it. I will stay and ... what would you have said in the Army? 'Hold down the fort'? You must choose what you will do, but as for me, I will stay here with Mr. Wiggins and the rest of your men and hold down the fort. And I know Megs will say the same." She crossed her arms and leaned back in her chair.

Nathan stared at her, mouth agape. Miss Abbey rarely pushed back against his wishes with such force.

He turned to Tom as if expecting him to chime in on his side, but Tom just shrugged.

"She's right, you know. Her place is here, along with Jim, looking after the people of Mountain Meadows. And right now, your place is going to Richmond to try and save Virginia. And my place, as always, is going with you. We may not like it, but that's the simple truth."

Nathan gazed back up at the ceiling, continuing to chew on the unlit cigar. He slowly nodded his head, then looked back at Miss Abbey. After a moment, he smiled, "Well, at least I now know where I got my courage ..."

Abbey smiled in answer.

 

"It's good to see you, Dr. Johnson. I'm sorry to come in such a flurry, but my Momma ... Miss Harriet, that is ... went to visit one of her friends. I feigned a headache to get out of going with her. There's no knowing how long she'll be gone, and it wouldn't look right if I were out of the house when she returned."

"Perfectly understandable, Miss Eve. Let's get right down to business then, shall we?"

They sat down at his kitchen table, their usual meeting place. He handed her a cup of hot tea, and offered a dish of cookies, which she politely declined.

"Thank you. First, let me tell you what I've heard concerning the plantations. I understand it has been a hugely profitable harvest, so several of the larger estates are looking to purchase more slaves. The problem being, of course, no one is looking to sell."

"Oh, there'll still be sales … the prices will just be way up. Not good news for us, as the slavers will be even more careful of their 'merchandise' than usual. However … when people are frantic to buy it puts us in a better position to … infiltrate the estates."

"Infiltrate? Whatever do you mean, Doctor?"

"Miss Eve … the level of courage and commitment some people demonstrate, for no reason other than the betterment of their fellow man, never ceases to amaze me. Would you believe, I have a whole list of *free* black men and women, who risk *all* on a regular basis—their freedom … even their very lives—to sneak into slave camps to spread the word of our activities, and to recruit more … *train passengers?*"

"Oh my! That is … so admirable and courageous … almost beyond words!"

"Yes … in fact, that's how your friend *Miss Cuba* heard about 'the *blue* house across from the *red* one.'"

They shared a smile. Dr. Johnson had just teasingly said it backward, the same as Violet had done, before they'd come here the first time, nearly ending in disaster.

"One of my freemen had infiltrated her farm and had spread the word among the leaders. Fortunately, he'd been able to escape again, but we haven't always been so lucky."

"But you mentioned the increase in prices would be beneficial in that regard?"

"Yes … it is a double benefit to us, though I must admit to a twinge of guilt about it. It seems much more like thievery than any of our other activities, despite the fact we are technically stealing someone's property every time we help a slave escape. Well … be that as it may … when prices are up, rather than having our freemen sneak into farms, we sell them. We use a private broker, who serves as the middleman, so there's little chance of tracing them back to us. We collect the money to help finance our efforts, less the fee to the broker, of course. And, we get our man into the farm we're targeting. Then, a few weeks later, he sneaks away, and we quickly relocate him to another 'train station' area. So it's unlikely he'll be recognized. I say 'him' because we don't ever sell the women. The risk of them being … well, let's just say … subject to abuse by their new master … is too high. So when women work for us, they usually try to sneak in and back out again without being noticed."

"That makes sense. And … yes, I can understand how you might feel a little guilt over that type of activity. But I guess when lives, and people's freedom is at stake, it's … *different* … somehow. Isn't it?"

"Hmm … yes, I suppose it is … at least that's what I keep telling myself."

"Well, anyway, here's a list I've made of the farms known to be buying now. I also listed one at the bottom that is said to be … *particularly abusive* … shall we say?"

Evelyn handed Dr. Johnson a tightly folded piece of paper she'd slipped into the back of her glove, and he thanked her with a bow of his head.

"Oh … before I depart … I've been meaning to ask you … have my reports concerning the regular whereabouts of Watchman Jubal Collins been helpful?"

"Oh, yes! Most certainly yes, thank you for that, Miss Eve. I've been remiss in not thanking you previously. It is very helpful for our activities to know where he will be at any given time during the evening hours—he is *the* regular police presence in this part of town."

"Oh good. He's a very nice, sweet young man, and … well, speaking of feeling a twinge of guilt, I fear he has taken a particular interest in me, which I have exploited mercilessly to get you this information."

"Yes … I'm afraid that is the burden you must bear for the types of activities we are engaged in, Miss Eve. We often have to be … *deceptive* … even sometimes to our loved ones, in order to carry out our vital mission. Oh, and … speaking of your young Mr. Collins … I wanted to warn you … though he's friendly and seems young and somewhat naïve, don't be fooled. He's a very clever young man. And he has the one attribute most dangerous to us."

"Oh? What might that be?"

"Curiosity! He is very inquisitive and won't stop asking until he's satisfied with the answers. Whenever I speak with him, he's always very nice and polite, but he quizzes me insatiably about my business and my activities. I … I actually have learned to develop a healthy fear of that young man, if you can believe it. I pray he gets moved to another part of town, before … well, let's just say before it's too late. Be careful what you say to him, Miss Eve. And don't assume he isn't suspecting something, despite his apparent feelings for you."

"Thank you, Doctor … I'll keep it in mind. I really must be going now. Was there anything else you wished to speak with me about?"

"Just one more thing. There are people I know who may be interested in speaking with you about a … *particular project* they have in mind."

"Oh? Who are these *people*, and what sort of project?"

"I'll say no more … not even to you. But have no fear … they will reach out to you, when the time is right. Then you can decide whether you wish to help them or not."

ಬಿಐಏೞಿಬಿಐಏೞಿಬಿಐಏೞಿ

"Captain! Captain, sir! Look what came today in the post!" Tom stood in front of Nathan breathing heavily, as if he'd finished running a race, which in fact he had, from his office upstairs to the library where Nathan sat.

He handed Nathan an envelope. It was addressed "Mr. Thomas Clark, Mountain Meadows Farm, Lewisburg, Virginia," in a neat, feminine hand. Nathan could see the envelope had been neatly cut open at the top.

"A letter for you, Tom … but …"

"It's from *Louisiana*, sir!"

"From Louisi—oh … *oh!* Then it's from …"

"Adilida! Yes, sir! It's from *her!* She wrote back!"

"Ah … well, I'm happy to hear *that*, Tom … I'm very pleased for you. But … what does she say, dare I ask?"

"Read it for yourself, sir. That is … if you wish to …"

89

"Oh, yes, most certainly, Tom! I'm fairly bursting with curiosity about it! Thank you very kindly."

He pulled the letter out of its envelope, opened it, and leaned forward to read.

My Dearest Thomas,

You cannot possibly imagine my great joy at receiving your letter! I screamed so loudly Uncle came running, sure a snake had bitten me!

My joy of your letter has only been matched this year by my sorrow of your sudden departure from New Orleans. I was so very low and feared you did not truly love me, though my heart did not believe it was so. But now, I know it is not true, and I am so very happy again!

Uncle said you must have had a good reason for leaving so soon, and now from your letter I see it was true. Oh, my dear sweet love, you saw me sitting with another man! For that I am so very sorry, as I know how it must have pained your heart to see.

A very handsome young man he is, too, and I was truly hugging and kissing him, even as you say. Only, he is Uncle's son, Phillipe, who surprised us at the hotel! He is my dear cousin, who I have grown up with like a brother, and whom I had not seen for a year and more. I told him all about you, and he was excited to make your acquaintance.

But now I know also you and your men were having troubles and had to leave quickly and with your guns on (or guns drawn? Is that the correct English?) Uncle was right about that too. He is such a clever man, and I do love him so.

Almost as much as I love you, Thomas! And, to answer your question, yes, yes, yes! I will come to you in Virginia as soon as ever I may, my love. I have spoken with Uncle, and he says we can come in the spring on a steamship when the weather at sea is not so dangerous! Won't that be wonderful?

Oh, please do write me back as soon as you may. I will be waiting breathlessly to hear from you again, my dearest beloved.

I am, now and always, your one and only True Love,

Adilida.

P.S. Phillipe might come also. He says he wants to meet you and apologize for kissing me in front of you! He is being very funny!

"*Well!* She doesn't mince words, nor tend to leave one wondering how she feels, does she?"

"No, sir. Most certainly *not!* She said some of those same things that night ... the night when ... well, before we left. Which of course has fairly stuck in my head ever since, making me doubt my thinking when we left there in a hurry.

"Her *cousin!* Can you believe it sir? Of all the dumb, bad luck! If he'd arrived at table *after* I had, all would've been well."

"Yes ... let that be a lesson to both of us, Tom. Sometimes things are *not* as they appear and there *really is* a reasonable explanation for something like that, even when it doesn't seem possible."

"Yes, sir. That's a lesson I will *not* soon forget, believe me!"

"Well, anyway, congratulations on your joyful surprise, Tom. That is wonderful news! I'm greatly looking forward to meeting her ... and her notorious cousin."

"Thank you, sir! Thank you very kindly!"

Tom leaned down, scooped up the letter, and headed for the door. But he paused in mid-stride as a different thought hit him. He turned, his happy expression suddenly turned serious.

"Oh ... Captain, have you had ... any correspondence from ... Miss Evelyn, sir?"

"No, Tom. She has not seen fit to reply to my letter."

"Oh ... I'm ... so sorry, sir."

"Never mind that, Tom. You should not let it dampen your joy or excitement. I'm exceedingly happy for you. It'll help put any troubles of my own clean out of mind, rest assured!"

"Thank you, sir. Very gracious of you to say."

"Not at all, Tom. Every word of it's true. So ... when do you think Adilida can set sail?"

"Well, when we were aboard ship between Galveston and New Orleans, I talked with some of the sailors about storms and whatnot. I recall them saying they tried to avoid the harsh winter weather between early November and ... end of March, I believe they said. So I'd say any time after April first would be safe, most likely. But I guess that will depend on when her Uncle can leave his business. Of course, that's the first thing I'll ask in my next letter. I will certainly let you know what she says, sir."

"Thanks, Tom."

"Thank *you*, sir. And goodnight."

"Goodnight, Tom."

ℰᏠᏠᏒᏒℰᏠℰᏠᏒᏒℰᏠℰᏠᏒᏒ

"So Jim ... tell me what you've come up with so far."

"Yes, sir. Well ... here's how I see it. We ain't got the manpower to watch the roads and approaches night and day, all winter, so we need to be strategic about it. Nor, in fact is it necessary to do so, I'm figurin'. You see, sir, if one applies a little reasoning, the problem becomes much simpler.

"Start with the date of it ... we know from the note, he'll not do it until you're gone to Richmond. That'll be ... oh ... January fifth at the earliest, but more likely the seventh, as he'll want to wait 'til you're good and gone before he starts anything. We can assume he'll have men somewhere along the road making sure you get on that train for Richmond, so he'll know for sure you're gone. And then, he'll not wait too long after, not knowing how long that 'special session' might last. So ... figure sometime within the first week or two of you leaving."

"All right, so that narrows it down to two weeks. That's still a lot of watching for the men, especially in cold winter weather."

"Well … I ain't done yet, sir."

"Oh, all right, my apologies … pray do continue, Mr. Wiggins."

"Thank ye kindly, sir. So … I'm also thinking … he's gonna want to get in and out quickly. So he's got to pick a day when there's no deep snow on the road. Nor any heavy rains nor snow melt turning all to mud."

"All right, then … clear weather, and a road that's been dry for … say *two* good days."

"Yes, sir … that's what I figure. Also … we can assume he won't risk it in the dark, neither coming, nor going. So figurin' in early January the sunrise is … oh, around half-past seven, and sunset a quarter past five—give or take—that means the earliest he can launch his attack is seven thirty. And he'll not want to risk getting pinned down and stuck here after dark, so he'll give himself plenty of leeway in the afternoon. So let's say two o'clock, at the latest."

"Yes … I see where you're going with this. You really only need to be ready for an attack for about … six or seven hours a day. And the number of days in early January likely to be dry enough for a mounted action has got to be only a handful at best."

"My thinking precisely, sir. So now you see, the task is suddenly much more manageable!"

"Excellent reasoning, Jim!"

"Thank you, sir. And … I've also got an idea on how we can increase our manpower, which could also pay off in other ways."

"Oh?"

"Yes, sir. I plan on recruiting several of the strong, healthy young black men, who's got little enough to do this time o' year anyway, to help with the watchin'. I figure, send out two or three together, so if they sees something comin', one can run back and report, while the others continue the watch. We can devise some sort o' relay system so nobody has to run all the way up the hill. Of course, for those that knows how to ride, we can keep a horse or two tied along the way."

"Yes … *I like it, Jim!* They've already seen what Walters is capable of. So it'll give them a feeling of defending their own people and homes, which can't be anything but to the good of all! And … it is one more lesson on what a freeman sometimes has to do: defend his hearth, home, and family."

"My thinking too, sir. Also, it's something Walters would *never* consider … since he'd never trust his slaves to be off on their own like that. Gives us a lot more men than he'll be figurin' on."

"Yes … another excellent point."

"I'm fixin' to have Billy train 'em up on how to do the watchin' without bein' seen. He and I can work out all the details later on — where to position them, and so on. Maybe even set up some kind of long-distance signaling system. But for now, it's at least the beginnin's of a plan, for keepin' an eye on our friends down the hill."

"Yes … very good, very good, Jim! Well done. I heartily approve. Keep at it!

"Now … tell me what sort of *unpleasant surprise* you have in mind for our dear friend Walters, when he finally shows up."

"Ah! I'm happy you asked, sir! Here's what I'm fixin' to do, so's to give him a proper Texas greeting …"

ഇ

"All right, Tom … so, now that the tobacco has been cured, stripped, and sorted for the year, I'd like to hear more about all these logging and mining ideas you've been working on."

"Yes, sir. So this year, given our impending departure for Richmond shortly after New Year's, this'll be more of an experiment and a proving-out exercise — not expecting a profitable operation. But if it proves reasonable, and not too onerous, we can talk about expanding the operation. We'll be better prepared for it *next* year, so it has a good chance of becoming a going concern."

"All right, that sounds reasonable."

"So first, the logging … I figure this year we'll focus on dead and dying trees, cutting them up for firewood only. I've had a look at the equipment we have to hand, and it is woefully outdated, and inadequate for any kind of large-scale operation, except by means of an excessive amount of manual labor, which is the one thing we're trying to eliminate. There are several whip saws in reasonable shape, which we can use for the felling, but the pit saws are terribly labor-intensive."

"Pit saw? What in the name of all's holy is that?"

"Oh … well, it's used to cut the logs into boards. The name comes from an actual pit dug into the ground for the purpose. They stretch a log over the top and secure it, so it won't slip or roll. Then one man gets down in the pit, and another stands atop the log. They proceed to rip the log into boards with a long saw. There's a handle on each end, one for each man, and the teeth are angled so the saw only cuts on the downstroke. That allows gravity to do most of the work, easing the burden on the lifting stroke. Still, it's slow, tedious, back-breaking labor, with the man in the pit becoming fairly covered in choking, hot sawdust."

"Hmm … that sounds like a nasty, tiresome business. But I understand steam engines are now easing the process?"

"Yes, sir. That's why I don't intend to do any lumber processing this year. I hope to buy and set up a small steam-powered lumber mill by next fall, so we can start getting into *that* business."

"But Tom … how on Earth can a steam engine power that … pit saw?"

"Oh, it won't, sir. They've now got a great round saw, like a wheel with teeth. The steam engine turns the great wheel, while pulling the log along. Quite ingenious."

"Oh … yes, I can picture it … very clever. Yes, let's do *that* … if we can afford it."

"I've been looking into costs, sir … and I reckon the entire setup can pay for itself in two years … three years at the most, after which it'll just be making money, less the cost of coal … oh, and the *labor*, of course."

"Yes … we mustn't forget *that* in our calculations! It is, after all, the whole point of all your mental labors, Tom!"

"Yes … believe me, I *never* forget *that*, sir! It's my daily motivation. Just the thought of handing those people their final manumission papers—granting their freedom. It's … well, it brings tears to my eyes just thinking of it!"

"Yes … I know what you mean, Tom. Me too."

"Okay … so only firewood this year … what about the mining? What've you discovered there?"

"Well, I'd been asking around, and doing some reading, and … of course there's plenty of coal to be found hereabouts. But it's generally found deep, and requires extensive, permanent excavations."

"Oh no, let's not do *that!* Sounds terribly dark, dangerous, and unpleasant. I've heard stories of such mines … like hell on Earth! I've no interest in asking our people to do *that* kind of work."

"Agreed, sir. Which is why I kept looking, and discovered limestone caves, such as you have up the hills on your property, have been yielding saltpeter. And it's relatively close to the surface."

"Saltpeter … you mean as in … preserving meat and dying fabrics, but most importantly in—"

"Gunpowder! Yes, sir. Saltpeter, when mixed with small amounts of sulfur and charcoal yields gunpowder!"

"Hmm … all this impending secession and war talk had nothing to do with you thinking of it, I don't suppose?"

"Well, yes, to be honest, sir. After the great success we had selling cotton, due to the fear about the secession, it occurred to me the demand for gunpowder must also increase with all this uncertainty."

"Well, I appreciate the idea, Tom … but I pray the need for gunpowder does *not* increase dramatically in the near future!"

"Amen to that, sir. Amen to that."

"But, even so …"

"So I did go out to one of the caves, took a shovel and a barrow, and collected some likely looking soil. I followed some instructions I'd found in the Lewisburg library: put it in a large pot, filled it with water, stirred it up, filtered out the soil, mixed in a little ash, and boiled it dry. I'm happy to report, the result was indeed saltpeter, sir!"

"Oh … well, that's marvelous, Tom! You are so very clever to have figured all that out. So what's next then, do you think?"

"Well, actually the cutting of firewood will not only be useful for keeping us all warm this winter, but is also necessary for processing the saltpeter. As you can imagine, if we're going to process it in sufficient quantities to make any money, it will require more than a kitchen pot on the stove! We'll have to set up a small operation—again, as more of a test this year—with large, wooden pots for boiling off the water from the soil. We'll figure out how to efficiently do it by experiment with different designs and such. I figure by the end we'll have a pretty good notion of how to build a real, full-scale operation for next year. Along with the lumber mill and tree felling, it'll give the men something to do during the winter months when there's little field work to do. And ... the caves, though cool, never get freezing cold, and the outside work'll be warmed by the fires needed to boil the pots. So ... in all, it shouldn't be terribly unpleasant winter work, I'm hoping. Of course, our little experiment this year should prove that out as well."

"Excellent! I heartily approve. Well done! Let's get started right away."

"Yes, sir. I was hoping you'd say that ..."

ഇഉഉരുങ്ങഉഉരുങ്ങഉഉരുങ്ങ

During a break in the tree felling, as the men sat eating their lunch, Jim stepped up in front of them. Resting one foot up on a recently cut stump, he said, "Young gentlemen ... while y'all are eatin' yer lunch, I have a matter of great import to speak with you about."

He immediately had everyone's attention; Jim was not a man one could easily ignore. All the white men already knew what it was about, so paid him little mind, other than a curiosity about what he planned to say.

But the black ones were intrigued. For one, they weren't used to being called "gentlemen," and it caught their attention. For another, they'd never seen Sergeant Jim step up and give a speech before. Normally only the Captain did that.

"Well, as y'all know, Mr. Chambers' rather nasty and disagreeable neighbor, by the name of Walters, recently made the

97

attempt to disrupt the very lovely weddin' the Captain had seen fit to hold at Mountain Meadows this past summer. An attempt that failed miserably, and in a most satisfying manner, I'm happy to say!"

He was pleased at the reaction to this … smiles and nods from the men, as they recalled the events of that memorable day.

"Well … it has come to our attention the damned fool is fixin' to try it again, just after the New Year. Only this time … well, men … not to make you fearful an' all, but it's time you knew the truth on it. This time that scoundrel Walters plans on bringing even more armed men. And he ain't just fixin' to cause some mischief neither … this time he means to murder as many of us as he can."

He could see an immediate, gratifying reaction to this … mostly shock and wide-eyed fear. But he also saw a few of the young men scowling and several had an angry look. *Good*, he thought, *they've got some backbone to them!*

"Well, I'm here to tell you, us *men* of Mountain Meadows— and when I say the *men of Mountain Meadows*, I *do* mean both the black and the white ones! Oh, and the *red*, countin' Billy, of course. Well, us *men* ain't goin' to sit idly by and let old Walters have his way and commit bloody red murder on our own land! Instead, we mean to turn things around on *him*, and put an end to his mischief once and for all! In fact, I'm personally fixin' to put a nice, round, lead ball right through the middle of his fat, ugly head!" He pointed his index finger at the center of his own forehead, mimed a pistol firing, and made a humorous, twisted face.

There were smiles and laughter all around, the white men also joining in.

"So … I know y'all ain't yet had no call to learn the shootin' o' guns and whatnot. But that don't mean your help ain't vital to the success o' this-here operation. In fact, the shootin' part is really the least important part of the whole business. The most important, critical, life-and-death part … is knowin' for sure when the ugly, poxy bastard and the rest of his unholy yahoos is comin' up our road, fixin' to kill us all. That's the most important thing, so's we can be prepared, and give him a proper, neighborly, *hot-lead* greeting!"

Jim was enjoying himself now, and he had his audience thoroughly captivated. Even Nathan and Tom were sitting back and smiling, enjoying the performance, though they'd known it was coming.

"So what I'm askin' for, and want a show o' hands on, is ... who'll volunteer to man the watch? It'll be in shifts, mind ... I ain't keen on anyone freezin' off his manly parts sitting in the cold all day. Just let me see those hands, now ..."

A few hands shot up right away, and then others soon followed. One of those that'd come up immediately was Tony, though Johnny and Ned, sitting next to him, had hesitated. He looked over and gave them a look and a nod of his head, so Johnny and Ned raised theirs as well.

In seconds every hand was in the air, including those of all the white men, who he hadn't even been talking to.

"Well, that's mighty fine, men! Damn! Mighty fine. You make me proud to know you, that's what you do! So soon as Mr. Tom has done with us cuttin' these here trees, and diggin' in them caves, we'll get started. In another week or two ... Billy and I'll take you out and show you where to go, and what to do, for the Mountain Meadows Watch! Thank you ... thank you, kindly. And, remember, you ain't just watchin' to save the Captain, or us white men, or the Big House or somethin'. That bastard Walters means to come here and murder your friends, your women, and even the little children. You men are about to learn what happens when some no good, whore-mongering, shitheel threatens a man's family. I tell you what ... he just goes ahead and kills the son-of-a-bitch!"

He looked around, and it gratified him to see the smiles, and nods of agreement. Several of the men exchanged determined looks among themselves, and quiet words.

At the end of the day, as they walked back toward the cabins, Johnny gave Tony a curious look. "Tony, if'n we's still gonna try an' escape to the North, why'd you go an' volunteer for that watch business anyway?"

"Ain't it plain, John? If'n we's out in the woods on this watch … ain't no white folks watching *us*. That way we can just walk away any time we please, and nobody's the wiser for hours and hours, 'til it's too late."

"Oh … I gets what you's thinkin', Tony. You's bein' right-clever, you was," Ned responded.

"I don't know, fellas … seems like things has been … well, getting *better* … more happy and friendly-like around the farm since the Captain come here. Maybe he means to do what he say and set us all free," Johnny said, shaking his head.

"Don't you see, John? He just doin' all that to keep us workin' hard, and not runnin' off. Like how that old Toby run the whole harvest for him. Hell, that just mean he don't have to pay some white man to do what Sickles was doin' 'fore he left. Now Toby gone and done it for nothin'."

"But … what about all this talk about this … *Lincoln* fella, what got hisself elected president? Folks is sayin' he fixin' to go ahead and free us all anyways."

"Yeah, and folks is also sayin' the white folks 'round here ain't gonna do what this Lincoln say. So they's gonna be a big ol' shootin' war. And us slaves is goin' to be right in the thick of the fightin'. Likely both sides'll reckon we's good for nothin' but target practice. No thank you … I'd rather be far, far North when any o' that happens. I even heard some say they's a place even farther north than America. It be called *Canada*. And there they ain't no slavery no how, even whether Lincoln like it or no."

"Well, okay. I see's what you mean on that, but … what about all Sergeant Jim said … about them men comin' to murder all the folks? Don't seem right runnin' out on them when they's in danger."

"Don't worry … we won't leave when there's danger … just when no one's lookin' at *us*. They'll find others to take up our watch, and it won't make no matter."

"Well … all right, Tony … I reckon you know your mind on such matters … I just hope to the good Lord you's right on all this."

"I am … don't you worry none, Johnny. I *know* I am."

"Hi, Stan ... how many times you cleaned that gun this winter without ever firing it?"

Stan sat on his bunk, running a small cloth up and down the barrel of his big Colt Walker revolver. He was a huge man—so large, in fact, they'd had to add an extension onto his bunk so half his legs wouldn't hang off the end. He was the only man on the farm larger than Nathan. Except maybe Big George, who wasn't quite as tall as Nathan, but was broader in the shoulders, and more muscular. Stan, whose real name was Stanislav, had made his way from Russia when just a young—but very large—lad. He'd come via a circuitous route, down the west coast of America, eventually making his way to Texas where he'd joined Nathan's regiment.

"Oh, hello, Captain. Oh ... have cleaned gun ... only twenty times—more or less. Is something to do when ground is all covered with the snow."

"I thought you were going hunting ... for bears, or something?"

"Oh, yes ... William and I went up into hills with Billy, but ... not hunting for the bears, Captain. Bears all sleepy in wintertime, hiding in caves."

"Ah yes ... I recall hearing something of the kind. Well then, what *were* you hunting?"

"Oh ... deer or ... hmm ... larger animal ... is *like* deer, only much bigger, but I am forgetting word in English."

"Elk?"

"Ah, *elk. Da, da*, Captain ... *elk*. But ... not finding any. Then cold rains coming down and are melting snow ... even Billy is not finding tracks in mooshie wet snow. Much better is freezing hard snow than cold, drippy rain ... nasty, nasty. Brrr."

"Yes, I can see that would not make it much fun."

"*Nyet!* No fun, Captain! So ... we wait for the raining to stop, then mebbe we try the hunting again, on other day. But not bears, *nyet*. Too sleepy."

"Well, that seems a good plan, Stan. But what I came here to talk to you about is Harry."

"Yes, Captain? Is something wrong with big dog?"

"Well … not at the moment but … I'm worried what's going to happen when I leave for Richmond after the New Year. Except when I'm inside the house, or in some other building, he's never let me out of his sight. Not since that first day we came here. I hate to think how the poor fellow will suffer when I leave without him."

"Ah … yes … seems he is very *fond* to you, Captain."

"Yes, well, I fear it goes beyond just fond. He's … well, not entirely *sane* about it, I think."

Stan laughed. "*Da*, Captain … is *crazy* dog. But … I *like* him … for some reason."

"Far as I can tell, you like everyone, Stan."

"*Nyet* … am not liking … hmm … *nenavistnyy* neighbor! Sergeant Jim says should put bullet in him if I see. Seems good plan, though maybe knife would be more … how you say? *Satisfying?* Either way, maybe would improve his humor … and looks!"

"Yes … can't disagree with you on that one. The world *would* be a better place if our *friend* Walters wasn't in it. And then … well, then Miss Margaret could just walk out of there without our help. Ah, well …

"But … I didn't come to talk about that, rather …"

"Dog … yes … what to do with big, crazy dog, eh Captain?"

"Yes, precisely. And the only thing I can think of is *you*. The animal seems to have a liking for you. Maybe because you're the only person who's bigger'n him?

"So … I was thinking. What if you worked with him a little in the next few weeks? You know, spent some more time around him. Maybe he'd take my leaving better."

"*Da, da* … is worth the trying, Captain. I will do as I can. And then …"

"Then … I guess we'll see."

"*Da* … then we'll see what we see, Captain."

Chapter 5. White Christmas Dreams

"Like snowflakes,
my Christmas memories
gather and dance —
each beautiful, unique,
and gone too soon."
–Deborah Whipp

Monday - Christmas Eve, Dec. 24, 1860 - Greenbrier County, Virginia:

Nathan, Tom, Megs, and the entire household staff gathered around the grand piano in the great room, singing, as Miss Abbey played Christmas carols. She played beautifully, just as Nathan had remembered from his childhood. He also thought the singing good, although he had to admit the whiskey he'd been drinking all evening might have had a positive effect on that!

Besides himself and Tom, he'd also shared out whiskey to the household men, the cooks Jeb and Ted. They were all now in a jolly mood, singing boisterously. Miss Abbey had likewise shared a glass of brandy with all the household women, who also seemed to be enjoying themselves.

They sang Christmas carols for hours—traditional favorites like "Joy to the World" and "Hark! The Herald Angels Sing," and even a new carol written just a few years before called "Jingle Bells."

Nathan had originally planned on taking the singing outdoors, having the whole farm gather around the bonfire and perhaps have William play the violin for accompaniment. But right before noon it had started snowing.

It'd only snowed twice so far, all winter. And that had quickly melted down at the level of the farm, though it had clung to the hills for a few days.

But now, getting late into the evening, the snow was over eight inches deep, and continued to fall thickly with no end in sight.

So they'd had to move the celebration indoors, and those not living in the Big House were left to come up with their own Christmas Eve festivities. Nathan didn't feel guilty about that, however; he'd already given them the whole week off, from Sabbath to Sabbath, and was anticipating some pleasant surprises he had in store for them in the morning.

And though he savored the sweet warmth of the whiskey, enjoyed the lovely and nostalgically familiar songs, and felt the loving embrace of genuine comradery, still he suffered a bittersweet hint of melancholy throughout the evening. He daydreamed of Mrs. Schmidt ... his dear, sweet Alisa, back in San Antonio. Imagining she might be missing him too at this very moment, he raised his glass to her in silent toast. He remembered spending one beautiful Christmas in her home with her and her children—a sweet and joyful occasion. He'd thoroughly enjoyed the German holiday traditions: the beautifully decorated Christmas tree, and other greenery and colorful decorations throughout the house. He decided to start adopting some of those traditions at Mountain Meadows, starting next year.

And he remembered Maria, his first real love, long ago, back in El Paso. So happy, so full of life. Until ... she wasn't. He shuddered as a horrifying vision of his last sight of her on Earth flashed in his mind's eye. He took another swallow of whiskey and shook his head to clear away the evil image.

But mostly he could not stop dreaming of Evelyn. Wondering what she was doing right now, what she was thinking, how she was feeling. Wondering if she was also thinking of him. Or if she was moving on with her life, now more concerned with other things ... and other people.

He contemplated her letter again, for the hundredth time. He'd finally received her reply to his letter a few weeks back, months after he'd mailed his to her. And though he'd read it through over and over, and now had it memorized, he still was not exactly sure what it meant. On the one hand, she still seemed to have strong feelings for him—love even. But, on the other hand, she made it clear she would not rejoin him now, and offered no suggestions of when, if ever, she would.

He now recalled it once more, trying to glean some new hidden meaning from its brief text:

My Dear Nathan,

I am so sorry for my tardy reply to your most gracious letter. I have no excuse, other than, like you, I have started this letter a hundred times. And each time I have set it aside for not knowing what to say.

I know I have caused you great pain, and for that I am most truly and profoundly sorry and beg your forgiveness. I want you to know you have never done anything wrong in any way. You have always been a true and wonderful gentleman, and even were my life dependent upon it, I could not find a single ill word to say about you.

All the fault for what happened lies with me, and only me. No woman could ever ask for a finer man than you, Nathan. I mean that most sincerely. And, much as I would like to explain to you what happened, I can't because I truly don't understand it myself. It is not something I planned or expected, but something that came on me suddenly, like an illness almost. But it is not truly so, as my health is perfectly fine.

And though I harbor great love and true affection for you, I know until I have reconciled myself of this struggle I am suffering, it would be too hurtful for both of us were we to try to be together, and have the same thing happen again.

I cannot ask you to wait for me, Nathan, that would be unfair to you. But I will tell you truly, I cannot imagine myself ever with another man. Whenever I dream of love, it is your face I see, strong and clear.

Your dear friend, and more,

Evelyn

P.S. I am so happy for you about the fine harvest. And, I do wish I had been there to see it.

P.P.S. I would like to wish you a most Happy Christmas, and please extend the same and my love to Miss Abbey and to Megs. I pray they can forgive me one day and don't hate me too much for what I have done.

At least the letter seemed to absolve him of any wrongdoing—of somehow inadvertently causing her sudden, unexplained departure. He supposed he should be relieved and happy about that, but … the more whiskey he drank, the more none of that mattered. In fact, at the moment nothing mattered to him, except being with her. Holding her close, gazing into her beautiful blue eyes, reveling in the glory of her dazzling smile, and kissing her soft, sweet lips. Hearing her musical laugh, sitting together on the swing down by the duck pond. Listening to the melodic flow of her words, not caring what she was saying …

And then she was there … gazing up at him, a soft, loving look in her eyes. She leaned up to kiss him. But even as their lips touched, her face changed, and she was Alisa Schmidt! He pulled back, intending to ask, "Alisa, my dear, what are *you* doing here?"

But it was no longer Alisa looking at him, but Maria. She gazed up at him, smiling brightly—as lovely and young as ever he remembered her. "Maria?!"

"*Si, mi amor … soy yo, tu amada, Maria,*" she said, and looked at him in that special way that had always made his heart race. But he shook his head, "No, Maria, it can't be you! You're long dead. I buried you myself and shed bitter tears on your grave. I can still feel the burning rage and the aching pain of it." But she said nothing, smiling brightly at him with her beautiful white teeth. Her eyes seemed to fade away to darkness, but the white teeth remained until … he was staring into the grinning face of a fleshless skull. He shuddered at the sight, and—

"Sir … *sir!*"

"What?! Oh … Tom. What time is it?"

"Time for bed, sir. The singing has come to an end, and I'm afraid you've nodded off in your chair. Come, let's go upstairs, Captain. I believe we've had enough 'Happy Christmas' for tonight."

Nathan looked around and noticed the room was empty. The others had discreetly departed leaving Tom to attend his Captain.

"All right. Thanks, Tom. That seems a sound idea."

They made their way up the stairs, arm in arm. Nathan decided he was a bit tipsier than he'd realized or intended, and was grateful Tom seemed rock solid by contrast.

By the time they reached the top of the stairs Nathan was feeling a bit steadier and more clear-headed. So he thanked Tom and said he could make it the rest of the way unaided.

"All right ... good night then, sir. I hope you sleep well. And thanks again for a very pleasant Christmas Eve. I can't recall enjoying another better." But even as he said this an image of sitting next to Adilida singing Christmas carols came unbidden into Tom's mind, clear and sharp, though they'd never been together for the holiday before, of course. He sighed for the bittersweet longing of it. But he also felt a sudden thrill of anticipation ... *maybe next year it will be so!*

"Thanks, Tom. I enjoyed it as well. Sorry I ... seem to have had a little too much ... *refreshment.*"

"Oh, not at all, Captain. You have as much right as any man to enjoy himself ... if not more!"

"Thank you, Tom. Good night then."

They parted, and Nathan went to his own room, opened the door, and went inside. He walked over to the bed and sat down hard with a sigh. He kicked off his shoes, and was about to lean back on the pillow, when he heard a soft knock on the door.

At first, he assumed Tom had thought of something else he wanted to say. But he shook off his sleepiness and the effects of the whiskey enough to remember Tom had a firmer, more decisive knock—never a soft, discreet knock. Someone else then, but who?

He'd decided it must be Miss Abbey, coming to check on him—the knock had a feminine sound to it. But when he opened the door, he was surprised to see Rosa standing there.

Despite his partial inebriation, he was reminded once again what a pretty young woman she was. And that she was one of his slaves ... and quite possibly his sister.

"Rosa ... what ... uh, how can I help you, my dear?"

"Oh, Captain. I'm so sorry to bother you so late at night, sir, but I ... I was noticing tonight you was looking ... well, down I guess—kind of sad like. And I was remembering how kindly you treated me when I was feeling low. So ... I thought you might like someone to talk to is all." She smiled up at him, a shy, hesitant sort of look.

Nathan stood there for a moment, trying to focus despite his current state of intoxication. For a moment he wondered if there were more to her suggestion than she was saying. It was a troublesome thought. But then he dismissed it as a likely effect of too much whiskey.

"That is ... very kindly offered, Rosa. Very thoughtful of you, and I thank you for your concern. But ... I think after a good night's sleep I'll be feeling much better come the morning. Have a good night, and ... happy Christmas."

She smiled again, and nodded her head, "Thank you, sir. And a happy Christmas to you as well. Good night."

But when he lay down in his bed, before he drifted off to sleep, the thought of Rosa continued to trouble him. Was she becoming more ... *fond* of him than was good for her? If so, should he head it off—nip it in the bud—by telling her his suspicions about them being siblings? But then he decided no, that would be unfair. He still wasn't sure ... what if it turned out to be untrue?

Suddenly tracking down Rosa's mother had become a much higher priority than he'd previously considered. *Well, one more thing to do in Richmond, as if we won't be busy enough.*

In addition to his senatorial duties, he'd already planned on visiting his aunt on his father's side, and his aunt and uncle on his mother's. Then there would be Margaret's parents. And ... of course ... at some point, working up the courage to visit Evelyn ...

Monday - Christmas Eve, Dec. 24, 1860 - Richmond, Virginia:

"Oh ... thank you ever so kindly, Mr. Evans ... but I must decline. I find I am fairly dead tired on my feet and cannot possibly dance even a single step more. But I promise, sir, I shall make it up to you next time ... I shall join you for at least two dances, if you wish, at the next ball."

"That would be most excellent, Miss Evelyn, I thank you. But you should not trouble yourself about declining my present invitation. It is perfectly understandable you being done-in at this point of the evening. May I extend to you my best wishes for a very Happy Christmas, Miss Evelyn?"

"Oh, thank you, Mr. Evans. And a Happy Christmas to you too, sir. And please extend my best wishes to your dear mother as well. She is such a sweet and lovely lady!"

"Thank you, Miss Evelyn, I shall certainly do so."

The young gentleman departed, disappointed perhaps, but at least feeling he'd not been rejected out of hand. He still held out some hope of future attentions from the beautiful young lady.

"Evie—I declare ... you must've turned down every gentleman in the room at least once, and probably several twice!"

"Oh, Bel! You exaggerate so! I *have* danced already ... a few times ..."

"Yes, but that was hours ago, and certainly was never enough to tire you out! Why, I've seen you dance all night on other occasions, and never appear to slow even a step. Are you not feeling well, dear one?"

"Yes ... and ... *no.* Oh, Bel ... I've held my chin up through so many of these functions ... smiling, playing the part of the happy, carefree young lady. But ... tonight ..."

"Tonight, you're missing *him*, aren't you, dear?"

Evelyn looked Bel in the eye, tears starting to well. "*Yes ...*" she said, in barely a whisper, as her voice choked up.

"It is ... *oh*, the hurt of it *tonight* on Christmas is ... almost *unbearable!* I keep dreaming of him, back at the farm. I picture snow falling outside, making everything beautiful and white—not gloomy and drippy like here. And I see him sitting by the fire, sipping whiskey, slowly smoking a cigar. Lonely … and maybe … dreaming of me, too …

"Oh, Bel! *What have I done?*"

She covered her eyes with her hand, and quietly sobbed, no longer holding back the tears.

Bel for once was quiet and thoughtful before answering.

"I'm sure I don't rightly know, Eve, dear. You've never been able to explain to me what happened between you two. And I wasn't there, though now I bitterly wish to God I had been. Maybe then things would've turned out differently. I'm so sorry I didn't go with you when you asked, but …"

"Oh, *no!* None of this is *your* fault, Bel. You were … well, just getting started with your own courtship. It really wasn't even fair of me to ask. It was just … I was feeling so nervous about meeting Nathan for the first time …"

Then she laughed and shook her head, wiping a tear from her eyes with a handkerchief. "Do you remember, Bel … how I imagined 'old Mr. Chambers' before I ever met him?"

"Yes … as I recall, you pictured him a short, round, gray-haired gentleman who was constantly red in the face from shouting orders at people!"

"Yes … yes, that was it. How ridiculous it seems now. Never before in the history of bad assumptions has anyone been so wrong about someone they'd never met! Nathan is nothing like that. He is—"

But once again her eyes teared up, and she couldn't complete her sentence.

Belinda reached over and patted her gently on the shoulder. "Oh, my dear sweet one … I'm so sorry you're suffering so. But I will always be here for you, dearest, if that helps any."

"Thank you, Bel … I know you will, and you've no idea how much I need that … especially now."

At that moment another man walked up to the table. But this one didn't come to ask Evelyn to dance, instead sitting down next to Belinda with a manner that spoke of ease and familiarity.

"Oh, Ollie! You're back. How was the men's talk out on the veranda?"

"Boring. All they want to talk about is politics, horse racing, and whatnot … nothing interesting like you women discuss … *all the latest gossip!*"

Evelyn and Belinda looked at each other and rolled their eyes. They couldn't count the number of times they'd said to each other they'd rather be out amongst the men—discussing more interesting things, like politics and horse racing, rather than being forced to listen to the ladies' gossip!

"Are you feeling ill, Miss Evelyn?"

"No, but she's rather done-in, I'm afraid, Ollie. Would you please be so kind as to go fetch our carriage? It's time for us to go."

But before he could respond, Evelyn said, "Oh, Bel … are you sure? I don't wish to spoil your evening on my account."

"Nonsense, Eve! I already have my betrothed! What need have I for more dancing and flirting?"

And to emphasize her point she leaned over and grabbed Ollie by the arm, giving it a tight squeeze that made him smile and blush at the same time.

"Speaking of … have you two settled on a wedding date yet?"

"Not yet, dear … but likely sometime in May or June. But whenever it is, you shall be my maid of honor!"

"Oh, Bel … thank you. I would be honored. You will be … such a *beautiful* bride! A very vision in white."

Bel beamed and squeezed Ollie's arm again. Ollie nodded his head and continued to smile … and blush.

™

Monday - Christmas Eve, Dec. 24, 1860 - Greenbrier County, Virginia:

Billy sat on an old stump, high up the side of a hill overlooking the farm. He saw the glow of lights from the Big House below, twinkling through the falling snow.

He'd cleared off a large enough space for him to sit cross-legged, leaving him still surrounded by snow on all sides. The stump was so large if he laid down on it and stretched his arms all the way above his head, his feet and hands still wouldn't reach its edges. And in Virginia he had seen many and many such trees, most still standing tall. They were an amazing sight to him when he'd first arrived, there being nothing even remotely so large in Texas. But now such things were almost commonplace to him.

What was not yet commonplace, and was the reason for his current exploration, was the snow. It had been falling heavily since midday. And now, as evening was spreading forth its dark wings, it had been nearly up to his knees as he'd worked his way up the hill. This was the third time this winter it had snowed, and the deepest yet, by far.

He still had not figured out what to make of it, and more important, how to read it. Just when he was feeling more confident about reading the complexity of the Virginia wilderness, along came the snow. If anything, the snow presented an even greater challenge than had the complex vegetation and moisture.

The snow added a baffling array of dimensions, all of which might be present and interacting at the same time: its depth, of course, but also the temperature, the consistency, and the amount of wind when it was falling. And then later, after it had lain on the ground, the different layers built up from various weather events: melting, freezing, more snow falling on top, more thawing, etc., etc.

Each time he looked at the snow it had changed in some way. In the proper conditions the tracks were so perfectly clear and sharp one might make out the smallest detail from the bottom of the foot that'd made them. And if the temperature and weather were right, these tracks could stay in place for days or even weeks. At other times, the snow was falling so heavily one might be walking along, look back, and not be able to make out one's own tracks even only a few yards away; or the snow had become so soft and wet it oozed like mud, quickly filling in any tracks that were made; or it would be a tall soft powder, like the finest sand, moving and flowing easily with the slightest touch or breath of wind.

There was a time when he might have been frustrated and anxious about this new challenge. But now, he knew he *could* master reading a new and foreign terrain, if he was patient with himself, and carefully observant. So he was feeling relaxed about learning the snow. It would take time—years likely—but eventually he *would* learn it.

Of course, even in Texas it occasionally snowed. He recalled seeing it three or four times in his lifetime. But … it was nothing like this Virginia snow! The snow he'd seen in Texas was a very thin, powdery coating, easily blown by the wind—what the white men called "just a skiff." It was interesting, but never lasted long enough to be of any concern, or to be worth learning about.

But earlier today, as he watched the snow falling once again, he recalled … somewhere in the very back of his mind … his grandfather talking about snow. But it was so long ago, Billy could not recall the words Grandfather had said. Had he been in a place with snow at one time, high in the hills maybe? Or had there been a time long ago when Texas was colder and had more snow? He couldn't recall.

That was part of why he'd come up here on the hill, in the middle of the snowfall. It was really quite beautiful, and not terribly cold, as there was no wind at all. And the snow seemed to create an odd silence, so silent, in fact, he could hear the soft, swishing sound the snowflakes made as they landed.

In this peaceful silence, he sat and closed his eyes. It was something Grandfather had taught him—he'd called it learning how to speak to the ancestors. But Billy wasn't sure if it was really that. Maybe it just enabled him to remember things said so long ago he could no longer bring them to mind. It didn't much matter either way. He'd learned to be still, and silent, and clear his mind of all distracting thoughts. Then to focus on the one person he wished to speak with, and sometimes they would come into his consciousness. Then he could silently "speak" with them, even asking them questions and receiving answers.

This time he focused his thoughts, thinking only of Grandfather; remembering how he looked, the way he walked, the sound of his voice, the things he used to say …

"Hello, Grandson … it is long and long since we have spoken."

"Hello, Grandfather. It has been long and long since you departed from this Earth, but still I am missing seeing you alive and walking around with the living."

To this, Grandfather made no answer. Billy wasn't sure what this signified. Maybe wherever it was Grandfather now lived, he didn't know he was dead. Maybe he thought he now lived in a different place where he could no longer speak to his grandson in the flesh. But if so, he had never told Billy anything about that place, even though Billy had asked about it often. Or maybe Grandfather was only a memory living in the deep dark places of Billy's mind, and no longer existed at all. Billy hoped that was not the truth of it. He preferred to believe Grandfather was in some other, far-away place.

"Grandfather, I have come to ask you about the snow. I remember you telling me about it one time, when I was a small boy. But now I cannot recall the words. And … this Virginia I am now in, which I have told you about before … has much snow, and it does not melt quickly like in Texas. I do not know how to read it, and I wish to learn what you would teach me."

"Yes … I have spoken of the snow with you before, long ago, Grandson. There came a bad time once, when I was young. The People were desperate and hungry, from war and famine. No … not 'The Breaking,' but another time—even I am not *that* old, Grandson! Ha!

"We were forced to flee to the high mountains and hide away, in places that were cold, and often covered in ice and snow. There I learned many of the things snow had to teach, though not nearly all. No man knows all that snow has to teach. The wise ones used to say, to learn all there is to learn from the snow and ice is to die— the great whiteness will only give away its true secrets to a man dying from its cold and frost. I don't know if this is true, but I believe it is.

"What is it you would learn from me about the snow, Grandson?"

"Everything, Grandfather … everything you would teach me, of course!"

The Christmas Eve celebration out in the bunkhouse was much more boisterous than that in the Big House. The original farmhands Zeke, Benny, and Joe where there, along with the former soldiers from Texas. But they'd also invited the grooms, Cobb, Sampson, and Phinney who lived in an adjoining room next door.

And Hetty, Cobb's wife from the "big wedding," also came along. She was a field slave, and had a cabin she'd slept in for years, along with several other women. But now she spent most of her nights in Cobb's bed, in the corner of the groom's room. They'd rigged up a privacy wall in one corner, made from some boards begged off Sergeant Jim, to provide a little discretion. Some of the other "newlyweds" from the big wedding had likewise changed their previous sleeping arrangements out in the cabins.

This evening, Jim had smuggled some glasses and a keg of whiskey out of the Big House, and had shared it out. So now all were in a holly-jolly Christmas mood! William pulled out his violin, or fiddle, as Jim called it, and played it with great vigor. He'd started out playing Christmas songs, but now was playing any rambunctious song that came to mind.

The men were singing to the songs, making up lyrics if they didn't know them, and taking turns dancing with Hetty. She just laughed or rolled her eyes at their mostly feeble and awkward attempts at dancing. But they were enjoying themselves and didn't seem to pay much attention to her scowling looks. They appreciated the company of a fine-looking women in the bunkhouse, not much caring she was already married to one of them!

Jim, more than half inebriated, even proposed to her at one point. But she giggled and said, "I'd likely take you up on that, sir, if'n I weren't already married!"

Everyone laughed, especially Cobb. Jim said, "Damn! All that fine dancin' for naught!" and then slapped his knee and had to sit down on one of the bunks, laughing so hard they thought he might choke.

They carried on in the same manner until well past the start of Christmas day.

It was early Christmas morning and Big George sat at the table, reveling in the view of his little family, still sleeping soundly. The sun was rising, and the light coming in the windows gave him enough illumination to make out their slumbering forms. His wife, Babs, the love of his life, still asleep in their tiny bed — more comfortable, no doubt, now that he'd gotten up and left it to her. And their two beautiful little girls, Annie and Lucy, sleeping like two little angels, sharing a single bed. He sighed, appreciating how lucky he was to have these three ladies in his life.

He was so used to getting up early, he didn't know how to sleep late, even when there was no reason to get up. It was almost beyond belief the Captain had given them another whole week off from working the fields or doing other outdoor chores. That was twice in the last two months. In his whole life before he'd never had even one!

Things were surely changing for the better ... and all thanks to the Captain's arrival. Then he shook his head and smiled, remembering all the rumors that'd been going 'round about how wicked the Captain was before he'd ever arrived. How wrong they'd been! The Captain was a good man and true to his word. They now had hope, for the first time ever. And not just hope — their lives were actually improving, day by day. It was a thing he could never have imagined, even only a year ago.

As he was contemplating these happy thoughts, there was a loud knock on the door.

He jumped up, and ran to the door, hoping to prevent another knock that might disturb his sleeping angels.

He opened the door and stood with his mouth agape. It was the most unexpected, and strangest thing he'd ever seen. There stood a man, taller than himself, dressed all in furs, from head to toe, with a long white beard, trimmed with garlands of holly and pine boughs.

"Happy Christmas, George!" the man exclaimed. "I'm St. Nicholas, and these are my helpers!" he said.

The voice sounded familiar, and George realized the man under the white beard, clearly made of cotton bolls sewn together, was none other than the Captain himself. Behind him stood the giant Stan, and two of the house maids.

The girls and Babs sat up in bed, looking confused, and bleary-eyed.

George said, "Well, come on in, o' course, Capt ... I means ... *Saint Nick*. I expects you's here to see these-here young'ns!"

"Yes, George ... that I am! Happy Christmas, to all! Happy Christmas Babs! And especially you two, Annie and Lucy! Happy, happy Christmas!"

The little girls sat up in bed, eyes wide. Of course, they'd heard of St. Nicholas all their lives, but never had imagined seeing him in person. Annie finally said, "St. Nicholas ... is that *really* you?"

"Well, yes, of course it's me, dear little ones! And I have brought gifts for you little angels ... and for your Momma and Daddy!"

He turned and signaled to the maids standing behind him. The maids Sarah and Cara quickly moved into the room, setting a ham, sweet potatoes, and green beans on the table in a heap, then turned and headed back out the door.

"I have brought you a fine Christmas dinner, but also ..." he flipped around a burlap sack he held on his back and reached inside pulling out several items. Then he walked over to Babs and handed her a bundle of cloth. She took it, saying, "Thank you kindly, sir!" When she unfolded it, she discovered a bright red, knitted woolen cap, with matching mittens. St. Nick gave similar bundles to George, and the two girls. Each unwound a similar set of hat and mittens—each a different bright color.

"Thank you very kindly ... St. Nick," George said, after unfolding his.

"Oh, you are most welcome, sir, most welcome! But I have more Christmas gifts ... for the little ones ..."

And he pulled out a smaller, cloth sack, and reached inside. He pulled out two small cloth bundles, handing one to each of the girls. They held them carefully, as if they were something precious, which, in fact, they were.

"Go on ... open them!" St. Nick prodded with a broad grin.

Annie, the older of the two, at all of five years, carefully unwrapped the twisted cloth, freeing the contents. Inside were two nearly identical tiny horses, carved of wood and brightly painted brown and white. She gasped and smiled with delight. "Oh my! Lookie here, Momma! They's horses ... the most beautiful horses ever! Oh, thank you, St. Nick! Thank you! I ain't never had anything so beautiful before!"

Then Lucy, age three, opened her bundle, and out came two carved cows, painted black and white. "Oh! Oh!" was all she said, gazing at them, then picking them up and hugging them close to her face, beaming from ear to ear.

St. Nicholas laughed with delight, "You're very welcome, my beautiful young ladies. And now my helper, the most magical giant Stan has something else to show you, that will be shared among all the children."

Stan stepped forward and held out something in his great hands. George looked, and saw it was a toy boat carved of wood and fancifully painted. But unlike most boats, this one seemed to have a house on top. And on the top of the house sat a brightly painted, white dove, with a piece of greenery in its beak.

"Why ... it's ... it's—" George started.

"Noah's Ark!" Babs completed his sentence for him. "It's ... just ... *beautiful* masters!"

The little girls came forward and gazed at it in wide-eyed amazement.

Then St. Nicholas said, "The animals I gave you are those Noah had in his Ark, two by two. Noah's Ark will be put up at the Big House. And later today, and every Sabbath hereafter, all you children can come up there and play at putting your animals in the Ark!"

The girls were wide-eyed with excitement, but George looked over and saw Babs gazing at them with tears in her eyes.

George caught the eye of St. Nicholas, and said, "Thank you sir … thank you most kindly … I don't reckon nobody ever done a kinder turn than that."

"You're most welcome, George. It is the least 'Old St. Nick' can do for you and your beautiful family … the *very* least. And more than well deserved. Happy Christmas to you all! Enjoy your dinner, the toy animals, and the rest of your Christmas day!"

He turned and headed out the door, leaving a joy, never before imagined, in his wake.

ℰ𝒰ℰ𝒟𝒞𝒢ℰ𝒰ℰ𝒟𝒞𝒢𝒞𝒢ℰ𝒰ℰ𝒟𝒞𝒢𝒞𝒢

The maids hurried back to the wagon to fetch another Christmas dinner. Nathan had considered serving out a fully cooked meal to each cabin, but finally decided the logistics of that would be way too difficult. And it would place an unfair burden on the kitchen staff. So in the end, he settled on providing each cabin with the means to prepare their own Christmas meal: a large ham, a helping of sweet potatoes, and a generous portion of green beans. It wasn't fabulous, but he knew it would be a great treat to those who'd rarely enjoyed anything half so nice. And, he ordered the exact same Christmas meal be served at the Big House, and to the men in the bunk house, later in the afternoon.

"Well, only nineteen more cabins, Captain," Stan said, and grinned, trudging along in the foot-deep snow.

"Yes … but what joyful duty, Mr. Volkov!" Nathan answered with a smile. He was pleased at how well the first cabin had gone and was now looking forward to doing the rest.

Jamie and Georgie came trotting up. "Hey … it's our turn now, ain't it?"

"Oh … so sleepy heads finally are getting out of the bedsheets!" Stan said with a grin. "Here, Irish … have a boat!"

He handed the Ark to Jamie.

"Thanks, Stanny-boy! So … how'd the wee ones like our little carved creations?"

"Oh … seems to me they were happier than little piggies rolling in the mud!"

"Well … that's good then, ain't it?"

"Yes, Irish ... it was very, very good ... and the Captain is making a magnificent St. Nick ... even *I* was believing it!"

Nathan had gotten the idea for it several months back when he discovered a full-length fur coat and matching fur cap in the back of his closet. He'd asked Miss Abbey about it, and she'd said it had belonged to his grandfather. But when Nathan tried it on, he'd found it was too short in length and in the sleeves—he must be a good half foot taller than his grandpa had been. But Miss Abbey laughed and said, "Why, Nathan, dear ... you look just like old St. Nick in all that fur!"

He had laughed it off and hadn't thought much of it at the time. But later an idea started to percolate, necessitated by a recurring nightmare he could not seem to shake. In it, the little slave girl Lonna was shackled by a thick chain to a massive log, rock, or other large, heavy object. And the object was sliding down into a ravine filled with raging water, or down a hill into the ocean, or into a pit filled with fire or snakes. He grabbed ahold of the chain and pulled with all his strength 'til his muscles screamed with pain and the skin peeled from his hands. He dug in his heels until his legs ached and his feet burned from digging deep ruts in the earth. Yet though he strained 'til his heart burst, he could *not* pull the chain free from the log, nor stop its inexorable slide. All the while the little girl looked him in the eyes, tears streaming down her face, begging him to save her. "I'm sorry ... I can't save you ... I can't ... I ... just ... *can't do it* ..." He'd awaken with a start, covered in sweat, and shaking.

During his waking hours he knew it was his guilty conscience talking to him in his sleep. He still believed he'd done the right thing; there was nothing he could've done to save her without helping to create more orphans like her. Unless he was willing to murder the slave traders, which he could not bring himself to do.

But ever since that incident he had thought often about the horrible ordeal of those children ripped from their mother's arms, still but babes. And no matter how much he thought about it, he could come up with no solution to the problem, other than an end to slavery itself.

But one day, while pondering the problem, two thoughts came to him, almost simultaneously. Firstly, it occurred to him he was now a state senator, and as such, would be one of those who made the laws. Perhaps it would be possible to at least reign in some of the more heinous activities, such as taking very young children from their mommas. Yes ... that might be possible. He could envision stirring strong emotions, even in otherwise hard-hearted men, with his story about Lonna. He'd have to test the waters on that once he arrived in Richmond.

Secondly, an entirely different, but related notion struck him. He might *not* be able to save the children on other farms, but he was entirely responsible for the ones on his *own* farm. Maybe in some small way he could make up for what was happening to those *other* children by giving his own children some happy, joyous moments to remember from their childhood at Mountain Meadows ...

He'd enlisted the aid of his men, and it was William — of course — who came up with the idea for Noah's Ark. Apparently, it was a popular form of toy in the North, especially among more religiously conservative families — those of the Puritan persuasion, who didn't believe their children should be indulged in a secular way. Because of its biblical nature, the Ark was considered an acceptable toy for their children to play with. So the men, bored and wanting something to do, set to work carving and painting two of each kind of animal they could think of: the typical, everyday ones like cows, horses, dogs, pigs, etc. But also some of the more exotic ones they'd seen only in pictures: elephants, giraffes, and zebras. Jamie and Georgie, who were the most experienced at building and fixing things, built the boat, and added the figures of Noah and his wife to the deck. It had been a true labor of love, and the men had embraced the idea with great enthusiasm, clearly taking pride in their work.

The result was, St. Nicholas now had a pair of beautifully carved and painted animals for each child on the farm, and several left over for general Ark usage. Nathan couldn't have been more pleased. The reaction of the little children was the true payoff on the whole scheme.

Friday Jan. 4, 1861 - Greenbrier County, Virginia:

Nathan, Tom, and William sat their horses on the drive just below the steps to the front door. Molly the mule was heavily packed with their necessities for the trip to Richmond, and their expected lengthy stay there. She was tied behind William's horse on a long lead.

The day was dry so far, and the road was clear of snow, the Christmas snow having completely melted off by New Year's Day. The clear weather and dry road lead Nathan and Jim to exchange a knowing look, recalling Walters' need for such conditions in order to launch his attack. In preparation for Nathan's departure, Jim had already had his volunteers out practicing the Watch he and Billy had put in place. But the weather was still cool, and heavy clouds filled the sky, threatening more snow.

Megs and Miss Abbey stood at the edge of the veranda, along with Jim, Stan, Jamie, Georgie, and Billy. Cobb was down on the drive, in front of Nathan's horse Milly, absently scratching her face while looking over at the others.

Harry the Dog sat on the lawn over to the side of the house, his eyes intent on Nathan, while his tongue lolled out to the side. The only thing unusual about his appearance this day, was the sturdy chain attached to a thick leather collar around his neck. The chain was connected on the other end to a large iron bolt embedded in the foundation of the house. Nathan felt a twinge of guilt at the sight. He feared the dog would take his absence hard, despite Stan's best efforts to befriend him. Nathan had chained Harry himself that morning, knowing the dog would not suffer anyone else to do it.

He hardened his heart, and turned away from the sight, looking instead up toward the people on the porch. "Megs ... Momma ..." he tipped his hat to them.

"You take care of yourself, Nathan dear. And come home safely to me ... as soon as may be. You've promised ... we shall always live here together ... *'happily ever after'* you said. I mean to hold you to that!"

Nathan smiled, and reached in his pocket for a cigar, which he poked into his mouth.

"Momma ... have no fear ... *nothing* in this world can keep me from returning to you—you too, Megs! Even should all the armies on Earth stand between us. I have made you a sacred promise, and I intend to keep it!"

"Thank you dear, just ... *be careful* out there. It seems like ... well, like the world has suddenly changed. It no longer seems ... *safe* ... like it used to."

"Yes ... I know what you mean. But that's part of why I have to go ... to maybe help make it feel that way once again, or at least to try.

"And, while I'm gone, you'll be in good hands. Mr. Wiggins ... I'll trust you to defend and protect my family while I'm away."

"Yes, sir. That I'll do sir, and with pleasure. I'll keep 'em safer than a new-born babe in his momma's arms! Or die in the trying."

"*No*, Mr. Wiggins ... I'll allow no dying on your watch ... is that clear?"

"Yes, Captain. Perfectly clear to *me* ... but I'm not sure I can speak for ... some *other* folks down the hill—namely our not-so-friendly neighbors. They may have a hankering for dying I'll be hard-pressed to talk 'em out of!"

"Well, I'm sure you'll do your best."

"Yes, sir ... though likely I'll be forced to give them just exactly what they're askin' for!"

Nathan chuckled.

"Stan, Jamie, Georgie, Billy ... until we meet again."

Then Jim squared up his shoulders, and said, "Atten ... *SHUN!*"

All five soldiers stood up straight, clicked their heels together, and snapped a salute at the riders. Nathan, Tom, and William sat up on their mounts, and returned the salute with grins.

Then Nathan looked down, "Cobb ... you take good care of Hetty—'Mrs. Cobb,' I should say—while we're away."

"Yes, sir ... but seems like Hetty don't rightly need much takin' care of." He chuckled, "And to hear *her* tell it, *I's* the one what needs lookin' after, sir!"

Nathan laughed, nearly spitting the cigar from his mouth.

"Prob'ly so, Cobb, prob'ly so! I guess that goes for most of us men when you think on it."

"Yes, sir. I reckon so."

They shared a warm smile.

"Well, anyway ... goodbye."

"Thank you kindly, Captain. I shall ... be lookin' forward to your return, sir."

"Thank you, Cobb. Me too."

They turned their horses and headed up the drive away from the house. They'd not got out of sight of it, not even to the cabins yet, when they heard a loud, mournful howling behind them. Nathan winced involuntarily. He suffered for the dog ... and feared he would hear that sad howling in his dreams and feel it tugging at his heart, for some time to come.

CHAPTER 6. ON UNFAMILIAR GROUND

"We become so used to the familiar
we begin to doubt the unfamiliar,
until our eyes are opened,
and we see."
– Ted Dekker

Monday Jan. 7, 1861 - Richmond, Virginia:

The special legislative session started precisely at noon, an exercise in punctuality greatly appreciated by Nathan's military side.

He sat toward the left side of the room facing the ornate raised wooden table at the front where the senate president, who was also the lieutenant governor, sat along with the senate clerk. Tom sat with the other secretaries and assistance in the back of the room.

The capitol building, which had been designed by Thomas Jefferson, was stately and impressive, sitting alone on a hill overlooking Richmond. Its most impressive feature, however, was not on the outside, but on the inside. The heart of the building was a large rotunda, lavish, and exquisitely paneled and painted, starting on the main level reaching up to the very top ceiling. It featured an unusual internal dome at the top, which wasn't visible from the outside, as it did not extend beyond the roof of the building.

But to Nathan's thinking, the most impressive thing about the rotunda was the life-size marble statue of George Washington, which stood in the very center of the room, sited high upon a large pedestal. They'd commissioned the statue while Washington was still alive, and it'd been carved using a life-mask of his face and the exact measurements of his body. The result was so eerily life-like it gave Nathan chills. He could easily imagine the great man standing there in person, in his elegant officer's uniform, issuing commands to his troops.

The special session started out auspiciously enough, with the reading of the governor's official proclamation of his previous call for a special session. It talked about various items of unfinished business from the previous session, and concluded with the words:

> ... the election of sectional candidates as president and vice president of the United States, whose principles and views are believed by a large portion of the Southern states to be in direct hostility to their constitutional rights and interests, and in consequence thereof, great excitement prevails in the public mind, and prudence requires that the representatives of the people of this Commonwealth should take into consideration the condition of public affairs, and determine calmly and wisely what action is necessary in this emergency; therefore, I John Letcher, governor, by virtue of the authority aforesaid, do hereby require the senators and delegates of the two houses of the General Assembly of the Commonwealth, to convene at the capitol in the city of Richmond, on Monday the seventh day of January, A.D. 1861, at twelve o'clock, to legislate upon such subjects as they may deem necessary and proper.

Nathan appreciated the governor's words. They recognized the reality—people *were* all excited about the results of the election—but it emphasized this situation called for the legislature to respond, "calmly and wisely." He prayed such would be the case.

Nathan's initial excitement and anticipation soon waned, as they filled the next several hours with reading the senate rules. These consisted of a dry, lengthy, excessively detailed set of instructions, including such mundane matters as the number of assistant clerks and their specific duties to the senatorial main clerk. Nathan assumed these employees were already well aware of their duties. If not, they'd soon be out of a job. Besides, none of those persons were probably listening anyway!

The reading also included a complete list of every senatorial committee, the purpose, and the minimum and maximum number of senators required for each. This even included, to Nathan's surprise and amusement, a "Committee to Examine the Lunatic Asylums of the Commonwealth." Did Virginia have so many of these it required a dedicated senate committee? But then an image of Elijah Walters came into his mind, and he had to suppress a wry smile. He decided he knew a likely candidate for one of those institutions.

Halfway through this recitation, Nathan found himself fighting down a very strong urge to yawn. He'd been used to a certain amount of etiquette and protocol in the military. But compared to this, any he had previously experienced seemed blunt, concise, and to the point. He decided if his enemies ever really wanted to make him suffer, they'd force him to listen to this sort of thing for days on end. Better to be stabbed in the eye with a red-hot poker, he figured.

At one point he casually turned and looked over his left shoulder toward the back of the room where Tom sat with the rest of the secretaries. They made brief eye contact, and Nathan raised an eyebrow at Tom, which elicited a subtle grin. From long years working together, Tom knew exactly what Nathan was saying with no words spoken.

Once this reading was, thankfully, finally completed, a senator with the last name Douglas made a motion for the chair to appoint a committee of three "to inform the governor that the senate is ready to receive any communication he may desire to make." This motion was immediately approved with unanimous *yeas*, and the chair, Lieutenant Governor Robert Montague, appointed Douglas, Senator Thompson, and Senator Rives to the committee. The committee left the room but returned almost immediately. Mr. Douglas addressed the chair, saying the committee had discharged the duty assigned them, handing him a letter from the governor.

Nathan thought this a ridiculous amount of rigmarole. Clearly everyone knew the governor had already written and sent a message, the whole committee charade being a mere formality.

The president read out the governor's letter. It was long, and rambling, touching on many different ideas concerning the present troubling state of affairs in the nation, and Virginia's particular place in it. Nathan was having a hard time deciding what he thought of Governor Letcher from this reading. On the one hand, his honor called for calmness, rational decisions, and patriotism, declaring the potential dissolution of the Union would be a terrible disaster, both politically and economically. But on the other hand, he declared that the Northern states, and their boldly anti-slavery rhetoric and actions had forced the South to defend itself. He proceeded to attack South Carolina in general, and its now-former governor specifically, in the most venomous terms. Chastising them for moving ahead without consulting the other slaveholding states and for attempting to coerce Virginia into joining them; after which he equally harangued the New England states for their actions, past and present, even proposing they be forcibly removed from a newly constructed, more congenial Union!

Nathan decided the governor must be walking a dangerously fine line. He seemed to have a clear grasp of the unmitigated disaster a disunion might trigger. But he was also likely under a lot of pressure to stand up to the external forces pressuring Virginia. And he had to appear strong in his support of slavery as an institution, regardless of how he might feel about it personally. Of the latter, Nathan had no idea, since he'd not yet spoken with the governor in person.

He'd intended to have a private meeting with his honor before the legislature ever convened, but the special session had made that all but impossible. When Nathan had arrived on Saturday, the governor's office was closed until Monday, when the special session would start. He'd sent a message with one of the senate clerks requesting a meeting at his honor's earliest convenience but had not yet received a reply.

But, still, the overall tone of the governor's text was hopeful of a happy outcome to the entire unhappy affair. Nathan found this encouraging. Virginia, at least, might not follow the monumentally disastrous path South Carolina had started down.

But he soon had cause to worry again. The next thing read out to the senate was a proposed joint resolution between the house and senate. This resolution, in a nutshell, resolved Virginia would oppose, in the strongest possible terms, any attempt by the federal government to hold the Union together by force.

That was worrisome. Nathan could not envision a scenario under which the president of the United States, be it Lincoln or any other man, would allow the secession to happen. Not without a fight. If he were president, he wouldn't.

ᏸᎧᏐᏣᏐᏣᏸᎧᏐᏣᏐᏣᏸᎧᏐᏣᏐᏣ

Tuesday Jan. 8, 1861 - Richmond, Virginia:

On the second day, they voted on the joint resolution from the previous day, opposing the use of coercion by the federal government, in its three parts. Nathan voted nay on all three. But he was almost alone in doing so. This surprised him and he suddenly felt discouraged; he'd assumed there'd be a larger number of pro-Union voters in the senate. He felt eyes on him, but so far none of the other senators had spoken with him. After today's session, he suspected that would no longer be the case — and it would likely not be in a friendly manner!

He had a harder time deciding about the resolution calling for a national convention to discuss constitutional amendments designed to resolve the current crisis. But if this conference proved unfruitful, which seemed highly likely given the divisiveness of the issues, the secessionists would have another excuse. So he voted against it.

When the senate adjourned for the day, Nathan rose and walked over to where Tom awaited him, in the back of the room. Tom had gathered up his writing papers, on which he'd been making notes, and stood to meet Nathan. They exchanged a serious look but said nothing, knowing full well anything they said would be overheard by any number of ears.

But as they turned to leave, two senators approached them. Nathan knew their last names, Mr. Stuart and Mr. Caldwell; they'd been named by the chair on several occasions during the session. As was his habit, he'd memorized any name that'd been associated with a specific face. Stuart was a handsome man of

129

medium height and build, with a kindly face that seemed inclined to an easy smile. Caldwell was of the same height, but of a much larger girth—a man who appeared to enjoy his libations. He also had a friendly disposition about him. Both men dressed in formal, dark suits, with elegant waistcoats, the same as all the other senators in attendance. Nathan smiled, thinking of the attire as the senatorial uniform.

He remembered Stuart had attempted to soften the wording on one of the joint resolutions. And Caldwell had voted with Nathan on one occasion. So he was pre-disposed to view them in a positive light.

"Mr. Chambers," Stuart said in low tones, as they approached, "I am Mr. Stuart, and this is …"

"Mr. Caldwell … yes, I know who you are, gentlemen. Pleased to make your acquaintance, sirs."

They shook hands, and met eyes with a serious, but genial look.

"Oh, the pleasure is ours, sir. And … that being the case, would you do us the honor, sir, of allowing us to accompany you from these halls? We would converse with you for a few moments once we have arrived at … a more … private location …"

But before Nathan could answer, he noticed three other gentlemen approaching, clearly also seeking his attention. Just before they reached him, Caldwell leaned in close, and whispered in his ear, "We are your *friends*, Mr. Chambers … these others … likely *not!*"

He stood back and smiled, and Nathan locked eyes with him. He saw sincerity there; the man meant what he was saying, and Nathan instinctively liked him.

The first of the other men to reach him, a tall, lean man with long graying hair, held out his hand and introduced himself, "Mr. Chambers, I am …"

"Mr. Thompson … an honor to meet you sir, and you Mr. Armstrong, and Mr. Paxton," Nathan said, extending his hand. Thompson seemed surprised he already knew their names. Nathan hoped it might set him a bit off his track.

"Oh … well, the honor is ours, Mr. Chambers. And … may I speak for myself and my esteemed colleagues in offering our condolences on the recent passing of your father. He was a highly valued, and much-admired member of this august gathering, and will be greatly missed."

"Thank you, sirs. Your kind words are greatly appreciated. My father would have been most pleased at your high regard for him."

"And, of course, Mr. Chambers, may I be the first to welcome you to the senate, assuming these other gentlemen have not already beaten me to it!"

"Thank you again, Mr. Thompson. And no, you are the *first*, sir."

"Ah, excellent. And would it be too much to ask, for a few moments of your time on the way out of the hall?"

"Oh … I must apologize, sir, and will gladly meet with you on another occasion, perhaps tomorrow before the session starts? You see, I have accepted an invitation to accompany Mr. Stuart and Mr. Caldwell from the hall this evening. Otherwise I would gratefully accept."

"Ah … yes, well, tomorrow morning would be fine. Shall we say half past eleven in the rotunda?"

"Excellent, Mr. Thompson. I shall be looking forward to it. Mr. Armstrong, Mr. Paxton. Good day, sirs."

They walked out into the broad foyer of the senate chambers heading toward the rotunda. Mr. Stuart turned to Nathan, and said, "That was neatly done, Mr. Chambers. I thank you. I am Alexander, but my close friends and associates call me Sandy, and this is Alfred."

"Nathaniel … but please do call me Nathan. And this is my assistant, Tom Clark. There is no need to thank me … I suddenly had a very strong urge to hear what *you* two gentlemen had to say, before listening to those others."

"I think that was wise, Nathan. And I believe you will agree once we've had a chance to converse," Caldwell said, and Stuart nodded his assent.

They walked through the great rotunda, and Nathan couldn't resist glancing up at General Washington once more, shaking his head in silent admiration. Tom seemed more impressed with the domed ceiling, gazing up with open mouth—the same as he'd done yesterday when they'd first seen it. They turned to the left, walked out the west entrance, and down the broad stairs on that side of the building. Various groups of people exiting at the same time began to separate and disburse in different directions. This afforded them a modicum of privacy as they walked along the gravel path leading downhill and in a southwesterly direction, leading toward downtown Richmond and their boarding house.

Sandy Stuart restarted the conversation, "Nathan ... may I assume, based on your votes today ... you are of a pro-Union disposition?"

"Yes, certainly ... I've no reason to deny it."

"Well ... as you no doubt surmised, that is why Mr. Caldwell whispered we were your 'friends,' before those other *most esteemed* gentlemen stepped up to you. We are also very much pro-Union. Mr. Caldwell considers himself a Northerner, being from Wheeling—in fact, the former mayor of that fair city, and a Lincoln Republican on top of it. And I ... well, I've been involved in the national government for many years, most recently as Secretary of the Interior to President Fillmore. And, in the recent presidential election, I worked for the Constitutional Union Party. So ... yes, we are most decidedly pro-Union."

"Ah ... well, glad to know it, gentlemen. And congratulations on your excellent records of service to the country. I sincerely thank you for that.

"Mr. Caldwell ... *Alfred*, I should say ... I happen know someone from Wheeling ... the Reverend Holing of the Methodist Church. I don't suppose you would know him?"

"Oh, my goodness, Mr. Chambers! Of course, I know him. He is the pastor of my very own church where I attend every Sunday, when not forced to be here in Richmond. How ever do you know the good reverend, sir?"

"Oh ... he recently performed a wedding ceremony for ... some *friends* of mine ... and we became well acquainted during his time in Greenbrier County."

"Well ... what a fine coincidence that is, I must say!"

"Yes, it certainly is. Please do be so kind as to give him my respects, and my best compliments, next time you see him, sir."

"That I will do, and gladly, Nathan. He will be so pleased to hear from you, I'm certain!"

They shared a smile, and a shake of the head at the surprising connection between them.

"So ... getting back to the ugly matter of politics, Nathan ..." Stuart said, "we'd like you to consider ... *softening* your pro-Union stance in the senate."

"Oh? Why do you say that, Sandy?"

"It is ... best if we ... are seen to go along with the majority at this point in time," he answered cryptically.

"And ... why is that, pray tell? Doesn't honor demand a man vote his conscience on such matters?"

"Well ... usually I'd say 'yes,' but sometimes ... well, sometimes the answer is 'no.'"

Nathan suddenly stopped, and the two senators had to stop in reaction, and turn back around to face him. Tom, who'd been walking two steps behind Nathan, avoided bumping into his back with near-heroic effort.

"What do you mean by *that*, sir? Why should I be untruthful in my actions in the senate? I'm not sure I like what you're suggesting, Mr. Stuart."

They stood still for a moment, Nathan locking eyes with Stuart. Stuart could see Nathan was heating up. He knew he needed to change his tack with this man ... to explain what needed to be done, but in a way the newcomer would understand and accept. Then it came to him in a flash, like a match struck in the darkness, and his face lit up.

"Nathan ... am I correct in my understanding you are a *military* man ... a West Point graduate in fact, and a former Army officer and war veteran?"

"Yes … you are correct. I've spent my entire adult life in the Army, up until only a few months ago, when I was informed of my father's untimely passing and was forced to return home to Virginia."

"My condolences on your recent loss, of course, sir. I have been remiss in not saying so earlier."

"Oh, yes, me as well," Caldwell agreed, "So sorry for your loss, Nathan."

Nathan nodded his head in acknowledgment but said nothing.

Stuart continued, "Well then, you being a military officer, let me ask you, sir; does honor demand you always attack your enemy head-on … in a frontal assault, and never employ … *other* methods?"

"Oh, well, most certainly not! In battle, if we can *flank* the enemy — that is … get around the end of his lines and get at him from his weak points on the sides or in back — we will *always* attempt to do so. It's a tactic as old as time, gentlemen, as I'm sure you already know. Why?"

"And … does honor require you to always let the enemy know what you intend to do on the battlefield? In the example you just gave, are you honor bound to tell the enemy you mean to flank him?"

"Of course not, what a ridiculous notion! We'd try to convince him of anything but. Like a feint to the opposite side or making a great show of preparing a frontal assault to pull off his strength. But what … *oh … I see …*"

Stuart smiled and folded his arms in a satisfied manner.

Nathan gazed up at the sky for a long moment. He looked down at Stuart, then over toward Caldwell, before returning their smiles.

"Well done, Sandy … well done. I am humbled, sir, *truly*. Gentlemen … I can now see I have much to learn about … *politics*. And it seems you two would make good teachers. I suppose … even outside the field of battle it is *not* always good to tell your enemies what you are about. Unless you wish to go down in ignominious defeat."

"You are a quick study, Nathan! It is a great pleasure to see. We shall get along famously, I have no doubts!"

"Thank you, Sandy. I thought I knew something about the world and dealing with all kinds of men. But these last two days in the senate I've felt like a child just learning to walk."

"Have no fear, Nathan ... we will help you navigate these treacherous waters ... and ... you are the largest *child* I have ever seen, what say you, Alfred?"

"Yes, certainly! I can't imagine any of the other senators insulting you, at the least, Nathan. You are ... a formidable looking fellow, if you don't mind my saying so."

"Well ... in the world I've lived in, a man's ability to kill other men is paramount. But I know that is of little value here."

"Oh ... I wouldn't be so sure of that!" Stuart said with a sly smile.

"So ... you say you wish me to soften my stance ... my military training demands me to ask, what is the *strategy* in it? What do we hope to accomplish by seeming to go along with the enemy?"

"Ah ... excellent question, Nathan! Now you cut right to the heart of the matter. You see, the governor, his honor Mr. Letcher, is also pro-Union, though he can never openly admit to it. His plan is to drag out the whole question of secession as long as possible. You see, every day that goes by is to the benefit of the pro-Union forces, and the detriment of the secessionists. Over time, cooler heads will surely prevail. And the new president will be given the opportunity to show he is *not* the three-horned devil they're making him out to be. The people will soon realize there is nothing to be gained by a disunion.

"To answer your question more specifically, we want to force the question of seceding, or *not*, to a specially elected set of delegates to a state convention, rather than have the issue decided within the General Assembly."

"Oh ... and why is that?"

"Because the General Assembly, especially the senate, is disproportionally stacked in favor of the Slave Power."

"Slave Power?"

"Yes … it's the name often given to the so-called 'Planter Class,' sometimes also referred to as the 'Slavocracy.' Those who have the most to gain by the continuation of slavery, generally considered to be those individuals who own twenty or more slaves."

"Well … I guess by those standards, I'd be included in that group."

"Yes, you most *certainly* would … and your Daddy was definitely of that persuasion. So I must admit we were caught by surprise you turned out to be … something *different*. I suspect our esteemed opponents were taken by surprise as well."

Nathan smiled.

"So … to finish answering your question, Nathan, we believe we can win in a special election of this type, where party loyalties are of little matter. Rather than oppose the Secession Convention, we intend to mold it to our benefit, and ensure it returns the result we want. Rather than opposing the election, we intend to support it while pushing for the apportionment of delegates on the white basis."

"White basis? What does that mean?"

"In the past, the Slave Power has insisted on representation based on population, with black slaves counting as 3/5ths, though obviously they can't vote. So the slaveholders have held a disproportionate representation in the legislature. In 1851 a new state constitution changed some of that. Now the House is apportioned based on the number of white men in a district, the so-called 'white basis,' rather than the old, distorted 3/5ths version. But the senate still uses the old method.

"So again … instead of standing against the election, we'll push for holding it on the white basis. This, plus the lack of party affiliations, will give us a distinct advantage in a special election. It'll shift much of the emphasis to the western side of the state, which either cares little for the Slave Power, or opposes it outright. We think there's a very good chance the election will result in a pro-Union majority."

"Oh. So instead of opposing a secession convention, you're saying I should support the idea, so we can win in the special election, and ensure the convention is pro-Union?"

"Yes, exactly!"

"And what about this proposed national Constitutional Convention? I'm concerned if it fails, which seems likely to me, it'll only lend more ammunition to the secessionists."

"Oh, you are correct; it will almost certainly fail. But that doesn't mean it isn't worth doing. A thing like that takes time to organize, to determine who can attend, get everyone there, decide on rules and whatnot. It'll likely take months, and ..."

"Nobody can make a move until it runs its course. Yes, I see that now. So I take it you also want me to support *that* notion?"

"Yes, certainly. As I said before, anything that drags things out is only to our benefit, regardless of the eventual outcome."

Nathan was thoughtful for a moment, "All right. That makes sense. I can go along with your plan."

"Good. There's one more thing," Caldwell said.

"Yes?"

"We want you to convince the Slave Power ... you're on *their* side."

ᴥᴥᴥᴥᴥᴥᴥᴥᴥ

When Nathan and Tom reached their boarding house, a large two-story house on the corner of Grace and Fifth Streets, William was already there waiting for them. It was an easy four-block stroll from the capitol building, so there was no need to ride their horses, which they'd boarded in a facility a few blocks over. In extreme weather it would be possible to arrange for a carriage, but so far that had not been necessary. Nathan was pleased they'd been able to obtain the rooms. Miss Abbey had recommended the place from her previous visits with Jacob, who apparently had also appreciated the short walking distance. Miss Abbey also spoke highly of the congenial proprietors, an elderly couple who treated their guests like royalty. So Tom had sent a telegram to the place shortly after they'd learned of the special session, to reserve the rooms before someone else asked for them.

"Hello, William, had a productive day?"

"Yes, sir, in fact I have!"

"Oh? That sounds encouraging. Tom, will you put up our things while I pour us a drink at the kitchen table? I'm eager to receive William's full report."

"Yes, sir ... I'll only be a moment, then I'll gladly have that drink with you. Sitting all day in the senate chambers is thirsty work!"

Nathan grinned, "Yes, I almost think I'd rather spend a whole day out in the hot Texas sun fighting Indians than half a day indoors fighting politicians!"

William gave him a puzzled look at first before realizing he was likely only speaking figuratively. But then ... considering the Captain's temperament ... *maybe not!*

The two men headed toward the kitchen, while Tom headed up the stairs to deposit the sheaf of papers and writing instruments he carried in a leather case.

Nathan opened a cabinet where he'd stashed a bottle of whiskey the previous evening while William searched several cabinets, trying to remember where they kept the glasses. But after he opened the third one, finding what he was looking for, he found himself chastised by the proprietress—she'd entered the room, having heard them rummaging about.

"Oh, *no*, Mr. Jenkins, Mr. Chambers! I'll not have my guests serving themselves! I'll be the disgrace of the neighborhood! For *shame*, sirs! Please allow a hostess to do her duty!"

She shooed them to the table, even grabbing the whiskey bottle from Nathan's hand before he sat.

They smiled, and politely answered, "Yes, ma'am."

She quickly placed two glasses on the table in front of them, then poured a generous splash in each before setting the bottle down next to the glasses.

"Thank you kindly, Mrs. Wilkerson ... and would you be so good as to set out one more glass? Mr. Clark will be joining us momentarily."

"Oh, yes, certainly, Mr. Chambers. And is there aught I can fetch you to eat while you refresh yourselves?" she asked as she set out another glass and filled it.

"Oh, thank you … but no, ma'am. We shall be content to await dinner in that regard."

"Very well, gentlemen. Enjoy your drink, and be sure to call on me if you need aught else."

"Yes, ma'am, thank you. We certainly shall."

Once Tom joined them, and they'd each had a sip, Tom said, "Well, out with it, William! Tell us of your expedition today, especially since you've said it was a success!"

"With pleasure, sirs. And though I am pleased to report on a successful mission of the day, I can't say there was any enjoyment in it for me. The thing was … on the whole, quite unpleasant— *upsetting*, would not be too strong a term for it, I suppose."

Nathan and Tom sipped their drinks, politely waiting for William to continue his tale.

"First, I've had quite a longer walk today than you gentlemen, and on the way back, mostly uphill. I nearly repented of my decision not to ride my horse. The address Tom gave me, Davenport and Company at 15th and Cary streets, is on the other side of the capitol building from here. In all it's about ten blocks east, and another three south. The building sits in a low, marshy part of town the locals call Shockoe Bottom, on account of Shockoe Creek running through the middle of the district before it empties into the James River. A dirty, noisome part of town, to be sure, and apparently the epicenter of the slave trade in Richmond. There are several slave auction houses and jails in the district, I am led to understand, but the Davenport Company appears to be among the largest. It occupies a great wooden warehouse a block back from the waterfront. One can imagine in the old days of the Atlantic slave trade, the Africans being marched in chains straight from the ships to this very building: the first place they ever saw in America."

"Hmm … not a very warm welcome, I'd imagine," Nathan said, with a hint of disgust.

"No, sir. It is in fact, a most *unhappy* place, I'm afraid. I had the ... great *dis*-pleasure of watching several auctions. The building has three fairly large auction rooms, each focused on a tall wooden pedestal with stairs leading up on one side. I was made to understand they had one auction room for field slaves, typically dressed as they would be on the farm, and another for domestic help, mostly women. Many were nicely dressed as if that might raise their value, I suppose."

"And the third?" Tom asked.

William looked at him for a moment, then over at the Captain, seeming reluctant to give the answer.

"The other was ... the most disturbing. There they have the women with small children—one or more babes in arms, or small tykes. They put them up for sale, either to be purchased as a package, or separately. It is of no matter to the auctioneers. I watched as they had to almost carry one nearly hysterical woman from the room, crying and wailing after they'd sold off her baby. It sickened me, I can tell you. I had to leave the room."

Nathan had a dark, severe look, but said nothing, so William continued.

"Anyway, they place the slave—man, woman, or child—sometimes a small family group—up on that platform, then allow the potential buyers to walk around and view them from all sides. They'll sometimes feel of a limb for firmness or ask the slave to walk about a bit if they suspect a limp or some sort of infirmity. Sometimes they ask the domestics a question or two about their household skills: cooking, sewing, and whatnot. Then they start the bidding. If it's a mother with child or a family group, they will ask a minimum price for purchasing the lot. If nobody bids the minimum, they split them up and bid on them separately. That happened on all of the groups I watched, I'm sorry to say. And a sad business it was, too."

"A damned *crime* is what it is," Nathan growled. "And the errand I sent you on?"

"Yes, sir ... I was coming to that part. I wandered about until I located the business office where they record the sales. They have a large shelf, stacked with ledger books—years and years of them from what I could see. Mostly collecting dust, but clearly a few had been taken down and dusted off from time to time. Anyway, I waited for a quiet moment, then asked about the woman Lilly you were interested in. As Tom had warned, at first the clerk gave me a blank stare, as if I were speaking in Greek—which I *can* do, by the way. Then in a bored tone he said, 'Sir, to find a single slave in this great stack of ledger books is an exceedingly difficult and onerous task.' But I reminded him I had the exact date of the sale, the price she'd been sold for, and of course the name of the woman and a fair description. That should make his search much easier, as I could see the ledger books were labeled by the dates of the sales within. I assured him, if he'd allowed me into the room, behind his counter, I'd find the information in a few minutes. But he was unmoved by my arguments, as Tom had predicted. I had to resort to … the *other methods* Tom had recommended."

"You bribed him, of course."

"Yes, sir, that's the naked truth of it. But the good news is I negotiated the price to only about half what Tom had suggested should be agreeable. I shamelessly used the fact it'd likely be an easy search to my advantage, even offering to conduct the search myself. But eventually we agreed on the value of his time to perform the search. And as I'd predicted, he located the pertinent ledger book in short order. He set it on the counter, blew off the dust, and we went through it carefully. He searched for the name Lilly—turns out it's a fairly common one. Then we looked at the prices, descriptions, ages, and whatnot, to make sure we had the correct one."

"And?"

"And … *we found her, sir!* Or at least, we found who purchased her back then. We can only hope she's still there after all this time. But fortunately, the farm that purchased her is not far away, as I understand, just north of Petersburg. I can ride there and back in a day, if you'd like."

"That was well done, thank you William. And … I'm not surprised, but that was also exceedingly honest of you."

"Honest, sir?"

Tom and Nathan shared a smile.

Tom answered, "William, many men I know ... even those I'd otherwise consider honest, would've negotiated the bribe, and pocketed the difference, considering it a fair fee for their efforts."

"Oh. Well, it never occurred to me to do such a thing, Tom. Nor would I have, even if it *had*. I'd not take the Captain's money if I hadn't earned it."

"Of course, you wouldn't William," Nathan said, "One more reason we hold you in such high esteem."

"Thank you, sir."

"Anyway ... to answer your other question: yes, I'd appreciate if you would ride out to Petersburg to see if Lilly is still there. I would be much obliged."

"Certainly, sir. Only ..."

"Yes?"

"Well, it might be easier to explain my interest in the woman if you told me why *you* are interested in her, sir."

Nathan met eyes with Tom before answering. "William ... do you remember the slave girl Rosa, who was nearly whipped by Sickles, on the day we cashiered him?"

"Yes, of course. She's working up at the Big House now, isn't she?"

"Yes ... that's right. The woman we seek is her mother. I wish to find her, as she is one of the few slaves my Daddy has ever sold away. I am considering reuniting mother and daughter if possible—in the name of Christian charity, and to make amends for her traumatic experience. You understand ..."

Nathan felt a little awkward with this explanation ... not that it wasn't true; it *was* true as far as it went. But he wasn't prepared yet to tell anyone other than Tom his suspicions about Jacob Chambers and the girl's mother. Not yet, not until he knew the truth, one way or the other, and he could speak with Miss Abbey about it before anyone else. He'd not risk her hearing some kind of rumor before the truth was known.

"Ah! All right, that's helpful, Captain, thank you. I will leave at first light tomorrow. Is there anything you wish me to do other than see if she is in fact there? Do you wish me to speak with her … ask her anything, or speak with the new owner to see if he would be interested in a sale?"

"No need to talk with the woman, but you'll probably need to explain to the owner your interest if you expect to get any information. You needn't say we're interested in purchasing her, but the new owner will assume it anyway. If she's there I'll ride out when next the Senate is out of session and have a word with her and her owner."

"Yes, sir. In the meantime, I'll see if I can feel him out on his willingness to part with her, without committing to anything on our part."

"That sounds fine, William, thank you."

The conversation then shifted, with Tom telling William all about the happenings in the senate, and their discussion with Mr. Stuart and Mr. Caldwell after.

While this was going on, Nathan continued to think about Lilly. He hadn't decided exactly what he wanted to do about her, other than speak with her about his father, to discover the truth about Rosa. He debated with himself about purchasing her, either way. If Jacob wasn't the father, there was still the mystery of why he'd sold her away when Mountain Meadows was actively buying. And he worried what Miss Abbey knew of it, and whether she'd had something to do with the woman's departure. If so, bringing her back might be very problematic. In the end, he decided it was too soon to make any definite plans. So he mentally shrugged; he'd just have to discover the truth first. Then, he'd likely have to broach the subject with Miss Abbey, even at the risk of reopening a painful wound.

ᏪᎯᏨᏧᏪᎯᏨᏧᏪᎯᏨᏧᏪᎯᏨᏧ

Wednesday Jan. 9, 1861 - Richmond, Virginia:

"Gentlemen, before you chastise me for my recent voting record, let me first explain my actions. Being in the Army all these years I've come to err on the straightforward side. In the military most of my problems were solved by a judicious application of hot lead and pointy steel! Not much subtlety to it, shall we say."

143

This prompted smiles from the three gentlemen sitting next to him. They sat on ornate stone benches set in a circle around the outer wall of the rotunda. It took an effort of will for Nathan to resist looking up at General Washington as he spoke.

"But … now, based on some conversations I've had since yesterday, it has occurred to me … some of my votes may have, inadvertently, been to the benefit of those who might naturally be considered on the opposite side of the political landscape from myself. Would you gentlemen agree?"

Nathan knew he was talking a fine line with these men. He was determined to get through this conversation without actually lying; it went against his nature to do so. But he also knew the stakes were high, and making them believe he was on their side might be of great benefit to the pro-Union side.

"Yes, that is very perceptive of you, Mr. Chambers," Thompson said. "And no blame on you for anything you've done in the senate in the last two days … you could not be expected to immediately be an expert in an unfamiliar landscape. I take it your conversation with Mr. Stuart and Mr. Caldwell was … eye opening?"

"Yes … certainly … based on my votes they considered me to be … well, let's just say other than what would be in my economic best interests. Gentlemen, I have recently inherited a sizable estate from my father, which includes over a hundred slaves. I'm sure I don't need to tell you the economic implications of that fact? My Granddaddy carved that farm out of the raw wilderness. And my Daddy expanded it to the large, highly productive estate it is today. They never could have done so without their slaves. Gentlemen, you can't truly believe a man in my position wouldn't do everything in his power to uphold the traditions and institutions that made all that possible?"

"Oh … certainly *not*, Mr. Chambers, certainly not. It's just … some of your votes did seem a bit … out of character, is all."

"Yes, I can understand that now. But you must excuse me on that. From my military training, if someone were to present a plan of battle, and I didn't entirely agree with it, detecting some flaw or other, I'd vote 'no,' until the issues had been resolved. In the

Army, this might mean the difference between victory and utter disaster. I've never before had to consider the idea of ... a *partial* victory or advantage. It has become clear to me I have much to learn in this arena, gentlemen."

"That is most understandable, Mr. Chambers. So may we assume you are *not* enamored of these radical Northern abolitionists, as embodied by the newly elected president?"

"Gentlemen, I have said this before on a number of occasions; forced abolition would be a disaster not just to my own farm and to the South, but probably in the North as well—the sudden collapse of the agricultural economy would have a continent-wide effect, I'm sure."

Nathan remembered saying almost that exact thing to Walters the first time they'd met, so it was a true statement. Though he'd said it before under the context of recommending a more gradual, controlled emancipation.

"Certainly, and well said, Mr. Chambers. Then ... can we count on your support when it comes time to push forward with secession?"

"Well, to be honest, I'd never even heard the idea of secession when I was out West in the Army. So it has caught me a bit off guard. As I said before, I must look out for what's in the best interests of my own household, first and foremost. So I'll need to be convinced this secession will benefit me before I'll agree to support it. But ... it does seem to me convening a group of knowledgeable men to discuss the matter at length and come to a decision, is a sound idea. So ... I'll be supportive of that notion.

"In any regard ... I will trust you gentlemen to help advise me going forward ... the last few days have been ... a new experience. I know a great deal about battles fought with guns and swords, but very little about the political kind of debates and votes."

"Certainly, Mr. Chambers. You can count on us to guide you on the proper course through these troubled waters, never fear."

"Thank you, gentlemen. I am much obliged."

As the meeting broke up, and the group headed toward the senate chambers, Nathan felt a sense of relief. He believed he'd convinced them he was either on their side, or at least leaning strongly in that direction, and never had to actually lie to do it. He had, however, allowed them to believe he was what they'd expected him to be, and felt only a tiny twinge of guilt about that. The stakes were too high to risk losing, and … he reminded himself the rules of battle; if you could outwit, outsmart, and deceive your enemy, so much the better. *All is fair in love in war*, he reminded himself. And this was certainly shaping up to be a war, though hopefully *not* the shooting kind.

ॐ๛๏ॐ๛๏ॐ๛๏ॐ๛๏ॐ๛๏

William sat on his horse, Bill, and gazed at the unexpected sight in front of him. He'd arrived at his destination: the Sam Monroe family farm a few miles north of Petersburg. But the place appeared as though it were entirely deserted, and had been so for some time. Most of the windows were shuttered, with a few even crudely boarded up. Unkempt and overgrown bushes lined the walkway to the house, which barely showed any gravel for its thick layer of darkened, decaying leaves. The lawn surrounding the house was brown and dead-seeming, overgrown with weeds. And weeds also seemed the only crops growing in the fields immediately surrounding the house, as far as William could see.

The outbuildings looked to be in a similar state of disrepair—several showing missing shingles, or gaping holes in the siding. All were in need of a fresh coat of paint, at the least.

It was a thoroughly depressing sight. William shivered, pulling his overcoat up tight under his chin to keep the chilly air out. Though it hadn't rained yet, as he'd been expecting, it was a gloomy, overcast day. A cool breeze rattled fitfully through the bare branches of the elms lining the roadway. William was thankful for Bill's warm body radiating heat up through his own frame, or he'd be suffering it much worse. Though curious if he might see anything of the inside through the shutters, he was not inclined to dismount and lose his nice warm seat.

He removed his glasses and wiped them clean with a cloth before risking a momentary cold backside; he stood in the stirrups and gazed into the far distance all around. To the south he spotted another farmhouse a few miles off—apparently the nearest

146

neighbor. Or better yet, maybe he was off his reckoning and this was *not* the Monroe farm at all. Maybe he'd just not reached it yet. He hoped it was true as he turned Bill around and headed back onto the main roadway toward the distant house.

As he rode, William reflected on how much his life had changed since his momentous decision to join the Army only three years ago. For starters, he'd never even ridden a horse before that, his family home being within walking distance of the college and anywhere he generally needed to go. He looked down at his apparel—the same rough riding gear he'd worn on their journey east through Texas, including well-worn riding boots, a long, oiled overcoat, and a broad-brimmed felt hat. To top it off, he had his loaded Colt revolver strapped to his right hip. Something he'd have never worn only a few short years ago now seemed so natural he felt naked without it. He shook his head and chuckled; what would his studious, college professor father think if could see him now? Even this little errand for the Captain would have caused him great fear and anxiety in his past life, but no longer. It was a good feeling, knowing he could handle just about any situation that might come his way. He had the Army … and the Captain … to thank for that.

He turned off the main road to the right, heading up the drive to the large, red farmhouse he'd seen in the distance. The land in this area was relatively flat, and the driveway ran straight as an arrow to the front of the house, less than a quarter mile distant. The closer he got the more hopeful the place looked: well-kempt grounds, solid-looking outbuildings, and a fresh coat of red paint on all.

As he approached the outbuildings, he heard a familiar, loud knocking coming from the far side of the building on his left. He rounded the corner and looked around the side. There he saw three black men splitting firewood from a large heap of cut logs piled up beside a barn. He steered his horse over to them and stopped. One of the three glanced back and saw him, reacting with a start. He grabbed the man next to him by the arm and shook him, pointing back at William. The other man stopped as well, and the three set down their axes, turned and stood in a row, facing William, their eyes cast down respectfully.

William still had a hard time getting used to this reaction. It didn't seem proper to him. He'd have much preferred a friendly hello followed by the usual exchange of names and handshakes with actual eye contact. But he knew this was the way things were here in Virginia, and he wasn't going to be the one to change it.

"Good afternoon, gentlemen. Can you please tell me the name of your master who owns this farm?"

"Yes, master," the taller of the three answered, "our master's name do be Johnston, sir. Jedidiah Johnston."

Damn! Not Monroe, William thought, but said, "Ah, thank you kindly. And can you tell me where the Monroe farm might be?"

"Yes, master. That'd be the old place just up yonder, next farm over," he pointed back toward the farm where William had just been. "But ain't nobody live there no more ... not since ... oh ... three, maybe four years back, I reckon." He looked at the others and they nodded their agreement.

William sighed a heavy sigh. *What now?* he wondered. *Well, perhaps Mr. Johnston knows something about where they went.*

"Would you fellas happen to know where your master is at the moment? I wish to have a word with him."

"Oh, yes sir, master ... he be up at the house now abouts, I reckon. He already done been out and about for the day and is likely gone in for his supper."

William tipped his hat at them, "Much obliged," then turned his horse toward the main house. He'd not gone past the next building before he heard them start back into splitting the wood, *thunk ... thunk ... thunk.*

When he reached the end of the drive, he tied the horse to a hitching post, and walked up the gravel path to the front porch steps. It was a large house, two stories high plus a full attic and basement, from what he could tell. But still, nothing nearly so grand as Mountain Meadows, or some of the larger plantations he'd seen on his ride today. And not nearly as well-supplied with labor, apparently; no grooms met him upon his arrival.

When he knocked at the door an elderly black maid greeted him and ushered him into a wide, simply furnished foyer. A couple of simple benches lined the walls, which contained hooks for hats and coats. He imagined Mr. Johnston sitting here to put on his boots before venturing out in the morning. The maid offered him a seat, but he declined; he hadn't been invited and didn't intend to stay long. She headed off down the hall—to fetch her master, he assumed.

In a few moments a middle-aged man appeared. He had thick, dark hair graying at the temples, and a bushy mustache. He had a burly build that reminded William somewhat of Sergeant Jim, though much older.

"Good afternoon, sir, I am Mr. Johnston."

"Mr. Jenkins, sir. Very pleased to meet you."

"Likewise, Mr. Jenkins, and welcome to my home. May I offer you refreshment? They've just brewed a fresh pot of coffee, and if you've been out long in this weather, I'd imagine you could use it!"

"Well, yes, now that you mention it, a cup of hot coffee would be just the thing to take the chill off. Thank you most kindly, sir."

"Nanna! Come take this gentleman's coat and hat, will you now?" he called back down the hall. Though it was clearly an order meant to be obeyed, the man had a manner that sounded friendly and almost jolly.

The elderly maid came back out, smiled, and took William's hat and coat. When William removed his coat, Mr. Johnston noticed the revolver on his belt for the first time. He raised an eyebrow, but smiled, and said nothing about it. He turned and ushered William down the hallway to a simple dining room, where he offered him a seat.

William liked the feel of the place—not grand and elegant like Miss Abbey's house, but more … *homey* feeling somehow. A fire burned brightly in a fireplace to one side of the dining room, a sudden warmth William greatly appreciated after his cold ride.

Johnston sat across from him. Before they could begin a conversation, a middle-aged white woman, in a nice but simple blue dress came into the room bearing two steaming hot mugs of coffee. William started to rise, but she said, "Oh no, sir ... stay seated, if you please. I'll just grab myself a cup and return to join you in a moment."

"Thank you most kindly, ma'am."

She set down the cups in front of the two men, smiled brightly, and exited the room, returning a moment later with her own cup. She took a seat next to her husband.

"Betsy, this is Mr. Jenkins."

"Pleased to meet you, and welcome to our home, Mr. Jenkins."

"The pleasure is all mine, ma'am. Thank you kindly for your hospitality, and your wonderful, warm coffee on this blustery day."

They each took a sip, before Johnston asked, "Ridden far today, Mr. Jenkins?"

William thought it a very gracious way to ask a stranger his business.

"Oh, no sir, not far. I've only come from downtown Richmond, where I'm staying in a boarding house a few blocks from the capitol. I'm presently in your neighborhood on an errand for my employer, Mr. Chambers. Mr. Chambers was interested in discussing a ... *business matter*, with your neighbor, Mr. Monroe. But I have come to understand, from talking with one of your servants outside, Mr. Monroe is no longer in residence."

"Oh, yes, that's true. He's been gone a good four years now, ever since he lost his farm, poor fellow."

"Lost it?"

"Well, ran it into the ground, really. It was his own fault. He kept insisting on growing tobacco on the place, as had his Daddy before him. But people 'round these parts have come to figure out if you grow the tobacco long enough, it finally gets to where the soil won't grow it no more. So you've got to plant other kinds o' crops for a spell, even though they don't bring nearly the cash. I kept warnin' him, but he ignored me, and each year his crop got worse. But he kept insisting it was just the amount o' rain, or lack of sun, or ... what have you, and nothing I said would change his mind. Finally came a crop so poor the bank just called in his loan and took the place, lock, stock and barrel. Not sure where Monroe and his wife went after that. I reckon he was feeling too sheepish to come speak with me, not wantin' to admit he was wrong, I expect."

"Oh … well, that is a sad tale … and having just come from there, I can testify it is a very sad place as well."

"Yes, unfortunately the bank has had a hard time selling the place, I hear, due to the crops failing. Nobody wants to buy a place that's gonna take several years to yield any cash crops. So there it sits, as you say, a very sad, lonely place.

"Not that it's any of my concern, Mr. Jenkins—and you may feel free to tell me so and no hard feelings—but I'm curious what your employer wanted to speak with Mr. Monroe concerning."

"Oh … I'm sure Mr. Chambers wouldn't mind my telling you. You see, Mr. Chambers recently returned from the Far West after learning he'd inherited a large plantation in western Virginia due to his father's untimely passing. Despite a well-earned reputation for being a hard-fighting military man, Mr. Chambers has a gentle side as well. It seems his father sold off the mother of one of his slaves several years back, and Mr. Monroe was apparently the purchaser. Mr. Chambers, out of pure kindliness and Christian charity, wishes to locate the woman with the hope of reuniting mother and daughter."

"Well! What a lovely notion!" Mrs. Johnston said, joining in the conversation for the first time. "Your Mr. Chambers sounds like a very fine, righteous gentleman to me."

"Yes, that he is. Thank you, ma'am."

"Jed … do you recall, when the bank held that auction down at the Monroe place, selling off all the equipment, livestock, and whatnot, they also sold off the slaves. And I seem to recall one man bought the whole lot of … oh, a dozen or so."

"Yes, now you make me think on it, that sounds right. I'll bet Ben would remember … that'd be our youngest boy Benjamin, Mr. Jenkins. Well … not really a boy any longer, now he's all of eighteen years! Anyway, he's always been a curious fella, and sharp as a tack. I recall him running all over the place during that auction, talking to everyone there, including … maybe, the fella you're looking for."

"Nanna!" Johnston shouted out down the hall.

In a few moments the old maid appeared in the doorway, "Yes, master?"

"Nanna, would you please go over to the wood pile, and ask one o' the boys to saddle up a horse and ride on out to the pond? See if he can locate Mr. Benjamin and ask him to come on back here now. I believe he took a fowling piece down this morning and went out to see if he might get us some duck for dinner."

The maid quickly departed, and a few moments later they heard her exiting the front door.

"Now, Mr. Jenkins—if you'll excuse my forwardness—from your appearance, and on account o' you mentioning your employer was a military man ... do I assume correctly you *too* are a military man? And unless I miss my guess, I'd say you've been out West fighting Indians, yes? Ah ... I *thought* so! That bein' the case, would you be willing to share a few tales of the West while we're waitin' on the boy? Betsy and I would dearly love to hear some of your adventures, sir."

William was almost shocked by this request. No one had ever asked him such a thing before. In fact, he'd never thought of himself that way before. He'd always been the studious, bookish type growing up, not someone who would've had any interesting adventures.

He smiled and nodded at Mr. and Mrs. Johnston, who seemed to be waiting eagerly to hear anything he might have to say. "Yes, certainly. I suppose I could tell you a few of the more amusing tales, while we wait." He realized to his own amazement, he *had* become *that* kind of man, and other people could now see it. And, on top of that, he actually *did* have some very interesting stories to tell from out West!

About a half hour later, William was winding down his latest tale—a humorous one about the time Big Stan jumped into a creek to rescue one of their fellow soldiers. He was a short but sassy fellow who couldn't swim—the story had Mr. Johnston laughing out loud and slapping the table, and Mrs. Johnston giggling and demurely covering her mouth.

At that moment their young son Benjamin stepped into the kitchen. He grinned broadly at the sight and motioned for William to stay seated and continue his tale, as he pulled up a chair and sat himself.

"So then Stan, having dragged the fellow to shore, holds him up by one ankle, and says, 'Hey! Look at ugly, odd fish I catch in creek!' The poor fellow is dangling upside down, sputtering and out of breath, water streaming off him. But Stan just laughs and says, 'Poor little fellow. Too bad he so small … maybe I just throw him back,' and he proceeds to dangle the man back over the water. The poor fellow squealed, pleading for mercy. Then Stan laughs and tosses the man onto the grass bank and strides off, leaving the rest of us laughing so hard we were gasping for breath!"

The elder Johnstons continued to laugh, Mrs. Johnston breaking out a handkerchief and rubbing her eyes. Young Ben, having missed all but the punch line just smiled, enjoying the sight of his parents' amusement.

"Your friend Stan sounds like quite the character … I sure do hope I get to meet him one day!" Mr. Johnston said, shaking his head and still feeling the effects of his raucous laughter.

"Oh, yes, sir, that he is. There's no one else like him, that's for certain."

"Sounds like I've missed out on all the fun!" The young man stood and extended his hand, "Benjamin Johnston, sir!"

William stood and leaned across to take the proffered hand, "William Jenkins. Pleased to meet you, Benjamin."

"Likewise, Mr. Jenkins."

Mr. Johnston wiped his eyes with his sleeve, still smiling and shaking his head, "Ben, William here is on an errand for his employer, Mr. Chambers from western Virginia. He's looking for information on one of the slaves that was owned by Mr. Monroe before he lost the farm. I was thinkin' you might recall the name of the fella that bought up all them slaves at the bank auction. I know it was a while back, but I recall you might've been talkin' to the fellow just before the sale."

"Oh! Yes … I do recall it. I was very excited, having never seen anything the likes of that auction before. Lots of folks around I'd never seen or met before. And I ... well, you know how I am Daddy; I have to know everyone's name, where they're from, their story, and whatnot. Speaking of ... I can't wait to hear your full story, Mr. Jenkins. Anyway ... you was asking about the fella that done bought them slaves. Hmm ... tall thin man ... slightly graying dark hair, neatly trimmed beard, nicely dressed in a dark gray suit. Said he owned a place over in ... Lynchburg, I think ... yes, *Lynchburg* it was! And his name was ..."

Ben was quiet and thoughtful for a moment as if thinking back.

William held his breath in anticipation. The success or failure of his mission hinged on the young man's ability to remember a name he'd heard only once, four years earlier.

"Hmm ... let me think ... *Benson* ... no ... *Bennett?* Hmm ... no ... but now I remember it did start with 'Ben' like my name ... *Ben* ... something ..."

"Benton?" Mr. Johnston offered.

But Benjamin held up his hand for quiet, not wanting his train of thought interrupted by helpful suggestions. He closed his eyes and was still for several more moments.

"*Benedict!* Yep, that's it. Mr. Benedict. Now I remember ... I was thinking it was like the name of the famous traitor from back in the days of General Washington: *Benedict* Arnold. Only this was the man's *last* name. Sorry, me bein' a kid and all, he never told me his first name."

"Oh, that's perfect, Benjamin! And never worry, I'm sure there can't be that many Benedicts owning slaves in Lynchburg. It'll be quite enough to find him. You've done very well, and I thank you most kindly!"

Benjamin beamed brightly, "Don't mention it, Mr. Jenkins. I'm most happy to help! But ... if it's not too much trouble, would you repay me by telling a few more of your tales from the West before you have to go?"

William smiled, "I suppose I could come up with one or two of the more *entertaining* ones, if your folks haven't tired of them yet ..."

CHAPTER 7. THE EYE OF THE STORM

*"I know there is a God, and that
He hates injustice and slavery.
I see the storm coming,
and I know that His hand is in it."*
– Abraham Lincoln

Wednesday Jan. 9, 1861 - Richmond, Virginia:

Nathan smiled ruefully, as he leaned back and caught Tom's eye. The senate president had just announced committee assignments. Common sense would say Nathan might be assigned to the Committee on Military Affairs or the Joint Committee on the Armory given his long military service. But he was learning things worked differently here. Instead, they assigned him to the Committee on Agriculture and Commerce, the Committee on the Library, and, most ironically, the Committee to Examine the Lunatic Asylums of the Commonwealth!

Clearly, they gave the new recruit the least interesting assignments. He decided he'd just have to make the most of it, and do his best, regardless of how mundane the duty might be.

Once they'd taken care of the committee assignment business, they held another round of discussions, motions, and amendments. These concerned the two highly-anticipated topics: "a state convention for consideration of relations with the federal government"—a.k.a., the "Secession Convention"—and "a proposal for a national meeting for the discussion of potential constitutional amendments to head off the present crisis"—a.k.a., the "National Peace Conference." This time Nathan voted in favor of both proposals, including Sandy Stuart's motion for the apportionment of the seats via the white basis.

It took about half the afternoon to finish the discussions and voting concerning the most momentous business the senate could possibly consider. After which, their focus devolved into dealing with the most *mundane* business the senate could possibly consider, from Nathan's viewpoint.

Nathan found this the most strange and peculiar contrast he'd ever seen. One minute the senate was discussing the most grave and important issue imaginable—the possible dissolution of the United States of America—and the next minute was discussing whether they owed Mr. Smith a tax refund of $31.24 from being overcharged for a particular herd of goats he owned. Or they owed Mr. Jones $23.45 because he'd been underpaid for work he'd performed repairing a fence around the local post office. Nathan now understood the purpose of the committees; most of these minor matters were immediately referred to the appropriate committee. Yet each matter had to be brought up and read out on the senate floor before it could be so assigned.

Nathan shook his head in wonder, and not for the last time wished he was back in Texas, fighting Moat Kangly, Gold-tooth, and the Comanche Indians.

ఴ౭ఔ౭ఴ౭ఔ౭ఴ౭ఔ౭ఴ౭ఔ౭

Nathan's request for a meeting with the governor had finally been answered, more than a week after he'd arrived in Richmond. He'd received a note upon returning to the boarding house after the senate session. It was from Mr. Templeton, the governor's aide, whom Nathan had met when he'd visited Mountain Meadows Farm the previous summer. The note invited Nathan to come to the governor's office an hour before the start of the senate session the following day.

So the next morning Nathan sat in a nicely padded chair in Mr. Letcher's office. Templeton was in a chair next to the governor's desk, his extensive bulk completely filling the seat to overflowing. The governor, a small, lean man by contrast, sat behind the large desk, leaning forward intently.

Both men had greeted Nathan warmly, and with great respect when he'd entered. He'd not known what to expect, given the circumstances, so was pleased with his reception.

"So Mr. Chambers, how are you enjoying your introduction to the senate thus far?" the governor asked.

"It has been … *interesting*, and … eye-opening, to be sure, your honor. I am quickly discovering I know nothing of political machinations. But … hopefully I am beginning to learn."

Mr. Letcher smiled, "Yes, I expect it is a bit different from the kind of life you've been used to out West in the Army. Someday when time allows, I would enjoy hearing about your exploits out in Texas. I'm sure they would be extremely interesting—*entertaining* even, I'd hazard to guess."

"Yes … I expect you would find some of our … *adventures* … amusing."

"Mr. Chambers, at the risk of being blunt, you have *not* turned out to be quite what we were expecting, when we asked you to fill your father's vacant senate seat."

"Yes … I'm not surprised. I'm actually not much like my father, when it comes right down to it. In fact, he and I had a serious falling out when I was a youth, and never really reconciled the rest of his life. I apologize if I've taken up his seat under false pretenses; it was never my intention."

"No fault to you, Mr. Chambers," Templeton answered, "you gave me ample opening to ask any questions. And I … well, I made certain *assumptions* that now appear to have been incorrect."

"Well, gentlemen, I'm sorry if I have disappointed you."

"On the contrary, Mr. Chambers," the governor replied with a smile. "You have been the most pleasant surprise of this special session."

"Oh? How so, your honor?"

"Mr. Chambers, have you heard the term 'Slave Power'?"

"I heard it earlier this week for the first time. I am led to understand it refers to the strong political influence exerted by the Planter Class—those having the greatest interest in preserving the 'peculiar institution' of slavery."

"Correct. It has been an all-powerful and pervasive force in the Commonwealth from the very beginning—so much so that a person in my position cannot openly stand against it. So when your father passed, him being a strong member of *that* camp, they exerted great pressure on me to replace him with someone equally ensconced in their cadre. But despite their power, they are a relatively small body of men. And most of those more politically inclined are already in the General Assembly, or some other government posting. So we were struggling to placate them. That's when our good Mr. Templeton had the idea of asking *you*. It seemed a stroke of genius at the time. Little did we know how fortuitous it might turn out to be. For, unless I am mistaken, Mr. Chambers ... I have been made to understand you are decidedly *not* of that political persuasion. And neither are you a wild-eyed abolitionist, as some others tried to persuade us."

Nathan scowled, "You are correct. And yes, I am aware my *good neighbor*, Mr. Elijah Walters paid you a visit. I am curious what he might have said about me."

"Oh, a great many things, none of which were very pleasant — nor very true, apparently."

"Yes ... Mr. Walters and I seem to have ... gotten off on the wrong foot, I suppose. And it has only gotten worse since, I'm afraid."

"Well, never mind about that. I found your neighbor thoroughly disagreeable, and we were inclined to disregard anything he had to say. However, we *are* pleased to learn from the good Mr. Stuart, you are strongly pro-Union, and not at all inclined to the Slave Power camp."

"Yes, Mr. Stuart has told it true. He also advised me to hold that knowledge close to the vest, though he did tell me you were of a similar mind — which I was very happy to hear."

"Yes, certainly, Mr. Chambers. Nothing good can come of a disunion of the states, especially for Virginia. It can only be a disaster for our economy, for starters. And should a general war break out — *God forbid* — we would find ourselves in the uncomfortable position of being on the very front lines. But as you say, we must keep such feelings close to the vest ... as much as possible, although in my position that is much more problematic. In order to get things done, I must attempt to appease the various camps. Which means I never make anyone completely happy. It is a hazard of the duty, I'm afraid."

"I can understand that, and my respect to you for performing a difficult job."

"Thank you, Mr. Chambers, but it's of little matter. So ... tell me, what was Mr. Stuart's argument for keeping your pro-Union feelings to yourself, did he say?"

"Well, your honor, I was quite reluctant about it at first, as you can imagine, being an Army officer and a gentleman. But he convinced me the stakes were too high for such niceties. The important thing is, as he explained it to me, getting the right people elected to the Special Convention. And ... if the Slave Power thinks I'm on their side, they won't put up a strong candidate against me when I run for the position."

"Oh! So you intend to run in the special election, so soon after just joining the senate?"

"I have given it much thought since my first discussion with Mr. Stuart. And ... well, to be perfectly honest, your honor, discussing Mr. Smith's tax refund, or Mr. Jones's fence line, when the entire country is falling apart all around us? I'm a man of *action*, sir; sitting on my hands doing nothing is just not in it for me!"

"Excellent, Mr. Chambers. Then I'm sure we shall get along famously. Only ..."

"Sir?"

"Just ... don't tell anyone about it, if you please."

‼‼‼‼‼‼‼‼‼

Sunday Jan. 13, 1861 - Richmond, Virginia:

Nathan, Tom, and William sat their horses on Cedar Street, in the far west end of Richmond, in front of a green and white-painted house. It was a relatively large residence, and Nathan noticed the yard was reasonably well kept, though not immaculate.

Since their arrival in Richmond for the special session they'd walked everywhere, but today they'd chosen to ride for several reasons. First, because this neighborhood was a good distance from their boarding house, nearly three miles—it would have taken the best part of the day to walk there and back. Second, Nathan's mare, Milly, and Tom's gelding, Jerry, hadn't been out of their boarding stables in more than a week and were badly in need of exercise. And finally, the weather was overcast, with a slight drizzle that threatened to turn into heavier rains at any moment. To Nathan's thinking, a heavy rain in January was colder and more miserable than any amount of snow or frost. So they'd donned their oiled overcoats, and their broad-brimmed traveling hats, and saddled up.

But contrary to Nathan's preferences for such a journey, they had *not* set out at first light. It was Sunday, and Nathan was feeling the need of some heavenly guidance. So they'd first attended the morning service at St. Paul's Episcopal Church across the street from the capitol building, just a few blocks from the boarding house. It was a beautiful church, in the Greek Revival style, featuring an elegant, columned portico, crowned by a tall, domed bell tower. Inside it was richly paneled and painted, with ornately carved hard-wood benches padded and covered in red velvet. It was very grand and had the look of a church much older than its twenty-five years.

They'd originally planned this particular outing for Saturday. But the senators had unexpectedly voted to hold a Saturday session, apparently feeling the pressure to move forward on the monumental decisions before them.

So they'd not been able to mount up until just after noon this Sunday. Nathan had written down the address, and the name of Margaret's father before sending off her letters to him last fall. And as far as he knew, John Emerson had never answered his daughter's letters. Nor had he answered the follow-up letter Nathan had sent a month later. He wasn't sure exactly what he would say to the man, but he meant to speak with him, nonetheless.

They dismounted and wrapped their horses' reins around the branches of a small tree growing near the edge of the lawn. They walked up the gravel path to the front steps, then up to the patio, where Nathan knocked firmly on the door.

After a few moments an elderly woman came and opened the door. She was heavy set, with gray hair, and walked in a hunched over manner. Incongruously, she wore a bright green dress, with a pattern of bright yellow flowers on it. "Yes? How can I help you gentleman?"

"Mrs. Emerson?"

"Yes."

"I am Mr. Chambers, and this is Mr. Clark, and Mr. Jenkins, ma'am. We've come to speak with your husband, if we may. Is he at home?"

"Yes ... come in out of the weather, if you please."

They stepped inside, into a small foyer just inside the front door. Water dripped off their coats and hats onto the slate floor.

"Thank you, kindly, Mrs. Emerson."

"John! There are three gentlemen here who wish to speak with you!" she called out down the hallway of the house.

Nathan noticed she did not invite them further into her house. *Well, she doesn't know us from Adam, after all,* he thought, and shrugged it off, though strictly speaking it couldn't be considered polite.

In a few moments, a thin, middle-aged man, with long gray hair came into the small room. He was a stern looking man, with bushy eyebrows and a thin, hooked nose. He greeted them with a puzzled expression.

"What can I do for you gentlemen?"

"Mr. Emerson, my name is Chambers, and these are my men, Mr. Clark, and Mr. Jenkins. I am here sir, because I am a friend of your daughter, Margaret, who currently finds herself wed to one Elijah Walters."

"Oh ... now I recognize the name. Chambers? Wrote me a letter, didn't you?"

"Yes, sir, I did. I was terribly concerned about your daughter, and in fact still am. Did you not receive her letters, sir?"

"Yes ... I received them. And what business is this matter of yours, pray?"

"As I said, I am her friend. It was I who mailed those letters on her behalf. I am concerned about her welfare and even ... for her safety. You see, her husband, Mr. Walters is ... well ... he is not a true gentleman, let's just say. He holds her a prisoner in his home, and I fear he will do her grave harm, if he hasn't already.

"I'm aware she beseeched you to come to her aid, to bring her out of there, with the law if necessary."

Emerson gave Nathan an odd look—as William would say, "as if he were speaking in Greek."

"What goes on in a man's house between himself and his wife ain't no concern of mine. And I can't see why it is of any concern of your'n neither. I paid her upkeep nigh-on twenty years, and with her bein' so bookish and unattractive, I'd feared I'd be payin' it the rest of her days. No sir, she's now her husband's to take care of, not mine."

Nathan was so shocked by this statement he was speechless for a moment.

"But, sir … she is your very daughter. Does it matter nothing to you she lives in fear for her life on a daily basis? Such is the way she described her situation to me the last time I spoke with her."

Nathan noticed Mrs. Emerson sat at the kitchen table in the adjoining room covering her head with her hands as she listened to this exchange. It occurred to him she likely did *not* agree with her husband's opinion on the matter but was helpless or unwilling to do anything about it.

"Oh, surely you don't believe such exaggerations from an emotional young woman, Mr. Chambers? Likely her wedded life is simply not the fanciful dream she'd imagined it would be, and now wants to run back to her Momma's skirts."

Nathan glared at the man.

"Sir … I can't imagine what woman you are speaking of, but it is clearly *not* your daughter Margaret. From what I've seen of her, she is the very picture of grace and level-headed thinking. I've never detected even the slightest glimpse of *'fanciful dreaminess'* in her makeup. On the contrary, she has proven herself one of the most thoughtful and clever persons I've *ever* met, man or woman."

Emerson looked at him a moment longer, then smirked.

"Oh! So *this* is what it's all about is it?"

"I … don't know what you mean by that, Emerson."

"I can see the motivation now. Bored of the mundane wedded life, she meets the handsome young stranger. And suddenly she

162

wants Daddy to come rescue her so she can pursue her girlish desires. Well, I can tell you, sir, I shall have no part in it!"

"What?!" Nathan's expression grew dark and threatening.

Tom caught William's eye, and made a motion that said, "get ready for trouble," to which William nodded agreement.

"This isn't going anywhere, sir. Perhaps we'd best be going now ..." Tom suggested.

But Nathan had his dander up and was not so easily swayed.

"You are ... *way* out of line, *sir!* I suggest you recant that statement immediately. Your daughter has never been anything but a most proper lady! And I ... I will not stand here and ... and have my honor impugned by the likes of *you*, sir!"

Mrs. Emerson had come into the room. She grabbed her husband by the arm, attempting to pull him away, but he shrugged off her efforts. Despite the growing danger, he seemed completely oblivious to the seriousness of his situation.

"This is *my* home, and *my* family, for me to do with as I see fit, *sir!* And I don't see what business it is of yours! If you're wanting to make a cuckold of Mr. Walters, dallying with his young bride, that is *your* affair, and none of my concern."

Tom knew Emerson had blindly taken that one last fateful step off into the abyss. He reached out to grab Nathan's left arm ... but an instant too late. Nathan was already moving forward. He grabbed Emerson by the front of his shirt, lifted him off the ground, and slammed him against the wall. A loud *thud* rattled the windowpanes. Nathan's face twisted in anger as he held Emerson up against the wall. Too late, the reality of his situation became crystal clear to Emerson. He turned pale, a look of shock and abject fear on his face.

"Tom ... give me a reason why I shouldn't crush this ... *insect* ... as he so richly deserves ..."

Tom stepped up beside Nathan.

"Yes, sir. He *does* richly deserve it ... no doubt. But if you kill him, they'll put you in prison ... or hang you. Then there'll be nobody to help Miss Margaret, sir."

Nathan continued to glare at Emerson. His face was red with rage, and it twitched slightly as he stared at the other man, who stared back wide-eyed, but said nothing.

Nathan closed his eyes and took a deep breath. Suddenly he simply let go, turned, and strode out the front door. Emerson slumped to the floor in a heap. Mrs. Emerson rushed over to tend him.

Tom and William looked at them, then toward the Captain's back as he exited the house. They exchanged a look, and a shrug, then turned and followed in his wake.

ഉ୬ଉୠ୯ଔୠୠ୯ଔୠ୬ୠୠ୯ଔ

Nathan was quiet for the first half of the ride, and the others weren't inclined to interrupt his solitude, preferring to let him cool down first.

But as they reached the western edge of the downtown area Nathan looked back and motioned Tom to ride up next to him.

"Sir?"

"Nasty business back there, Tom. Thanks for talking me out of doing the fellow an injury. I'd have felt badly about it later, of course, knowing he was no worse than a *damned fool* shooting off his mouth."

"Yes, sir. Never mention it."

"Now I just feel sad for Margaret. And I dread seeing her and having to tell her those hurtful words from her own father. But honor, friendship, and even common sense, demand I tell her the truth, painful as it may be. I'd not have her thinking she can count on the man for anything."

"I agree with that, sir. Not a pleasant conversation to have, though, I'm sure."

"Yes. And speaking of unpleasant conversations I'm dreading … I keep debating with myself about paying Evelyn a visit. I can't decide whether it would be good to see her, or if it would just be painful—re-opening wounds, as they say. I've read through her letter in my mind a thousand times, but still can't decide the matter. I know it's none of your concern, but if you have any helpful thoughts or suggestions for me, I'd be most grateful."

"Oh … well, as you say, it really is none of my business. But … I can tell you from my own situation … the not-knowing is the hardest part of it. So maybe even if it ends up being painful, that might be better than the wondering."

"Yes … that makes sense. But still …" he pulled a cigar from his pocket, stuck it in his mouth and lit it. He took several puffs, seeming deep in thought.

"I thank you, Tom, and I'm sure you have the right of it. But I'm obliged to first visit Daddy's sister, Aunt Annie, since I'm here and haven't seen her in over twenty years. And after that Momma's brother and sister, whom I can't *ever* remember meeting.

By then it'll likely be time to return to Greenbrier for the special election. So I believe I'll hold off doing anything about Evelyn until we return to Richmond after."

"That seems reasonable, sir," Tom said. But what he thought was, *I've never known the Captain to put off something unpleasant or difficult before … this woman surely has a strong hold on his mind!*

❧☙☀❧☙☀❧☙☀❧☙☀

The letter was innocuous enough, though it had arrived hand-delivered by a courier, rather than coming by the normal post.

Dear Miss Evelyn,

I have heard many very gracious compliments spoken of you by individuals we know in common, and yet I have never had the pleasure of your acquaintance. It is my fond wish to rectify this unfortunate situation as quickly as may be arranged, and I am hoping you will feel the same.

I would be greatly pleased and honored if you would come to tea on Wednesday, at 11:00 a.m., at my residence listed below.

Sincerest regards and best wishes for a future friendship,
Mrs. Jonathan Hughes (Angeline)

The letter arrived on Saturday. So Evelyn had half a week to ponder it, wondering all the while whether it really was as innocent as it seemed, or if there were something more to it. She kept remembering Dr. Johnson's mysterious words, *"there are people I know who may be interested in speaking with you about a ... particular project they have in mind."* Could Mrs. Hughes be one of the "people" Dr. Johnson had been speaking of?

She stepped up the stairs onto the wide porch. It was a grand house, in the wealthiest neighborhood of Richmond. It was a full three stories, made of red brick with brightly painted white and black woodwork. Like many mansions in and around Richmond, it featured massive columns on the front portico, giving it a traditional, Greek look.

She knocked at the door. An elderly black butler, dressed elegantly in a black suit with white gloves, answered. He bowed her into the house in the formal manner, "Please, do enter, miss."

He led her into a broad foyer with marble floors and opulently paneled and gilded walls and ceiling. It featured a beautiful multi-level chandelier hanging down from the ceiling three floors up. Elegant matching curved staircases ran up both sides of the foyer to the second floor. They apparently reached the third floor by another stairway further back in the house; only a railing could be seen up at that level from the foyer below. The whole effect was breathtaking, which was, of course, the whole point of it. Evelyn tried hard not to gawk, but it was the most impressive entrance she'd ever seen. It made all others she'd known, even the elegant one at Mr. Chambers' Mountain Meadows house, seem plain and simple by compare.

The butler led her to a room with wide, glass-pained double doors. Inside were massive mahogany cabinets and bookshelves, a full two stories high. And these shelves were not empty; on the contrary, nearly every inch of bookshelf space was filled. A ladder on wheels leaned against a highly polished brass track that circled the room, allowing access to books too high to reach from the floor.

Evelyn couldn't recall ever seeing a sight as imposing—so many books! It made the library at the Chambers' house seem tiny by comparison.

The butler motioned for her to take a seat—a large, chair intricately carved of mahogany, with heavily padded seat, back, and armrests covered in a dark, violet-colored velvet. Several other chairs, similarly magnificent, were positioned around the room. A wide, two-story-high window on the wall opposite the door was elegantly covered in velvet the same color as the chair, but with gold embroidery and trim giving the whole a regal look.

"May I assume, I have the pleasure of welcoming Miss Evelyn Hanson?" the butler asked, with a bow of his head.

"Oh, yes, you may!" Evelyn said, suppressing a giggle. Though she'd been to many sophisticated formal functions, she'd never been treated quite so royally before.

"Very good, Miss Evelyn. The Mistress of the House has asked me to say, she and the Master will be joining you momentarily, and tea will be served shortly thereafter. I am called Sam, if you should require anything at all, mistress."

"Thank you, Sam."

He bowed, and backed out of the room, in the traditional, formal manner.

After only a few minutes, a man and woman entered. The man was of medium height and build, middle-aged, with sandy-colored hair and a neatly trimmed beard. Evelyn thought his was a handsome face, though nothing to compare with Nathan's. She silently scolded herself … she must stop comparing every man to Nathan, or she would soon go mad, and cease to function!

The woman was elegantly dressed, tall for a woman, with a thin, pretty face and build. She wore her silver-white hair done up in a knot on the top of her head.

Evelyn rose to greet them, and they both smiled warmly, seeming genuinely happy to make her acquaintance.

"Miss Evelyn, I am Jonathan Hughes, and this is my wife, Angeline."

Evelyn curtsied deeply in the formal style the circumstances seemed to call for, "Very pleased to make your acquaintance, Mr. and Mrs. Hughes."

Mrs. Hughes smiled, and said, "That was most prettily done, Miss Evelyn. But please be seated and at your ease. Despite appearances, we do *not* intend this to be a stuffy formal meeting. We have ... important business we'd like to discuss. But first, we wish to become better acquainted, which I find most difficult when there's too much formality, wouldn't you agree?"

"Well, yes, certainly. And ... thank you so much for inviting me into your home. I am entirely at your service, of course."

"So in keeping with a less formal tone, do feel free to just call us *Jonathan* and *Angeline*, if you please."

"Oh. Certainly, if it pleases you. And you may call me *Evelyn*, if you wish."

They sat back down, and Jonathan said, "Evelyn, we've been most impressed with you ... from afar, of course. The good Dr. Johnson speaks very highly of you, and he is not one to exaggerate or lightly hand out compliments."

"That is most kind of you to say, Jonathan. Dr. Johnson is a very admirable man—quite courageous, and yet humble. I have great respect for him and for ... the *things* he does."

"Yes ... as do we. And we are well aware of those ... *things* ... you speak of. You see, we are major sponsors of his activities, providing both monetary and human resources for his projects. And we understand you've begun to make a positive impact as well, for which we thank you most sincerely."

"Oh ... well, I feel I've done so very little, but thank you for saying so. I have come to believe ... the way things are in the South is ... immoral and unconscionable. So a person must do what little she can to help. Well, at least to help *some* people, if she can ..."

She found it difficult to put into words the way she was feeling, and what was motivating her. It went so contrary to the general views of the society she'd been raised in that it was hard to explain why she was doing it.

But Jonathan just smiled, "You needn't justify yourself to *us*, dear. We know exactly how you're feeling. And you needn't be so modest. We know you've been providing valuable intelligence to Dr. Johnson for some months now. We have spoken of you often, and how—"

But he paused in mid-sentence, as two black maids came in, setting out silver trays of tea, and various small pastries. They poured tea for the three of them before departing again.

"As I was saying … we have been discussing how we might make better use of your abilities."

"Oh? And what abilities is it you believe I have, that you could make better use of?"

Jonathan seemed to blush at this, so turned to his wife, as if expecting her to answer this question.

She smiled, "Evelyn, a man may fight with his fists, use his strength and his skill with weapons to defeat his enemies. But we women … well, we must employ *subtler* methods. Fortunately for us, these methods are often more effective than the manly kind!"

She looked over and shared a smile with her husband, who rolled his eyes.

"You must pardon me for being forward, Evelyn," she continued, "but you possess beauty, charm, and upper-class sophistication we rarely have access to in our … *business*. And you have already proven your ability to play a role, to convince people to confide in you who might not otherwise. We want to groom you for an even more important task than aiding the Underground Railroad."

"*More* important? What do you consider more important than that? And, also … forgive *my* bluntness, but how is it you can be so heavily involved in this *business* while you clearly keep several slaves yourselves?"

But Jonathan smiled, and did not seem put off by her query. "You ask good questions, Miss Evelyn. Cutting, and to the point. That serves you well. Of course, you must not share what I tell you now with anyone outside this room. Every person of African descent you see in this household, or anywhere else under our 'employ' is in fact a freeman. Their service is entirely voluntary, and we pay them the same wages as any comparable white laborer."

He chuckled, "In fact, it's partially because of that fact my people have given me a secret 'code name,' I suppose you could call it, at the risk of sounding overly dramatic. They call me '*The Employer*,' because I appear to be a slave owner when in fact I am merely their employer, paying them a fair wage. By the way, that name should never be used in association with *me*, lest our adversaries make the connection.

"So you see, my dear, we actually *do* practice what we preach! We are secretive about it because … well, I think you can deduce that one for yourself. It tends to deflect suspicion away from us if we are assumed to be in the *other* camp, let's just say."

"Oh! Well, now I *am* impressed. That is most admirable of you, and … also quite clever. Nobody walking into this house would ever dream of your connection with your *other* activities. Speaking of … you didn't answer my other question; what could be more important than the *business* we are currently involved in?"

"I had not forgotten, but that question requires a longer explanation, beginning with our family background and business. You see, my family is from Boston, and has been in the shipping business for three generations now; four if you count our three sons, and their young cousins back in Boston, who are even now learning the trade.

"My father was the younger of two sons. When my grandfather became elderly it came time to decide what to do concerning his sons' inheritance and the family business. So the two brothers got together to solve the problem for him. They wished to settle the matter amicably and to the profit of all. My father, being the younger, volunteered to relocate to Richmond. You see, they were already doing considerable commerce here through third-party agents. But they wanted to start a branch of the family business here, so the company would have a more solid representation in both cities. So my Daddy and Momma moved here just before I was born.

"Well, as you can see, the business here in Richmond has done exceedingly well, thanks in large part to our strong ties to the company back in Boston, now run by two of my cousins, with whom I am personally quite close. You see, when I was young my parents visited Boston often, not wanting to feel isolated from the rest of the family. When I was an older lad, they would sometimes send me alone to spend months with my cousins—to keep the family connection strong, and to learn the ins and outs of the business there. Of course, as you are no doubt aware, Boston is the very epicenter of the abolitionist movement, and anti-slavery sentiments in general; so I've been strongly influenced in that regard most of my life. Our company has always quietly endeavored to avoid profiting the slavers whenever possible, though it is a difficult challenge with so much of the South's exports being agricultural. At any rate, I tell you this tale, so you will understand; though I was born and raised in Richmond, my loyalties lie rather in the North, and with the United States and all it stands for."

"Thank you, Jonathan. Now things are making more sense to me. But what of you, Angeline? Though you speak most eloquently and beautifully, a true Southern lady ... am I not correct in detecting a slight *Northern* accent in your speech?"

Angeline laughed, "Again, you prove most perceptive, my dear! Only a few of my closest friends are aware of it. But yes, I am from Boston, born and raised. I met Jonathan on a long visit there when we were just sixteen. At the time, I was enamored of one of his cousins. But as soon as we met, the poor cousin was quickly forgotten!"

"Yes ... dear Theodore still hasn't forgiven me," Jonathan said with a chuckle, shaking his head.

Angeline rolled her eyes at him, and continued, "We were married two years later in Boston. I sailed back to Richmond with Jonathan to begin our new life together. It was difficult at first, but I've worked hard to fit in and not sound like an outsider. Now my own family pokes fun at me for my odd accent whenever we return to Boston."

"What a lovely story! One day I should like to hear more of the details. I'm sure it was all very exciting and romantic."

Angeline smiled and let out a heavy sigh, "Yes … that it was, dear. The two years waiting to be married were the longest of my life. I can remember endless days and nights pining for my handsome 'Sir Galahad' to return aboard his ship."

Jonathan beamed, but she turned to him and said, "Don't let it go to your head, dear … you haven't always come off so heroic!"

But he just shrugged and continued to smile, taking another sip of tea.

"So my dear … with that background, we can answer your earlier question," she continued, now in a more serious tone. "We believe, despite the best efforts of a great number of good-hearted men, the South *is* going to secede, including Virginia. And when that happens, there will be a war such as this country has never seen before!"

"Oh my!" Angeline's statement gave Evelyn a sinking feeling in the pit of her stomach. "Surely not! Surely common sense and decency will prevail, and an armed conflict may be averted!"

"Well, we certainly hope for the best. But hoping for a thing will not make it so, I'm afraid," Jonathan responded. "In the shipping trade, many things can go wrong, sometimes *terribly* wrong, as you can well imagine. So we've developed a saying, 'hope for the best, but plan for the worst.' In this case, if we plan for a war, and a war never comes, it has cost us but little. The other alternative is far worse; if we do nothing, and a war comes, our enemies have gained a step on us. Or at least we haven't gained a step on *them*, which we dearly wish to do."

"But, Jonathan, what is it you hope to accomplish by planning for a war? I must assume you aren't talking about raising armies and purchasing arms, or you would not be speaking with *me!* I have no knowledge whatever of such things, I can assure you."

Angeline laughed, "No, we don't expect you to shoulder a musket, Evelyn! Nor do we plan on Jonathan or any of our boys doing so. Jonathan has been telling everyone of a serious health problem he has for some time now, so when the time comes no one will expect a man in such 'ill health' to serve in the military."

"Oh, I'm so sorry to hear you are not well, Jonathan."

He chucked and shook his head, "Oh no, Evelyn, I've never felt better!"

"But then ... *oh* ... I see. Another ruse? Hmm ... again, very clever."

Angeline nodded her head in answer, then continued, "And we've sent our boys off to Boston indefinitely, so there will be no pressure on them to fight for the ... *wrong* side."

"That seems prudent."

"So to answer your question—as I hinted at earlier, we women must employ other methods to aid in the fighting."

"All right ... not weapons or fighting—then what? What are you planning to do that will aid the North in the coming war?"

Angeline took a deep breath and looked over at Jonathan. The two exchanged a meaningful look. Then Angeline turned to Evelyn and said, "We mean to spy on the Southern government and its armies, to the benefit of the Northern Union."

For the second time in as many minutes, Evelyn was shocked. Gathering gossip from slave owners and reporting it to the Underground Railroad was one thing. But spying on the government and its soldiers? That was a *whole* other matter! They would hang you for *that* kind of spying. If they caught you.

"Oh ... I see. And ... what do you imagine my role would be in such an endeavor?"

Jonathan blushed again and looked to Angeline for an answer.

"Evelyn, we wish you to use all your beauty, wit, and charm—and the fact you are an *available* young woman—to gain the confidence of men running the government, and the Army," she said. She held Evelyn in a serious gaze, as if to gauge her reaction.

"You want me to ... *court* these men ... in order to get information from them? Oh ... I don't know about that. I would feel so ... *unclean* somehow. Like a woman with loose morals—teasing men ... playing with their emotions and feelings. It seems so ... wicked ... *vile* even. I'm not sure I could do *that*," she shook her head, imagining the terrible pain she'd likely inflict on the unsuspecting men.

Jonathan and Angeline were quiet for several minutes, leaving Evelyn to her thoughts.

Finally, Jonathan spoke, "Evelyn ... we would never ask you to do anything ... *immoral*. But we understand there will be young men who'll have their feelings hurt. Likely even what might be termed a 'broken heart.' But ... think of this; the information you might provide could save hundreds, even thousands of lives of young soldiers on the Northern side. I believe it's worth risking a few hurt feelings to possibly save so many lives ..."

"Yes ... I can see that. But ... what of the young men on the Southern side? If I were to provide information to the Union side ... how many of *those* young men might die as a result? It is a horrific trade-off."

"Yes ... war is a horrible thing. The most terrible thing known to man, except maybe ..."

"Maybe, what?"

"I was going to say, except maybe ... *slavery*. I think the black men we've been helping would say they'd rather die young in a war for freedom, than live to a great old age in slavery. Never forget, Miss Evelyn: if a war comes, it will ultimately decide the issue of slavery for years to come. And only if the North wins will it be decided in the way we would wish."

"Yes ... I understand. I have a feeling Nathan would also agree with you on that."

She'd been thinking of Nathan and how he'd feel about all this but hadn't meant to say anything out loud.

"Nathan?"

"Oh ... excuse me ... I mean, my ... *friend*, Mr. Nathaniel Chambers."

"Nathaniel Chambers? You mean the new state senator from Greenbrier County?"

"Yes, that's him. He and I are ... *very close* ... or at least, we *were* at one time."

"Oh! Isn't he one of the West Point men? Angeline, don't we have Nathaniel Chambers slated for one of Virginia's generals, should war break out?"

"Yes, that's correct, dear. He's expected to be high in the military command of Virginia, and likely the entire South. He has extensive combat experience—a decorated veteran—and long service in the Army out West. There are only a few who can match his pedigree ... Robert Lee, certainly, and his nephew Fitzhugh Lee. Hmm ... Joe Johnston perhaps ... and a handful of others. I would have to consult my notes for the full list ..."

"Well then, Evelyn, if you're already close to Mr. Chambers, that would be a good starting point. You could continue your relationship with him, and report any military information he might let slip ..."

Evelyn shook her head and laughed. "No ... you misunderstand. I *know* Nathan Chambers. He *hates* slavery. He intends to free all his hundred-some slaves as soon as practical, and ..."

"And?"

"And he would *never* fight against the Union ... *never in life!* He loves the United States, is very proud of carrying her flag into Mexico long ago and would never take up arms against her. Of all the things I *might* know, this thing I know *for sure."*

"Oh! Well, that *is* news to us. Well Momma ... we must make note of that ... Nathaniel Chambers on the *Union* side! That is ... *most interesting.* I wonder if the *other* side is aware of it?"

"I don't know," Evelyn answered, "he can hold things close, until he trusts people completely. It is possible the other side assumes the same as you, because of his father. I ... just don't know. Like I said, we were *close* ... at one time, but ..."

"What is it, dear?"

"I ... think I've said too much already. Suffice to say one of the reasons I hesitate to accept your plans for me is because of *him.* I ... have strong feelings for him, and I believe he returns those feelings. To speak more plainly ... if God appeared before me and said I had to marry *someone* today ... it would certainly be *him.* I don't want to do something that might jeopardize our ... *potential* relationship."

"Oh ... but ..." Jonathan had a puzzled look, and glanced over at Angeline for help, but she also seemed at a loss, "why then are you two not engaged, or married even? I'm sorry to intrude on your private affairs, but ... we need to *know* these things."

"It's all right … I don't blame you for being confused about it. I'm confused myself. And dear Nathan is probably the most confused of all. He was on the verge of asking for my hand, I believe, but I … I don't know what came over me. I … suddenly had a feeling I needed to *do something* before I could marry him. Like God was speaking to me … or something.

"Maybe this thing you're suggesting is what I'm supposed to do, I don't know. All I know is, a little voice in the back of my mind keeps telling me I need to find out who *I am … me …* all by myself, before I can become Mrs. … *anybody.* I know it makes no sense, but … that's how it seems to me."

She felt foolish, and embarrassed to admit her troubles in front of these people who she barely knew, and who were most admirable in so many ways.

But Angeline surprised her by smiling and saying, "I understand *exactly* how you feel, my dear. And I admire you for it."

"You do?"

"Yes, certainly! Most women are content being the wife of an important or wealthy man. There are very few of us who need something more: to be someone in our own right! An individual person first, and a wife second! It took Jonathan a long time to understand this need in me. But now he has come to accept this is the way I am. So now he includes me in all his major decisions, and we are co-conspirators in all our plans and schemes. Even these … most *clandestine* ones."

Jonathan smiled, "Yes, Evelyn, I understand you better than you could have imagined before coming here tonight. As you can see, I have a wife very much like you. And … if it helps … I love her none the less for it. And I'm sure if your Mr. Chambers is the man you believe he is, he'll come to accept it as well."

"Thank you, Jonathan. You're the first people I've talked to who seem to understand what I'm going through. It's … a very great relief. As if a large weight has been lifted from me. Thank you, most sincerely."

"Never mind that, dear. Now that we understand Nathan Chambers is most likely on *our* side, let us talk about how you can aid us in getting information from those who are ... most certainly *not!*"

"You must keep looking, Billy! Try harder ... do not give up so quickly!" Stan was becoming heated—snappish even—which was unusual for him.

But Billy just looked up at him and shrugged. "A man can only do what a *man* can do, Stan. He cannot be a god, nor fly like a bird, no matter how much he may want to. The trail is gone—buried under the snows of these hills—and nothing you or I can do will bring it back. If we go further, we may even die, buried ourselves. Perhaps our shades could find the dog in hell that way, but never on this Earth."

Billy put hands on hips and stared up defiantly at the man who was a foot and a half taller, and several hundred pounds heavier. It aided Billy's argument that he currently stood in snow nearly up to his waist, and each step forward required herculean effort.

Stan strode past him, forging ahead another ten feet or so before stopping, and staring ahead. The route they were on headed further up slope, which only promised deeper snow. He gazed about in all directions for several minutes, before striding back down to where Billy stood.

Billy was surprised, shocked even, to see tears welling in Stan's eyes.

"Damned dog! Why he run off like that? Damn him!"

Then he looked down at Billy, "Sorry, Billy, I am being big stupid jerk. You have done more than man should be asked ... thank you. This is *not* your fault ... only *mine.*"

"No, Stan ... the animal has a mind of his own, and no man can understand it. He has chosen his path, and short of keeping him tied forever, or killing him, you could not sway him from it. I think maybe even a god could not do it."

Stan nodded at Billy appreciatively. He knew it was true. He'd kept the animal tied for almost a week, enduring the crying and howling nearly non-stop every day, even when he sat out on the cold, wet, or snowy ground next to Harry. Miss Abbey had come out and given him an exasperated look at one point, but all Stan could do was shrug his shoulders apologetically.

No amount of attention or bribery with food would console the creature. In fact, he showed no interest in the food offered him, to the point Stan feared he would lay there and starve himself to death. Finally, having no other option, he let Harry off the leash. The dog shook his great head, looked up at Stan for a long moment, then turned and ran up the drive at full speed, howling the whole way.

Stan hoped Harry would return after being unable to sniff out the Captain's trail. But the next day went by with no dog. So Stan recruited Billy to help him search, and they started out at dawn the following day. Billy had no trouble at first, and they followed the dog's trail for many miles up into the hills. They were amazed Harry seemed to be following an easterly route, which was the direction of Richmond. But he was *not* following the road the Captain would have taken. It was as if something in the dog's instincts knew where the Captain *was*, but not the route he had taken to get there.

They were at it until it began to get dark, so they stopped and spent the night in a cave Billy had seen on a previous outing. But this morning when dawn broke, they stepped out of the cave to find snow falling heavily, already four or five inches deep. They'd continued several more hours in the direction the dog had been going when they'd left off the previous evening. But they were going steadily uphill, and the snow got deeper with every step, until Billy finally had called a halt to the expedition.

"Come, Stan, let us return to the farm. When these snows melt, we will come back here and try to pick up the trail again."

"All right ... thank you, Billy. Yes ... we must try again later. *Damn* ... what will Captain say when he learns I lose his dog?"

Billy thought about it a moment, then said, "He will say you did everything a man can do ... and no man could have done more."

Chapter 8. Opening Moves

"We all play chess with Fate as partner.
He makes a move, we make a move.
He tries to checkmate us in three moves,
we try to prevent it. We know we can't win,
but we're driven to give him a good fight."
– Isaac Bashevis Singer

Sunday Jan. 27, 1861 - Greenbrier County, Virginia:

"So, Jim … no sign of our friend Walters yet, I presume?" Nathan asked.

"No, sir, but so far none's been expected. As you saw when you rode in yesterday, the road's been a sloppy, muddy mess. Either knee-deep in snow, or ankle-deep in mud, depending on the weather. Never more than two days in a row without some sort of precipitation on it. Not that I'm complaining, mind … I'm happy to have old Walters' plans stymied, at least for the moment."

"Yes … me too."

"But despite the unlikelihood of an attack, we've continued to hold the Watch several days a week—just to keep everyone in practice, and not forgettin' what they're supposed to do, or why they're doing it."

"Good idea, Jim. I wholeheartedly agree."

Nathan leaned back in his chair and blew a long stream of smoke from a cigar high overhead. Jim did likewise. They were enjoying a brief break in the weather to sit out on the veranda and enjoy a smoke. But they'd had to wipe down the wet chairs before they sat, and they wore heavy jackets pulled up tight under their chins to keep out the chill. It was overcast once again, but Nathan couldn't decide if it was threatening rain or snow, or a mixture of the two.

"Captain … you don't suppose he'll try to get at you … you know, while you're away from the farm campaigning and whatnot?"

"Hmm … I suppose that's always a possibility … but I think it unlikely. The information we got hinted he wanted to eliminate any witnesses to his nefarious activities, so I doubt he'll try anything so blatantly public. Pretty hard to kill off all the witnesses if you're in the middle of Lewisburg."

"Yes, I reckon not. Still …"

"Still, prudence would suggest we at least allow for the possibility. Let's have a couple of the men armed up and riding along to provide an escort. And Tom'll be there as well. He can also go armed. And I'll just keep that small Colt in my pocket. I still want *you* to stay and keep an eye on things here. I wouldn't put it past him to try something here while I'm out campaigning, if the weather should improve."

"Aye, sir. If he does, we'll be ready, don't you worry none."

"Oh … I'm not worried for *you*, Mr. Wiggins … but those fellows planning to give you a fight … well, that's another matter!"

They shared a grin and took another puff.

"Oh … and I'd be remiss if I didn't say I'm sorry about your hound dog, sir. It's a damned shame he done gone and run off like that."

"Oh, yes … thank you, Jim. But I can't say I'm too surprised. That animal has a strange infatuation for me, bordering on obsession. What I *am* surprised about is how hard it hit Stan. He seemed very low and downcast about it, even after I assured him he wasn't to blame."

"Yep, he took it hard to heart all right. For a such a large, fearsome fighting man, he surely does have a soft side—especially for the little children and pet animals." He laughed, "No sorry son-of-a-bitch who's ever been on the receiving end of one o' his barroom fights would believe it, that's for sure!"

"Well, anyway, now I'm home for a spell, perhaps Harry'll come back. Then we can come up with a better plan for him. Perhaps putting him in that old dog kennel might suit better."

180

"Maybe, sir. But he's so durned strong he'd likely just knock down the fence. But, it's worth a try. At least he'd be farther from the house, and not so distressing to Miss Abbey."

"Yes … and speaking of, I'd best get back inside, Jim. I told Miss Abbey I'd have lunch with her today, and it's about that time. You're welcome to join us, if you will."

"Oh … thank you, but *no*, sir. I'm of a mind to get back to the barracks and talk with the men on keepin' you safe, while continuing to guard the farm. I've got a few different ideas, and I want to discuss them while it's all still fresh in my mind."

ಬಿಎಲ್‌ಆರ್‌ಜ‌ಬಿಎಲ್‌ಆರ್‌ಜ‌ಬಿಎಲ್‌ಆರ್‌ಜ

In the end, they decided Georgie and Zeke would serve as the Captain's escort, along with Tom. The rest would stay home this time. Zeke had proven himself a reliable hand and proficient with both rifle and pistol. He said he'd done a lot of hunting with his Daddy growing up. Nathan liked Zeke and had a growing confidence in him—almost as much as with the regular soldiers.

But when it came right down to it, and there was any possibility of a threat against Mountain Meadows and Miss Abbey, he wasn't taking chances. He wanted as many of his soldiers on hand as possible to deal with it.

They arrived at the courthouse in Lewisburg at half-past twelve, with the speeches by the candidates scheduled to begin at 1:00. When they entered the courthouse, the other candidate, Nathan's opponent in the election, greeted them. His name was Orville Taylor, a small, mousey looking man, with long gray hair that was thinning badly on the top of his head. He was also clean shaven, so had no beard to help offset his balding, as some men opted for.

He greeted them cordially, though Nathan thought him a bit shy for a person running in an election. Nathan's armed escort seemed a surprise to him—he'd come by himself. Mr. Taylor had been a delegate in the Virginia General Assembly a few years back. He'd recently campaigned on behalf of the Constitutional Union Party and their candidate John Bell during the presidential campaign. Nathan felt a little sheepish about the special election.

He couldn't help feeling dishonest about the whole affair, even though the scheme hadn't been his idea. After all, he had gone along with it, after agreeing the stakes were too high to risk losing.

As part of the overall strategy for convincing the Slave Power Nathan was one of them, it was necessary for the pro-Union side to put up another candidate—someone to run in opposition to him. Otherwise the other side would be suspicious as to why they were giving up without a fight. The pro-Union side intentionally chose a man who, though trustworthy and reliable, was not an especially inspiring candidate.

Nathan felt badly for Mr. Taylor; he knew nothing about the scheme and was running for the position in good faith. He was a pro-Union, anti-secession candidate and naturally assumed Nathan was the opposite. Again, Nathan had never actually lied about his position on these matters, but rather had allowed others to assume what they were naturally inclined to assume. His only dishonesty was in not correcting those false assumptions.

But Mr. Taylor was another matter, as he was actually on the same side as Nathan and was in for a bit of a shock. The planned speech to the electorate in Lewisburg was the point where Nathan would set all pretenses aside and reveal his true position. He'd have never agreed to be dishonest to the voters, and fortunately it wouldn't be necessary. From this day forward, his true feelings and positions on the major issues of the day would become public knowledge. The pro-Union side had cleverly set up the Greenbrier election as a *fait accompli*; no matter which candidate won they would have gained a pro-Union seat. After this, there was no longer a reason for Nathan to promote or allow false pretenses—unless he intended to become a spy in the enemy camp. He would've refused that in no uncertain terms, though no one had ever asked it of him. If they'd considered it, likely they'd thought better of the notion, having a fair idea what Nathan's reaction would be. A short-term deception was one thing—like a feint on the battlefield. But becoming a spy? That was a whole different matter in his mind.

The thing that was *not* a foregone conclusion in Greenbrier County was the second item on the ballot. In addition to voting on the candidates for the Special Convention, the ballot also included the question of whether the people should have the final say concerning secession. In other words, even should the convention vote for secession, should there be an election in which the people had the final say on the question? The Slave Power was working hard for a no vote on this issue, and conversely the pro-Union side was pushing hard for its passage. So in addition to promoting themselves as candidates, both speakers were pushing for the passage of the people's referendum question. Ultimately the decision on that ballot question might prove more important than which representative they elected.

Lewisburg, with about a thousand residents was the only sizeable town in Greenbrier County, whose entire population was around twelve thousand scattered about in numerous rural pockets. It was also the county seat, and the place where the voting would take place on February fourth. As such, many of the residents in the surrounding countryside had come into town to listen to the speakers.

So despite a light dusting of snow on the streets and low, heavy-looking clouds threatening more, there was no place large enough to hold the gathering indoors. So everyone gathered on the street in the broad square in front of the courthouse. Nathan and Mr. Taylor stood on the steps of the courthouse, as thousands of people filled the square, the connecting streets, and every window of the surrounding buildings.

They'd scheduled the speeches for 1:00. Several entrepreneurial individuals had rolled out beer kegs, and were doing a good business, so the crowd was getting noisier.

Despite Nathan's lack of concern, Tom was nervous for his safety. If Walters wanted to murder Nathan, this would be a pretty good place to do it, he decided. If someone fired a shot from within this crowd, it'd be difficult to tell where it came from. And even if one could tell, it'd be nearly impossible to get at the shooter, and they'd dare not return fire into the thick crowd. Tom sent Georgie and Zeke out into the audience, to watch for trouble—as much as possible—while he stayed next to Nathan.

About ten minutes to one, Georgie came back and grabbed Tom by the arm, whispering something in his ear before turning and merging back into the throng.

Tom stepped over to Nathan. "Sir ... Georgie says he has recognized at least two of Walters' men in the crowd, fairly close to the front."

"Oh? Any sign of Walters?"

"Not that he's seen so far. Oh, and he says Walters' men don't appear to be armed ... at least not openly."

"Well, that sounds hopeful. Let's have a quick look."

Nathan casually stepped up to the small platform where they'd be speaking and gazed out at the crowd. He smiled, and waved at people he knew in the audience, as if he were simply being friendly and welcoming. But Tom could tell Nathan was methodically scanning the gathering. The Captain had an uncannily keen eye and memory for faces and details, such as no one else Tom had ever known. If Walters or his men were there in the audience, Nathan would spot them.

Mr. Taylor looked surprised, as if he couldn't imagine standing up there and casually waving at people. He looked nervous and fidgety, and Tom guessed he had never addressed such a large audience before. Likely the elections he'd been in previously had been much less interesting, drawing much more modest crowds.

After a few minutes, Nathan turned, and walked back to where Tom waited.

"I see three of them. Two were in the raid on Mountain Meadows back during the big wedding, and the third I have seen with Walters at church. All three are within the front ten rows, but not standing together. There may be others further back, but I can't tell. No sign of Walters."

"Could be they are just here for the show, and not on Walters' behalf, sir."

"Yes ... that's possible. But if it were so—being well acquainted—wouldn't they tend to stand together, instead of being spread out?"

"True ... sounds intentional, all right. Like something we'd do, actually."

"Yes, precisely. Well, nothing to be done now but carry through with it, and hope they're not inclined to start trouble."

"Yes, sir. But you can be sure my holster will be unbuttoned!"

Nathan smiled at Tom and reached out to give him a friendly pat on the shoulder. "Good man."

Nathan and Taylor had briefly discussed the order of their appearance, and had decided Taylor would go first this time, him being the more experienced candidate. This suited Nathan perfectly, as he wanted to allow Taylor to have his say before he shocked the man with his apparent change of position.

At approximately five minutes after one, Mr. Taylor stepped out onto the platform. This lack of punctuality annoyed Nathan— if he'd gone first, it would've started precisely at one. But he held his tongue, and kept his patience, allowing the man to proceed as he would. Taylor held up his hands for quiet, and the crowd began to settle down after much shushing, especially aimed at some of the more boisterous and drunken attendees.

"Fellow citizens of Virginia, and Greenbrier County ... my name is Orville Taylor. Many of you already know me from the time a few years back when I had the honor of representing this county as a delegate in the General Assembly. I welcome you and thank you for allowing me to speak to you at this most solemn and monumental moment in our history. Great matters of state are being contemplated, such as have never before been considered since the very beginnings of our Commonwealth.

"I stand here before you a simple, humble man. A loyal Virginian, a patriot, and a strong believer in the Union of the United States of America. I am also a firm believer in the intelligence and trustworthiness of the common man, and in the principals of democracy—of one man, one vote.

"My opponent will likely speak of such things as states' rights, of the time-honored rights of Virginians to own black Africans as slaves, and how the Northerners and their new president will take all that away. But he'll likely *not* mention the time-honored tradition of such slave owners running the Virginia government as they see fit—setting the taxes to their advantage and writing laws for their own aggrandizement.

"I do not hold with such beliefs. I do not believe the rights of slave owners are greater than the rights of other men. And I certainly don't believe we should break apart our great nation at the whim of such men, and to their benefit alone, and to the detriment of all other men.

"For, my friends, let me assure you, the dissolution of our great Union would be a disaster of epic proportions. A disaster for our economy, cutting off our most important trading partners in the North. A disaster for our own individual rights, as the Slavocracy would use the crisis to solidify their hold on power.

"And most importantly, it would be a disaster for our very lives. Virginia would likely find herself on the front lines of a devastating civil war. Are you ready to sacrifice your brave young sons on the altar of the Slave Power? That they might continue lording it over you and running our beloved Commonwealth for their own personal profit? I for one am not.

"If you are of like mind, I ask for your vote, that I might represent your opinions in Richmond. Along with others of the same beliefs, I mean to prevent this looming disaster, and ensure our great state serves all the people, not just the Slavocracy.

"I also ask you to vote in favor of the referendum allowing the people a vote on any proposed secession. Any arguments against such a notion are clearly undemocratic, disingenuous, and purely aristocratic in nature. There can be no legitimate, reasonable argument against allowing the people to have the final say on such an all-important, life or death matter.

"Thank you, and may God grant us the wisdom to make the right choices for our great Commonwealth of Virginia."

Though he was not an inspiring speaker—performing his speech in a nervous, hurried, and monotone manner—he projected his voice well, and the words clearly struck a chord with many of those present. Mr. Taylor received an enthusiastic response, with many applauding loudly, along with shouts of "amen," "hear, hear," and "we the people, we the people!"

Taylor came back to where Nathan stood and glanced at him in what seemed an apologetic manner, as if it had made him uncomfortable to so openly criticize his opponent. But Nathan just smiled at him warmly and offered his hand. Taylor looked surprised but took the proffered hand and shook it as Nathan leaned in close and said, "Well said, Mr. Taylor, well said!"

But Mr. Taylor seemed shocked, looking up and meeting eyes with Nathan, "Uh ... thank you, Mr. Chambers. Very ... gracious of you to say."

Nathan waited a few minutes for the applause to die down, then stepped forward onto the platform.

"Good afternoon, fellow Virginians, and fellow Americans. I am Nathaniel Chambers, your current state senator. As many of you know, the governor asked me to fulfill my father's term in office after his recent passing ..."

He was suddenly interrupted by a shout from someone near the front of the audience, "You're not your father, Chambers! You're nothing like him!"

Nathan glanced down and saw it was one of Walters' men who'd shouted.

"... and now I am asking you to vote for me to represent you in the coming Secession Convention."

"But you're really one o' them Black Republicans, I heard!" another man shouted. It was another of Walters' men.

So ... that's their plan, is it? Nathan thought and smiled. If that was their strategy for attacking him, they were in for a big disappointment.

"As Mr. Taylor said, the men you elect to this Special State Convention will help decide whether Virginia stays a part of the Union of the United States. Or if she breaks off to join her Southern brethren in a new confederation ..."

"Ha, Chambers! I heard you was really a Union-lover in disguise! I heard you don't care a bit about Southern rights, or the rights of *true* Virginians to own slaves!"

Nathan paused in his speech and pointed right at the man.

"This fellow up front thinks to disrupt my speech and make me out a liar. But in fact, ladies and gentlemen, he speaks the *truth!* I *am* a pro-Union man ... to my very core; and I also have no love of slavery, nor of the Slavocracy. So, no, I am not at all like my Daddy—thank you for pointing that out, sir!

"It's true, I do own more than a hundred slaves, but not by *choice*. I recently inherited them when my father passed away, and I intend to free every last one of them—man, woman, and child."

Walters' man was wide-eyed. Not only were people now staring at him, many with angry looks, which he hadn't expected, but Chambers was actually agreeing with him. That wasn't supposed to happen. Not knowing what to do or say, he broke eye contact with Nathan, and stared down at his shoes, looking embarrassed and uncomfortable.

"My friends, I am not a politician of any kind. I've been a soldier almost my entire life. I proudly marched with the Army to Mexico in that great war, when all Americans stood together against a common foe. And I can tell you, when Americans do that ... no power on Earth can stand against us! Ask General Santa Anna, if you don't believe me!

"We were outnumbered and surrounded by enemies, thousands of miles from home in a foreign land—yet still we prevailed. Against overwhelming odds, your own brave fathers, uncles, brothers, and sons ... fought for the Army of the *United States of America!* We fought together ... not as Virginians, or Texans, or New Yorkers, but as brothers in arms—as *Americans!* With the specter of General Washington watching proudly over our shoulders, we bested the enemy in every skirmish and every battle, driving him back step by bloody step all the way to the walls of his own capital city. And there, in desperate battle against a mighty fortress of stone, even still *your men* were victorious!

"I was just a young lieutenant, but never will I forget the thrill of standing at salute as the Stars and Stripes rose above the capitol building in Mexico City—a thousand, thousand miles from home!

"My friends ... George Washington was proud to be a Virginian, there can be no doubt. As am I, and as are all of you. This no man may question. This is the land where we were born and bred, and we love her like no other. And yet if he were alive today, and you were to ask him, General Washington would say he was even more proud to be an *American!*

"Virginia didn't defeat the British. Massachusetts didn't drive the enemy into the sea ... *Americans* did that ... all of us ... *together.* Not once, but *twice* we defeated the greatest nation on Earth! Ask the British how they enjoyed their fight down in New Orleans against General Jackson, a Tennessean, and his volunteer army of *Americans* from many different states.

"Together we are strong, proud, and fiercely free—more than a match for any power on Earth. Ask the Barbary Pirates what happens to despots who think to despoil American ships at sea and seize Americans for ransom. President Madison, another great Virginian, had an answer for them: a fleet of *United States* warships, bristling with cannon!

"Split apart what are we? Nothing but a scattering of independent states, each floating alone in a great sea of mighty nations, at the mercy of the next petty tyrant who comes along and decides he'd like to acquire a new colony."

As he spoke, he made eye contact with members of the audience, and he could see he had their full attention. Many had a mesmerized look, and he saw several grown men with tears in their eyes.

"So now these ... *slavers*, unapologetic aristocrats, want to break up this great country just to line their own pockets with more gold! They care nothing of *you*, the common men and women of Virginia, the people who work hard every day, doing their *own* labor with their *own* hands. They care only for their own comfortable lives, forcing others to do their labor for free. And then paying fewer tax dollars than you, while enjoying more political influence.

"I have come back from the Army in the West knowing little of such things. But I have suffered a quick education. People ... there are men with great power in this state who would martyr your sons in a desperate war against the North. And for no better reason than to propagate their desired lifestyle in perpetuity. I say don't give them their desire! Deny them! Vote as true Virginians, true *Americans*, with your hearts and minds. I say ... *defy them!"*

Nathan pounded his fist in his open hand for emphasis, and there was a spontaneous eruption of cheering and shouting. He acknowledged the applause with a shake of his upstretched fist. Nathan noticed Walters' men working their way out of the crowd. He also noted Georgie eyeing them suspiciously as they skulked away.

"And as Mr. Taylor says, these slavers don't believe in democracy. They don't believe you people should have a say in your own future. I say to them, 'for shame, for shame.' Allow the people to have their say, as George Washington fought for, and for which Thomas Jefferson spoke so eloquently. These great Virginians stood for *'We the People'* ... not for slavers who would subjugate all of us, no better than what King George attempted.

"My friends and neighbors, will we allow a few fat greedy men to rule over us, tell us how to run this state, and this country? Tell us how to vote, when to fight, and when to die?"

The crowd responded to this question with a resounding, "NO!" along with more enthusiastic cheering and hooting.

"Well, then, I ask you to do as Mr. Taylor has suggested, and vote in favor of the referendum proposal, to ensure the people will have their say!"

There was more cheering and shouting.

But after several minutes Nathan raised his hands for silence and held them up until the crowd had quieted to near a whisper.

"Ladies and gentlemen ... I speak no more than the simple truth here today ... it is up to you what you do with that truth. I would like to remind you, in the Bible ... John chapter eight, verse thirty-two, our Lord Jesus Christ himself said, *'And ye shall know the truth ... and the truth shall make you free.'*

"Thank you. And may God bless each of you, the great Commonwealth of Virginia, and the United States of America!"

He waved and bowed, then stepped back, and was met by thunderous applause, shouting, and cheering. He continued to wave and bow for several minutes, before stepping back to join Mr. Taylor, and Tom back on the courthouse steps.

"Well done, Captain. Well done!"

"Thank you, Tom."

"Yes, Mr. Chambers ... I must say that was ... *surprising* ... and quite inspiring. I was led to believe we were ... opponents, but I can see now I was misinformed."

"Yes, well ... I apologize for *that*, Mr. Taylor. I'm sorry to have caught you off guard. But I'm happy we're on the same side, after hearing your most eloquent speech earlier."

"Very gracious of you, as I said before, Mr. Chambers. But I can hardly hold a candle to you, sir, in that regard."

They stepped down the stairs together, and were greeted by the throng of enthusiastic, smiling men, quickly surrounding them. Many reached out to shake their hands or pat them warmly on the back. It was a heady experience for both men, neither of whom was used to such attention.

Tom just shook his head in wonder. He had expected much more opposition, heated even. He had never imagined the people of Virginia would greet Nathan's ideas with such enthusiasm.

"Thank you, thank you, good to meet you, very good to see you," Nathan said over and over until he was nearly out of breath. He felt great hope swell in his breast — the slavers had been called out, and these Virginians at least, had utterly rejected them!

Nathan and Taylor spent the next two days in Lewisburg, meeting with smaller groups of people, and giving additional speeches, but none as large and boisterous as that first one. Walters' men made no more appearances, though the Mountain Meadows' men never let down their guard and stayed alert against any re-appearance of them. The men even declined Nathan's offer of whiskey in the evenings — it was a sore test and a great sacrifice, Georgie declared, to which Zeke agreed. Tom just rolled his eyes and smiled.

On the third day, they rode up to White Sulphur Springs and gave another round of speeches, this time to a group of several hundred. After that, Nathan finally returned to Mountain Meadows, well satisfied with the campaign.

When February fourth dawned, Nathan and Mr. Taylor were once again in Lewisburg, greeting voters and shaking hands. The election itself was anti-climactic, since the two candidates were essentially on the same side. But the sun came out in the morning after overnight snow flurries had painted the roofs white; and the beer vendors still managed a brisk business.

In the final tally, Nathan received 65 percent of the vote, to Taylor's 35 percent. The referendum vote was a stunning success, with 86 percent in favor, and only 14 percent opposed. Nathan prayed the rest of the state had gone so well, but that seemed unlikely. Western Virginia had relatively few slaves, so little reason to love the Slave Power. The eastern part of the state might be a whole other matter.

ॐॐॐॐॐॐॐॐॐॐॐ

Saturday Feb. 9, 1861, Covington, Virginia:

Nathan, Tom, and William sat in one of the passenger cars on the train headed back to Richmond. They'd just settled in for the day-long ride, after loading their horses and gear aboard at the Covington station.

Tom leaned toward Nathan and said, "Well, I'd have to say that was a successful mission, sir."

"Yes, I'd say so, Tom. I'm feeling much more hopeful about Virginia heading to Richmond this time around."

"I sense it too, sir. And from the rumors I heard back at the train station, it seems like the rest of the state voted our way as well. At least that's what everyone was talking about, including some folks just arriving from Richmond."

"Oh! You don't say? After our success I was assuming the western part of the state would go our way, but I had no great hopes for the eastern side. That *is* good news, Tom, if it's true! Guess we'll know for sure once we arrive in Richmond."

"Yes, sir, I expect so. But at least for now, the world seems a bit brighter, and more hopeful."

"True ... except ..."

"Except?"

"Don't forget ... Walters is still out there scheming against us. And if anything, the results of the election will motivate him further."

192

"Yes … that's true. But I'd have given a twenty-dollar gold piece to see his face when his men reported back to him, telling how you turned the tables on them at your speech in Lewisburg."

"I wouldn't! Likely just his usual, bland, unreadable expression. Why pay good money to see *that?*"

They shared a smile.

"But, it's the second time he's played right into my hands, despite his worst intentions. I fear our good fortune against him can't last forever. And speaking of, I'm sure you noticed the storm that blew through just before the election has now given way to some clear, dry-looking weather."

"Yes, sir … I'd noted it and discussed it with Jim. He figured if it kept up for a couple more days … well, then it would be time to keep a *very* sharp watch."

Nathan nodded, and reached into his pocket for a cigar, which he lit. Yes, Walters' looming threat was still a dark cloud on the horizon.

And though he didn't feel like talking about it just now, he was still anxious about the disappearance of the dog, Harry. Nathan felt sorry for the animal, of course, but maybe even more so for Stan. The big man had taken it surprisingly hard. He acted downcast, and for some odd reason that Nathan could not quite comprehend, it had shamed him. And now he seemed hesitant to speak with Nathan or make steady eye contact with him. This despite Nathan's emphatic assurances it was *not* his fault, and he was *not* to blame.

Nathan had a sudden thought and smiled. Tom noticed and gave him a quizzical look.

"I was thinking about Stan. It occurred to me just now, what he really needs is a *good fight* to cheer him up!"

Tom smiled and nodded, "Yes, I think you're right, sir. And it almost makes me feel sorry for Walters and his men. They have *no idea* what kind of trouble they're in for!"

They shared a chuckle, and William, who'd been listening, nodded his agreement, and laughed along with them.

♏♏♏♏♏♏

The next afternoon Nathan, Tom, and William sat around Mrs. Wilkerson's kitchen table in their boarding house sipping whiskey, along with an unexpected guest.

They'd just finished their noontime meal after returning from the morning church service, when Sandy Stuart came by the boarding house to pay Nathan a visit. They welcomed him with great enthusiasm—the Mountain Meadows men being eager to hear what he had to say about the election.

Since their arrival at the Richmond train station the evening before, it had been the talk of the town. They'd confirmed the rumors of an overwhelming pro-Union victory.

"Yes, it was a success beyond our wildest dreams, gentlemen," Stuart confirmed, beaming. "The election of delegates exceeded all our expectations, but the referendum vote ... well, it was almost breathtaking. I know you men are new to politics, so let me put it in perspective for you. In any election, a difference of 10 percent, that is 55 percent to 45 percent, is considered a runaway success—a 'landslide victory' some call it. Gentlemen, the referendum election results were 69 percent in favor, 31 percent opposed—a variance of 38 percentage points! It is not just a strong message against the secession, but a slap in the face to the Slave Power."

"Oh ... how so?"

"Nathan ... the Slave Power was desperate to defeat that referendum because they know if the people vote, they'll lose. They practically threw money at it, and pulled out all the stops, including having Virginia's national legislators speak out in opposition. But to no avail! The people have spoken!"

"It does seem like exceedingly good news, Sandy. But what about the convention delegates? I've heard it was overall a pro-Union outcome, but I don't know the details."

"Well, according to our calculations, it breaks out like this; of the 152 delegates elected, hardline pro-secessionists account for only 20 percent, versus unwavering Unionists at 33 percent—we consider you in this number, Nathan. And myself, of course."

"Hmm ... I may not be a brilliant mathematician like my man William here, but I do believe you've only accounted for just over half. What of the others?"

"The remaining 47 percent we are considering 'conditional' Unionists."

"Conditional? That doesn't sound so very reliable to me, Sandy. What are their *conditions?*"

"Ah ... now you cut right to the crux of the matter, Nathan, and the reason we can't just hold a vote on the first day of the convention and have done with it. This middle group would prefer Virginia remained in the Union, but they want ... certain assurances."

"Assurances? Assurances of what?"

"Well, that varies by individual, of course. Some want assurances the federal government won't try to interfere with slavery. Others want to see guarantees the fugitive slave laws will be enforced in Northern states. Still others are concerned about trade tariffs the national Congress has put in place that tend to harm the Southern states. Many would like to see one or more constitutional amendments passed on these issues, which will likely be the focus of the Peace Conference led by former President Tyler."

"Well, from what I've read about Mr. Lincoln, I doubt he would be resistant to any of those ideas, so there should be little issue."

"Yes, I'd agree, but ..."

"Yes?"

"The biggest issue that will sway the majority into one camp or the other, is how the new administration reacts to the states that've already seceded."

"Hmm ... I *have* noted a strong opposition, in the senate chambers at least, to the federal government using force to bring those states back in line."

"Yes ... that is, I believe, the most critical matter. Regardless of how the other issues are addressed, I think the way the new president deals with the seceding states will be the deciding factor. But on that matter, I am most hopeful, Nathan. I and a few others have ... certain connections in Washington ... and they say there's a strong sentiment growing against the use of force in the secession crisis. The thinking now is the seceding states can be persuaded to come back through a combination of negotiation and certain assurances being put in place."

Nathan scowled.

"I see you disagree with something I've said, Nathan. May as well have out with it, sir!"

"Sorry, Sandy. I know you *believe* what you're saying, and I don't doubt your *connections* believe what they're saying, but ... Hmm ... maybe it's just a product of my long years of military service, but I just can't envision a new president, be it Lincoln, or anyone else, coming into office and immediately bowing to this kind of political pressure. *Blackmail* even, one might call it. Regardless of the eventual outcome, it would immediately make him look weak and ineffectual, and give solace and encouragement to his political enemies. Which I understand are numerous, even in the North. No, sorry, I just can't picture it. If I were president, the first thing I'd do is muster the troops!"

"Well ... then I guess we should be happy you are *not* the new president, Mr. Chambers!" Sandy said in good humor and smiled.

But Nathan continued to scowl, "Maybe, Mr. Stuart ... maybe."

ഇൽൽൽഇൽൽൽഇൽൽൽ

Wednesday Feb. 13, 1861, Richmond, Virginia:

The Special Convention convened in the main hall at the Mechanics' Institute in Richmond, just across from the capitol building, at the foot of Capitol Hill. Since the General Assembly was still in session, the capitol building itself wouldn't be available until they officially adjourned — probably sometime in April.

The mood among the pro-Union faction was enthusiastic and upbeat, and they wasted no time in electing one of their own as president of the convention: John Janney of Loudoun County.

The secessionists, by contrast, were sullen, and downcast. Nathan could feel a particular venom directed toward himself, but he shrugged it off, trying not to take it personally. He'd expected it, after all, because of his perceived deception prior to the special election. And he had to admit to some extent he deserved it. He couldn't recall ever doing anything quite so dishonest. Despite Mr. Stuart's clever analogy about deceiving the enemy on a battlefield, somehow it still wasn't the same, despite the high stakes.

By contrast, he was now the darling of the pro-Union side, especially the unconditional Unionists. Only Stuart, Caldwell, and a few others had known the truth about him prior to the election. So the others saw his apparent defection from the enemy camp as a particularly satisfying coup. He received countless enthusiastic handshakes, and pats on the back that first day, along with multiple invitations for dining and drinking.

In the days since the election the pro-Union side had received even more encouraging news from the other "border" states. On February 9th, Tennessee voters had decided not to hold a secession convention at all. And two days later, the Kentucky legislature had adjourned, also refusing to call for one. And although both Arkansas and Missouri were holding elections for their own secession conventions, it was now expected they would both seat pro-Union-dominated gatherings. It appeared the other border states were following Virginia's lead.

The two diametrically opposed camps, the secessionists, and the unconditional Unionists, set out to sway the large middle group to their side of the argument. A series of speeches and discussions ensued, which Nathan found interesting at first, but soon found tiresome and repetitive. Yet again, he found himself longing for a good old-fashioned battlefield, in which the issue could be settled timelier—and less painfully, to his way of thinking.

ℰʊℰϽℭჳℭჳℰʊℰϽℭჳℭჳℰʊℰϽℭჳℭჳ

Evelyn picked up the elegant, delicate-looking china teacup. It had a lovely intricate flower pattern on it and gold trim around

197

the lip. She blew lightly on the hot tea to cool it before taking a sip.

"So Angeline … are you and Jonathan relieved now it seems Virginia will *not* go along with the secession after all?"

They sat together once again in the same sitting room where they'd first met. Jonathan had not joined them this time, having other business to attend to.

"You mean the results of the special election, dear, and the referendum vote? Well … it is *very* encouraging I must admit. But, my dear Evelyn … I've been around Virginia politics long enough to know nothing is ever for certain. And, never underestimate the Slave Power. They may seem down and defeated at the moment, but I can't imagine Governor Wise going down without a fight!"

"Governor *Wise?* I thought the governor's name was Letcher?"

"Yes, dear, Mr. Letcher is the *current* governor, and not a bad fellow, all in all.

Mr. *Wise* is the *former* governor, and a whole *different* kind of man, I'm afraid. Not really a nice man at all. Oh, he's nice enough in public, of course. He can be quite charming and witty, in fact. And he'll be very nice to you in private too, if you're on his side— we should know!

"But if he considers you an enemy, or even just someone in his way … woe be unto you! He is not a man to let a little thing like democracy, or the rule of law, get in his way. Though he is no longer governor, he continues as the political leader of the Slave Power. A man like that won't give up due to a minor inconvenience like losing an election."

"Oh, I see. Then … you still think there could be a war? You still want me to carry through with the plan we discussed before?"

"Of course, dear! Like Jonathan told you last time; better to be prepared and have nothing happen than to be caught off guard and at the mercy of our enemies. Yes, we wish you to continue as planned. If no war comes, then it has cost but a little of your time, and perhaps a few young men with hurt feelings. As we discussed before, small price to pay for the possible benefits.

"And it's not just *you*, Evelyn. We have many others performing related *services* for the cause … though not in your specific capacity. As you can imagine, it's not easy recruiting a young woman of your station without risking exposure. Don't underestimate how fortunate we are having you with us in this endeavor, Evelyn."

"Thank you, Angeline. I hope I can live up to your expectations."

"Oh, my goodness, dear! You've already exceeded our expectations with your Underground Railroad activities. Jonathan and I have talked about you many times. We continue to marvel at what a stroke of good fortune it was you happened upon that runaway slave girl. And decided to help her rather than turning her over to the authorities, as many other young women would've done."

"It just seemed ... like the *right* thing to do, not something extraordinary."

Angeline smiled at her. It was a warm, genuine smile. Evelyn really liked this woman. If it weren't for their great age difference, she could envision they'd have been the best of friends. Then again ... maybe the age difference didn't matter so much.

"Be that as it may, you give us a 'weapon' in our arsenal our enemies won't expect."

"Well, all right then, Angeline. You said today you'd have a list of ... 'targets,' did you call them?"

Angeline smiled, "Yes ... I know it sounds a bit extreme, but if you think in those ... military-type terms, it may make it easier for you. If they are 'targets' of our activities, as opposed to 'eligible men,' it may help you keep things in the proper perspective."

"All right ... I see what you mean. Shall we look at your *target* list, then? Likely I will already be acquainted with a number of them."

"Yes ... I expect so."

Angeline stood, and walked over to a large, elegantly carved mahogany desk on the other side of the room. Instead of opening a drawer as Evelyn had expected, she leaned over on the left-hand side of the desk and reached down. Evelyn heard a quiet, clicking, followed by the sound of a piece of paper being lifted. And then another click. *A secret compartment!* Evelyn realized. She also noticed they'd placed the desk in a corner of the room where it couldn't be seen either from the door, or from any outside windows. *Very clever. Very clever indeed!*

Angeline came back with a sheet of parchment paper that appeared to have writing on one side.

"You can never be too careful in our business, even in your own home. Remember that Evelyn. If you ever have need to keep anything in writing, find a private, secret place to store such messages from prying eyes."

Evelyn nodded her understanding.

"Now … let's have a look at this list," Angeline sat in a chair next to Evelyn, and spread the page out on the small table between them.

"I have written the names, ages, current occupations, and … expected or possible future occupations in a government or army in opposition to the Union. All are single men, either unmarried, or widowers. We have excluded married men and divorcees—you should not be seen with such men. We must maintain your high, proper reputation, both for our purposes, and for your own. At some point you will no longer be … in our *business* … and must still have your reputation intact!"

"I appreciate your concern for me in that regard."

"Of course, my dear. We know we're asking you to *risk* a great deal … but we would never ask you to do something certain to bring you harm."

ᛥᚸᚱᚳᚸᛥᚸᚱᚳᚸᛥᚸᚱᚳᚸ

The three informal camps at the convention soon began to coalesce behind natural leaders. For the unconditional Unionists, besides Sandy Stuart, this was George Summers of Kanawha County, and John Brown Baldwin of Augusta County. Baldwin was Sandy's brother-in-law and an inspiring speaker in his own right. George Summers was a highly respected former U.S. Representative and district judge. Rumors said he had a strong personal connection with a major player in Washington—a man expected to be in Lincoln's cabinet once the new president took office.

Former Governor Henry Wise from the Tidewater region led the secessionists along with his trusted crony, Lewis Harvie of Amelia and Nottoway. Nathan found Wise particularly disagreeable: arrogant and condescending. He had intense eyes and a lean, hawkish look to his face, with long thinning dark hair. Gray streaks were beginning to show his fifty-four years. When angry, as he frequently was at this convention, he had the deadly look of a man not to be crossed lightly.

Nathan had to admit, however, the man was sharp as a tack and knew his way around parliamentary procedure better than Nathan knew his way around a battlefield. Despite his faction being badly outnumbered, he had an uncanny ability to manipulate the conference to his own purposes, and somehow managed get more speaking time than anyone else. Nathan found him a most entertaining speaker—always witty, urbane, and humorous. Often bringing the entire floor to laughter, including those who greatly despised him personally.

The conditional Unionists, being less firm in their position were less clearly organized. Robert Conrad of Frederick County, Robert Scott of Fauquier, and William Preston of Montgomery were generally their speakers and nominal leaders.

But it was the unwavering Unionists, with the support of the middle group, who clearly dominated the conference. On the third day, President Janney appointed the Committee on Federal Relations, which would be the focal point of the secession debate. And to no one's surprise, there were only four pro-secessionists included. Robert Conrad was appointed its chairman—recognizing his role as leader of the most numerous faction at the conference.

The opening days of the convention comprised a series of speeches from the leaders of the three factions, elucidating the various arguments for and against secession versus preserving the Union.

For his part, Nathan gave just one formal speech, something very similar to his election speech in Lewisburg. It was well received, the delegates on both sides appreciating the marshal theme of it. He received a standing ovation, and formal acknowledgment and thanks from the chair for his heroic service to the nation. It was most gratifying, but he wasn't convinced it had swayed anyone one way or the other.

Sandy and the other hardcore Unionists focused all their energy in small groups and private meetings. Their goal was to negotiate various compromises and proposals to ensure the conditional Unionists would ultimately vote their way.

Nathan focused all his efforts on trying to convince the conditional Unionists to become *unconditional*. He had little faith in convincing the federal government in Washington, and particularly its new president, to accept a series of demands and conditions for Virginia's loyalty. He considered their chances much better if they could get enough delegates to accept the notion that nothing was bad enough to justify secession and civil war.

So he took it upon himself to hammer on that theme with every Delegate he met. Fortunately, he knew of what he spoke, having witnessed the horrors of total war up close. So he could paint a realistic and gruesome picture of it for the other representatives — emphasizing how they'd feel if their own sons were lost in the conflict.

Several other hardcore Unionists, especially men from western Virginia—like John Carlile from Harrison County, and Chester Hubbard of Ohio County—often joined with him in these discussions. Besides their unwavering support for the Union, he could sense a great deal of animosity between these men and their eastern Virginia counterparts. It surprised him one day when he overheard several of the western Virginians grumbling that if Virginia seceded, maybe there'd have to be another secession, this time *within* the state. It was the first time he'd ever heard *that idea* mentioned … but it was far from the last.

The back-and-forth speeches and debates and negotiations continued for days on end to the point Nathan almost wished he were back in the senate chambers deciding whether the state owed farmer Jones a tax refund!

But then one morning Sandy Stuart came in with a face like a storm cloud, which piqued Nathan's interest. So he walked over to see him, along with several others, curious to find out what it was about.

"He's gone too far this time!"

"Who has, Sandy?"

"Wise! He's an unrepentant demagogue! Thinks he's above the law. Now he's pushing for Virginia to seize federal facilities throughout the state—Harper's Ferry Armory, Norfolk Naval Base—even as we debate in this convention! Multiple people have reported hearing him promoting these seditious ideas in public venues. Word is he's also hired any number of young hoodlums to roam the streets of Richmond shouting pro-secession slogans and threatening anyone who speaks up in opposition! I'll not stand idly by in the face of such blatant lawlessness!"

Sandy's anger pleased Nathan. Though serious-minded, Sandy had always seemed calm and in good humor. It was gratifying to see him fired up over something. And Wise was just the man to do it! Nathan had previously heard rumors of Wise's hired bullyboys but hadn't seen them himself.

True to his word, shortly after the session began, Sandy Stuart stood up and addressed the convention, challenging Wise to explain his nefarious remarks about seizing federal facilities. He pointedly accused Wise of promoting lawlessness and sedition. And that he'd been attempting to circumvent the legal proceedings of the Special Convention. He also chastised him for promoting and paying for unruly and lawless behavior by young men around Richmond in the name of the secessionist movement.

Nathan thought it well said—forceful, direct, and likely all true. It received enthusiastic applause and approval by the majority of those present.

As expected, Wise immediately stood and responded. He adamantly denied every allegation and assumed the humble and righteous demeanor of a man falsely accused. Nothing could be further from the truth, he stated. Surely the duly elected delegates could not *believe* such slanderous accusations leveled against an honorable former governor. He would never stoop to such tactics, being a staunch advocate of the democratic process, the rule of law, and so on, and so forth.

In the end Nathan had to shake his head in admiration. Wise was good—*very, very* good. So good, in fact, though Nathan was almost certain the things Sandy was saying were true, he still felt a very strong inclination to believe Wise. He had to combat that compunction with a physical shake of the head, and a determined force of will.

If Sandy was telling the truth, Nathan wondered what Wise would do if the convention ultimately voted against him. A man like that would surely stop at nothing to get what he wanted. He began to wonder if his own military skills might not come in handy after all, if things went sour. He began to wish they'd brought additional guns and ammo with them from Mountain Meadows. And more of his men ...

Chapter 9. Betrayal and Redemption

"I have blotted out, as a thick cloud,
thy transgressions, and, as a cloud, thy sins:
return unto me; for I have redeemed thee."
– Isaiah 44:22

Wednesday Feb. 13, 1861, Greenbrier County, Virginia:

Tony crouched behind a bush at the edge of the lawn surrounding the Big House. He held still, suppressing the urge to shiver in the midnight cold by sheer force of will. Listening for any sounds, he strained his eyes into the darkness for signs of movement. He'd picked a moonless night, so there'd be little chance of being seen.

He'd also wanted a night with no rain or snow for his purpose. It wouldn't do to get soaking wet tonight. For one, he'd risk freezing to death with winter temperatures hovering right around the freezing point. And for another, he'd likely drip all over the floor of the Big House, leaving telltale signs of his presence. No one must ever know he'd been there. The weather agreed with his plans this evening: a mostly clear sky with even a few stars sparkling out, giving off just enough light to see where he was going.

He still held a deathly fear of the Captain's great hound, even though the beast had disappeared shortly after the Captain had gone to Richmond the first time, and nobody'd seen it in weeks, not even when the Captain returned home.

Tony gazed into the deeper shadows surrounding the house but saw nothing. He realized if the hound was there, he'd never see it until he stepped right on it. Well, nothing for it then, he must either risk it, or give up and go home. He moved out from behind the bush, and moved swiftly across the lawn, making as little noise as possible. The grass, though cold and wet, felt soft under his bare feet, which he appreciated—much nicer than running along the gravel road. He might've chosen to wear his shoes, it being plenty cold enough this time of year, but he knew he could move much more quietly through the house without them.

He'd decided to use the back door rather than the front for several reasons. First, if someone saw him, they might not think twice about a slave coming in or going out the back door. Likely they'd assume he either had legitimate business, or at worst was keeping a secret tryst with one of the house slaves. A vision of Rosa flashed unbidden through his mind at the thought. He shook his head, trying to clear away the image—he couldn't afford any such distractions now.

His other reason for choosing the back door was its proximity to the closet where the groom had said the Captain kept his guns. On the downside, he'd have to pass close by the rooms where the house slaves slept. If someone was awake, or restless, they might see him. But there was nothing he could do about that. He'd just have to chance it.

Using the front door wouldn't do at all … he couldn't imagine any plausible explanation for a field slave doing *that*, and neither would anyone else. It would certainly look suspicious.

So he'd worked his way around the back of the house through the woods before starting out across the lawn, moving straight toward the back door. He saw no lights on in the house. That was a good sign, at least.

Once inside, he'd have to risk lighting a candle, he could think of no way around it. He'd never been inside the Big House, and though he knew the path to the closet in theory from talking with the groom, he'd need some light. It'd be impossible to be sure he'd found the right door in a pitch-black house. The groom said the hallway ran straight through the house from the back door halfway toward the front, before taking a right-hand turn. Then another left turn to the foyer and front door.

He also understood the maids slept behind the first door on the left, the male house slaves behind the second door. After that, the back stairway led up to the second floor on that same side. On the right were the kitchen and then the dining hall. The storage closet was down the hall, on the right side somewhere past the right-hand turn. But the groom had been unclear on the distance.

He planned to walk down the hallway, quietly touching the wall on the left side with his fingertips to make sure he went in a straight line. That way he could tell when he passed the slaves' rooms and the staircase. Then he'd risk lighting the candle. The white folks would all be sleeping upstairs, so there'd be little to worry about from that direction.

He hurried across the lawn and paused in the deep shadows next to the house, trying to quiet his breathing to listen for any sounds. After a few minutes, satisfied nothing moved near him, he slipped quietly up the back stairs to the veranda. When he stepped on the fourth step, it made a small squeak. He stopped and stood still again, listening.

He continued to the top of the stairs and hastened across the veranda to the back door. Now for the moment of truth. According to the groom, they never locked any doors at Mountain Meadows, but Tony didn't believe it. So he reached up and slowly turned the doorknob. It moved easily, making only a slight clicking noise as the latch cleared the door frame. He pulled it open cautiously, happy he'd thought to ask the groom which way the door swung. For reasons he did not understand, the front door swung into the house, while the back door swung out onto the veranda. He opened it as deliberately as possible, praying it wouldn't squeak. When it was wide enough for him to slip inside, he silently thanked whichever slave kept the hinges oiled—he apparently did his job well!

Moving inside, he pulled the door closed, straining to move deliberately and quietly. The door slid back into place without a sound, and once again, made only the slightest clicking sound when the latch returned into the door frame.

He paused to steady his breathing before turning and carefully orienting himself in a direct line away from the door. With his left hand he reached out until he lightly touched the wall. He moved out down the hall, continuing to run the tips of his fingers along the wall to his left. In this way he encountered the first door (the maids), and then the second door (the male house slaves), relieved to discover both closed. Then he felt empty air and knew he'd reached the stairway.

He walked another five feet past the stairwell before crouching and setting his back to the wall. Reaching into his pocket he pulled out a candle and a match. He struck the match, rubbing it against a small stone he'd brought for the purpose. It flared up with a brightness that appeared blinding in the darkness, and the hiss of the match igniting sounded like a gun going off in the silent house. Tony cringed at the sound, silently willing the match to make less noise. After a moment the match obeyed, and burned with a quiet, steady blaze. Tony held the candle out and lit it, then shook the match to extinguish it. He made sure it was completely out before stuffing it into his pocket. It wouldn't do to leave behind a telltale matchstick.

In the dim candlelight he looked down the hall and nearly jumped; a man stared back down the hall right at him! He stifled a sigh of relief as he realized it was only a painting hanging there on the wall where the hallway made its right-hand turn. It was an elegantly framed painting of a neatly dressed, serious-looking white man with gray hair. The Captain's grandfather, maybe?

Tony hurried down the hall and turned the corner. The hallway widened here, in this in-between area, before turning left again and running straight up to the front door. But Tony wasn't going that far. He looked along the wall on the right-hand side of the short, wide hallway, and found the closet door, just as the groom had said. He moved over to it and gripped the knob. Again, he expected to meet resistance from a locked door, and again, the groom's words proved true; the knob turned easily until the latch clicked free.

He eased the door open and held the candle out into the entrance for a quick look inside. To his relief, the closet was large—the kind meant for a man to walk into rather than just reach into. So he slipped inside, and pulled the door closed behind him.

He gazed around the room. Shelves lined two walls from floor to ceiling, filled with all kinds of things. From the thin coating of dust and trailing spider webs it was clear most of the items had been there a long time. Hats, gloves, shoes, boots, pots and pans, jars and bottles filled the shelves along with many other odd things he did not recognize, and for which he could not guess the purpose.

He wondered if anyone even knew all of what was in this closet. He shook his head in wonder. There were more things forgotten in this one small room than all the goods he'd owned in his entire lifetime. And his Daddy's lifetime as well.

But he remembered his purpose and pulled his gaze from the various mysteries on the shelves. He began searching the room for the thing he sought. At the end of the room, on a wall with no shelves he saw rows of hooks, from near the ceiling to within a few feet of the floor. He came over closer and held the candle up for a better look. The hooks were of a dark metal and perfectly smooth—large enough to wrap around the lower part of a man's arm. They lined up in perfect rows each row about a foot apart, with four hooks per row. It puzzled him at first, unable to discern the purpose of the hooks. Then a sudden thought hit him, and he took a step back to get a better look at the whole thing.

Of course! *Damn!* These hooks were where they hung the rifles. Two hooks for each gun, two guns each row. But the hooks were empty! Tony's heart sank, and he sank to the floor, still gazing up at the empty hooks.

Fool! he scolded himself. He remembered Sergeant Jim saying he'd keep the soldiers prepared at all times for an attack by the wicked neighbor Walters. Clearly, they'd not be prepared if their rifles were shut away in this closet! They must've moved them out to their bunkhouse, along with the bullets and powder. Tony knew there'd be no hope of sneaking in there and lifting a rifle right out from under the noses of the soldiers. And even if he did somehow manage it, they'd be sure to notice the missing weapon straight away. Then there'd be hell to pay for sure.

Well, no point in moping over something he could do nothing about. Best to get out of here before someone caught him. He'd just have to risk the run without the weapon. Still, it made him shudder to think of that great dog coming at him out in the woods, with nowhere to run, and no way to fight.

He stood and turned toward the door, when something on the shelf to his left caught his eye. The thing he'd seen was a beautiful red, velvety material. He reached out and touched it, enjoying the wonderful softness of it. But then he noticed the material was wrapped around something. He looked down its length ... something very, very long. His heart began to beat wildly ... could it be?

He carefully set the candle on a shelf, making certain it wouldn't tip. He reached out and gingerly lifted the thing wrapped in the cloth, setting it gently on the floor. The red cloth had been sewn like a great long sleeve, with one end sewn shut. He moved down to the open end and slowly pulled back the cloth. His breath caught. The end of a shiny black gun barrel now poked out from the red sleeve!

He carefully pulled the sleeve the rest of the way off, then stood and retrieved the candle. He squatted back down for a better look. The rifle was long and thin, with beautifully polished wood, and shiny brass trim all along the gun workings. Its maker had delicately engraved it with intricate, swirling designs. And Tony could see there was writing in the engraving, though he could not read the words. He sat back in wonder, gazing at the beautiful object. But he'd seen this rifle before. There was no mistaking it, with its great length, elegance, and most notably the odd, crescent moon shape of the buttstock. He'd seen the Captain shoot it out on the target practice range. The men called it "The Governor's Rifle," though he didn't know why. Fortunately, he'd been curious to learn everything he could about operating the guns. So he'd noticed the odd way the men held this particular gun due to its great length and the oddly shaped buttstock. He closed his eyes and pictured it in his mind—the Captain tucking the buttstock into the crook of his elbow, rather than up against his shoulder as with the other rifles. *Yes ... thanks to you, Captain, I know how this-here gun works!*

The discovery of the rifle excited and re-energized him. He stood and looked around the shelf for the other things he'd need and quickly found them. On the same shelf where the rifle had been, he located a full powder tin, a small pouch of percussion caps, and a synch bag with cloth patches. A little more searching turned up a small tin box of Minni balls.

He'd planned ahead, knowing he'd need all these other things, not just the rifle. So he'd brought along a small burlap sack, like the kind they used to pick cotton, looped around his neck to free his hands. He quickly stuffed all the accessories into the sack. Then, after taking one last admiring look at the gun, he slipped the red sleeve back over it. He felt a twinge of guilt at his thievery. It wasn't what he'd planned on taking. He would have preferred one of the other, more business-like rifles. Now he had no other choice. But this was an object of great value, and in his mind, it made the crime more serious.

Then he stiffened his resolve, thinking, *Maybe it be a fair trade for him taking something of great beauty from me. Maybe it begins to make up for him taking her away ... for taking Rosa.*

He stood, lifting the rifle with him. The heft of it surprised him. Despite its delicate appearance it was still a wicked, deadly weapon!

He moved toward the door, but quickly froze. He'd heard a quiet noise from outside and now saw the doorknob turning. A dim light shone in under the door!

Various options ran through his mind in an instant: blowing out the candle, attempting to hide, putting the gun back and coming up with some story, overpowering whoever it was and making a run for it. But just as quickly he rejected all as unworkable. There'd be no place to hide in the small closet. And if he tried to run for it now, the soldiers would catch him before he got two miles. Besides which, it was the middle of winter and he'd have none of the warm clothing, food and supplies he'd prepared. Also, he had no desire to harm one of the household slaves, which he'd likely have to do to get past them. So in the end he just stood where he was, staring at the slowly opening door, awaiting his fate.

It was difficult to tell which face expressed more surprise when the door cracked open, and Rosa looked in. Her eyes went wide, but to her credit, she didn't cry out or make any sound. She quickly recovered from her shock, stepped inside the closet, and closed the door. She held a candle in her left hand, and a broom in her right.

"Tony … what are you doing in here?" she whispered. "I was restless and heard a soft noise out in the hallway. I reckoned it was a rat, so I grabs a broom, figurin' to give it a whack. But I saw a light coming from the closet … well, I ain't yet met a rat knew how to light a candle!"

Then she noticed he held something long, wrapped in a red cloth. "What is that, Tony?"

"Rosa … I's … I's fixin' to go away. Up to the North," he answered back in a whisper. "I was fearing the Captain's great hound might chase me, so I was thinkin' to protect myself." He held up the rifle in its sleeve, and her eyes widened with recognition of what was inside.

"You's running away? But *why*, Tony? Captain says he gonna free us. Why you wanna run?"

"'Cause I don't believe him, Rosa. I think he just be telling tales to get us all to work harder for him. Or to stop doing 'The Way,' so's he'll make more money and have less troubles.

"And also …"

"Also, what, Tony?"

"Also, on account o' *you*, Rosa."

"Me? Tony … just cause I ain't said I'd marry you, don't mean we ain't still friends. Gosh, Tony … we done know'd each other since we was babies. When you asked me … the *thing* you asked me before … it was such a surprise. I just ain't never thought of you and me … *that* way before."

"Yeah, I understand all that, but I ain't a fool. I know you *do* think on the Captain *that* way. I ain't fixin' to stay here to see *that*."

Rosa was stunned. What had given him that idea? But even as she pondered the question, she realized there might be a small grain of truth in it. She had been feeling … *differently* about the Captain lately, in a way she didn't entirely understand.

"Look, Tony. That just ain't so. The Captain … and *me*? It ain't like that …"

But Tony just stared at her and slowly shook his head, "So, Rosa … what now? You fixin' to turn me in to Sergeant Jim for tryin' to steal one o' the Captain's guns?"

212

But she looked back up at him, tears in her eyes, "No, Tony, I ain't. Like I said, we been friends our whole lives, and I'd like to keep it that way, if I can …"

Her tears softened Tony's heart. "Rosa … *come with me!* We can go up North and be free. Start a new life. Have a family in freedom. Not be … whatever it is we gonna be if'n we stays here."

But as soon as the words were out of his mouth, he knew he'd wasted the breath.

Her face hardened, "No, Tony. I ain't gonna run. I'm fixin' to stay, come what may. But if you's insistent on goin', I ain't gonna turn you in, neither. Best you be gettin' now, 'fore someone else hears something."

♏♏♏♏♏♏♏♏♏♏♏

Walters and his column of men rode across Howard Creek as the night sky turned to a lighter shade of black, well before dawn.

Bob noticed his boss had a grim, determined look on his face, not his typical bland, unreadable expression. This did not bode well for the Mountain Meadows men, he decided. He shivered at the thought of the murder and mayhem they'd planned. He didn't like the thought of it, but would hold up his end, no matter how distasteful it became.

The fiasco of their abortive raid on the slave wedding the previous year had left Walters determined not to repeat his mistakes. He'd planned much more carefully this time, holding endless battle conferences with Bob and Sickles, discussing every detail of the operation. Sickles' knowledge of the layout of the Chambers' farm, and of the individuals likely to be guarding it, had proven invaluable.

Bob now understood how foolish they'd been the last time, blindly riding right into Chambers' trap. He was an experienced Army officer, with men fresh from fighting Indians in Texas. Walters' men were only a bunch of farmers. And yet they'd figured they could just ride up and have their way with Chambers. In hindsight it seemed worse than ridiculous.

But to Walters' credit, he'd taken it much more seriously this time. For one, he'd purchased a supply of new, military style

213

rifles, and had drilled his men relentlessly on their usage, holding target practice for hours on end. He'd also purchased new revolvers—Remingtons, which had an advantage over the Colts in that the shooter could easily swap out a spare cylinder without tools. This meant each man would not only have a full six shots loaded in his pistol but another six already loaded in a spare cylinder. They could quickly reload this weapon even under combat conditions, unlike its Colt counterpart.

And rather than riding right up the main road, as they'd done before, this time they'd go up the back way—up the rough elk trail to the top of the mountain. He'd send scouts ahead this time, to make sure they didn't ride into an ambush. At the crest of the hill they'd be able to reconnoiter Chambers' farm. If what they saw didn't look right, as in a high state of preparation, they could still abort the attack without taking casualties.

And to ensure a safe retreat, he'd leave a couple of men behind to guard the approach to the hill at the start of the elk trail.

And finally, and maybe most importantly, he'd planned the attack when Chambers would be away from home in Richmond. Without their leader, Walters' action was much more likely to succeed. And Walters seemed to like the idea of wounding Chambers to the core better than killing him outright.

So on this frosty, crisp morning which promised more dry weather, stars still sparkled in the lightening sky as the column of mounted men turned east onto the main road toward Mountain Meadows Farm. Bob turned and looked back. Yes, a much more determined and formidable looking group of men this time, to be sure. Twenty men in all, each held a rifle and had a pistol in a holster at his waist. These men had a confident demeanor—none of the nervous twitchiness he recalled from the last time. Walters had even recruited a couple of ex-soldiers. They'd helped immensely with the rifle training and had instilled confidence in the farm boys.

Bob turned back around and glanced ahead at Walters. He was the only one without a rifle, but he had two pistols on holsters strapped to his waist. Bob had to suppress a smile when he noticed Walters wore older boots this time, not his shiny new ones. *Guess he learned that lesson as well,* he thought.

☙℘ℭ℞☙℘ℭ℞☙℘ℭ℞

Tony shivered in the pre-dawn darkness, wrapping his arms around himself and rubbing the sleeves with mittened hands in a vain attempt to keep warm. Johnny and Ned huddled next to him, their breath coming out in steamy gusts. Despite the cold, they weren't allowed a fire for fear the smoke would give away their position. But they'd dressed warmly, so other than a little discomfort, the cold didn't feel deathly.

Tony looked up at the sky, turning lighter each minute with the approaching dawn. He looked over at where the trail led down the hill and could now make out a few details: bushes, stumps, and tall grass. *A few more minutes, then it'll be time to go,* he decided.

He'd secured the rifle three nights ago, so he'd just been waiting for the right opportunity to make their run for it. They'd held the Watch several times since Christmas. But this past week, with the drier weather, it'd been worked in earnest every day from well before dawn until nearly sunset. Fortunately, they'd designated their threesome a team, so they always went out together. This morning their post was at the top of the hill overlooking the farm. Tony would've preferred to start their run closer in. They'd need to cross back behind the farm buildings to retrieve their hidden gear before heading north. They'd also have to be careful to avoid being seen by any of the other watchers, or by any of the white hands.

But he'd decided it was more important to start at first light. That way they'd have an entire day to run before having to halt for the night. They never knew until the night before where they'd be positioned, or at what time, as Sergeant Jim seemed to like to mix things up every day. So last night, when they'd learned they had the pre-dawn shift, he'd decided to run as soon as it got light enough to see. There'd still be another three hours or so before the Watch would be shifted, so they'd have a good start before anyone noticed them missing.

215

He stood, brushed off his backside, and said, "Time to go."

Ned stood immediately, but Johnny continued to sit. He looked up at Tony, and said, "You sure we oughta do this now, Tony? What if them bad fellas shows up just as we's leavin'?"

Tony scowled at him. "Don't you see it, John? They ain't comin'. It's just another tale meant to make us believe the Captain's takin' care of us, so we oughta be grateful."

Johnny stood, but for once wasn't smiling and jovial. He looked Tony hard in the eyes, and said, "I sure do hope you's right about this, Tony."

But Tony was sure; and besides, he was tired of arguing about it, so he just turned and headed for the trail, Ned close behind. Johnny sighed a deep sigh, shrugged his shoulders, and followed.

☙℞◖℞◖☙℞◖℞◖☙℞◖◖℞◖☙℞◖℞◖☙

It was an hour past dawn, and Jim was on his way back from the hog pens. One of the slaves had reported a sow with a limp from a wound she'd gotten rubbing against a broken board, and he worried it might be festering. Jim had gone to have a look, though he knew little enough about pigs beyond enjoying their meat. The sow did look a bit gimpy to him, and the wound looked pretty nasty. He was wishing William was here to have a look, then remembered him cleaning the Captain's wound with whiskey. He was just wondering whether that would also work on a pig, when Georgie came riding around the corner of the barn, yanking his gelding to a sudden stop, just short of trampling Jim.

"They come, Sergeant Jim!" he shouted.

"What? Walters? All right, I'm coming … no reason to run me over, Georgie!"

"No! You don't understand, sir; something went wrong with the Watch … they're here! They're here, *now!*"

"*Shit!* How'd that happen?" Jim said, rushing forward and jumping up behind Georgie on the horse.

Georgie jerked hard on the reigns, turning the horse and spurring it back in the direction he'd come.

"Looks like some of our men deserted their post, sir."

"Deserters? Which ones was it?"

216

"Tony's, at the hilltop."

"Tony's?! *Damn!* I reckoned him one of our *most* reliable hands!"

"Yep, we all did, sir."

"Damn, but that's a bitter pill."

"Yes, sir. The others did their bit, though, and started the alarm relay. But since we was missing one post on the hill, the poor fellow who discovered it had to run 'til he was like to burst. 'Fore he arrived at the next station Walters was already coming down the hill. By now I reckon he's down on the main road between here and the bottom of the hill."

Georgie continued filling Jim in on the details as the gelding's hooves pounded along the path toward the horse stables.

"How many?"

"Our men counted eighteen, all mounted. Each armed with rifle and pistol."

"*Damn it!*"

"Jamie went to the barracks to rouse the others. I told him to meet us at the stables. Fortunately, I passed Cobb on my way in and told him to saddle up the horses. They should be ready by now."

"*Damn it all to hell!*" Jim said, and spit to the side, still fuming over the failure of the Watch from the desertion of Tony and his men.

They pulled up to a stop at the stables, and Jim jumped down. The others were already there, leading horses out. Though they showed no panic, the men looked worried and harassed, especially the farmhands, Zeke, Benny, and Joe.

Stan trotted over and handed Jim his gun belt, along with two fully loaded Colts. Stan did *not* look concerned. He flashed Jim his great wide grin. "Hey, Sergeant Jim—is good day for shooting *wolves*, no?"

Jim shook his head. Stan was a wonder, there could be no doubt, "Yep, I reckon so, Private Volkov. I reckon it's as good a day as any for it."

Jamie handed Jim the reins of his horse. He climbed into the saddle. The others did likewise. He motioned them to line up for a quick inspection.

Fortunately, part of Jim's plans had included the ability to respond quickly in an emergency. It'd included keeping the horses bridled, and each horse stabled during the day with its saddle next to it. He'd even drilled the grooms, timing them on how quickly they could get the horses saddled in a crisis.

His preparations had also included keeping a rifle and two revolvers for each man, fully loaded and holstered all day, every day. And having the men in the barracks where they'd not need to be gathered, anytime they weren't needed out with the Watch. He'd even had the men fashion a rifle holster to attach to their saddles. It allowed them to carry a rifle on horseback without encumbering the rider, freeing his hands for reins and pistols while riding.

He looked down, pleased to see each man had his pistols strapped on, his rifle in its holster, and his horse saddled and ready to go. It was then he realized one of their number was missing.

"Hey ... anybody seen Billy?"

"He went down the main road at first light, for to check on the Watch down there, don't you know? Figure they've slipped past him after going up over top o' the hill," Jamie answered.

"*Damn* ... we surely could use him! Well, can't be helped now I reckon. Anyway men, seems our plans for laying a trap have gone to hell ... as such things will do in battle. But, if Walters reckons on riding in here and having his way with us, he's sorely mistaken. I still mean to bloody him good.

"Ain't time for much of a plan, so here's what we're gonna do ..."

They moved up the road at a fast trot. As Jim had ordered, they formed up in double file—Stan and the three farmhands on the right, Jim, Jamie and Georgie on the left. They passed the slave cabins and the old oak tree and table where the Captain had

218

famously chopped up the whip. They'd seen no sign of the enemy ahead, and Jim wondered if he should worry about Walters laying a trap of his own this time. But, he decided, there hadn't been time for that; and anyway, Walters had no way of knowing where they'd be. And since they'd not sounded the alarm, he probably reckoned he'd managed to catch Mountain Meadows flat footed this time.

They continued up a gentle rise, Jim hoping they'd get to the crest of the rise before Walters did. He'd much prefer a downhill cavalry charge! He picked up the pace a bit, and the men responded in kind.

They neared the top of the rise. Still no sign of the enemy. Then, just as they reached the top, they saw a darkness moving toward them on the roadway ahead—Walters' column. Jim calculated they were about two hundred yards out and closing fast … time to go!

He turned toward Stan, and caught his eye, "Now, Volkov!" he said, and spurred his horse. As it lurched into a gallop, he dropped the reins and reached for his pistols.

ೞഗ೧൝ೞഗ೧൝ೞഗ೧൝

Bob became more nervous the closer they got to the farm buildings. There they meant to get off the road, and circle back behind the house, coming at Chambers' men from a direction they'd not be expecting.

Amazingly, they'd made it up to the top of the hill without encountering any of Chambers' people. They'd paused long enough for Walters to survey the farm below with his spyglass. He turned around with a rare grin, "Quiet as a baby in a cradle. We've caught them with their pants down this time, boys."

They'd gone down the winding path from the hill, and the thickly wooded trail helped ease Bob's concerns; there'd be no possibility of them being spotted from below. They reached the bottom of the hill and headed down the well-worn trail toward the main drive. Still no sign of trouble.

They were on the main drive leading to the farmhouse now, moving along in two rows, Walters leading one row, and Sickles

219

the other. They'd ridden up and down several shallow rises, heading up another when someone shouted, "There they are, sir!"

Bob looked ahead, around Walters and saw riders coming. Like Walters' men, the riders came in double file, but he couldn't tell how many they were. They were closing fast, riding at a gallop.

Walters raised his hand bringing the column to a halt. He pulled his pistols and fired off several shots. Sickles did the same. But these shots appeared to have no effect on the approaching riders.

Of course, the rest of Walters' men, Bob included, drew pistols, but couldn't fire at the enemy without risking hitting the men in front of them. So only Walters and Sickles fired at the enemy. And apparently neither of them hit their mark. Bob realized with a sudden sinking feeling this terrible disadvantage was *not* accidental. Again Chambers had gained the upper hand—this time without even being here!

The riders closed to within fifty yards, before returning fire. Bob saw puffs of smoke in front of the riders followed by the distant pop of pistol fire. Something buzzed past his right ear like an angry bee. He heard a hard *thud*, and someone screamed behind him. More bullets came whistling in, ripping through their ranks. Their column wavered. Horses flinched and balked nervously to the sides. One man fell to the ground. Then another.

The riders were upon them—flashing by on either side—a thunderous noise of galloping hooves, and a deafening sound of gunfire. The riders passed, a cloud of gun smoke swirling in their wake.

Bob realized he'd never fired a shot. He wondered if the others had.

He looked back to see if the riders would return. But instead they peeled off to the sides of the road. *What now?*

He looked at their own column and saw five men down, their horses prancing about nervously or already bolting away. Two others remained in the saddle but clutched at bullet wounds.

He looked again to see what Chambers' men were doing. They pulled rifles from saddles, jumped from their horses, and scrambled for cover on either side of the road, less than twenty yards away.

A sudden chill went down his spine. Walters' men were exposed, out in the open. It was a death trap! And they were about to be slaughtered.

He looked up and was dismayed by Walters' blank, shocked expression. Bob realized the man was incapable of taking command in this type of emergency. He glanced over at Sickles, but he stared open mouthed at Walters, as if expecting *him* to do something.

Bob stood in his saddle, and shouted, "Ride! Ride or die where you sit!" Even before Bob had finished yelling, the last man in the column took a rifle bullet to the side of his head. Blood splattered over the man next to him.

Bob spurred his horse forward. With a lurch, it launched itself right between the glazed look of Walters, and the panicked, slack-jawed stare of Sickles. "Ride or die!" he shouted at them. He continued spurring his horse while ducking low in the saddle. He didn't look back to see if anyone followed.

༄ఠ৯ ৫৯ ༄ఠ৯ ৫৯ ༄ఠ৯ ৫৯

Tony pushed his way past another bush and felt a hand grab him from behind. He turned, and gave Johnny an annoyed look, "What now, John?"

But instead of answering, Johnny put his finger to his lips, and gazed upward, as if listening for something. "There ... there it is again!"

"What?"

"Listen, Tony!"

Tony had been breathing hard from his exertions and hadn't heard anything. So he slowed his breathing with an effort and listened. Then he heard it ... a faint, distant ... *popping* sound. Repeated multiple times.

"What you reckon *that* is, Tony?"

By now Ned had caught up with them and leaned in to hear what they were discussing.

221

"Damn!" Tony exclaimed, a strange, frightened look coming over his face. "Good, holy, *Goddamn!* We've got to get back!"

"What? What you talking about, Tony? What is it? Get back? Why?"

Tony looked them both hard in the eye, "I was wrong … *dead* wrong. They's attackin' Mountain Meadows! And it's all my fault! I's goin' back!"

Without another word he took off at a run back up the trail they'd just worked their way down. Johnny and Ned exchanged a shocked look, then turned and ran after him.

ಬಿಬಿಎಲ್ ಬಿಬಿಎಲ್ ಬಿಬಿಎಲ್

As he watched Walters and his remaining men gallop off toward the Big House, Jim realized the fatal flaw in his plan. Up to that moment it'd come off beautifully, and he'd been feeling pretty smug about it. They'd killed half a dozen of the enemy on that first furious pass. Then a couple more immediately after with their rifles. They'd forced the enemy into complete confusion, milling about, thoroughly disorganized. They appeared incapable of further fight, and in a few minutes the deadly crossfire from the rifles would've surely finished the job.

But one rider had extracted himself and taken the lead. And instead of retreating toward Walters Farm, as Jim had expected, he'd spurred in the opposite direction. The others quickly followed.

It was the worst thing that could've happened. And now Jim and his men didn't even have their horses to follow.

Well, nothing to be gained by crying about it now, he decided. So he jumped up, and shouted to the men, "Load one round in your rifle, then follow me. They's headed for the Big House, and we must follow's best we can." He hadn't fired his last loaded rifle round, so he headed off at a trot, rifle in hand.

He pulled out his pistols as he ran and tossed them to the ground, along with his extra pistol ammo. There'd be no time to reload them, and their weight would only slow him down. He felt a strong urge to run faster, but he was much more used to walking, or riding a horse. He knew he'd have to pace himself to have any hope of making it there without collapsing.

Once they were clear of Chambers' trap, Bob realized they now had the initiative; the Mountain Meadows men had abandoned their horses to fire their rifles from cover. The road to the Big House lay wide open.

Walters' original plan, to eliminate all whites as witnesses, was no longer possible. They'd never beat the Mountain Meadows men in a gunfight now that they'd lost the benefit of surprise, and of superior numbers. But Bob thought they might still make it out alive if they were clever. Like, maybe taking Miss Abbey hostage, and using her to bargain for their escape. He had no great hopes of getting out any other way, since there was no way back to Walters Farm without going past Chambers' soldiers.

He slowed his pace and fell back next to Walters' horse. Walters continued to look dazed and had shown no sign of taking charge.

"Sir, we're now cut off from retreat, our numbers badly depleted."

Walters scowled and said, "So? What do you expect me to do about it?"

"Well, sir, I'm thinking it may still be possible to make it out of here. We can ride up to the Big House and take Miss Abbey hostage. Chambers' men won't dare fire on us if we hold her. Then we can negotiate our safe passage back to the main road in exchange for her freedom."

Walters perked up at this suggestion.

"Take Miss Abbey? How?"

"Well, sir. I believe the men who attacked us on the road are all they have. And if that's so, they all abandoned their horses, figuring to finish us off right there or as we tried to escape past them back the way we came. I don't reckon they figured on us riding out of their trap in *this* direction."

"Yes … yes, that makes sense. You may be right, Bob! Perhaps they have no more men and have left Chambers' house unguarded. Let's ride ahead and see."

He turned and waved his men forward. They moved into a trot, though two of the men were clearly in great pain, nursing serious gunshot wounds.

They slowed as they came to the area of the slave cabins, nervously pointing their guns in all directions. But nothing moved. No faces looked out from the cabins. Unbeknownst to them, Sergeant Jim had also drilled the slaves for this emergency. They knew they must act the moment they heard gunfire. They were to grab the children and run into the woods—far back into the woods—and hide until he gave the pre-arranged all-clear signal.

Walters' men continued past the farm outbuildings, moving slowly and cautiously, expecting an ambush at any moment. But nothing happened, and they saw nothing other than the occasional chicken skittering past.

They rode up the circular drive to the front of the house, still feeling anxious. Walters looked all around, then smiled incongruously. He holstered his pistols and got down off his horse. "Nothing, Bob! Seems you were right; Chambers' men are all back up there on the road. Come, Sickles. Let's see if Miss Abbey is at home and kindly invite her to take a little ride with us."

Sickles dismounted, but looked around nervously, clutching his pistol, as if still expecting an attack at any moment.

Walters smiled at him, and said, "And maybe we can see what color blood the Chambers' house slaves have. That won't lessen Miss Abbey's exchange value none, will it Bob?"

Bob swallowed hard, not wanting to think about what Walters had in mind. "No, sir, it won't, but ..."

"But?"

"Well, just thinking it might be best to hurry, lest some other of Chambers' men arrives, is all."

"Bob ... you worry too much. Besides, they'll not dare attack now we hold the house."

Sickles had moved ahead of Walters, still gazing around anxiously. He stepped up the stairs to the veranda, looking all around, then turned back toward Walters, shrugged, and finally holstered his pistol.

"Guess you're right, boss. Nothing here to worry about," he said.

Just then a rifle shot rang out, and a large, round, red spot appeared in the center of Sickles' chest. He opened his mouth, gazed down at his chest, and collapsed, rolling down the stairs, coming to a stop at Walters' feet.

Walters stared down in shock.

"It came from the woods!"

"They's out in the woods around the house!"

"We're surrounded. Let's get outta here!"

The men looked around anxiously, especially out toward the woods from where the shot had come.

Walters stared at Sickles' body for another moment, then without a word, trotted over and jumped on his horse.

Bob had already been working on another escape plan in case things went sideways. He decided they might ride through the fields off to the west of the road on past the place where they'd first been attacked. From there they might cross back over to the road and make good their escape.

"Come, sir. I think I know a way out. Follow me, if you please."

"All right, Bob. Lead the way."

ಐಏ〇೫〇ℬಐಏ〇೫〇ℬಐಏ〇೫〇ℬ

Megs looked out an upstairs window and watched Walters and his men riding off across the fields. She had a pretty good feeling they'd *not* be back. She came downstairs and called for Miss Abbey, who'd been sitting in the library the whole time. As soon as they'd heard the gunfire in the distance, Miss Abbey had sent all the household servants out the back door to hide in the woods.

She'd refused to go herself, telling Megs, "This is my home. I'll not be driven from it by murderous cutthroats. If they can fight through our men, then they may take me. Go now, Megs."

But Megs was every bit as stubborn as Miss Abbey, "No ma'am! For once in my life I'll *not* obey your wishes. If you stay, I stay. But …"

"But *what*, dear?"

Miss Abbey noticed Megs had her hands behind her back. She brought them out, palms upraised, and Miss Abbey saw she held two small Colt revolvers, such as the one Nathan often carried in his pocket.

"Captain done give me these before he left for Richmond and showed me how to load and fire them. He said to break them out and load them up if they was trouble, and to give you one. He said he thought you knew what to do with it."

Miss Abbey smiled. "Thank you, Megs. Yes, I do at least know which end is best avoided."

So throughout the crisis Miss Abbey sat calmly in the library, sipping tea, the loaded Colt revolver on the table beside her. Megs strained to see anything she could from out the upstairs window.

Megs now cautiously opened the front door, and the two of them stepped out. They walked over to the head of the stairs and looked down to see Sickles lying crumpled at the bottom. They noticed three field slaves walking toward them across the lawn. At first, they thought little of it. Just men returning from the woods now that the crisis was over. But then Megs' breath caught, and she grabbed Miss Abbey by the arm, "Look! Look what he carries!"

Miss Abbey looked over and saw the young man in front carried a great, long rifle over his shoulder. The three men walked up to the stairs and nodded respectfully to Miss Abbey.

"Your name is Tony, isn't it?" Miss Abbey asked the one carrying the rifle.

"Yes ma'am. That's right."

"And … do I assume correctly it was you who shot this man, scared off the enemy, and saved us from … well, from God-knows-what wickedness?"

"Well, yes ma'am. I did shoot this man. I don't know nothin' 'bout them other things, though I reckoned he weren't up to no good."

"Tony, you just saved Miss Abbey from that no-good scoundrel Mr. Walters with that-there gun," Megs said. "You done *good*, son. Real, real good!"

But despite these glowing words, and Miss Abbey's obvious pleasure and gratitude, Tony did *not* look at all pleased. Instead he stared at his feet and muttered something to himself.

Megs and Miss Abbey looked at each other in puzzlement. Maybe the young man was shaken up on account of killing a man for the first time. Nathan had told Miss Abbey how it was sometimes hard on the young soldiers the first time in battle.

Just then Jim came running up with his rifle, red faced. He stopped, placing his hands on his knees and gasping for breath. The rest of the men soon followed, all in a similar state of exhaustion.

They gathered around, looking down at Sickles' body. Jim looked over toward where Walters and his men had ridden off into the fields.

He looked up at Megs, "They gone?" he managed between gasps for breath.

"Yes, Sergeant Jim, they's gone. When Tony here put a bullet through that scoundrel Sickles, they done lost their nerve, and skedaddled outta here."

Jim looked over at Tony for the first time and noted the rifle. Tony looked up and they met eyes.

Miss Abbey looked back and forth from one to the other as the two men locked eyes. It seemed to her some secret manly communication must be going on that she could not fathom. The other men stood and watched, saying nothing. Miss Abbey guessed the men knew exactly what was being said, with no sound coming out.

Finally, Jim spoke aloud, "Well done, soldier. Shot him from the edge of yonder woods, did you?"

"Yes, sir. I'd o' come closer, but there weren't no time for it. He was about to go into the house, and I thought … well, I thought that'd be a mighty bad thing, likely. So I sits down right on the grass where I was, out yonder. Then steadied the rifle, as I seen the other soldier-men doing out on the target range. And I squeezed the trigger. Reckon I was more surprised on shootin' him than he was on bein' shot!"

Jim stepped over to where Sickles' body lay crumpled—face down at the bottom of the stairs. He gazed a moment then rolled the body over with the toe of his boot.

Jim whistled, "Dead center of the chest."

He looked over toward the woods. "Son ... I reckon that's a good ... hundred ... maybe hundred-fifty-yards. That-there's a fine shot for *any* man. Don't think I ever heard of a better'n on the first try. Nor one timelier nor more righteous. Likely avoided us a very *prickly* situation up here at the house. Yep ... well done I reckon ... very, *very* well done, son."

Tony stepped up and handed Jim the rifle, then his burlap bag of accessories.

"Thank, you kindly, son. I'll just put this back where it belongs ... 'til we might need it again."

"Thank you, sir," Tony said softly. He again stared at his feet, no longer meeting eyes with Sergeant Jim.

Miss Abbey continued to stare at these two men, still not sure what she was witnessing. It seemed to her there was much more *not* being said, than what *was*. Like, for instance, why did the young slave man have a rifle in the first place? There must be a story behind that! And why weren't the men being more effusive in their praise of him? Clearly, he'd been a hero ... *hadn't he?*

But since Sergeant Jim didn't seem inclined to talk about it just now, she decided not to pursue it for the moment. But she'd get the full story out of him later.

ཀ૭ᅠᏆᎠᏕᎥᏕᎥᏕᎥᏕ

It was a sorry-looking, bedraggled group arriving back at Walters Farm that afternoon. Margaret silently rejoiced as she watched from her window. Although her fondest wish, that Walters himself would *not* return, had not come to pass, it was apparent he'd suffered another defeat at the hands of Mr. Chambers.

She wasn't sure the exact numbers he'd left with in the morning, as it had been too dark to see clearly. But one horse now carried a dead man tied across its saddle, and another man was obviously in great pain, requiring assistance down from his horse. She was fairly sure Walters had taken more men than this, so it was very likely several others had *not* come back. The slaves would eventually get the whole story, and then she would.

For now, it was enough to know the raid had failed. She wondered if her encrypted note had made it through to Mr. Chambers, and if so, if it had helped. She prayed it was so but wondered if she would ever know the truth.

As she watched, Walters walked toward the house. Then he paused and looked up toward her window. He gave her what could only be described as an evil glare. She knew there'd be hell to pay for *someone*, maybe even her.

ʚϡʗʒʚϡʗʒʚϡʗʒ

Two days later, Nathan received a telegram from Jim. He sat with Tom and William at Mrs. Wilkerson's table, and they read it together:

> *Our long-expected guest called, bringing 18 items. He left behind 8, including one that used to be ours. Happily, we gave nothing in the exchange. Miss A. sends love and thanks for the small gift horse. Regards, J.W.*

Tom whistled. "Can't wait to hear the full story. Killed eight of eighteen, with no casualties on our side. Sent the rest packing apparently. Must have been one helluva fight."

"Oh, I doubt *that* very much," Nathan answered, "clearly Jim sprung his well-laid trap on them, just as he'd planned. Sounds like it went off like clockwork. More like a turkey-shoot than a real fight, I figure."

"Yes, I expect you're right, Captain. Still, it would've been great to see."

"Yes, you'll get no arguments from me on that one, Tom."

William nodded agreement. "I picked up on the enemy numbers, and the casualty counts, but what did he mean by 'one that used to be ours'?"

229

Nathan turned to him with a smile, "Apparently our men have managed to bag our old friend Mr. Sickles."

"Oh … that *is* good news, sir … I suppose. Though it doesn't seem … properly Christian to rejoice over someone's killing."

"When he's a nasty, sneaky bastard like Sickles it is," Nathan answered. "Don't forget, William, in the Bible there are plenty of times when God is more than happy to slay the enemies of his people, if it's called for."

"Yes, sir. I'm sure you're right about that."

Then Tom asked, "I get everything except the part about the small gift horse. You didn't really give Miss Abbey a horse for a gift, did you?"

Nathan laughed, "No … Jim's attempt at being witty. You see, I left a pair of small Colt revolvers, like the one I keep in my pocket, in Megs' care. I gave her a quick lesson on their loading and use then instructed her to keep one and give the other to Miss Abbey—in case Walters came calling. Apparently, Megs carried out my instructions, though I doubt they were ever in any serious danger."

"Oh, small horse—*pocket Colt*—now I get the joke. Very clever, Mr. Wiggins!"

"Unfortunately, seems like they weren't able to get Walters himself. Too bad …"

"Yes, but I'm sure it wasn't for lack of trying on Jim's part," Tom said with a smile. "I can picture him emptying every cylinder he had trying to get the man and then throwing the empty gun at him for good measure."

"Yes … and Walters was likely doing the same trying to get back at him. I believe there's no love lost between those two. Especially since, as I understand it, in the aftermath of the big wedding Jim made Walters and his men walk all the way back to their farm, including wading Howard Creek."

They shared a smile imagining Walters' seething anger at being forced to wade the creek in his shiny new riding boots. And Jim's fuming frustration at failing to shoot Walters, despite the lop-sided victory.

Chapter 10. The Truth that Cannot be Seen

"For we walk by faith, not by sight"
– 2 Corinthians 5:7

Saturday Feb. 24, 1861 - Richmond, Virginia:

"Gentlemen, I am sick to death of the smug, self-confidence of these abolitionists, just because they won a single election. One election … in seventy-two years of the Commonwealth! They misunderstand … true Virginians can weather any storm and won't let a minor setback deter them."

The other men in the room agreed with Henry Wise, and even if they hadn't, were unlikely to say so. He was their acknowledged leader but also a man not to be trifled with.

"We'll continue to do what we can here at the convention. But I have no great hopes for things going our way with all these damned pro-Unionists in it. Gentlemen … we must make other plans to ensure the success of our venture."

Lewis Harvie, Wise's right-hand man, asked, "You mean more of the noise and harassment in Richmond, your honor?"

"Well, yes, more of that certainly, and I intend to increase the incidents and level of violence, and the threats … but it isn't enough. We must also take *action*. Action to ensure Virginia's secession, despite what the convention decides … or how the people vote. I care little for such inconsequential matters, my friends. We are the *true* Virginians, the true heirs of Washington and Jefferson. These … northern transplants … from western Virginia … pah! Newcomers, who care little or nothing for our long-honored traditions. Well … I for one won't stand for it!"

"So … what is it you're planning, sir?"

"Not just planning, my dear Mr. Harvie … *doing!* I have already made certain … arrangements with men in position to take charge of local militia. When the time is right, they'll forcefully take charge of key federal facilities."

No one spoke for a moment, and several looked wide eyed by this admission—something he had vehemently denied before the entire convention less than a week earlier.

"Oh, don't look so shocked, gentlemen! Is it better to let these … *lesser men* … strip us of our honor … of our very way of life? To allow Lincoln and his noisome herd of abolitionists to run roughshod over our gentile and time-honored traditions? I say *no!* Not as long as there's a breath left in my body!"

No one spoke, so he continued, "But … that's not all, gentlemen. Certain key individuals have informed me the governor of South Carolina is ready to send us troops to support our secession, at a moment's notice.

"And … I have also been considering a … competing convention to this one."

"Competing, sir? What do you mean by that? How can you hold another convention without a vote of the people?"

"The people? *Pah!* You mean the same *people* who just sent a large, uncouth rabble of Black Republicans to the Secession Convention? *Those* people?! I care nothing for such chattel. I'll take one true Virginian over a thousand of such creatures!"

"But, if not through an election, then how, your honor?"

"I see this new convention not as something official, called by the government, but rather … something … *spontaneous*—true Virginians so outraged by what's happening they come together to hold their own convention and voice their own opinions! Yes … that seems good to me … we'll call it 'The Spontaneous Peoples' Convention,' and I promise you, there'll be no Goddamned abolitionists in it!"

There were smiles and nods of agreement in the room, with a general sense of approval, so Wise continued. "Then, if this current convention votes down the secession … well, let's just say … then it will be time for *us* to have our say! Come, gentlemen, let's put our heads together and figure on how to get this thing accomplished!"

They spent the next several hours planning Wise's "spontaneous" convention: where to hold it, who to invite, what to put on the agenda, what sort of mischief to cause after hours, and so on, and so on.

As the meeting was winding down, and men were gathering their belongings to depart for the evening, Wise stopped them, "Oh! I nearly forgot; I have one more item to discuss. If things do go our way, as I fully intend, it's likely there will be a general war. And when that happens, Virginia, and the South, will need all the loyal military men we have … and must prevent any *disloyal* ones from joining the North. I wish to compile a list of all the pro-Unionists who have military experience and have them watched. When the time comes, I want them forced to choose; either they are with us … or … they must be *eliminated!*"

No one responded to this, and several men gazed at their feet sheepishly. It was a time-honored tradition in Virginia, the birthplace of General Washington, to honor military veterans above all else. To speak of … *murdering* them … it was almost unthinkable, even for these men. But Henry Wise seemed undeterred by the looks he received.

"Come now, gentlemen … we must be realistic. We cannot allow experienced Virginian military officers to fight against us! Everyone knows Virginians are the finest soldiers, and we certainly don't want any as enemies if we can avoid it! And speaking of … I am particularly unhappy with this … *Chambers*. He has lied to us about his loyalties, gentlemen, tricking us into promoting him for election to the convention, then betraying us! And he has the gall to smugly stand up before the convention and play the war hero! *Pah!* I want him brought low, gentlemen. He must either return to the fold … *or else …*"

He left the last part of his sentence unsaid, but they all knew what he meant.

ဆံဆလ၆ဆံဆလ၆ဆံဆလ၆ဆံဆလ

Despite Sandy Stuart's chastisement and Henry Wise's protestations to the contrary, thuggish, lawless behavior in the streets of Richmond continued to increase. The pro-secessionists at the convention denied any involvement in the activity. They claimed it was simply a popular uprising by the people, over which they had no control, and for which they carried no blame. No one on the pro-Union side believed them for a moment, especially in light of the recent lopsided election victory. Clearly, the vast majority of Virginians did *not* want immediate secession! If there were a popular uprising, logic would say it should be *anti*-secession in nature, not pro.

But so far, they'd confined these activities to downtown Richmond and the unlucky neighborhoods immediately surrounding the central core. There had been no disruption near the capitol itself. Today, however, something had changed. Nathan and several other delegates were leaving the capitol grounds, heading up Franklin street, when they saw a group of eight or ten young men loitering on the sidewalk. They could see people ahead of them approach the group, then turn and cross the street to avoid them, before continuing on their way.

"Well, what now, do you suppose?" Sandy Stuart said, as they continued coming closer.

John Carlile, who was walking with them answered, "More of Wise's young toughs, I'd say. Looks like your dressing him down on the convention floor the other day was to little effect."

"Yes, maybe so ... but surely they wouldn't dare molest members of the convention?"

Nathan responded, "Oh ... they'd dare all right."

They continued along the sidewalk until they were within a few steps of the group of young men.

The presumed leader of the group, a great lanky fellow, taller than Nathan, with long stringy hair and nasty, yellow looking teeth leered down at them. "This here sidewalk's only for *loyal* Virginians. Ain't no northern abolitionists allowed."

"Stand aside," Sandy ordered him, "we are sitting delegates at the Special Convention, and may not be molested in the course of our personal affairs."

But the man just grinned. "We know who *you* are ... and we know who the *loyal* Virginians is. And we mean to hinder the one and help the other. All you Union lovers got to cross over to the other side o' the street if you want to pass."

"Well! If Wise thinks he can get away with this, he has another thing coming!" Sandy was now getting fired up, and his face was reddening.

"Governor Wise is a true and loyal Virginian. We'd let him pass any day ... but we don't answer to him, and he's got nothing to do with us bein' here."

Carlile laughed, "Spoken exactly as *he* told you to say it, no doubt. Probably word for word, as you doubtless haven't the wit to come up with the words yourself!"

The tough scowled at him and repeated, "Y'all traitors ain't passing this way. You got to cross over t'other side of the road if you wants to go further."

Sandy turned and looked at Nathan, Carlile, and the three delegates who'd been walking with them, "This isn't the end of the matter. I shall ask Convention President Mr. Janney to censure Wise and his cronies for this! Come, gentlemen, we are wasting our time here. We may as well cross the street and get on with our business."

He turned and stepped off the sidewalk, heading out across the cobblestoned street. The others in the small group, turned and followed. It wasn't until he was nearly halfway across Sandy glanced back and realized Nathan had *not* followed. And his two men, who'd been walking slightly behind the others, now stood next to him.

"Mr. Chambers ... aren't you coming?" The other members of Sandy's group stopped and also looked back.

But Nathan didn't immediately answer, slowly reaching into his pocket, pulling out a cigar and lighting it.

"No Mr. Stuart, I don't believe I am. I'm not of a mind to cross over to *that* side just now. My boarding house is on *this* side. If I crossed the street here ... then I'd just have to re-cross it further down. No, sir ... I believe I'll just continue in *this* direction."

"*But ...*" Sandy began. Then it occurred to him he'd been viewing Nathan as any other of the politicians, lawyers, and merchants he was used to dealing with. Nathan had acted the perfect gentleman the entire time Sandy had known him. So it was easy to see him in the same light as any of the others.

But Nathan was *not* like the others, Sandy reminded himself. Before he came back to Virginia, he was ... *something entirely different.* And his men, though neatly dressed as proper young gentlemen, appearing to be nothing out of the ordinary, were also ... likely *not* what they seemed.

The street was presently empty of any traffic. So Sandy and his group stood where they were, in the middle of the street, waiting to see what would happen. Several other men who'd crossed the street before them stopped and turned to watch. Others who'd been following behind Nathan's party also paused, safely back out of the way, wondering what would develop.

Nathan turned and looked at the young men, who glared back at him, but said nothing, daring him to make the first move.

Tom touched him on the sleeve. "Sir ... it wouldn't be proper for a gentleman of your station, representing our county in an official capacity and all, to be seen brawling in the streets."

Nathan looked at Tom with surprise. It wasn't like Tom to suggest backing down from a fight, but ... he had a valid point. "What are you suggesting then, Tom? Do you believe I should allow these ... *vermin* ... to insult me and tell me where I can and cannot walk?"

"No, sir. Not at all. What I'm suggesting is ... let William and I handle this. We're your men, sir ... that's why we're here."

He gave Nathan a serious look. Nathan saw the sincerity and determination in the young man's eyes. They'd insulted his Captain and purposely obstructed his legitimate passage. Tom could not allow *that* challenge to go unanswered.

"Very well, Tom. We'll do it your way."

"Thank you, sir. William ..."

They exchanged a hard look, and William nodded, "I'm with you, Sergeant."

They stepped in front of Nathan, between him and the miscreants. Tom walked to within two steps of their leader, who towered over him. He wasn't as tall as Big Stan, but nearly so, though not as muscular. William stepped up beside Tom.

Tom looked up at the man and spoke in a loud clear voice intended to carry—not only to the men blocking the way, but to all those watching. "You men clear out of the way *now* and let this gentleman pass. You've no legal right to block this path, and he is an important man with no time for such nonsense!"

But the big man grinned, along with his fellows, "Yeah? And what you fixin' to do 'bout it if'n we don't, little man?"

Tom gazed up at him, as if the sight was intimidating, then turned around facing the Captain. He gave William a meaningful look, winked at Nathan, and shrugged. Nathan tilted his head and raised an eyebrow but said nothing and continued puffing his cigar.

Tom stepped back and pivoted, slamming his right fist into the man's stomach.

The big man grunted in surprise and pain, doubled over, and grasped his midsection with both hands. Tom hammered his left fist into the man's right temple, *whack!* The big man crumpled to the ground onto all fours, moaning and quivering.

It had happened so fast the other men standing by hadn't reacted. The one nearest Tom, thick as an oak barrel, glanced down at his fallen comrade, then lunged at Tom, *"Hey!"*

William's right fist caught the man under the chin, snapping his head back. He stumbled sideways into his fellows. Two men caught him and lowered him to the ground. His eyes looked dazed and his legs wobbled.

The ruffians backed away from the strangers in shock. These meek-looking, smaller men, who appeared easy meat, had taken down the biggest and strongest among them in mere seconds and with seeming ease. It completely dumbfounded them and left them leaderless, confronted by the unfathomable.

Nathan stepped up between Tom and William, still smoking his cigar. The tall man, down on all fours on the sidewalk gasping for breath, blocked the way. Nathan casually reached out his boot, set it against the man's midsection, and pushed. The fellow collapsed onto his side on the ground, with a groan. His eyes appeared unfocused, and he'd vomited down the front of his shirt.

Nathan stepped over him and walked straight through the other men, who offered no further resistance.

"Come gentlemen, you've had your fun for today. I have more pressing matters to attend."

"Oh? What would that be, sir?" Tom asked, rubbing his left hand, which had gone numb from the force of his blow to the tall man's head.

"Well ... for one, I'm parched, and there's a fine bottle of whiskey back at the boarding house calling out my name."

Tom and William fell in behind him, glaring at the men around them as they passed through. The larger group of gentlemen who'd been waiting behind followed closely on their heels. All stepped over the fallen man and strode smiling through the remaining thugs. Even Sandy's little group came back across the road to make a point of passing through the hooligans.

ဆၣၢၣၤၢၣၤၢၣၤၢၣၤၢၣၤၢၣ

A man sitting at the kitchen table surprised them when they arrived back at the boarding house. He'd been waiting on them, and apparently helping himself to Nathan's whiskey.

"Well, hello Georgie! Where'd you come from ... and what are you doing with my bottle of whiskey?"

"Directly from Mountain Meadows, sir ... by way of the train, of course. And as for the whiskey, well ... I was just getting the cork loosened up for your arrival, sir!"

"Well, yes, I can see that. But ... though it is a pleasure to see you, of course, more to the point would be to ask ... *why are you here?*"

"Oh, well, as for that sir ... I was only following *orders*, sir."

"Orders? But I never ..."

"*I* told him to come, sir," Tom answered. "After we received news of Walters' abortive attack last week, I sent a letter telling Georgie to come as soon as he could."

"Oh. Why did you do that?"

"Well, sir ... what I've heard and seen in Richmond since we arrived this time has made me uneasy for your safety. Rumors of all kinds have been swirling around, about things happening or going to happen. And I ... well, to be blunt, sir, I don't trust the opposition to behave in a civil, orderly, lawful manner if things

238

don't go their way. So I figured we could use another hand, since things back at Mountain Meadows are presumably safe for now."

"Hmm ... well, after our little *adventure* walking home today, I'd say you were right on the mark there, Tom."

"Adventure?" Georgie asked.

"Apparently the opposition has seen fit to hire groups of disreputable young men to roam Richmond's streets threatening and harassing anyone who's not pro-secession. We'd heard of them but hadn't seen any until today. On the way home, we found our path blocked by one such unfriendly gathering."

"Oh? So what happened, sir?"

"What happened? One might say Tom and William gave the young toughs a lesson in manners they'll not soon forget ... if they can remember it at all given their aching heads! Suffice to say it was not the genteel, intellectual lessons William learned in his college classrooms. Rather the more straight-forward Texas Army style."

"Ah! *Damn!* Sorry I didn't get here a day earlier, so's I could o' got in on some of that 'lesson teaching' myself! Sounds like a good time was had by all ... 'cept maybe the students!"

They shared a laugh.

"Speaking of missing out on a bit of good fun, we were all sorry to have missed your little 'turkey shoot' back home," Tom said.

"Turkey shoot? Oh, you mean Mr. Walters' attack. Well ... it turned out okay, and I can see from the bare facts one might reckon it went all our way, but ..."

"*But?*" Nathan suddenly had a sinking feeling his home had *not* been as safe as he'd assumed.

"Well, Captain, let's just say it didn't come off exactly as planned. Have a seat, sir, you too Sergeant Clark, William. Pour yourselves a drink, and I'll tell the whole thing from the beginning."

For the next hour Georgie gave them the details of that eventful day. They stopped him from time to time to ask questions about various details and finer points, but mostly just listened as he told the tale. As Georgie described them running after Walters on foot, fearful for Miss Abbey's safety, Nathan stood up from the table and paced anxiously around the small kitchen.

Georgie finished his story at the point right after Tony handed the Governor's Rifle to Sergeant Jim.

Georgie reached out and took a drink. He'd been so caught up in telling the tale he'd forgotten to take a sip, and now his throat was parched.

"That was a close thing ... much too close for my comfort. Now I almost regret not staying home to keep an eye on things," Nathan said, a worried expression creasing his brow.

"Well, please don't be too hard on Sergeant Jim, sir. He took charge and rallied the troops in what looked like a terrible-bad, desperate fix. We was outnumbered nearly three to one, and had totally lost the element of surprise, having no time to set a trap for 'em.

"At that point all we had left was manly courage, old-fashioned fighting spirit, and Sergeant Jim's quick thinking. And it would've carried the day, too, if'n it hadn't been for them retreating in a direction we'd never expected. Anybody'd o' figured when caught exposed in a deadly cross-fire, near half their men already shot full o' holes, they'd turn and run for home. We couldn't hardly believe it when we saw them ride off the *other* way, toward the Big House."

"Hmm ... I agree, Georgie. My apologies ... in my fear and anxiety for Miss Abbey, Megs, and the others I misspoke. If I'd been there, it'd likely made little difference. I wouldn't have done anything differently from what Jim did, and likely wouldn't have done nearly as well."

"Thank you, sir. But I'll tell you, we was all sure wishing you *were* there that day. That goes for Tom and William as well. But such as we were, we did what we could."

"And a damned fine job you did, too, Georgie. My heartfelt thanks for defending my home at risk of your own life. I shall *not* forget it.

"But tell me ... what did Sergeant Jim do about Tony after?"

"Oh, well ... I could tell he was in a great quandary about that, sir. On the one hand, the man deserted his post, intending to run away, which left our defenses down at the worst possible time. Walters nearly caught us with our pants down. But then, just as the day looked darkest, he returned, stepped up, and shot old Sickles dead through the heart at more'n a hundred paces, even as the scoundrel was fixin' to go into the house and grab Miss Abbey.

"Finally, after puzzling on it several hours, Sergeant Jim says to us, 'Gents, I know I been left in charge, so it's my decision as to what should be done about the lad. But I ain't got the wisdom o' old King Solomon, and I'll be damned if I can figure what to do. I ain't never seen someone do something so lowdown, dishonorable, and despicable one minute, then turn around and do something so admirable, courageous, and heroic the next! What should you do with such a man?'

"So in the end he decided to do nothing at all and leave it for you to decide on once you get back to home, sir."

"Hmm … wise man. Clearly the Army has taught him well; when in doubt, let someone else deal with an impossible decision," Nathan said with a wry smile.

"Anyway, sir, a few days after Sergeant Jim sent off his telegram to you, we receives a letter back from Sergeant Clark giving me my new marching orders. Though a curious letter it was …"

Tom smiled knowingly but said nothing.

"The first part was plain enough. It was addressed to me from Sergeant Clark, and it said, 'Georgie, take this letter to Miss Abbey. She has the key.' The rest was three full pages filled with letters, all scrambled up like a broken egg. I couldn't make heads, nor tales of it, and couldn't figure what he meant by Miss Abbey having a key. *What good is a key for reading a letter*, I was wondering."

Nathan looked at Tom, and they shared a smile, "Ah … good idea, Tom."

"So not knowing what else to do, I went to Miss Abbey as instructed. She took one look at the letter, and squealed with delight, like a schoolgirl just handed a puppy! Well, sir, she goes over to the desk, takes out paper and pen, and starts counting and writing. I had no idea what she was doing, so I sat down and stared wide eyed in wonder as she worked. About an hour later she handed me my instructions all written out as neat as you please. I must o' had a look of amazement on my face, because she started laughing, in that fine, musical way she has, if you know what I mean, Captain, sir. Meaning no disrespect.

"So here I am, and have brought the extra horses, traveling gear, supplies and clothing, and all the other things Sergeant Clark instructed."

"Other things?" Nathan raised an eyebrow, looking over at Tom.

"Oh, yes, sir! I put all them things upstairs already, before you got here. An extra pistol and a rifle for each man, and plenty of powder and lead."

"You can never be too careful, sir!" Tom responded with a shrug.

Nathan smiled, "Tom, sometimes it amazes me how much we think alike. Well done. But what of the traveling gear? I was considering riding back through Lynchburg to check on Rosa's momma, but I hadn't decided yet, so hadn't mentioned it. How did you come up with the idea?"

"Well, sir, I hadn't considered Rosa's situation, I must admit. Though now you mention it, it seems a fine idea. No, I was more concerned about … well … I'd started worrying; what if things were to really come unraveled here in Richmond? We could find ourselves unwelcome guests in the city and might want a way to slip off quietly rather than going the expected way by train."

"Good thought, Tom, though I really don't expect it to come to that. But if you'd have told me a week ago we'd be molested by thugs in broad daylight in downtown Richmond, I wouldn't have believed *that* either. These are very strange times we're living in, and you can't be too careful. Better safe than sorry, I suppose. Well done, Tom. And … thank you for giving Miss Abbey such joy with your letter. Although that wasn't the main purpose, I'm sure you were aware it would be one result."

"Never mention it, sir. It seemed the right thing to do, and if it also brought her a little pleasure, so much the better."

William chimed in for the first time, "Georgie … I have to ask; how is Stan doing now you've had your battle? We had all conjectured a good fight was what he needed to bring him out of the doldrums."

"Oh, yes, he's back to his old self now, joking and cracking wise with Sergeant Jim for the first time since the dog ran off. It's surprising how much of a relief it is to the rest of us. I guess having Big Stan down so low was dragging the rest of us down as well. That and the stress of not knowing when Walters would make his move. Yep, things are now much happier all around back at Mountain Meadows, and everyone is in a much better humor."

"Thanks, Georgie, that's a big relief. Oh! And speaking of humor … I had nearly forgotten," William reached inside his jacket and pulled out a folded newspaper. "I reckoned you'd all find this story I read in the newspaper today amusing. Especially you, Georgie."

He unfolded the newspaper and scanned through it until he found the article he was searching for. He folded it back and laid it out on the table.

"The headline reads, 'Tragic Hunting Accident in Western Virginia Mountains,' and the article goes on to say:"

> Mr. Elijah Walters, of Greenbrier County, has been obligated to report, with great sorrow and heavy heart, the loss of nine of his employees in a tragic accident in the mountains of western Virginia. The men were on a hunting expedition in the hills to the east of Mr. Walters' estate near Lewisburg, Virginia, when they were struck by an avalanche of snow, and buried under a veritable mountain of same. Two men were rescued, but suffered serious injuries, of which one later died at Mr. Walters' home. The remaining eight bodies could not be recovered due to the steepness of the terrain, the depth of the snow, and the continuing threat of further dangerous conditions in the region. A memorial service will be held to honor the fallen, at the Episcopal Methodist Church, Lewisburg on Sunday next. God rest their souls.

Georgie shook his head and chuckled, "That's the first time I ever heard of a gun fight called a 'hunting accident'! I guess they was *hunting* us and got themselves killed by *accidentally* gettin' in the way o' our bullets!"

They shared a laugh and shook their heads at the absurdity of it. They did have to hand it to Walters; he *had* come up with a *very* creative excuse for why he'd suddenly lost so many men, whose bodies he could never recover.

ဧသၢၣသၢၣသၢၣသၢၣသၢၣ

Evelyn's mother, Harriet, had become an unwitting partner in the game she was playing with Mr. and Mrs. Hughes. Evelyn had looked through the "target" list and decided she'd start with someone she already knew. His name was Peter Stevens, presently a member of the Virginia House of Delegates, heir to a large estate, and an elected representative to the special Secession Convention. And more important, a committed member of the Slave Power, as was his father.

He was also a West Point graduate, who'd resigned his commission as a first lieutenant in the Army four years ago after suffering an extended illness. From what Evelyn could tell, he had fully recovered from whatever had ailed him.

He was a little older than Evelyn, in his late twenties, and his long blond hair, along with rugged good looks, drew plenty of attention from the young ladies. The Hugheses figured him for either a mid-level government official or a colonel in the Southern Army if the secession happened. He wasn't the highest-ranking person on their list, but they were already acquainted and he'd previously shown interest in her. So it seemed a relatively easy starting point. Better learn to walk before trying to run, she'd decided. If nothing else, it'd be good practice.

So she mentioned to Harriet her possible interest in the man, and her mother happily took the bait, immediately setting to work making the necessary arrangements. Evelyn felt more than a little guilt for involving her momma unknowingly in the scheme in such a way. But she knew Harriet would never approve of her new activities, and it would seem suspicious if she were to suddenly start making her own arrangements in these matters.

It was now Tuesday morning, and Mr. Stevens had agreed to accompany her to a ball the next Saturday. A wealthy Richmond family with an eligible young daughter close to Evelyn's own age was hosting the event. The family was known for being apolitical, so they expected that people from both sides of the secession divide might attend. It could make for a raucous function, especially if the drinks were flowing freely, and the gentlemen got to talking politics.

Harriet had arranged everything, so Evelyn was a little surprised when a courier came to the house with an invitation for tea with Angeline Hughes. She'd walked the half-dozen blocks to the Hughes mansion, and now stood on the veranda, knocking on the door.

The same elderly black butler who'd been there each time she'd called greeted her. *A freeman, not a slave*, she reminded herself, and smiled.

"Good morning, Sam."

"Good morning, Miss Evelyn. Won't you please come in, Miss? The mistress is expecting you."

"Thank you, Sam."

She entered the house, stepping into the grand foyer. No matter how many times she saw it, it still impressed her and left her awestruck. Such grandeur and elegance! Sam led her to the library where, to her surprise, both Mr. and Mrs. Hughes awaited her. They stood as she entered, greeting her warmly.

After they'd exchanged the usual pleasantries, Evelyn turned to Mr. Hughes, and asked, "To what do I owe the honor, Mr. Hughes?"

"Please, have a seat, my dear. I wanted to speak with you myself, before you attend the event at the Richardson's house on Saturday."

"Oh? What is it you wish to tell me, Jonathan?"

They sat, and he gazed steadily into her eyes before continuing.

245

"Evelyn ... I have it on good authority ... your friend, Mr. Nathaniel Chambers, has also been invited to this event. And he has signified his intention to attend."

"Oh!"

She looked at her feet, not making eye contact with Jonathan while she digested this news.

"That ... will make things ... *difficult* for me," she said.

This time Angeline responded, "We assumed so ... which is why we wanted to tell you in person. If you want to make your excuses and wait for another event, it will be understandable."

"No ... I am eager to get started ... the longer I wait and only ... *think* about it, the harder it will be. But ... I should like to somehow tell Mr. Chambers what I'm doing so he won't believe ... well, *you know.*"

Angeline and Jonathan shared a look, then turned back toward her, and he continued, "We ... wouldn't advise it, Evelyn. You see, we have also heard ... our adversaries are looking ahead toward a possible war, even as we are. And they're targeting men who might *not* be loyal to their cause ... especially *military* men. We have information Mr. Chambers has been specifically mentioned by our enemies. It seems he has attracted the particular ire of Mr. Wise, who believes he has betrayed their cause, being a slave owner who's promoting the pro-Union cause. To be plain, Miss Evelyn, we now know Nathan Chambers is being watched by the enemy."

"Watched? What does *that* mean? *Why* do they watch him? What do they seek to gain by it?"

Again, Jonathan did not immediately answer, and looked over at Angeline before responding.

"Miss Evelyn, you must promise to let me handle this matter, before I speak further. Will you trust me on this, Evelyn?"

"Yes ... of course, Jonathan. At this point, it wouldn't be too great an exaggeration to say I am trusting you with my life."

"Good. Then I'll tell you what I know. It comes down to this: if the secession happens, and Mr. Chambers refuses to join with them to fight for Virginia ... they mean to murder him if they can!"

"Oh!" she put her hand to her mouth to cover her shock, and tears began to well in her eyes. "Oh *no* … surely not *that?*! Oh no, *no … it can't be …*" she finished in a whisper, her voice choking with emotion.

"Yes, I'm afraid so. But here's where you need to trust me, Evelyn. For starters, consider the fact I'm privy to the information I have just shared with you …"

"Yes … it means … it means you have someone … someone like me … in Mr. Wise's camp. It means you know what he plans to do almost as soon as he does."

"Yes, that's right. So believe me when I tell you … we also intend to watch Mr. Chambers, and to keep him safe if trouble comes. So have no fear. We will take care of him like his own private guardian angels, if worse comes to worst."

"Well, that makes me feel a *little* better, but still, it seems to me he needs to be told."

"Yes … it may be that the time will come when we will tell him of the threat … but not yet. Sometimes … well, sometimes it's better people don't know about such things too soon. It can cause them to change their behavior and give away the fact they know something they shouldn't. That could make guarding for him more difficult. And, he may assume he can look after himself better and may not trust us to do so."

"Yes … I can see Nathan thinking *that*, all right. He trusts his own men to take care of him. He'd be suspicious of your help."

"Exactly. Fortunately, we have time to wait and see what happens. Anyway … the *other* reason the enemy is watching him is … they wish to gather a list of people he associates with here in Richmond. One can easily imagine how they intend to use such information if things go south."

"So … you're saying, not only can't I tell Nathan what I'm up to … but I must appear … *unfriendly* with him? Oh … I don't know … I don't know if I can do that … I … that would be … *painful*, and … *difficult* … for both of us, I think."

Jonathan didn't respond but nodded.

"You truly love this man, don't you dear?" Angeline asked.

"Yes … I *think* so …" she answered, again looking at her shoes.

"Then perhaps you should beg off from this function, my dear. There will be others."

"But what if he is also at the next, and the next, and the one after that? Shall I never go out again, never do for you what I have said I would do, for fear of running into him?"

Angeline didn't respond, waiting for Evelyn to answer her own questions in her own time.

"No ... I must face him sometime. But I can't hurt him in this way, I *won't* do it! I must figure a way to let him know what I'm doing isn't *real*, without giving him any information that might endanger our activities."

Jonathan and Angeline again exchanged a concerned look. Jonathan turned back to Evelyn and sighed. "Very well, Evelyn. We will trust you to handle this. But you must use the utmost discretion ... so much is at stake. You are now known to associate with us, so if you fall under suspicion, so will we. Everything we've worked for could come undone. Do you understand? No one must ever see you two together in a friendly way and never assume he's not being watched. Even the slaves should not be trusted. Many will bring information to their masters to curry favor, or out of fear, even to the detriment of their own people, I'm sorry to say.

If possible, you must never meet in person, but only correspond through a trusted third-party, or by an innocuous, indecipherable written message."

"I understand. I will give it a great deal of thought before I act, and I will be careful. You asked me earlier if I trusted you ... now you must trust me."

Angeline answered this time, "We *do* trust you, Evelyn. More than you know. You're one of the few people in this enterprise we've spoken to in person. Most of the people in this 'business' working for us don't even know who we are, or where we live. But we recognized early on you were someone special, someone we could bring into our circle of confidence. We know you will not betray our trust."

"Oh ... thank you, Angeline, Jonathan ... of course I never will. Never in life!"

In the weeks leading up to the new president's inauguration, a brewing national crisis pre-occupied the convention delegates. A small U.S. Army fortress on a tiny rock, with a name nobody including Nathan had ever heard of, was suddenly on everyone's lips. Fort Sumter, occupied by a small garrison of soldiers commanded by U.S. Army Major Robert Anderson, was located in the harbor of Charleston, South Carolina—the very hotbed and epicenter of secessionism. The governor of South Carolina had demanded President Buchanan evacuate the fort, but he had refused, and had unsuccessfully tried to re-supply the fort's defenders. The fort was now cut off from all aid by the federal government.

With the president-elect ready to take office in a few weeks, the question on everyone's mind was what Lincoln would do about Fort Sumter.

Ironically, the pro-Union members were hoping for an evacuation to avoid a military crisis that might trigger a full-scale war, and push Virginia into secession. And just as ironically, the pro-secession forces were praying Lincoln would attempt to re-supply the fort and instigate an armed confrontation.

Nathan felt torn. On the one hand, Sandy Stuart and George Summers were adamant the new president must *not* make any move to trigger a clash of arms. They reasoned the fort had no military necessity, so evacuation was the only sensible course, and the course that would keep Virginia from joining the secessionists.

Nathan wasn't so sure. The military side of him believed it was never wise to show weakness before the enemy. If he were Lincoln, what would he do? He was pretty sure he knew the answer.

Henry Wise, on the other hand, was almost giddy about the prospect of an armed confrontation over the fort, and said so to anyone who would listen. He was convinced Lincoln would send in the fleet the first chance he got.

But toward the end of the week, in a private meeting of the pro-Union leadership, George Summers told them he had received assurances from Henry Seward himself; the fort *would* be evacuated.

"Henry Seward?" Nathan asked.

"William Henry Seward. Next to Mr. Lincoln, he is the leading Republican. He's said to be actively assisting the president-elect in building his new cabinet, and it's assumed he'll have a leadership role. Mr. Seward, unlike Mr. Lincoln, is an experienced Washington politician, and probably the most influential person in that city at this moment. It must be assumed he is in the know about any plans the new president is making, and any decisions he intends to make."

"Ah! Well, then. It seems we have nothing to fear about Fort Sumter, after all."

"I'm not convinced," John Brown Baldwin said. "Until we hear from the president himself ... we won't truly know."

"I disagree, John," George answered. "I've known Henry Seward a very long time and have always found him most honorable and trustworthy. If he says it is so, I for one, believe him."

"Come, gentlemen," Sandy Stuart said, "let's trust in what George is telling us, and move forward on that assumption. The alternative is ... well, is something we will find extremely difficult to counter."

"I don't know," Nathan said, "I still think we should do everything in our power to sway delegates to the unconditional camp. No matter what your Mr. Seward says, I still can't believe any president would sit on his hands and do nothing when his nation is threatened. Especially when his soldiers are besieged in their own forts."

ဆၯၩၒၮၒဆၯၩၒၮၒဆၯၩၒၮၒ

Saturday Mar. 2, 1861 - Richmond, Virginia:

Nathan and Tom sat at a small table in one corner of a large, elegant ball room in an elegant mansion in the wealthiest neighborhood in Virginia. In an alcove to one side were musicians, playing a minuet. Out on the brightly shining hardwood dance floor, under the light of an immense, spectacular crystal chandelier, couples moved neatly to the rhythm of the music.

On the side opposite them they saw young ladies dressed to the nines, sitting on intricately carved and padded benches, chatting with each other, or watching the couples out on the floor. Occasionally a young gentleman would come over, speak briefly to one of the young ladies, and hold out his hand and lead her to the dance floor.

Nathan observed the spectacle in a detached manner, slowly sipping a glass of whiskey. He'd commandeered a bottle from the butler via a small gratuity shortly after their arrival. "I don't know why I let you talk me into this, Tom. I'm feeling like a fish out of water. The only formal dances I've ever been to have been for officers and their wives. At those gatherings everyone knows their rank and place, who they can talk to and who they can't, and what the topic ought to be when they do.

"One could dance with the young daughter of a colonel or general only by invitation, and then under his watchful eyes the entire time. This ... *Southern ball* ... it is ... chaotic to my eyes. I'm unclear how I'm expected to behave. Am I supposed to approach the young ladies and ask them to dance? It seems ... ludicrous, somehow, with all that's going on. And most of them seem like ... silly *little girls* to me, after all we've seen and done out West."

"Oh, come now, sir. Even though the world may be falling apart all around us, it doesn't mean one shouldn't still have a little fun. All the ladies at this ball are of age. They wouldn't be here if their parents weren't ready to see them married off. And, I've noted how they've eyed you since our arrival. Any one of them would be thrilled if you paid them even the slightest attention."

"Well, I don't intend to, so they'll just have to suffer going without. Come, Tom, let's take this bottle out on the veranda and have a smoke. Then—"

Tom looked up at Nathan, wondering why he'd paused in mid-sentence. His expression had changed from mild annoyance to shocked surprise, as he stared out across the room.

"What is it, sir?"

"It's … it's *her*, Tom. She's here."

"Her? *Oh!* Miss Evelyn …"

Tom waited to see what Nathan would do. Would he jump up and go talk with her, or would he head for the door? Both options seemed equally likely in his mind.

After several minutes went by, Tom finally couldn't stand the waiting any longer, "What … what are you going to do, sir?"

"*Do*, Tom? I will *do* nothing. It appears she is escorted by a … young gentleman. And if I'm not mistaken, he is … yes … he is one of our *adversaries*. Peter Stevens … a former Army officer, and one of Wise's protégés."

Nathan had a scowl on his face, a dark expression Tom knew all too well. It often preceded a violent outburst, if not ruthlessly suppressed.

"Come, Tom. I've had enough of this farce. Let's go find someplace quiet to drink our whiskey and smoke our cigars. I'm suddenly not in a particularly … *festive* mood."

"Of course, sir," Tom stood, but couldn't resist a glance across the room for a glimpse of Evelyn with her escort. He suffered a shock; they were approaching the table, clearly intending to speak with Nathan.

Nathan had already stood from the table, put on his hat, and turned toward the door, when Tom hissed, "Captain … *she* comes!"

Nathan stopped and turned slowly around. He now presented a calm demeanor, to Tom's surprise. But Tom knew Nathan was displaying this pacific expression through great force of will.

"Miss Evelyn … it's such a … pleasant surprise to see you," he said with a slight bow. She held out her hand and curtseyed. He took it and kissed it. Being this close to her, smelling her sweet perfume, kissing her bare hand after all the endless nights dreaming of her—it was like a bolt of lightning flashing through him. His heart threatened to burst in his chest.

She wore a blue velvet gown with black trim and a low-cut V in front. And on her head she'd arranged an intricate black bow with blue lace from which her lovely golden hair hung down in long curls.

And the change in her face from the last time he'd seen her was startling. When she'd departed Mountain Meadows the previous summer, she'd been so emotionally distraught she could barely speak, her body racked by uncontrollable sobbing, her eyes puffy and red from crying.

The woman he looked at now was entirely different— confident, composed, and … if not entirely happy, something close to it. Gazing at her lovely face and admiring the difference, he couldn't help but smile. She returned his smile with an utterly dazzling one of her own. The sight of it nearly took his breath away and made his heart race in his chest. He had to admit she looked … *magnificent!*

Nathan realized in that moment she was the most beautiful vision he'd ever seen. How could he possibly live without … *that?* He took a deep breath, desperate to control his emotions, reminding himself she was presently standing next to a young man who was obviously her escort. Never had he suffered such mixed emotions … typically either he loved people, or despised them, or felt nothing at all, never anything like this …

"Mr. Chambers, it is such a *pleasure* to see you again, sir. Mr. Clark, it is good to see you as well. Have you gentlemen met Mr. Stevens?" she said, gesturing toward her escort.

"Yes, we've met. Stevens …" Nathan held out his hand politely, and Stevens shook it firmly, giving Nathan an ironic grin. Tom reached out and shook hands with Stevens as well. Stevens wore a dark formal suit, nearly identical to the one Nathan wore. He had a young, vigorous appearance, augmented by long, blond hair and neatly trimmed beard. Nathan assumed the women found him handsome, though he was gratified to note the man was several inches shorter than himself and not nearly so broad in the shoulders. Not that he was making comparisons …

"Miss Evelyn … how is it you and Mr. Chambers are acquainted, if you don't mind my asking?"

"Oh! Didn't I say? Mr. Chambers' momma and mine are old and dear friends from the time when Mr. Chambers' momma lived here in Richmond. Isn't that so, sir? Mr. Chambers is … an old friend of the family."

Nathan gave her a bland expression, and nodded, but said nothing. The truth was he could think of nothing to say. Was that all he was to her now? "An old friend?" He felt such conflicting emotions he didn't trust himself to speak. Only one feeling seemed clear and simple at that moment ... a very strong urge to strangle Stevens with his bare hands right there on the spot!

But finally, he decided it would be easiest to just go along with whatever game Evelyn was playing, "Well, I was just preparing to retire for the evening. It was ... good to see you again, Miss Evelyn. Please do give my regards to your Momma, Miss Harriet. Stevens ..." he tipped his hat and turned to leave.

But Evelyn had an odd, unreadable look on her face. She suddenly stepped forward and grasped his arm, looking him hard in the eyes. Again, he experienced that shocking thrill, despite everything ... gazing intently into those dazzling, blue eyes. "Oh, Mr. Chambers, please *take my love* ... to your dear Momma, Miss Abbey."

And then she stepped back. Nathan's head was swimming. Did she linger on the word *love*? And wasn't it an odd way to say it, "*Take* my love?" Wouldn't one normally say, "*Give* my love?" Or was he imagining things he wanted to hear?

He gazed at her for another moment, and Tom could see him struggling mightily with his emotions. He tipped his hat to her, turned and strode for the door without a backward glance. Tom looked over at Evelyn, who stared steadily back at him. He thought it a meaningful look, but it was beyond his ability to decipher that meaning. So he too tipped his hat to her and to Stevens, turned and headed for the door, following in his Captain's wake.

As they walked, Nathan drank whiskey straight from the bottle he'd grabbed off the table. Between swigs he puffed a cigar like it was the last one on Earth. But when they were about halfway home, he stopped and turned to Tom.

"*What the hell* was that about? Damn it, Tom, if she's not the most confusing, exasperating ... *magnificently beautiful* woman God ever put on this Earth, I don't know who is! Damn it, she leaves my head spinning! There she is standing next to another man, telling him I am nothing but 'an old family friend.' And at the same time her eyes are telling me ... *something completely different!* And then she reaches out to touch me, looks in my eyes, and says the word *'love'* in a way no man can possibly mistake. What ... the ... *hell*, Tom?!"

"Sorry, sir. I wish I knew. I'm afraid women are as much a mystery to me, so I'm not a great deal of help to you."

"Damn it, Tom! I sure as hell can't go back to the boarding house like *this!* I'm all wound up like Big Stan itching for a fight. Let's go find a saloon down on the waterfront somewhere and see if I can't get some sailor to insult me."

Tom looked him in the eye and slowly shook his head. "You know I enjoy a good fight as much as the next man, sir, but ..."

"Yes, yes ... don't say it. I *know*—it's a really *bad* idea. But still ... where are Wise's damned street thugs when one could really *use* them?"

He reached into his vest pocket for a match to light another cigar. "What the ...? What's this?" he pulled a small, folded piece of paper from his pocket. "What in the seven hells ...?"

He unfolded the paper and could see writing on one side. There was a gas streetlamp about halfway down the block, so he strode over to it and held the paper out in the light. He gazed at it for several minutes before handing it to Tom.

Tom read:

> *All is not as it seems. Trust not your eyes, but rather your heart. - E.*

"What does it mean, Captain?"

"How the hell do I know, Tom? 'E' is clearly Evelyn. She must have slipped it into my pocket when she reached out to grab my arm. *'Trust not your eyes ... rather your heart ...'* well, right now my eyes are entirely befuddled, and my heart feels like it's been kicked by a mule. I have more than half a mind to march right back there and ask her what it means straight out!"

"I can understand the desire, but it seems to me she went to a lot of trouble to give you that message secretly. Which implies she has a good reason for ... I don't know ... for not revealing her true feelings, maybe? 'All is not as it seems' reminds me of the episode with Adilida and her cousin; we believed we knew what we were seeing, but later it turned out to be something entirely different. Think about it, sir ... she obviously gave this a good deal of consideration, writing it out ahead of time, folding it neatly and concealing it on her person. Which means ..."

"She *knew* I would be there!"

"Yes, clearly. And she was also determined to speak with you ... as soon as we got up to leave, she came straight to our table."

"True ..."

"And ... you said her words didn't match the expression on her face, and I felt something of the same, though I don't know her as well as you do."

"Humph! I'm beginning to think I don't know her at all! Still ... what you're saying makes sense. But *why*, is the bigger question. What is she up to that she doesn't want people to know she has feelings for me, if she really does? Is she fearing I'll frighten off other suitors?"

"That would be the obvious answer, but from what I've seen and heard, women usually *like* men to compete for them, even fight over them. If that's true, then she should be more inclined to make the other men envious of you, rather than to turn the cold shoulder to you."

"True ... what then? I'm sure I've made some bad enemies since we've been in Richmond—Henry Wise for sure, which implies that Stevens fellow as well. But she'd have nothing to fear from that. Such men, as despicable as they might behave toward you and I, would never harm an upper-class lady like her. Unless she has a liking for this Stevens and is afraid he'd take it badly if she appears too kindly disposed toward me?"

"Could be, I suppose, sir. But while you were understandably distracted ... by the suddenness of the moment, the mixed emotions, and whatnot I was able to observe the whole thing a little more ... *objectively*."

"Oh? And what did you observe?"

"I may be wrong, but she did *not* appear especially enamored of Stevens. In fact, I would go so far as to say she doesn't even particularly *like* the man. If I had to hazard a guess, I would say it was something Miss Harriet arranged, and Evelyn was going along with it to placate her mother. And ... I'm guessing she's friends with the Richardsons' daughter who told her you would be in attendance. She wrote the note, so you'd know she wasn't serious about Stevens."

"Hmm ... that *could* be a plausible explanation. When we first arrived at the function and were introduced to the Richardson girl, it occurred to me she and Evelyn were of a similar age. I wondered if they might be acquainted."

"Well, if nothing else you're making me feel better, Tom, for which I'm much obliged."

He took another long drag on the cigar, letting it out slowly as he gazed up into the dark sky. When he looked at Tom again, his expression had softened.

"What is a man supposed to make of all this, Tom?"

"I'm sure I don't know, Captain. But I'll be happy to sit here on this bench and think on it with you ... if you'll share that bottle."

"What? Oh, sorry, Tom. I forgot I was holding it. Here, you take it."

"Come ... sit, sir. Let's finish this bottle, and a few more cigars. And see if we can't figure this thing out ... and all the rest of the world's problems while we're at it."

"All right, Tom. That seems as good a plan as any."

☙❧♋♌☙❧♋♌☙❧♋♌

Harriet was sitting up reading a book under the light of an oil lamp when Evelyn arrived home. One nice thing about an escort by a well-to-do young gentleman was she got to ride in an elegant carriage all the way there and back. Miss Harriet wouldn't have to spend the money to hire one out and didn't have to come along for the ride.

"How's the book, Momma?"

"Interesting. It's a new one by Dickens called *A Tale of Two Cities.*"

"Ah ... yes ... '*It was the best of times, it was the worst of times ...*'"

"You've read it? I wasn't aware ..."

"Oh no, only *started* it ... but found myself too distracted, so never finished. Perhaps one day I shall try again."

"So ... how was *your* evening? Did you find Mr. Stevens to your liking?"

"It was ... also *interesting*, Momma. And as for Mr. Stevens, he is a pleasant enough gentleman ..."

She suddenly smiled.

"What is it, Evelyn?"

"Oh ... concerning Mr. Stevens; I was just thinking ... I'm not sure how I feel about a man who believes I am surely the *second* most beautiful person in the world *after himself!*"

She giggled, and Harriet smiled. Harriet had met Stevens, and she had to agree he was a man who was entirely too fond of his own good looks.

Evelyn removed her hairpiece, shook her hair free, and sat in the chair across from Harriet. She sat quietly a few moments, and Harriet noticed she had a thoughtful, far-away expression.

"What is it you're *not* telling me, dear?"

Evelyn looked at her and sighed. "*He* was there, Momma."

"He?"

"Nathan."

"*Oh!* I see. And ... did you speak with him? That must have been ... *awkward*, I'd imagine."

"Yes ... very much so. Especially for him, I'm afraid. We spoke only briefly, just as he was departing ... on my account, I'm sure. I don't imagine he much enjoyed seeing me escorted by another man."

"No ... I should think *not!* A man like *that!* I'm surprised it didn't come to blows."

"Oh ... I'm pretty sure it nearly did. But Mr. Chambers controlled himself admirably," she smiled, with a wistful expression.

"And how did *you* feel about it ... about seeing *him* again?"

"It felt … it felt just the same as before … he looked … *divine*, and when he briefly smiled at me, I thought my heart would leap from my chest. He still has those dark, intense eyes—like he's looking deep down inside me … down into my heart … into my very soul, maybe—if that's not too trite to say. *Oh Momma*, no other man ever makes me feel like *that!*"

"Then … what on *Earth* is the matter with you, girl? Why aren't we busily planning a wedding, instead of sitting here talking about how you're still in love with this man? I swear, Evelyn, sometimes you are even more exasperating and confounding than your Daddy *ever* was! What are you thinking?"

But Evelyn put her head in her hands, and stared at her shoes, "I wish I knew, Momma. I sure do wish I knew."

A few minutes later Evelyn went off to her room for the evening, but the book had caught Harriet's interest, so she stayed up reading a while longer.

When she finally blew out the lamp and headed for bed, she heard a noise coming from Evelyn's room, though no light shone out from beneath the door. She leaned her head close to listen and heard the unmistakable sound of sobbing. There was a part of her that wanted to comfort the girl. But it was not her way. The girl needed to straighten out her own mind. After that, all would be well. She let out a heavy sigh, shook her head in bewilderment, and continued down the hallway to her own room.

Chapter 11. The Edge of the Abyss

"I implore, gentlemen …
whether from the South or the North …
to pause at the edge of the precipice,
before the fearful and dangerous leap be taken
into the yawning abyss below,
from which none who ever take it
shall return in safety."
– Henry Clay, 1850

Monday, Mar. 4, 1861, Washington, D.C.:

The week before the new president's inauguration had been filled with unsettling news, endless rumors, and a growing sense of unease. This was especially so among Nathan and his allies at the convention.

First, congress failed to pass the seven-part constitutional amendment proposed by the Peace Conference. Ironically, the Slave Power and the radical Republican abolitionists combined to kill the potential compromise. Then, congress turned around and passed a proposed constitutional amendment that declared slavery could not be interfered with by the federal government in states where it already existed. If ratified by the states, this would become the Thirteenth Amendment. But everyone agreed it was probably not enough to sway the seceding states from their chosen course. This seemed to be confirmed when days later Texas was admitted as the seventh state in the newly formed Confederate States of America, or C.S.A. They chose Montgomery, Alabama as their capital.

Rumors ran rampant of an imminent invasion of Washington city by forces of the C.S.A. to prevent or disrupt Lincoln's inauguration. In response, President Buchanan ordered General Winfield Scott to call up the troops to protect the capital.

Newspapers reported armed soldiers patrolling the streets of the city, and cannons positioned on the high ground of Capitol Hill.

"And what news of Fort Sumter, Sandy?" Nathan asked, as they sat at Mrs. Wilkerson's kitchen table sipping whiskey after a long day at the convention.

"Well … still no news of an evacuation, but George Summers insists Mr. Seward has promised it will happen shortly after Lincoln takes office."

"Hmm …"

"You're still skeptical, I see."

"I won't deny it, Sandy. Everything I've heard and read about Lincoln tells me he has a stout backbone. I still can't picture the man giving in on this fort. Even if holding it is militarily untenable, I believe he must try … it's the *principle* of the thing. If he backs down now, he will have been the first to blink, and his enemies will think him easy game. No … I still can't see it happening, Sandy, I'm sorry. I just pray whatever happens, our fellow delegates will see reason and not overreact to it."

"Agreed, though I fear if Lincoln is seen as instigating a military conflict it will go badly for our side here in Virginia. Well, I guess we shall just have to wait and see, Nathan."

"Yes, that we will, Sandy."

ಬಿಞಜರಿಞಜಿಬಿಞಜರಿಞಜಬಿಞಜರಿ

Despite the unrest, the sixteenth president was sworn in without a hitch. Lincoln and President Buchanan rode down Pennsylvania Avenue from the White House to the Capitol Building in an open carriage. Reports said federal troops lined the streets, and riflemen could be seen on the rooftops, along with the cannons on the Capitol grounds. But nothing untoward occurred.

Lincoln was sworn in on the steps of the unfinished Capitol building by chief justice Roger Taney. Taney was, ironically, a pro-slavery judge who'd written the infamous majority opinion in the Dredd Scott case several years earlier. The case had affirmed that enslaved people of African ancestry had no constitutional rights. They were in fact property, no different from a horse, a cow, or a piece of farm equipment.

The new president delivered a half-hour address, which was politely, though not enthusiastically, received by those present. Afterward he walked back to the White House as part of the inaugural parade.

In the days following the inauguration, the talk at the Virginia Special Convention centered around the new president's inaugural speech. The Slave Power declared it a call to war, while the pro-Union side argued it was just the opposite: a call for calm and level-headed reflection, concluding with the words, *"We are not enemies, but friends. We must not be enemies. Though passion may have strained it must not break our bonds of affection."*

Finally exasperated by all the talk, John Carlile rose and gave an impassioned speech defending the intentions of the president and lambasting the secessionists. "Is there anything in this inaugural address to justify for a moment the assertions that have been made upon this floor, that it breathes a spirit of war? Read it again, gentlemen! Mr. Lincoln has told you ... that no war will be made upon you, that no force will be used against you—none whatever! I protest against this wicked effort to destroy the fairest and freest government on the Earth. And I denounce all attempts to involve Virginia to commit her to self-murder, as an insult to all reasonable living humanity, and a crime against God!"

The majority greeted this speech with great enthusiasm; both Nathan and Sandy congratulated John when he returned to his seat, shaking his hand and patting him on the back.

But the Slave Power was undeterred and continued every effort to provoke the pro-Union delegates and to foster a sense of unease and discontent.

ℬ๏๏ฆ๏ℬ๏๏ฆ๏ℬ๏๏ฆ๏ℬ๏๏ฆ๏

Throughout the rest of March, Nathan felt as if life were standing still, breathlessly waiting for something momentous to happen, which never did. Each day seemed like a repeat of the day before. The two opposing sides would give no ground in the convention. The pro-Union side continued to support a compromise, something like the Peace Conference proposals.

And the Slave Power attempted almost daily to present a motion for immediate secession, which the majority easily quashed.

Nathan also had no further contact with Evelyn, adding to his own personal sense of unending, intolerably stressful waiting. He'd decided Tom was right about Evelyn having some good reason for not wanting anyone to know her true feelings. So he was hesitant to write to her or go to her house uninvited. But what he was still unsure about were her motives. Though Tom's suggestion that it had been a simple attempt to placate her mother had seemed reasonable at the time, Nathan was now beginning to have his doubts. It seemed to him there must be more to Evelyn's actions than something so simple, else why wouldn't she have written him a letter? Or arrange to meet him somewhere? But he couldn't quite put his finger on what her motives might be. It was baffling, and it troubled his mind almost constantly—more than he would admit to any of his companions, even Tom. He'd experienced nothing like this before in his life, and so had no prior experience to draw upon.

He now realized he'd developed a burning desire to be with her. The long period of forced separation had *not* diminished it; if anything, it had strengthened it. The incident at the ball had only taken it from a slow simmer in the back of his mind to a full boil at the front.

This made the monotony of his days in Richmond even more galling. Nathan was a man of action, and yet no action was forthcoming. His time was filled with endless, repetitive debates and speeches at the convention during the day, and at night, fruitless, unsolvable speculation and anxiety about Evelyn.

And all the time, the thought on everyone's mind whenever it wasn't in at the forefront of discussion was: *what of Fort Sumter?* The days dragged on with no news either of an evacuation, or of an effort to reinforce the fort. Nathan now believed all the speeches, arguments, and discussions at the Convention were so much tiresome, wasted energy. Despite their best efforts, it would all come down to one thing: what the president did about this small fortified rock in the middle of Charleston Harbor.

As each day passed with no news concerning the fort, Wise's assertion that the president intended to reinforce the fort seemed more plausible. And it seemed more certain such an attempt at reinforcement would make it the flashpoint for a military conflict leading to a general civil war. Even the pro-Union side began to worry have their doubts; if Lincoln intended to evacuate the fort, what was he waiting for?

Then, on April 3rd, in a state of great agitation, George Summers called a secret meeting of the pro-Union leaders. He brought to the meeting a man named Allan Magruder, a native Virginian practicing law in Washington. He had arrived in secret with a message from the president, requesting Mr. Summers come immediately to the White House on urgent business. Mr. Magruder claimed he did not know why the president had called the meeting, despite very insistent prodding by George Summers, Janney, and the others.

They all discussed and debated the meaning of this news. Sandy suggested it might be Mr. Lincoln wanted assurances the Virginia Convention would adjourn without a call for secession in return for evacuating the fort. After some discussion, there was a consensus amongst those in attendance this was the most plausible reason for the president requesting the meeting. But they did not know how they could promise anything of the kind. They decided there was nothing for it but to send George to meet with the president and see what he wished to discuss. But George was reluctant to leave the convention at present. He had been the most influential pro-Union member throughout the month of March. His eloquent and timely speeches had continued to fend off repeated attempts by the Slave Power to call for a vote on secession. So they agreed to send John Brown Baldwin in his stead. Mr. Baldwin departed for the rail station to catch the next train north for the capital.

Despite their best efforts at secrecy, the next day there was a different mood at the convention, like something profound had changed. A feeling something was finally about to happen. John Baldwin's sudden, unexplained absence did *not* go unnoticed, and the continuing lack of news from Washington seemed to embolden the pro-secessionists. This time when Harvie Lewis called for a vote on secession, the question was not immediately tabled. The time had come to put the matter to the test.

A full day of debate followed, at the end of which they called for a vote. To the great relief of the pro-Union side, the vote was forty-five in favor, ninety opposed. Once again, the Slave Power had suffered an overwhelming defeat.

George Summers appeared relieved, and Sandy Stuart was ecstatic, "Well ... that should put an end to the secession, once and for all!"

But Nathan wasn't convinced. "Yes ... we've won a great battle. But don't forget, the war's not over yet; the enemy has not been driven from the field. He may be defeated for the moment, but he is not destroyed. And ... lest we forget ... Fort Sumter still looms. And what of John Baldwin's meeting with the President?"

Sandy couldn't argue against Nathan's reasoning, but seemed miffed he would spoil the victory celebration with such gloomy talk. Still, he had to admit it was now a matter of awaiting John Baldwin's return. Hopefully he would have more good news, and they could finally put the whole matter to rest.

The next day, Friday, April 5th, a tired, and worn-looking John Baldwin returned to Richmond, and the pro-Union leaders immediately called another meeting. But instead of bringing good news, Baldwin seemed baffled and perplexed, bringing no news at all.

"Gentlemen ... I ... don't know what to tell you. When I met with the president, he seemed distracted—appeared tired and careworn. He seemed lost in his own thoughts and paid me but little mind, though I stood in the same room. He asked me general questions about the Secession Convention but did not discuss any specific proposal. Nor did he offer any kind of 'deal,' such was we had anticipated. To be honest, gentlemen, at the time I couldn't figure out *why* I was there, what the purpose of the meeting might be. But since leaving the White House and thinking about it on the train ride home ... something he said has jumped into my mind. At one point he said, 'I wish you'd come sooner. Now I fear it's too late.' He didn't explain what he meant by it, and I didn't push him on the matter. But now I believe … well, maybe when he initially sent for George, he'd not yet made some decision. But before I arrived at the White House, something had changed. Gentlemen, I believe events have been set in motion now that cannot be undone. We can only wait and see what transpires."

They left the meeting feeling very anxious about what may be happening in South Carolina. It was possible the president had already ordered the fort's evacuation, and so had nothing further to discuss with Mr. Baldwin. It was also just as likely the president had ordered the re-supply and re-enforcement of the fort, which might trigger a battle in Charleston Harbor.

The following day, Saturday, April 6th, rumors of military action swirled around the convention. Reports had been circulated of war ships departing New York harbor. And no news of an evacuation. Wise and Harvie seemed re-invigorated, telling anyone who would listen they had been right all along. The president had ordered ships to wage war against the South. And the sooner Virginia joined with her Southern brethren, the better she'd be able to defend herself against a Northern invasion. Even the pro-Union side had tired of the waiting, the rumors, and the not knowing. So President Janney called for a special three-man delegation to travel to Washington to meet with President Lincoln to ask him straight out his intentions concerning Fort Sumter. The convention hall was filled with tension, which led to uncharacteristic outbursts of ungentlemanly behavior, threatening to come to blows.

And to be expected, Henry Wise and the Slave Power once again demanded immediate secession, despite their overwhelming defeat only two days earlier.

Mr. Janney called for calm, and ordered the convention adjourned until Monday. Before they departed, he requested that all present use the next day, a Sunday, as a day of prayer for Virginia, and for the nation.

಻಻಻಻಻಻಻಻಻

On Monday, Janney chose the three delegates to send to Washington to meet with the President. He selected a representative from each of the three camps in the convention: Sandy Stuart for the pro-Union side, William Preston of the conditional pro-Union camp, and George Randolph of the immediate-secession cadre.

The three departed the next day for Washington amid a torrential downpour. It took the better part of three days to reach Washington; heavy rains had washed out the main railroad bridge to the capital, forcing them to backtrack and travel by boat.

After they finally arrived, they arranged with Henry Seward, now Secretary of State, to meet with the president on Friday the twelfth. But for some unknown reason the meeting was moved to Saturday the thirteenth.

When they arrived for their meeting with the president, he informed them Fort Sumter had been under bombardment since earlier in the day. This had occurred after a failed attempt to re-supply the garrison with food and other non-military essentials. Lincoln was understandably pre-occupied, and ended the meeting abruptly with the words, "Gentlemen, an unprovoked assault has been made upon Fort Sumter. I shall hold myself at liberty to repossess, if I can, any and all federal forts that the Confederacy seized, before or after the Inaugural."

Sandy left the White House feeling dejected, like everything he had worked for was coming unraveled before his eyes, and there was nothing he could do to prevent it. George Randolph, the pro-secessionist of the delegation was, by contrast, almost giddy; with a military conflict underway, victory was at hand.

♏♐♏♐

Back in Richmond, on the floor of the convention, on Saturday April 13th, President Janney suddenly stopped all debate.

"Gentlemen ... I have just received a message from Governor Letcher. In it he says he has today received a telegram from Governor Pickens of South Carolina that states 'the war has commenced.' Mr. Pickens has gone on to ask his honor, Mr. Letcher what Virginia now intends to do. Our governor has answered, 'the convention now in session will determine what Virginia will do.'"

The floor of the convention erupted at this news, and Henry Wise loudly demanded the convention immediately vote on an ordinance of secession. "Gentlemen, fellow Virginians, combat has begun! The time for talk is over, it is now time to *act!*"

But the pro-Union side was not yet ready to concede defeat. They called for more information and demanded questions be answered before any precipitous actions be taken. What had actually happened? Were the reports of military conflict true? If so, did South Carolina, in their hot-headed secessionist fervor, start the whole thing, which seemed more than likely?

Again, tempers flared, and shouting matches threatened to turn violent.

John Baldwin moved the convention be adjourned until Monday, that the news might be verified, and tempers might be cooled. The motion carried, so a recess was called until Monday.

A gloomy mood of impending doom settled over the pro-Union camp, that no amount of wishful thinking could dispel. Sunday would once again be a day for fervent prayer.

ಖಿ⅀⦾⦿⅀ಖಿ⅀⦾⦿⅀ಖಿ⅀⦾⦿⅀

Monday Apr. 15, 1861 - Richmond, Virginia:

Monday morning did not bring calm to the convention floor; if anything, the opposite. Not only had the bombardment of Fort Sumter been confirmed, but the end of the day Sunday had brought the news of its surrender.

By midday on Monday, rumors once again began to circulate on the convention floor. This time, it was said President Lincoln had issued a Proclamation of Insurrection, asking the states, including Virginia, to furnish 75,000 soldiers to suppress it. Once again, the convention adjourned early that the veracity of this news might be verified before any action was taken.

ಖಿ⅀⦾⦿⅀ಖಿ⅀⦾⦿⅀ಖಿ⅀⦾⦿⅀

"Gentlemen ... though events seem to be finally moving in our favor, still I fear the abolitionists will continue to dither and delay from now 'til perdition. Were it left to them, our grandchildren

268

would still be discussing the secession long after we're dead and gone!"

"But, Governor Wise ... despite Lincoln's proclamation, we are still badly outnumbered at the convention. What do you propose we do?"

"Mr. Harvie ... if the convention doesn't vote for an ordinance of secession by tomorrow ... or the day after at the latest ... I intend to force the point. Gentlemen, the members of the People's Convention are prepared to move on the capitol, forcefully close down the Secession Convention, and arrest Governor Letcher. They will then declare a state of secession!"

There was a hushed, shocked silence.

"The local militias I spoke of earlier are in place to seize key federal installations within Virginia the moment I give the word. I also intend to telegraph Governor Pickens of South Carolina asking for C.S.A. troops to reinforce our actions. Gentlemen ... whether the Convention votes for secession, or it doesn't ... either way, Virginia *will* secede. And it *will* join with the Confederate States of America, and our sacred way of life *will* be preserved, so help me God!"

ༀༀༀༀༀༀༀༀༀ

"Damn it, Templeton! After all our work, all our plans, schemes, and behind-the-scenes maneuvering ... all is destroyed ... all is for naught, because of *this!* This one piece of paper negates everything we've worked for all these months and gives Wise his victory. That's the most bitter pill of all. The insufferable man believes he's still the governor, and I'm some sort of pretender! The nerve! The unmitigated gall!"

Governor Letcher slammed the piece of paper down on the desk in disgust. It was a telegram from U.S. Secretary of War Simon Cameron, confirming President Lincoln's Proclamation of Insurrection. In it he asked Virginia to provide three regiments of militia, 2,340 officers and men—their portion of the 75,000-man force the president had called for.

"Yes, your honor. It seems our hands are now tied, I'm sorry to say."

Templeton shifted his heavy bulk to a more comfortable position in the padded chair opposite the governor, who now stood on the other side of the desk. Templeton for once had no suggestions to offer and seemed thoroughly beaten down.

"Do you know Wise has been badgering me incessantly, for the last week or more, to pre-emptively seize federal installations within Virginia? On the possibility there *might* be a secession! He practically called me a traitor and a coward to my face! I had him thrown out of this office! If I was the sort of man who believed in such things, I'd have called him out for a duel of honor like in the old days."

"I doubt it would do any good, your honor. Henry Wise is so stubborn and mean the bullets would likely be unable to penetrate his thick hide!"

But Templeton's attempt at derisive humor was lost on Letcher, who sat back down in his chair heavily, shaking his head slowly from side to side. "I can see no way out of this now, unless the convention stands firm and declares some form of neutrality."

"Not likely, your honor. There's been no discussion of such a position to date, from either camp, so I can't imagine the idea gaining any traction at this late hour."

"No … I suppose not. But what then am I to do? If I attempt to give Lincoln his troops, Wise will stir up a lynch mob, and I'd not last a day. Hell, I might even agree with them! What was Lincoln *thinking*? Why did he *do it*? I … just don't understand. It would've been so easy … simply withdraw from Fort Sumter! What is it to him, anyway? Just a barren rock with stone walls, in a harbor that needs no fort to begin with!

"Or, since South Carolina started the shooting, he could have called up the troops for defense of the capital. He might have made up a story about an imminent invasion by the hot-headed, out-of-control government of South Carolina. Under such circumstances I might have complied and still saved face, given South Carolina's track record of reckless and uncircumspect action. But troops to put down the secession? The *people* of Virginia won't allow it, never mind Henry Wise. It's an unadulterated disaster, Templeton!"

"Yes, your honor."

Letcher sighed heavily, then reached for a piece of parchment and his pen. "May as well get it over with. Come over here and help me draft my response."

Executive Department, Richmond, Va.
April 15, 1861
Hon. Simon Cameron
Secretary of War

Sir:

I have received your telegram of the 15th, the genuineness of which I doubted. Since that time, I have received your communications mailed the same day, in which I am requested to detach from the militia of the State of Virginia 'the quota assigned in a table,' which you append, 'to serve as infantry or rifleman for the period of three months, unless sooner discharged.'

In reply to this communication, I have only to say that the militia of Virginia will not be furnished to the powers at Washington for any such use or purpose as they have in view. Your object is to subjugate the Southern States, and a requisition made upon me for such an object — an object, in my judgment, not within the purview of the Constitution or the act of 1795 — will not be complied with.

You have chosen to inaugurate civil war, and, having done so, we will meet it in a spirit as determined as the administration has exhibited toward the South.

Respectfully,
John Letcher
Governor, Commonwealth of Virginia

ഇരുഗരുഗഇരുഗരുഗഇരുഗരുഗ

On Tuesday, April 16th, the Convention President barred all reporters and private citizens from the convention hall. The convention would meet in secret session to discuss an ordinance of secession, against the wishes of the leadership of the pro-Union camp. Their majority hold on the convention was slipping, and Nathan felt a definite change in the wind. Many who'd previously been receptive to his point of view had now switched sides, claiming Lincoln had declared war on the South. He found it a helpless and depressing feeling, like slowly sinking under water without the ability to swim.

Henry Wise spoke forcefully that military necessity required not only immediate secession but also immediate seizure of federal military facilities, even before any ratification vote by the people.

The Slave Power once again proposed an ordinance of secession, asking for an immediate vote.

Sandy Stuart, just returned from Washington, spoke forcefully against Wise. "Secession is not only war, but it is emancipation, it is bankruptcy, it is widespread ruin to our people!"

John Baldwin joined him, with an impassioned plea to do all in their power to avoid what would surely be a disaster for the state. He was a forceful, eloquent speaker, and convinced a slim majority to adjourn for the day, that the delegates might give serious thought to how they might vote on the following day.

Henry Wise, though on the very brink of achieving his goals, left in a huff, his desires put off for at least one more day. He sent a message to the leaders of the Peoples Spontaneous Convention stating he believed the convention *would* approve the Ordinance of Secession on the morrow. But since he wasn't certain, he issued specific instructions on what to do under either eventuality.

He also issued his pre-arranged orders to seize federal military installations at Harpers Ferry and Norfolk; this despite Governor Letcher's refusal to go along with the idea, and despite his lack of any legal authority to do so. Wise would force the secession, regardless of how tomorrow's vote turned out.

ဢ∞ఴరిఴဢ∞ఴరిఴဢ∞ఴరిఴ

Wednesday Apr. 17, 1861 - Richmond, Virginia:

The first order of business was the reading of Governor Letcher's response to Simon Cameron, U.S. Secretary of War. This response had a thoroughly chilling effect on the pro-Union delegates. If the governor had given up, what hope was there?

But the delegates from western Virginia surprised most of those present by adopting a new stand; if Virginia seceded from the Union, the counties of western Virginia would refuse to accept it. Nathan had heard this mentioned from time to time in private meetings or small groups, but it was the first time it'd been spoken before the entire assembly. The representatives from the western Virginia counties demanded to be heard. One after another they warned a vote for secession would result in the dissolution of the state of Virginia!

Nathan hadn't given this idea much thought previously, but now he started thinking on the idea in earnest. If Virginia seceded from the United States ... could the western side of Virginia secede from the state and re-join the Union? It was an intriguing idea, now that he gave it proper consideration. But he set the idea aside for the moment ... Virginia *must not* secede! Everything depended on it. The alternative was ... unthinkable.

But then, following the predictable speeches for and against, it came time to vote on the Ordinance of Secession. The final tally was eighty-eight in favor, fifty-five against. Nathan sat with Sandy Stuart and John Carlile as they announced the tally. It was a shocking and sobering outcome, and afterward the three men sat in their chairs shaking their heads in disbelief. How could everything have suddenly gone so wrong? How could their overwhelming majority have suddenly turned into a fatal minority?

Henry Wise stood and delivered a gloating speech in which he announced the takeover of the federal armory at Harpers Ferry, and the naval base at Norfolk.

The pro-Union delegates rose to their feet as a group and shouted their disgust, calling Wise a lawbreaker and usurper. John Baldwin was the next to speak, and denounced Wise as a demagogue, a criminal, and a traitor to democracy and the state of Virginia. He declared the people must have the final say, that no action could be taken until after the referendum was held.

But Wise sat back in his seat with a smirk on his face. He'd won, and they'd lost, and everyone knew it. And unless Governor Letcher had the backbone to have Wise arrested, and to countermand his orders, which nobody believed would ever happen, he'd get away with it too.

As Nathan and the other pro-Union delegates sat in a state of disbelief, an aide ran up to George Summers and whispered in his ear.

George stood and demanded to speak. President Janney recognized him immediately.

"Gentleman, I have just been informed a rabble, claiming to be from the *so-called* Spontaneous People's Convention even now surrounds this building. They threaten to hang anyone who objects to Mr. Wise's thoroughly illegal activities! Mr. Janney, I insist Mr. Wise be censured in the strongest possible terms. And I request the governor be notified and requested to call out of the proper authorities to disperse these lawless ruffians post-haste!"

But the pro-secessionists jumped to their feet and shouted down Summers, drowning out anything additional he tried to say.

Finally, Henry Wise held up his hands for silence, and a quiet fell over the Convention.

"Gentlemen ... you may not like it, but clearly the people have spoken ..."

But Nathan stood and pulled the small Colt revolver from his pocket, holding it up for all to see. "Surely some others of you have come to this meeting armed, given all that's been happening? Let us sally forth and put a stop to this lawlessness! If we shoot a few of the ring leaders, the others will disperse quickly enough!"

But none of his own party responded. Even Sandy Stuart looked at him as if he'd gone insane, leaving him standing alone, gun held over his head.

Wise stepped up to confront him face to face. "Surely, Mr. Chambers, you don't intend to walk out and commit cold-blooded murder, simply because the citizens of Virginia disagree with you?"

Nathan gave him a withering glare, *"No*, Mr. Wise, I intend to commit very *hot-blooded* murder! And since no one seems inclined to join me, I shall leave this building now and will *not* return. But … I must warn you, *sir*, if anyone attempts to bar my way, or threatens violence to me or my friends, I *will* put a bullet between his eyes. And then … I will come back into this building, and the next bullet will be for you, *sir!* This I swear on the Bible of Abraham, and the Gospels of our Lord Jesus Christ!"

He aimed the pistol straight at Wise's forehead and pulled back the hammer with a *click*.

A look of shock and fear replaced Wise's smirk. But it quickly passed, and he scowled.

Nathan lowered the hammer, turned, and strode from the room, pistol still in his fist. As he passed the back of the room, Tom, William, and Georgie fell in behind him. They too drew pistols from holsters concealed beneath their jackets. Men backed out of their way as they left the chambers.

🐮🐮ℂℋ🐮🐮ℂℋ🐮🐮ℂℋ

In the end, Nathan's exit from the capitol building was anticlimactic. Whether his reputation had preceded him, or Wise had given orders not to hinder him, or their open display of firearms had been sufficient intimidation, he never knew. But in any case, when he and his men left the building, and walked down the steps, the crowd parted a way for them. They were not molested, either verbally or physically, despite the look of disdainful disgust Nathan graced them with as he walked through their midst.

They returned to the boarding house without incident. But they had to endure the sights and sounds of the Slave Power's victory celebration the rest of that afternoon and evening. This included cannons firing, bonfires burning, and parades marching through the streets, all instigated by the so-called delegates to the Peoples' Spontaneous Convention, many in a drunken state.

Nathan was thoroughly disgusted, and turned in late that evening in a foul mood. He awoke the next morning with a pounding headache, having imbibed too much whiskey the night before.

But despite the headache, he awoke determined to fight back against Wise and his followers. They meant to usurp the democratic traditions of Virginia for their own purposes. And in so doing they'd split the country apart, no matter how many laws they had to break in the process. But there was still the referendum. The people would have the final say, not the Slave Power. And if the earlier election were any indication, he reckoned the pro-Union side should have a better than even chance to win that election.

He dressed and went to see Sandy Stuart, his three men in tow. Stuart had taken on the role of his mentor in the senate, and later at the convention. He'd helped steer Nathan through the treacherous and unfamiliar waters of politics, while always maintaining an optimistic outlook. Sandy was one those rare people who seemed to always have a smile and a kind word for the people he liked. And a sharp, witty, acerbic tongue for his enemies.

But when Sandy opened the door to his room this morning, the contrast with his usual demeanor was shocking. He'd not yet dressed, wearing a silk robe and house shoes, though it was already several hours past sunrise. His hair was disheveled, and his eyes looked red and puffy, as if he'd been up all night, or had been recently crying. Or both.

"Sandy … may I come in?"

"Nathan … sorry, yes … yes, of course. Come …"

Nathan entered the hotel room. Tom and the others stayed outside to afford them privacy and prevent any interruptions.

It was one of the nicest hotels in Richmond, and Nathan remembered feeling impressed with the furnishings the first time he'd seen it. Not nearly as large and elegant as the St. Charles in New Orleans had been, but then … nothing else was. Still, for Richmond, it was extremely nice, and he'd felt it suited Sandy perfectly. Now as he entered, he saw clothing laid haphazardly across a chair and shoes tossed into the corner. The stale remains of the previous evening's meal was still on the table.

"Excuse my appearance ... and that of my rooms ... with all the noise and whatnot I ... slept but little."

"Understandable ... if it hadn't been for a healthy dose of whiskey last night, I'd probably not've slept a wink! Are you ... not feeling well, Sandy?"

Sandy sat down heavily in a chair and gave out a great sigh. "No, Nathan ... I'm *not* feeling well. Oh, I am fine *physically*, other than a great tiredness. But I must confess, I have rarely in life felt this low. I am not a man used to losing, and I find I am not well suited to it."

"Ha! I hear you there, sir! In my previous line of work losing meant bloody and painful death ... for myself and everyone around me I cared about. No, sir ... I don't care at all for losing, I can promise you that! Which is why I'm here this morning. I'm not of a mind to give up yet. Wise may have won the convention, but there is still the referendum. I figure if we muster the troops, and get out campaigning, traveling the state, giving speeches and meeting with the people ... perhaps we can still win the day. What say you?"

But to Nathan's surprise, Sandy put his head in his hands, and did not immediately answer.

"You don't understand, Nathan. We've lost ... don't you see? Lost utterly and completely. Wise has already had federal facilities seized, and Governor Letcher has all but declared war on Lincoln. There's no turning back now, no matter how much you and I might want to."

"But the people ... they still have a say ..."

"The people?! Who do you think voted against us at the convention yesterday, after Mr. Lincoln made his call for troops? Those conditional Unionists we'd been working so hard to turn to our way of thinking are nothing but a reflection of the people of Virginia as a whole, much more so than you and I or Wise, even. They're the ones who matter, the ones who'll carry the vote. And they've decided they'll *not* join in Mr. Lincoln's war to re-unite the country but rather will fight against it."

"But … will you not at least come with me? See if we can rouse the others … Mr. Summers, Baldwin, John Carlile … surely they'll want to keep up the fight."

"Maybe John Baldwin … he was here briefly last night. Said he was determined to return to the convention today to try one more time to convince the delegates to change their minds. It is a fool's errand, and I told him so. But you should go see him after the convention convenes to see what came of it, and whether he wants to continue campaigning. I for one, am done. I'm sorry, Nathan, but sometimes one must recognize defeat and bow to the inevitable."

"I will go see Mr. Baldwin this afternoon … if *he* will continue the fight, will you join us?"

"If he and George Summers wish to continue, come back and see me and we'll talk again. But I doubt you will find much interest in the idea. We've lost. It's time to come to terms with it."

"Well, as I said, I'm not one to easily accept defeat and stop fighting, not until I'm cold and dead at any rate. But … if we really have lost, and Virginia goes to war against the Union … what will *you* do, Sandy? Where will you go?"

"Do? Go? I will do what I've always done, my dear Nathan. I will help run this state. I'm a Virginian … I have nowhere else to go. This is my home."

"Go west … go north, anywhere but here! If war breaks out, Virginia will be the very front lines … it will be destroyed, and you with it!"

"Then … so be it. I will not leave Virginia in its hour of need."

Nathan stood and shook his head. "I don't understand such reasoning. Good day to you, Sandy. I hope we meet again under more pleasant circumstances. But if not … I have appreciated your help, advice and … your friendship."

He extended his hand, and Sandy looked up, gave him a wan smile, and shook his hand. "Thank you, Nathan. I have also enjoyed our comradeship. I assume you will return to the West?"

"Not until all hope of victory is lost. Then … yes, I suppose I'll have no other course than to return home and … await whatever transpires."

Nathan went to see George Summers at the house where he'd been staying, but the proprietress said he had left the house early. She did not know where he'd gone. The streets were eerily quiet throughout Richmond, especially considering the raucous commotion of the previous night. He assumed those that'd stayed up all night noisemaking and carousing had finally gone to bed.

Next, he called on John Carlile. The contrast between John and Sandy was startling. John was not downcast; on the contrary, he was fighting mad.

"Wise and his ilk disgust me, Mr. Chambers! They never had any intention of following the will of the people. I've just learned the so-called People's Convention was an elaborate plot to take over the government if the Convention failed to give them their secession. They'd planned a veritable *coup d'état*, dispersing the convention with violence and arresting Mr. Letcher if things didn't go their way!

"But fortunately for them, the rest of us handed them their victory without a fight. Well I, for one, won't stand for it, sir!"

"That's the spirit, John! I visited Sandy earlier, but he's so downcast he refuses to continue the fight. Can we get the others to join us, do you think? Summers, Baldwin, Janney? It seems to me the way the last election turned out we should have a good chance of winning the referendum if we work at it."

But John turned and looked at him as if he'd suggested they jump to the moon.

"My dear Mr. Chambers ... you don't understand what has happened here! Though I can't agree with Mr. Stuart's resignation on the matter, still ... the reality is, Virginia is lost—lost to the Union. And if we continue the fight here in Richmond, we put our very lives at risk for no good purpose."

"I'm not afraid of Wise and his bullies," Nathan said with a scowl. "I'll not be moved from my course by threats of violence from such vermin. Violence is a business I know *much* better than they, I can assure you!"

"Yes ... that I can well believe, Mr. Chambers, that I can well believe. But still, there comes a time, even in your former occupation, when a man must admit it's time for a strategic retreat. A retreat to a place where he can regroup his men, and then ... like our dear General Washington used to preach ... live to fight another day."

Nathan thought on this a moment, then said, "Back to the West, you mean? And what then?"

"Nathan ... even before the fatal events of this past week, many of us in the West have felt disaffected with the government of Virginia. Many of the counties on the other side of the mountains feel more connection and kinship with the North than they do with Richmond. And since the convention started, the idea has been slowly growing ... if Virginia decides to commit self-murder ... perhaps it's time the western side go in another direction."

"Go ...? Oh ... yes, I heard the talk at the convention, but I'd assumed it was only idle threats made in anger. Do you mean the idea has received serious consideration?"

"And why not? I'm sure you noticed almost every representative from west of the Alleghenies voted against the secession ... *both times!* And I can assure you they have no love for Henry Wise, and no desire to join in this insane confrontation with the federal government. No, Nathan, I will not spend my energy, and risk my life trying to convince these eastern Virginians not to kill themselves. I would rather retreat to the West and see what can be done on our own. In fact, a meeting has already been scheduled, in less than a week's time in Wheeling, to discuss the options. I should very much like you to attend. We can certainly use a man of your leadership qualities, and ... likely your martial skills as well."

"Hmm ... I will consider it. What of the others? What of George Summers? He's also a Westerner ... from Kanawha County. Does he also plan to attend this gathering in Wheeling?"

"George is even more downcast than Sandy. He feels betrayed by his friends in Washington, and by the new president. He is ashamed that he continued to assure us about Fort Sumter to the bitter end, though myself and several others assured him he is blameless. In my opinion, he's a thoroughly beaten man. I spoke with him last night, and he would barely look up to meet my eyes. He refuses to come to Wheeling, and today he is settling all his affairs in Richmond, so he can take the first train out of town tomorrow morning. I believe he will return to his home and stay out of public life. It saddens me ... he is a *truly* great man, but now he seems ... *broken* by what's happened."

They were quiet for a moment. Nathan had also admired Summers, thinking him the greatest among them. Now he was a "thoroughly beaten man"? It was hard to digest.

"And Baldwin? Sandy said he was going to try again to dissuade the delegates from their course today."

"Oh ... he will make a good argument, and many will be moved to agree with him, but it won't serve to change the outcome. And in the end, he, like Sandy, is a Virginian, and a politician. He will stay here and try his best to steer the state through these troubled times."

"I can't believe these men would ... go along with this madness. Why not just leave the state, or go to the West?"

"It's their home. They don't want to leave."

"Well, I can understand that, but ... in the end a home is just a piece of dirt with some boards thrown together on top. A man must ... stand for something *more*, it seems to me. A place is just a place, but *America* ... our country ... it's something greater. It's an idea, a symbol ... of how men should treat each other. How they should live together under a government *of the people*. And though it's clearly not perfect, it's the best thing by far that's ever been in the long history of the world. To throw that away ... to turn your back on *that* for ... a *place* ... for a *piece of dirt?* It makes no sense."

"Not to you, and maybe not to me, but to these men ...?" he shrugged.

☼♋♐☙☼♋♐☙☼♋♐☙

Sunday Apr. 21, 1861 - Richmond, Virginia:

When Evelyn had first heard the news of the convention's vote for secession, it sent a chill down her spine. Was the war really going to happen after all? Apparently, Jonathan and Angeline had been right to be skeptical, despite all the positive-sounding news up to that point.

She still didn't understand exactly what had happened to turn things around so suddenly. It had something to do with the dispute over Fort ... *Something*. She could never remember the name for some reason. And when someone had described the place to her it seemed so insignificant she couldn't imagine it triggering a war. Nonetheless, it apparently had.

Her next thought was fear for Nathan's safety, remembering what Jonathan had said about the Slave Power watching him and threatening his life if he didn't go along with their side. She was certain he would *never* do that, so ...

But then she'd remembered about the referendum. The secession couldn't happen until the people voted on it. And they'd announced that wouldn't happen until later, toward the end of May. So Nathan would surely be safe until then ... wouldn't he?

But now it was Sunday. And though the vote for secession by the convention had only happened on Wednesday, everyone was now talking and acting as if the final decision had already been made. Someone told her the Virginia militia had seized federal military installations within the state. She'd also heard the convention delegates from west of the mountains were beginning to leave the city, feeling threatened by the Slave Power's increasingly lawless behavior.

When she heard this her thoughts turned to Nathan. If he was preparing to leave the city, Wise would hear of it and ... *then what?*

She sat in church, listening to the pastor drone on about ... something, but she had no mind for listening. She was consumed by a growing fear for Nathan. He must be warned! His life was in danger ... had Jonathan's men told him? How carefully were they watching him, with everything else going on? Should she warn him herself? Would that help, or make matters worse? The more she thought about it, the more fearful she became, to the point she was fidgeting in her seat. Miss Harriet noticed and leaned over to ask her in a whisper if she was feeling unwell.

Then something in the back of her mind told her she should listen carefully to what the preacher was saying.

"Now I should like to close with a reading from the Book of Ecclesiastes chapter four, verses nine through eleven ..."

> *Two are better than one; because they have a good reward for their labor. For if they fall, the one will lift up his fellow: but woe to him who is alone when he falleth; for he hath not another to help him up. Again, if two lie together, then they have heat: but how can one be warm alone?*

A chill ran down her spine ... she knew *exactly* what these words from God meant; Nathan *must not* face these men alone, without his friends, or surely he would fall, and cold death come over him! She must go to him at once, not abandon him in his greatest hour of need. She must find him and warn him to keep his men close by and well-armed, night and day.

As soon as the service ended, Evelyn turned to Miss Harriet, "Forgive me, Momma, but there is something I *must* do immediately, before even returning to the house. Will you be all right walking home alone?"

"Well, of course I will. I'm no invalid! I'm as capable of walking home as you are. But what is it you must do all of a sudden? Where are you going, and why?"

"Oh, Momma. Please don't ask ... I ... don't wish to speak on it now." But she knew she had to give Harriet something, or she would never let it go.

"Let me just say it concerns ... a certain young gentleman who ... I believe may have mistaken my intentions. And I ... simply can't be at peace until I set the matter straight. Please do trust me on this, Momma."

"Well ... all right, dear. I'll trust you can take care of ... disabusing the young man. But you be careful out walking the streets and come straight home after. These are strange times. I've heard there are some rough and lawless men out and about these days."

"Thank you, Momma. And don't worry, I shall be most careful and avoid any such men."

She stood and made her way from the church. She headed straight for the Hughes house, some ten blocks away, walking as quickly as she could, resisting the urge to run.

"I understand your concern, Evelyn, dear. But Jonathan has assured me he has at least one man, and often more, watching over your Mr. Chambers night and day."

"Thank you, Angeline, but … what if they are not enough? What if Mr. Wise sends more men than they can defend against? What if these men somehow slip past Jonathan's watch? Angeline, it's past time we warn Mr. Chambers of the danger he's in, so he and his men can prepare to meet it!"

"Well … I see your point, Evelyn. I shall speak to Jonathan when he returns later this evening and see what he says."

"*No!*"

Angeline looked up in surprise. She'd not expected the agreeable young woman to contradict her so strongly. "Excuse me?"

"*No, Angeline!* It can't wait for Jonathan. And I'll not accept no for an answer. I will go to him myself, *now*, only … I don't know where he's staying."

"Oh! Oh … all right … yes, I see how important this is to you, dear. And … I can't say I blame you. I know if someone were threatening harm to my Jonathan … there's nothing I wouldn't do to protect him.

"But … I'm afraid I don't know where Mr. Chambers is staying either. Nor do I know who Jonathan has set to watching him. I've never thought to ask, not thinking it was something I'd have any need to know. Hmm … Jonathan won't be back until late this evening, and I have no way of contacting him before then. I wonder who else might know …"

She was quiet and thoughtful for a moment, then looked up, "There's a man named Sandy Stuart … Alexander H. H. Stuart, to be exact. I seem to recall hearing he's been working closely with your Mr. Chambers at the convention, so he might know where he's been staying. Mr. Stuart always stays in the same hotel whenever he comes to town. It's the Hotel Elizabeth, on Main Street between 5th and 6th streets. If you go to him, he may be able to tell you where to find Mr. Chambers."

ಬಿಲ್ಡಿ ಬ್ರೆ ಡಿ ಬಿ ಡಿ ಬ್ರೆ ಡಿ ಬಿ ಡಿ ಬ್ರೆ

Even as Evelyn sat fidgeting in church across town, Nathan too sat in church at St. Paul's next to the capitol. His three men sat next to him.

And even though he too had many things on his mind, he listened intently to the preacher, hoping to glean some inspiration from the message. Some divine sign, perhaps, of what his next steps should be. He still felt the proper course was to stay and fight the secession—campaign against it. But it was becoming increasingly obvious he'd be almost alone in that effort if he were to do it. Still, if it were the right thing to do, should that deter him? And then there was still the problem of … what to do about Evelyn?

And though he concentrated as best he could on the pastor's words, still he found no inspiration in them. He thought it a good and timely sermon. It spoke of not succumbing to fear in these times of trouble, and of trusting in God. Still, there was no specific guidance in the words.

But then the pastor looked up at the congregation. And it seemed to Nathan that this man, whom he did not know and had never met, looked directly at him and locked eyes with him. He said, "And now, I shall read from the Book of Isaiah, chapter forty-one, verse ten …"

At these words, Nathan felt a chill run through him. In that moment he was certain, without a doubt, God spoke directly to him, through the mouth of this preacher:

> *Fear thou not; for I am with thee: be not dismayed; for I am thy God: I will strengthen thee; yea, I will help thee; yea, I will uphold thee with the right hand of my righteousness.*

285

Tears began to well in his eyes; it was the very verse he'd used to calm his people after Walters' failed raid on Mountain Meadows during the great wedding. And he knew *exactly* what it meant, as if God himself had whispered in his ear; it was time to return home and see to the wellbeing of his *own* people, setting aside his fears for Virginia and for the country. He must trust *those* momentous issues to the almighty hand of God.

But before he went, he knew he must also speak with Evelyn. He needed to learn the truth of her feelings, as he had not done back at the wedding, nor any time since.

Even before the service ended, he turned to Tom. In a whisper he said, "After the service, return with the men to our rooms and gather our things. We leave for home *today*, as soon as everything is made ready. While you're packing our things, I must go speak with Miss Evelyn. I *must* know the truth from her before we depart. If she still has feelings for me, as I suspect … then I intend to persuade her to come with us, if I can. I fear we may not be coming back here for a *very* long time."

"Oh! All right, Captain, only …"

"Only?"

"Only I finally received word from Adilida about her arrival. She's scheduled to leave New Orleans on a steamship at the end of this month and arrive here in Richmond a week or so later."

"Oh … then you must figure out a different port, something more … *Northerly*."

"Yes … I'm sure you're right. I will send her a telegram straight away to change her destination … New York maybe, or Boston? I should like to look at a map and see which is the closest port to Mountain Meadows without going through Virginia proper."

"That'd be Baltimore."

"Oh … yes, of course. Thank you, sir. But … as for you going to see Evelyn, I will go with you. The streets aren't safe."

"*No*. There are some things a man must do by himself. I'll not have keepers with me when I go to speak with … with the woman who I hope to make my wife one day!"

"When you put it that way … I can see your point, sir. But … you will be careful?"

Nathan grinned at him and patted the vest pocket where he carried the small Colt revolver, "Of course; you know what a cautious fellow I am!"

Tom rolled his eyes in response.

In his concern for Nathan's safety, Tom had raised his voice a bit too much; several parishioners nearby turned and gave them chastising looks, which stifled any further conversation.

ཀྵ།ༀ།ཀྵ།ༀ།ཀྵ།ༀ།ཀྵ།

Nathan strode briskly down the street, his mind focused on what he would say to Evelyn—what arguments he would make if she refused to leave Richmond with him. He still didn't understand what had happened to her back at Mountain Meadows. But he was now almost certain she was still in love with him. He'd had nothing but time to think about that, and her follow-up letter. And then there was their odd, uncomfortable meeting at the ball in Richmond, followed by her puzzling note. It all seemed to confirm his suspicions.

He now believed her hesitation stemmed from … *whatever it was* that had happened during the wedding back at the farm. He was determined to convince her he would be there for her, to help her deal with … whatever difficulties might arise.

The alternative … well … he feared once he left town, events would drive him ever farther from Richmond. He could easily imagine a scenario where vast armies stood between them. That they'd be on opposite sides of a great conflict. The thought of it made him shudder.

This uncomfortable train of thought so captivated his attention he nearly strode right past a man who stopped in front of him and called his name. He looked up and nearly jumped in surprise.

"Colonel Lee!"

"Hello, Nathaniel!"

They embraced and exchanged a firm handshake. Nathan greeted his former commanding officer, mentor, and fellow Virginian, Colonel Robert E. Lee, with warmth and affection.

"It has been … well, it will have been two years … last Thursday … since we last saw each other!" Nathan said.

Lee shook his head in wonder, "Still have that amazing memory, I see."

"Yes, sir. These things seem to stick in my head … somehow. Anyway … I was so disappointed by your absence when I came to visit you in San Antonio on my way home."

"Yes … I felt the same when I heard you'd stopped by headquarters while I was off to Fort Brown chasing Cortina. Never did manage to run the rascal to ground. But we did make things hot enough down there the Mexican authorities agreed to go after him themselves and curtail his activities … so we'd curtail ours! I suspect they feared we'd cross the border and come after him, and had no taste for how that might come out."

They exchanged a smile at this; they had a shared memory of the last time the U.S. Army had crossed the border. And it had *not* turned out well for the Mexicans. Nathan smiled at a vision of the Stars and Stripes flying above the Mexican capitol building.

Then Nathan noticed, despite the smile, and the warmth of the greeting, Colonel Lee's handsome face seemed … older somehow, more careworn. His hair and beard appeared whiter than they'd been. Much more so than the two years absence should have accounted for. He wondered what may have happened. Some illness perhaps? As he pondered these thoughts, something else about the man's appearance suddenly hit him like a bolt of lightning from the blue. The man was wearing a nice, dark-colored suit with waistcoat similar to the one Nathan was wearing.

"But … but sir … you are out of uniform!"

Even as he said this, a cold chill of fear ran through him, "and … why are you here in Richmond … may I ask?"

Lee broke eye contact and looked down at the ground for a moment.

"I … I have resigned my commission, Nathaniel."

"Oh?! I … I can hardly believe it, sir! I always imagined you … well, and myself for that matter … a lifelong officer. When

288

General Scott finally retires, I'd always believed you would be the perfect man to replace him in command of the entire Army."

This statement made Lee wince, as if it were hurtful, though Nathan had intended it for a compliment.

When Lee looked back up at him, his expression reflected a deep emotional pain.

"It was ... the most difficult thing I've ever done in my life. But I ... I just ... couldn't do it. I couldn't do it ... you will understand, being a Virginian."

"Couldn't do *what*, sir?" Nathan had a sickening feeling he knew what Colonel Lee would say, but prayed he was wrong.

"General Scott ... *did* in fact offer me command of all the armies ... but I just couldn't lead those armies ... not against *Virginia.*"

Nathan was quiet for a moment, absorbing this new, shocking news. He didn't know what to say. Finally, almost in a whisper, he asked, "And ... then why are you *here*, sir?"

They locked eyes for a moment before Lee answered. "I am here at the request of Governor Letcher. He wishes ... to speak with me about the defense of Virginia."

Nathan took a deep breath, reached in his jacket, and pulled out a cigar, which he lit. His mind was in turmoil. The man he had idolized for the past ... six years at least ... was now a ... a ... *traitor!*

"Colonel ... we swore an oath, you and I, when we first put on the officer's uniform. A *sacred* oath ... under the very eyes of *God*, sir! To serve and defend the United States against *all* opposers ... and to obey the orders of the *President* of the United States! I don't recall any part of that oath that says ... *'until it becomes inconvenient to do so'!"*

Nathan's tone had turned hard, and his words no longer carried any warmth.

The careworn look Nathan had noticed earlier seemed to increase. They continued to stare at one another.

"Some things are ... more important than those words ..."

Nathan stared at him, open-mouthed. "*Virginia*, you mean? What is Virginia, compared to the *United States of America?*

Virginia is a piece of land … nothing more than a whole lot of *dirt!* And what are Virginians? Well, in the last few weeks I have learned Virginians are not all that admirable, faithful, honest, or democratic. They are selfish, aristocratic, and … foolish beyond belief!

"And now it seems … they are also not particularly *loyal*, and do not feel it is necessary to keep their word, even when solemnly sworn before God!"

Lee's face turned red, "I don't appreciate what you are insinuating, sir!"

"I am not *insinuating* anything, *sir!* I am speaking it plainly. What you're talking about doing is treason, *sir!* Outright *sedition!* Not just refusing orders of a superior officer in the face of the enemy, refusing to *fight* when your commander is in his hour of greatest need. Even worse, going over to the enemy side!

"In the Army *I* am familiar with, we'd shoot a *private* who behaved in such a craven manner. But … apparently *colonels* are *exempt!*"

Lee again looked at the ground. It seemed to Nathan he had struck a nerve. It occurred to him Lee had already entertained the same thoughts.

But seeing the turmoil and pain on the man's face, Nathan softened, recalling the man he'd loved and admired all these years. "Please, sir … I *beg* of you … reconsider what you've done! I've just spent the last four months here in Richmond … and I can tell you in no uncertain terms these men are *not* deserving of your sacrifice, nor your fealty. *They are simply not worth fighting for, sir!*

"Please, Colonel … come away with me. Let's board the next train for Washington and tell General Scott you have reconsidered. I'm sure he'll reinstate your commission, and the offer of command he presented you. I'll re-enlist, then you and I can lead an army back here and put an end to this madness! I promise you, sir, nothing good will come from this secession. Not even the preservation of slavery. Only death and destruction."

"I care nothing of slavery, Nathaniel, as you know. I have always intended to free my slaves as soon as I could make sure my family would be able to … make do without them."

"Yes, I know, sir. I'm also planning to free my slaves. So why fight and die for the sake of men who want to perpetuate this *evil* forever, and care nothing for the wants of you or I? Come, sir. Will you join me? Uphold your sacred oaths and reject this insanity?"

Lee was silent for a moment and again looked down at his feet. But when he looked up, Nathan could see tears welling in his eyes, "I'm sorry, Nathaniel ... I can't. I can't turn my back on Virginia, no matter the circumstances. But you ... I must ask *you*, Nathaniel, as a true Virginian ... to join *me*. Help me lead the state through these troubles—steer her toward a better day after."

"*Never!* Never in life would I choose Virginia over the United States! I do *not* break my sworn oaths, sir! And though I resigned my commission to look after my family, I *never* would have done so had I known my country was on the verge of *war!* And when I swore the oath to protect the United States and obey their president, I don't recall saying, 'until such time as I resign my commission'! When I said that oath, I said it for *life*. No, sir, until I am cold and buried in the ground, I will *never* break my oath!"

"Well, then I am very sorry we may well be on opposing sides in any coming conflict. But still I wish you well, Nathaniel."

But Nathan was now angry—wounded and betrayed. He could not bring himself to say any kindly words, and he refused Lee's outstretched hand.

Finally, he answered, "For the sake of our *former* comradeship, I pray I never see you over the sights of my rifle. Good day to you, sir."

He stepped past Colonel Lee and continued down the street. He never looked back, but after a few moments he found it necessary to wipe his eyes; likely some dust had blown into them.

☙℥ℨ℧℥℞℧℥℥℥ℨ℧℥℥℥℞℧℥

He paid but little mind to the walk from the time he left Colonel Lee until he stood in front of Evelyn's house—the same address Miss Abbey had given him to write his letter to Evelyn. His mind was in a state of turmoil over the meeting with Robert Lee, and he couldn't shake the distressing thoughts from his head. Not only did he feel personally betrayed, but he knew General

Scott had exercised perfect judgment when he'd offered command of the armies to Lee. From Nathan's years in the Army, he knew Lee was head and shoulders above the rest of the officers in the United States Army, of any rank. Now the Union had not only lost their finest officer, but worse than that, he'd joined the enemy!

If Nathan hadn't been so distracted, he might have noticed three other men on the street. These men, by some surprising coincidence, seemed to be walking his very same route through Richmond, only a block behind him; this despite several turns he'd taken. And if those three men hadn't been so intent on their quarry, they might have noticed their own footpad. But he was a man rarely noticed by the typical citizen, an ill-kempt and disreputable looking fellow, often seen passed out on a sidewalk, and usually seen with a bottle in his hand. He too appeared to be following the very same course.

Nathan hesitated for a moment, breathed a heavy sigh, stepped forward and knocked on the door. It was a small, neat, though unspectacular house, in a neat but unspectacular neighborhood. The type of place a common laborer might afford after he'd worked at his job a few years. Nathan now understood Miss Harriet's strong motivation to see Evelyn married to a man such as himself.

After a moment the door opened, and an older woman, with spectacles on her nose peered out. She said, "Oh!" putting her hand over her mouth, and patting her hair, as if to make sure it was properly in place. She removed the glasses, and looked more like the Harriet Nathan remembered, though more casually dressed than she'd ever been when she was at Mountain Meadows.

"Mr. Chambers! What a pleasant surprise! Please ... you must forgive my appearance ... I have just been relaxing and reading a book and was not expecting visitors."

"Oh, never mind that, Miss Harriet; you look lovely, as always. I find it is sometimes good to relax and dress more comfortably. Never worry over that, my dear lady, it is all my fault for coming unannounced."

"Oh, nonsense, Mr. Chambers, you are always welcome in our ... ever-so-humble home. Please, please ... do come in, sir."

He removed his hat and bowed to her, "Thank you, ma'am," and he entered the room.

She led him through the small entry room to a sitting room and offered him a chair. He sat, and she asked if she could make him tea, or offer him any other refreshment, which he politely refused.

She sat in a chair opposite him, "Miss Abbey is well, I trust?"

"Yes, Miss Harriet, thank you very kindly for asking. She is quite well, though anxious for my return I'm sure."

"No doubt, no doubt. From what I understand, you and the other delegates, have been in Richmond for three or four months now. I can imagine she is missing you terribly by now."

"Yes, and to tell the truth, I am also quite eager to see her, and home as well."

"Oh, yes, I expect so, Mr. Chambers. I can't imagine Richmond would be much to your liking."

"No, ma'am. You are quite correct on that count."

They were quiet for a moment. Then Harriet said, "Well, Mr. Chambers, as much as it is a pleasure to have your company, I'm sure you came here hoping to speak with Evelyn."

He smiled, "Yes, of course, Miss Harriet, though no offense intended to you. It is a pleasure to see you again as well."

"Thank you for saying so, Mr. Chambers. And no offense taken. I understand there is a ... *special* connection between the two of you."

Nathan didn't know how to take this, so just nodded his head.

"But as you no doubt have discerned, Mr. Chambers ... Evelyn is currently out, and I'm not sure how long she will be gone. She was ... not especially forthcoming on exactly what errand she was about, or when to expect her. So I apologize, but I can tell you very little of what you would like to know. Neither where she currently is, nor when to reasonably expect her return."

Nathan couldn't disguise his disappointment at this news. He'd told Tom to be ready to leave this afternoon. But he never considered Evelyn might not be at home. Well, nothing he could do about that now. He *would not* leave without speaking to her, so their departure might have to wait another day.

"But … of course you are more than welcome to wait here until she returns …" Harriet offered.

But Nathan couldn't imagine sitting in the tiny house making small talk with Miss Harriet, potentially for hours, while awaiting Evelyn's return.

"Thank you, kindly, Miss Harriet. But I do have other business requiring my attention. You see, I am preparing to depart for home shortly, but I … wished to have a word with Miss Evelyn before I did."

"Yes, I understand. Is there … some message you'd like me to give her?"

He thought about this a moment. How much should he tell Harriet? He knew Evelyn was unlikely to do anything without her approval, so maybe if he told her what was on his mind it might speed up the whole process. But he decided *no*; there were some things you needed to tell a person to their face—things they should not hear from another, and this *clearly* fell into that category.

"Thank you, Miss Harriet. If you can please just tell her … I wish to speak with her as soon as may be. And … you may tell her I will *not* leave town without speaking with her first. If she returns today before the hour is too late, and if she is of a mind, she can come see me at the place I'm staying. You too, of course, Miss Harriet! I shall be there the remainder of the day. I will write down the address for you, if you have pen and paper handy. And if she can't come today, I will come here again tomorrow morning, say … nine o'clock?"

ᔥᒼᑐᒉᔥᒼᔥᒼᑐᒉᔥᒼᔥᒼᑐᒉ

Evelyn knocked firmly on the hotel door. She'd had to sweet-talk the proprietor downstairs into telling her which room Mr. Stuart occupied. But when he hesitated, despite her best charms, she'd shamelessly hinted Mr. Stuart was … "expecting her" … but had forgotten to give her the room number. She prayed Mr. Stuart's wife never heard about *that!*

In a few moments the door opened, and a man looked out. When he laid eyes on her a look of shock came over his face. He pulled together the sides of the blue silk robe he was wearing and ran his fingers through a disheveled head of dark hair. Despite his current appearance, she could see he was a handsome man, though old enough to be her father.

"Oh! Excuse my appearance, miss. I … haven't been feeling well today and … and I wasn't expecting company. Please … do come back momentarily after I've had a chance to … make myself more presentable."

He started to push the door closed, but she stuck her foot across the threshold, and placed her hand firmly in the center of the door.

"*No!* Please, Mr. Stuart … I must speak with you *now* … most urgently!"

He paused and returned a puzzled expression.

"But miss … I don't believe we've ever met before … what urgent business could you possibly have with me?"

"Please let me come in at once, Mr. Stuart! It concerns our mutual friend, Nathan Chambers and is … a matter of life and death!"

"Oh? Nathan's in trouble? Please do come in then, miss, and tell me what it's about."

She came in and he closed the door, ushering her over to the same chair Nathan had sat in the day after the secession vote, earlier in the week.

"Now then, Miss …?"

"Evelyn, sir. Evelyn Hanson. I am a very dear … *friend* … of Mr. Chambers."

"Oh, well … I'm not surprised Mr. Chambers has a … *friend* … like you, Miss Evelyn. He is, after all, a very handsome, dashing fellow."

She blushed at what Stuart was implying but couldn't deny it.

"Never mind about that just now, Mr. Stuart. It has come to my attention through certain … *friends* of mine … that Mr. Henry Wise and his associates have men following Mr. Chambers in anticipation of the secession. And once things have been decided … as now appears to be the case—him being a military man of some reputation, they intend to confront him. They mean to force him to decide which side he'll fight for."

"*Oh!* I see. Well, there's no doubt which side *that* will be, and it surely won't please Mr. Wise!"

"Precisely, sir."

"Then … what is it these *friends* of yours say Mr. Wise and his cronies intend to do if Mr. Chambers refuses to fight for Virginia?"

"That is the urgency, Mr. Stuart. *They intend to murder him!* I must warn him at once! He must not go anywhere without his armed men guarding him until he leaves Richmond. But … I don't know where he's staying. It was suggested *you* … also being a friend of his … might know where that is."

"Oh! Yes, certainly … give me but a moment to dress and I will take you there, my dear."

"Oh … thank you ever so kindly, Mr. Stuart. But … please do hurry, I fear the worst and I believe there's not a moment to lose!"

ּﬡﬡﬡﬡﬡﬡﬡﬡﬡﬡﬡﬡ

Nathan strode back toward the boarding house, head down, deep in thought. He nearly walked right into a man standing on the street in front of him, speaking his name.

He stopped and looked up. Not Colonel Lee, but *three* men this time, and his initial reaction was not so positive. He recognized the one on the left as Peter Stevens, the handsome young gentleman who'd escorted Evelyn to the ball where he'd last seen her. Stevens was also a former Army officer, and a member of Wise's cadre. Nathan suppressed a strong desire to strangle the man, a feeling he'd also experienced that night at the ball.

Stevens grinned, but Nathan didn't return the smile. The other young men, also dressed as gentlemen, did *not* smile. They looked nervous and gave him non-committal looks.

"Stevens …"

"Mr. Chambers. Well met, sir. May I introduce Mr. Miller and Mr. Baker."

296

Nathan nodded toward them but didn't offer his hand. Miller and Baker tipped their hats to him, but likewise didn't extend their hands.

"Well, I'm sure it's my pleasure to see you again, Mr. Stevens. But if you'll excuse me ... I'm in a hurry just now and have important matters to attend."

"Please, Mr. Chambers ... I've been looking for you and wish but a moment of your time."

Nathan eyed him with suspicion. He could think of no *good* reason for Stevens to seek him out but could easily imagine several *bad* ones.

"Oh? And what is it you wish to speak with me about, pray, Stevens?"

"Mr. Chambers ... now the secession is a ... *fait accompli*, as they say ... some friends of mine would like to know you're thinking on certain topics, sir."

"Hmm ... by friends I assume you mean our *esteemed* former governor, Henry Wise? I can see no reason why Mr. Wise would seek my opinion on *any* subject whatever; he certainly has shown no inclination for doing so in the past."

"Mr. Chambers ... he knows you're a man ... such as myself ... of great military experience, even heroic service to the country. He begs you to consider lending your ... considerable martial talents ... to the wellbeing of Virginia in her hour of need."

Nathan gave him a bland look, and said, "I was unaware *you* had served during the late Mexican War, sir ..."

Stevens blushed. "Did I say so? No ... I simply refer to my time doing my duty in the military, same as you."

"Maybe not *quite* the same. But be that as it may ... I prefer to keep my own counsel concerning my plans, if it's all the same to you ... and Mr. Wise."

"But, sir ... will you not do me the honor of allowing me be the first to hear your intention to come to the defense of the Commonwealth? I should be most honored, sir, to give the good news to my friends and associates regarding this matter."

Nathan knew he was being baited into disclosing his true intentions, but at this point he was having a hard time caring.

After all the recent calamitous events he felt thoroughly disgusted with the whole affair and not particularly inclined to equivocate.

He reached into his pocket and pulled out a cigar. It seemed to him the man on the right flinched when he did this. But it'd been out of the corner of his eye, so he couldn't be sure. He stuck the cigar in his mouth but didn't light it.

"Mr. Stevens … you may tell Mr. Wise and the rest of your *friends* I have no intention of fighting for Virginia — now, or *ever.*"

Stevens frowned at him, "Then … you will fight *against* us, sir? You will be a traitor to your own home of Virginia?"

Nathan took the cigar from his mouth and pointed it at Stevens.

"Let me tell you the difference between you and me, Stevens, aside from the fact I actually fought in a war, while I understand you took to your sick bed. *I don't break my sacred oaths!* You and I swore an oath to the United States and their president. I don't break my oaths, sir! While you … you dare call *me* traitor, when in fact, it is *you*, sir, who is the traitor! You and all your slaver *friends* speak nothing but treasonous sedition."

Stevens' face turned red. Nathan knew he'd struck a nerve.

"Gentlemen, I tire of this conversation. In fact, I am sick at heart, and wish only to return to my home and there pray to God cooler heads may yet prevail. Good day to you, sirs."

But when Nathan put the cigar back in his mouth, and attempted to move past them, he found himself staring down the barrels of three pistols.

Stevens glared at him, "I'm sorry you feel that way, Chambers, as it will not go well for you. Now you will please just hand over that Colt you keep in your pocket and come with us … *sir!*"

Nathan met eyes with each of the three. The looks they returned told him Stevens was the only one who'd ever drawn a gun on a man. The other two had no experience — neither military nor police.

"Or *what*, Stevens? Will you murder me, right here in broad daylight, on this street in the middle of town? With … God knows how many people watching out their windows, or from down the street? Secession or no, there'd be a *noose* in it for you."

Stevens hesitated a moment, then said, "Of course not, sir. We only wish you to accompany us, that we might discuss this matter more thoroughly ... in private."

Nathan could readily imagine the tone of that conversation and had no wish to take part.

But Stevens and company had unwittingly stepped into Nathan's trap. He'd forced them to consider how bad it might go for them if they murdered an unarmed man in the street. It was the slight edge he needed.

"Now, if you would be so good, Mr. Chambers; please do reach in your pocket and hand me that Colt ... nice and easy like ..."

Nathan glowered at him for a moment, then shrugged. He carefully peeled back the right side of his jacket and slowly reached across with his left hand. Using only two fingers, he lifted the small pistol out of his waistcoat pocket.

He grasped the barrel in his left hand and held it out handle first. Stevens reached forward to take it. As his hand touched the handle, Nathan punched him hard in the face. The blow *crunched* bones in the man's nose and he staggered backward.

Nathan swung at the middle man to pistol whip him. But the man's cowardice saved him; he'd already backed away, so the strike missed his face by mere inches.

Nathan's mind raced, already on to the third man, behind him and to the right. He envisioned a trigger about to be squeezed.

A sudden blinding pain struck the top of his head—a searing hot bolt of lightning. It streaked down his back and legs to his feet. His knees buckled, and his sight grew dark. Excruciating agony like knives and needles shot through his arms and chest. Brilliant, mind-dazzling, multi-colored lights flashed and sparkled in the darkness. The world became a swirling dream, and the hard earth rushed up to meet his face.

Chapter 12. Behind Enemy Lines

"I feel safe in the midst of my enemies,
for the truth is all powerful
and will prevail."
– Sojourner Truth

Sunday Apr. 21, 1861 - Richmond, Virginia:

Tom was upstairs in his room nearly finished packing his things when a noise from downstairs made him pause. It sounded as if someone called his name. He held still to listen. Mrs. Wilkerson's voice was coming from out toward the front door, and she did *not* sound pleased, like she was angry with someone and shouting.

Then he heard it again, this time without doubt—a man's voice, "Mr. Clark! Mr. Clark, if you are here, I must speak with you! It is most urgent, sir! *Please!"*

What the devil ...? he thought and headed for the door at a trot.

As he moved down the hall to the head of the stairs the commotion downstairs continued. Mrs. Wilkerson yelled, "You can't come in here, sir! Please go away or I shall call for the authorities!"

But the man seemed to ignore her, and continued to shout, "Mr. Clark! If you can hear me, sir, I *must* speak with you!"

Tom arrived at the front entry and a most amazing sight met his eyes. Mrs. Wilkerson had her shoulder against the door, and was pushing with all her might, using her considerable bulk. But a man outside had one boot, and half an arm wedged into the doorway, keeping her from closing the door.

Tom shook his head in amazement and had to suppress the urge to laugh out loud at the sight. Instead he said, "It's all right, Mrs. Wilkerson, you can let go now ... I'll see what the gentleman wants."

She looked over at him, "Oh! Mr. Clark, thank God you've arrived. He's a mad man, I tell you! I told him he couldn't come in here ... a man like *that* ... in a proper place like *this!* But he wouldn't listen and tried to push his way past me."

"Thank you, Mrs. Wilkerson, but I'll take care of it now, if you please."

"Well, all right, if you say so, Mr. Clark ..."

She left off pushing and stepped back, moving quickly around Tom to put him between her and the stranger.

The man opened the door and began rubbing the arm that he'd wedged in the doorway. "I must hand it to you, Mrs. Wilkerson ... you're a strong woman! I thought I'd lose the circulation in my arm if the conflict continued much longer."

His words and manner of speaking contrasted sharply with his appearance. His ragged dirty clothes, floppy hat, and unkempt hair and beard gave him the look of a common vagrant of around forty years. But now as he stepped inside Tom saw he had clear, keen eyes that betrayed the rest of his appearance.

"You are *not* what you would appear to be ..." Tom said. It was a statement, not a question.

"Very perceptive of you, Mr. Clark. I can see now why Mr. Chambers puts so much faith in you. That's good, because now he needs you more than ever before, sir!"

"What do you mean?"

"I've been charged by ... a *certain important individual, who's known as 'The Employer'* ... to watch over your Captain."

"Watch him? To what end?"

"To keep him safe, Mr. Clark."

Georgie poked his head into the room, followed by William. They'd heard the noise and had come to see what it was about.

"Safe? Safe from what ... or whom?"

"From the Slave Power, sir. It came to our attention they intended to confront him over his loyalties once the secession was decided. They don't want any military men joining the *other* side, you see."

"So ... then why are you here, instead of watching over him?" Tom had a sinking feeling about where this was going.

The man gave Tom a serious look, "I am here because I ... *I have failed in my duty* ... the enemy has taken your Captain! I have come here because it was quicker than seeking out my own friends ... you must come with all haste if you wish to save his life!"

"What?!"

"Men have confronted him on the street, just minutes ago, and there was a fight. Your Captain came against three armed men. And though he downed one with a great blow from his fist, another struck him hard on the head with a pistol. Mr. Chambers fell like a stone.

"I was ... caught off my guard by the suddenness of it. I'd been following these men, even as they followed Mr. Chambers. But when they confronted him in the middle of a busy street in broad daylight, I felt little concern. I thought—wrongly it's now clear—they only planned to call him out as to his loyalties.

"I was not expecting them to put him at gunpoint. Before I could even think to come to his aid the fight was over, he was unconscious on the ground, and the scoundrels were carrying his inert form away. I followed them to an old, abandoned warehouse only a few blocks away. I debated going in by myself, but if I failed, there could be no further help for him. So I ran here as fast as ever my feet would carry me!"

"Then we must go to him, as fast as *our* feet will carry *us*, Sergeant!" Georgie said, eyes wide with fear.

"*Wait!* How do we know you tell the truth and are not just leading us out to bushwhack *us*? For all we know, you're in league with those who attacked Captain Chambers ... or you've made the whole story up to trap us."

The stranger breathed a heavy sigh, "Your thoughtful caution does you credit, sir, but ... now you must decide ... to trust me, or not. If you hesitate, I promise you, *Nathaniel Chambers will die.*"

Tom stared at him another moment, then made his decision, "All right. Georgie, William ... fetch our guns."

Before he'd finished the sentence the two men were running back up the stairs.

Tom turned back to the stranger, "Do you have a name, sir?"

"Not one I'm willing to share. But if you must call me something, you may call me Joseph, though it is *not* my real name."

"Well then, *Joseph* ... if this is a trap, I swear by God, I'll shoot you first."

"As it should be, sir, as it should be."

ℰℐℯℴℭℬ℮ℐℯℭℬ℮ℐℯℭℬ

Sandy and Evelyn hurried along the street toward Nathan's boarding house and were only one house away when Sandy suddenly stopped and grabbed her arm.

"What are you doing, sir?"

"Shhhh ... listen ..."

She tried to quiet her own breathing, so she could hear what he was hearing. At first, she heard nothing, and was ready to hurry him on. Then she heard it: the sounds of shouting. Men arguing loudly with a woman ... and it seemed to be coming from the boarding house.

Sandy put his finger to his mouth, and led her cautiously forward, until they were at the edge of the house.

"You open this door, old woman, or we'll kick it in. We have business with Mr. Chambers and his men, and we'll not wait outside. Open up!"

"Mr. Chambers ain't here. Go away, you scoundrels, before I sick the dogs on you!"

The man laughed, "We know you ain't got no dogs, ma'am. Now open up!"

There came a loud scraping noise, and a squeal.

Evelyn looked at Sandy, eyes wide, and whispered, "We must go to her aid, sir! Are you armed?"

Sandy stood up straight, and answered, "Of course, madam! I am *always* armed, for I have my sharp tongue. And I can assure you it is a wicked cutting weapon, such as few men can endure! It has rarely failed me, and I don't expect it to now. Stay here, my dear, and I shall see what is amiss."

"But ..."

303

"No, Miss Evelyn! ... Mr. Chambers would never forgive me if I allowed you to step into harm's way. Fear not, I will handle these ruffians."

She reluctantly nodded her head, and he tipped his hat to her, then trotted up to the front of the house, and hurried up the stairs.

Evelyn waited in a state of great anxiety. Now besides Nathan, she was fearful for Sandy, and the poor woman in the boarding house. The men confronting them did not sound gentlemanly in the least. Not for the first time, Evelyn wished she were a man, with pistols strapped to her hips, that she might march into the house and put an abrupt end to any ill doings. But if she entered now it would likely only make matters more difficult for Mr. Stuart.

After about five minutes, men came out the front door, and down the steps. She moved back from the sidewalk and hid behind a bush that they wouldn't see her standing there. The men turned and headed off down the street in the opposite direction from where she crouched. She was tempted to go inside, but it occurred to her she didn't know how many men had gone inside, so couldn't be sure all had left. So she waited for Sandy to come out.

In a few more minutes he came out the door and down the stairs. She stepped out from her hiding place.

"There are strange doings afoot today, my dear. I fear you were right about Mr. Chambers. Mrs. Wilkerson, the proprietress says a man came by less than an hour ago—some kind of vagabond, if you believe what she says. Anyway, she says this man came bursting into her house calling for Mr. Clark, claiming armed men had attacked Mr. Chambers on the street and taken him captive. Of course, I am piecing together the story from her rantings, so it could be I have some of it wrong. At any rate, it seems clear something serious is happening. Mr. Clark and the other men left with this stranger, fully armed."

"Oh! Oh, no ..." tears began welling in her eyes, but she fought them down. It was not the time to become emotional, she needed to keep a clear head, "... and what of these men just now? Who were they, and what were they about?"

304

"Clearly more of Wise's bullies, though they didn't say so. Of course, they wouldn't say why they were there. But surprisingly, they didn't seem particularly interested in Mr. Chambers. They were quizzing Mrs. Wilkerson, and then me about Mr. Clark's whereabouts. I can't figure why that would be. Anyway, I told them I was a personal friend of Governor Letcher and ordered them to depart, posthaste! At first, they laughed derisively, calling him 'Letcher the traitor,' and 'Letcher the fool.' But I reminded them Wise only *acted like* the governor, while Mr. Letcher actually *was* the governor, and as such commanded all the law officers and militia in the state. And though he might seem mild mannered, Mr. Letcher was not feeling especially well disposed toward Mr. Wise at the moment. He'd love nothing better than an excuse to string up a few of Wise's troublemakers. That seemed to motivate them to head for the door."

Evelyn thought for a moment, "Hmm ... the only reason they'd be interested in Tom Clark ... would be to keep him from helping Nathan. That's got to be it! These men were supposed to keep Tom from leaving the boarding house to help Nathan. But apparently, they arrived too late; Tom was already gone! That's good news, at least. But ... where did he go? And ... was he in time to help Nathan?"

"I'm sorry, dear ... I don't know anything else, and I'm sure Mrs. Wilkerson will be of no further help. She is quite shaken-up by the day's happenings, and it was a challenge to pull from her the little bit of information I did."

"Thank you, Mr. Stuart. I know you did your best, it's just ... I feel so helpless. I ... I can't think of what to do next." Tears were again welling in her eyes, both of fear and of frustration.

"Well, sometimes there's nothing one can do, except wait ... and pray."

"Yes ... I'm sure you're right but ... well, I can at least go visit ... *my friends* ... to see what they know."

"Shall I accompany you there, dear? I hate to think of you out alone on these streets with all these strange happenings."

She briefly considered it. But as much as she would appreciate having his companionship, she knew she shouldn't lead anyone

305

to the Hughes' house without a specific invitation. And though it was clear they knew Mr. Stuart, it was unlikely he was aware of their ... *particular activities.*

"Oh, thank you ... but no, Mr. Stuart. I shall be perfectly fine, and you have done more than enough already. It is, after all, broad daylight. And though these men may have ill intentions toward Mr. Chambers, they will pay me no mind, I'm certain."

He raised an eyebrow in a curious expression but didn't argue with her. Clearly, she wasn't comfortable telling him who these knowledgeable *friends* were. But he decided that might be for the best.

"Well, if you're sure you'll no longer have need of me, I intend to see if I can locate Mr. Letcher on a Sunday. I wish to prompt him to finally take action against this rampant lawlessness in the streets. Proper gentlemen accosted at gunpoint in the streets?! Ruffians forcing their way into a decent woman's home?! *Indeed!* I should like to think my threats of a few moments ago were not entirely empty, else what's this world coming to, anyway?"

�❧☙☙☙☙☙☙☙☙

Nathan was vaguely aware the dream had changed somehow. The images were sharper than they'd been, and the leering, ugly, angry-looking face covered in blood in front of him was almost ... *real.* The visage also was speaking, but Nathan couldn't understand the words. Maybe in his dream these strange monsters spoke in their own demonic tongue. But then he thought he recognized one word. This word was familiar somehow, but he couldn't quite remember why ...

"Chambers! Chambers! Can you hear me? Wake up!"

Chambers. That was the word ... he should know that word for some reason, but ...

Then he felt an odd, cold sensation all through the dream, something like swimming in frigid water, only he wasn't swimming because he didn't have a body. Only muddled thoughts floating through a darkness that wasn't completely dark, having odd, swirling and flashing lights and colors. And a sensation of sharp pain, only it emanated from no place in particular and everywhere at once.

Then he heard the word again … and now he remembered. *Chambers … that's me. I'm Chambers … it's my name.* He thought it odd, and probably not a good thing; the dream creatures knew his name. Then the bloody, ugly face appeared again, only this time it was more distinct. And it vaguely reminded him of someone … someone he once knew. He couldn't remember who, but he remembered he hadn't much liked him. It made some sense a dream demon would have a face he didn't like. But the face kept staring at him and saying words. It seemed to him he was starting to recognize more of the words, only they were all jumbled and garbled, like Miss Margaret's cipher poem. Who was Miss Margaret, anyway? The name had jumped into his mind. Then he remembered her. Nice lady, very smart. And he remembered she was also in the dream world somewhere, locked in a tower by another demon. But not this ugly one talking … a different one, but who and where? He needed to go look for her. But he didn't know where she was, or even how to move, since he didn't have any legs or feet.

"Chambers … time to wake up … so I can hurt you!"

Why should I wake up for that? I'd rather sleep. And why would a dream creature want me to wake up, anyway? But the demon kept putting his face in view and kept talking. Then it suddenly occurred to him who the creature reminded him of … "Stevens …" he croaked.

"Yes, it's me … or what's left of me. You broke my nose, you bastard! Now you'll pay! I'm gonna cut you up bad, before I kill you, you son-of-a-bitch!"

Then suddenly the dream was over, and he was awake, though he wished he wasn't. He became aware of several extremely uncomfortable sensations. Firstly, a biting pain from his wrists and arms. He glanced up and saw his wrists tied above his head by a strap of leather. They'd looped the strap around a rusty-looking hook embedded in a dark beam above him.

The room was spinning around sickeningly. He tried to stand to take pressure off his wrists, but his legs ignored his commands.

They were limp, though definitely not numb—a burning pain shot through each leg. And he was dripping wet. Obviously Stevens had thrown cold water on him to rouse him. He could tell he had vomited on himself at some point, both from the smell, and the sour taste of bile in his mouth.

But worst of all was a searing pain that emanated from the very top of his head. It streaked down inside his skull where it throbbed with a pounding, mind-numbing sensation, sending a stabbing pain along his spine. Never in life had he felt such pain throughout his body. It made him queasy and he knew he'd vomit again, which he did. Almost immediately another splash of icy water hit his face.

"You disgust me, sir! Have you no self-respect? Stop soiling yourself and stand up like a man to face your punishment!"

Despite the overwhelming pain, complete lack of strength, and swimming, fuzzy sight, Nathan felt the old fire beginning to burn. He'd never been one to lightly take insults from another man, and he wasn't about to start now. He looked up at Stevens and scowled. Then he spit on the man, a bloody spittle wreaking of vomit. "Untie me. We'll see who has self-respect, *coward!*" It came out in a raspy whisper, but Stevens seemed to get the gist. He punched Nathan hard in the face, sending him back to the dream world.

After a while, he again felt cold water on his face and running down his body. But this time he knew it wasn't a dream, but another dousing by his captors.

He slowly opened his eyes a crack. The room still spun, and his sight wouldn't focus properly, but now he remembered where he was.

Again, Stevens leaned in close and held up something shiny in front of Nathan's face. He couldn't tell what it was. His eyes refused to focus on the thing. But Stevens said, "You hurt me, Chambers, and now I'm going to hurt you … only a whole lot worse. I'm going to cut you until you beg me to kill you."

Nathan spat at him again, but this time Stevens had anticipated the move, and stepped back in time to avoid another soiling. Then he stepped up and grabbed the front of Nathan's shirt in both fists, and ripped it open, exposing his bare chest.

But Nathan was in such overwhelming, mind-numbing pain already, the knife held little fear. He thought he might not even feel it. Stevens pressed the blade up to the skin of his chest and poked him releasing a thin stream of blood. Stevens looked at his face to gauge the reaction. But though Nathan's mind was aware of the sensation, it was such a trivial, insignificant pain compared to that already wracking his body it was of little concern. Rather than flinch at the new pain, he smiled at Stevens.

This enraged the man. His face turned a deep red, "Oh, so you think this is funny? We'll see how humorous it is when I cut your guts out and feed them to you!"

He pressed the tip of the knife blade to the center of Nathan's abdomen, just below the sternum. He leaned forward to push in the blade.

There was a sudden ear-splitting noise in the small room. The door burst in, banging against the wall. Stevens turned toward the noise. Tom pulled his trigger, *boom!* The bullet caught Stevens in the upper part of his right arm. The knife clattered to the floor. Tom fired again at Stevens' chest. He staggered back and collapsed.

Miller moved to draw his pistol. William and Georgie shot him point blank. Miller slumped to the floor. His pistol never cleared its holster.

The third man, Baker, stepped back and raised his hands in surrender. He'd seen his comrades go down without so much as a fight and wanted no part of these strangers.

Georgie held him at gunpoint, while Tom and William moved quickly to Nathan.

Tom knelt in front of him to look at his face. Nathan opened his eyes, and croaked out, "Oh … hello, Tom. When did *you* join the party?"

Tom smiled with relief and shook his head, "Hang on, sir. We'll have you down in a moment."

William examined the back of Nathan's head and winced. Dried blood matted the hair into thick black clumps. The collar of his white dress shirt showed a large red stain that flowed onto his fine black suit. There it made a dark shiny streak that ran halfway down his back. Near the top of his head William found a large, gaping wound, four or five inches long, still oozing blood. It'd need tending as soon as possible. But he'd not be able to work on it until they found a safe place to lie Nathan down for a several minutes.

Tom picked up the knife Stevens had dropped. William grabbed Nathan around the chest to prevent him falling, as Tom cut the thongs holding his wrists to the ceiling. He immediately collapsed into William's arms, and Tom reached over to help settle him to a sitting position on the floor.

"Water …" Nathan whispered. The sudden cutting of the cords on his wrists brought a fresh wave of intense pain. It left him shaken and out of breath. His throat was sticky dry and burned from the vomiting.

Tom found a small cup sitting on a side table and dipped it into a half-empty wooden bucket sitting on the floor. He took a sip himself first, to ensure it was drinkable, then held it up to Nathan's lips. He downed several swallows before coughing and shaking his head that he could take no more.

Joseph looked over at Tom and said, "The gunshots may have been heard outside. We must not tarry, others may come. Your men may have to carry him."

"Yes … of course, you're right. Georgie … get over here and help William set the Captain on his feet. We must leave immediately."

Georgie looked at him and said, "But … what about this fella?" he waved his gun at the third assailant, still holding his hands in the air.

Tom gave Georgie a scowl, by way of answer. He drew his pistol, held it to the man's head and pulled the trigger. The sound of the gunshot rattled the quiet room, and smoke swirled in the air once more. The man fell to the ground, a neat red bullet hole right between his eyes.

"Dead men tell no tales! We've already committed two murders, one more is of little matter."

Georgie and William stared at him, open mouthed, in shock at the sudden ruthlessness of the action. It was not what they'd expected from their typically mild-mannered master sergeant.

"He's right," Joseph said, "these men meant to murder your Captain, bloody and painful. A quick death is *far* better than they deserve."

William continued to gaze at Tom in disbelief. But Georgie smiled, shrugged his shoulders, and holstered his pistol, "You're the boss, Sergeant!"

Nathan turned toward them and spoke in a weak, raspy voice, "Gentlemen ... there must be no more killing. This is Virginia ... it's ... *civilized*. Not like West Texas ... we can't just kill people in our way. No more killing ..." he slowly shook his head.

But Tom took a knee and looked him in the eye.

"No, sir!"

It startled Nathan. Tom had never refused an order. "What, Tom?"

"I said, *NO*, sir!"

Nathan seemed confused, and Tom could tell he was having trouble focusing.

"Captain ..."

Nathan's eyes looked foggy, and he gazed around the room as if not seeing it clearly or perhaps wondering where he was.

"Nathan!"

He looked at Tom. Tom disobeying an order was one thing, but ... he *never* called Nathan by his given name! The strangeness of it seemed to cut through the fog, and he gazed at Tom with more clarity.

"Sir ... like it or not, there's a war on now, and we're soldiers behind enemy lines. We've no chance of reinforcement, and don't know who we can trust. This may still be *Virginia*, sir ... but we're no longer in the *United States of America!* If we have to fight our way out, then that's what we'll do. If they catch us now, we will surely hang."

Nathan stared at him a moment longer, then said, "Yes ... yes, of course. You're right Tom. I ... I don't seem to be thinking clearly. Sergeant Clark … take command, and … get us home, if you please."

"Yes, sir. That I *will* do. Men …" he motioned for them to help Nathan from the floor. With Georgie under one arm, and William under the other, they raised him to a standing position. He could move his legs a little, but they wouldn't bear any weight. And his entire body continued to suffer shooting, stabbing pain, regardless of whether he moved or stood still.

Joseph stood by the door, looking out nervously. It was then Tom noticed for the first time the man also held a small pistol in his hand. It reminded Tom to have a quick look around for the Captain's pocket Colt. He didn't see it laying around anywhere. But a quick search of the bodies soon revealed its hiding place in Stevens' jacket, so Tom stuck it in his own pocket. Then he grabbed the other pistols from the dead men, keeping one and distributing the others to William and Georgie, who tucked them into their belts. He made a quick search for any spare ammunition and powder, pocketing that as well.

"Please … we must hurry, sirs," Joseph pleaded.

ಬಿಡಿಂಡಿಂಡಿಂಡಿಂಡಿಂಡಿಂಡಿಂಡಿ

Tom decided to make straight for the horse stables before attempting to return to the boarding house to collect the rest of their belongings. Fortunately, they'd stored most of their traveling equipment—tents, cooking gear, oiled overcoats, etc.—at the stables, there being no good place to keep them at the boarding house. So they'd have the basic necessities they'd need to travel cross-country, at least. Tom had already ruled out the train station—it was too likely to be watched, and the westbound train for Covington only departed in the morning. And, since the Captain had said he wanted to leave today, that meant traveling by horseback.

Now he prayed the enemy hadn't thought to watch the stables. Joseph led them in a circuitous route, staying away from the major streets and cutting through back alleys as much as possible to avoid unfriendly eyes.

When they were a block from the stables, he told Tom to stop while he went on ahead to check if it was safe. But before he left, Tom caught his eye and said, "Whatever else happens, I would thank you for what you've done today. If not for you the Captain would already be dead. I can *never* repay you for that."

But Joseph smiled, patted Tom on the shoulder, and headed off toward the stables.

A few minutes later—what seemed an eternity to those waiting—Joseph returned, slightly out of breath.

"All is well. The stables are clear ... come!"

They headed out, moving as quickly as they could manage, with Nathan unable to support his own weight. When they arrived at the stables, they moved inside and found a room that was relatively clean with a table. They laid Nathan on the table, face first so his head wound could be examined and tended. Tom sent Georgie to collect the gear and see to the horses, and Joseph to watch the door for anyone approaching.

William was already tending to the Captain; Tom hadn't needed to give *that* order. William had thought to grab his medical necessities, including a small bottle of whiskey, even though they'd left the boarding house in a great hurry. He was pouring whiskey onto the wound, and wiping away the crusty blood with a clean, white cloth that was quickly turning dark red. The Captain moaned softly but didn't flinch or try to pull away.

Seeing the treatment was well underway, and having no stomach for William's handiwork, Tom went to find the proprietor to arrange for paying off their bill. He'd not had time to bring any money with him, so the man would have to trust his word that he'd send payment as soon as he could arrange it. Hopefully, the Wilkersons would pay it once Tom explained the situation and gave them bank notes to cover it.

An hour later, Nathan's wound was stitched, the horses saddled and packed, and the proprietor satisfied. So they prepared to leave for the boarding house.

Tom shared a quick look with William before they stepped outside, raising a questioning eyebrow and tipping his head toward the Captain. William shook his head slowly, and then shrugged, as if to say, "Not good, but we shall have to wait and see."

Tom decided they should ride from this point, in case they needed to make a quick getaway. Nathan and his men would ride four horses, which left two spare horses and the mule, Molly. One of the spare horses they packed but lightly, leaving the saddle open, so Joseph could ride with them as far as he would.

They carefully helped Nathan into the saddle, but he was very unsteady and wobbly, having a hard time with his balance and controlling his own muscles. So Tom dug into his pack and pulled out a length of rope.

He reached up toward Nathan, and said, "Forgive me, sir, but I must tie you in the saddle, lest you fall. I know it's undignified, but I can think of no other way. If we put another man on to help steady you and we must run for it, Millie can't be expected to keep up carrying two riders."

Nathan gave him a look and a wave of his hand, a gesture that meant, "just get on with it and stop apologizing," so Tom set about firmly anchoring Nathan to the saddle.

Once again Joseph led them by the back alleyways to avoid detection. And again, when they were within a block of the boarding house, he signaled a halt. He dismounted, and said, "I shall return shortly. Be prepared to move when I do. Either we will go straight to the boarding house and collect your belongings, or we will ride directly out of town."

Tom nodded, and Joseph trotted out into the lengthening shadows of the evening. Tom was grateful the sun would soon set, to help cover their movements.

In less time than Tom had expected, Joseph came trotting back, and jumped back into his saddle.

"We must away ... men watch the house."

"Damn. How many?" Tom had half a mind to risk it if they weren't too badly outnumbered. He hated to leave behind their things, especially the bank notes and the food he'd carefully packed away for the road. Without that they could be badly slowed trying to forage, with no way to purchase any supplies along the way.

But worst of all, they'd have to leave the rifles. Georgie had brought one for each man, including two of the nice new Springfields. Without those they'd be at a severe disadvantage in an extended gunfight, and they'd not be able to hunt for game in the woods.

"Too many. Though none are in or around the house, and they try to make it look clear … it's a trap. I've been doing this long enough to spot them, without them spotting me. Six at the least, spread about the neighborhood. Maybe more. And though they try to disguise it, I could tell several were armed, so I must assume the others are as well."

"*Damn* … damn it to hell! Well, there's nothing for it then. But which way shall we leave town? I meant to study the map just after packing, but you interrupted us before I could do it."

"*South … we must cross the James before heading west.*"

Tom was surprised … the answer came from Nathan not Joseph.

"I have studied the map … I know the way," he said, almost in a whisper.

"Yes, sir, but … due west would be quicker, don't you think?" Tom wasn't sure how much he should trust the Captain in his current state.

"Mr. Chambers is right," Joseph responded. "Mayo's Bridge heading south is the last across the river for more than fifty miles. If you're north of the river you must follow a narrow track as the river bends in a northward arc. Or travel many miles out of your way even further north. On the narrower track you will be easier to follow. And if they get ahead of you, they can guard the few crossings, knowing at some point you must get across to arrive at the mountain passes leading into the West. If you cross the river now, the countryside will be wide open to you, and you can take many different paths to avoid capture."

"Very well, lead on then, if you're willing to guide us."

Joseph smiled and turned his horse by way of answer. But to Tom's surprise, he walked his horse rather than trotting. Tom moved up next to him, "You seemed in a great hurry before … why do we move so slowly now?"

"Appearances, Mr. Clark. It is something I know a great deal about."

"Appearances?"

"If you behave in a way people think normal, they will never even see you. But if you move quickly, people will take notice, and wonder why. Moving slowly, even if they see us, they will think nothing is amiss. Plus … it will give time for the sun to set before we arrive at the bridge, in case it is … *watched*."

"Do you think it will be? Surely they'd not know we're headed that way?"

"I have made the near fatal mistake of underestimating the enemy once today, Mr. Clark. I don't intend to do so again. If they hold the bridge against us, we may have no choice but to shoot our way through. I assume you and your men are willing to do so?"

Tom just snorted a laugh, and Joseph smiled, "Thought so. But … wait for my signal before you start any gunfire. Even if the bridge is watched, they may not be as diligent as their masters might like. There should be plenty of traffic, and we may blend in if we act inconspicuous."

Again, Joseph led them on a circuitous route, avoiding the main roads, though it meant taking longer to arrive at the bridge. Tom was becoming more anxious with each mile, imagining their enemies closing in around them like a noose. But he was pleased when the sun finally set, and near darkness closed around them, providing good cover.

Eventually Joseph led them on 15th Street in the direction of the water, though it was one block further east that they'd needed to go, the bridge being at the end of 14th —another way to avoid potentially prying eyes. But finally, the point came when they were out of options, having reached the river's edge. Now they must cross back to over to 14th, and head out onto the bridge.

As they reached 14th and turned left, they saw the bridge entrance ahead of them, torches burning brightly on posts to each side of the entrance. Joseph looked over, giving Tom a meaningful look. In the torchlight they could see men lounging about on either side of the bridge entrance, as if … waiting for something.

"They watch, but aren't especially attentive, as I'd hoped. There is a steady stream of traffic, and they may not know we're on our way. Let us see if we can bluff our way past."

Tom saw what Joseph meant. Though not extremely crowded, still, a fair number of horses, carriages, and wagons were crossing the bridge. The men loitering off to the sides appeared to be paying but scant attention. As they rode closer, it seemed they might be able to blend in with the other traffic and pass onto the bridge unmolested.

But as they closed to within fifty yards, they heard men running on the street behind them, and shouting. Looking back, they saw a group of a half-dozen or so men, running down 14th Street in their direction. As he watched, Tom saw a man pull out a pistol and aim it right at him. He resisted the urge to duck; it was more than a hundred yards, so there was little chance of being hit. He heard the loud *pop* of the pistol going off, and a puff of smoke rising. He looked forward and saw the bridge watchers jump up at the sound and scramble up onto the roadway. The man who'd fired the pistol was waving and shouting, "Stop those men … stop those men! Don't let them cross the bridge!"

Tom exchanged a hard look with Joseph, who pulled out his pistol and cocked the hammer, "Yes, it's time, Mr. Clark."

Tom dropped his reins, and pulled one pistol from its holster, the other from where he'd tucked it into his belt; pulling back both hammers as he did. William and Tom had seen the movement and didn't need to be told to do likewise. They dropped the leads on the mule and the spare horse. There'd be no need to guide them now, and the leads might get in the way or become tangled. By training and instinct, the pack animals would follow the other horses, once the action started.

"Men … when I open fire, spur into a gallop, and shoot anything that moves!" Tom ordered.

He looked over at Nathan, clutching Millie's reins and looking wobbly but determined. "Lead on, Tom. Don't worry, even if I pass out, Millie will follow with no help from me. I'm sorry, but I don't think I can hold a pistol just now."

"It's all right, Captain, that won't be necessary. Just stay in the midst of us, where we can guard you, if you will."

Then, with another quick glance at his men, Tom turned and fired at the men watching the bridge, spurring his horse. He continued firing both pistols as he rode. William and Georgie also fired pistols with both hands, and Joseph fired his single pistol, as they galloped toward the bridge.

That first pistol shot from the men coming up behind had gotten everyone's attention. But the sudden thunderous firing of multiple guns and the pounding of galloping hooves, stirred those in and around the bridge like a stick in a hornets' nest.

The bystanders scrambled for safety. Those already on the bridge moved at a run toward the southern end, away from the mayhem. Those not yet on the bridge scattered off the roadway as best they could. The bridge watchers attempted to return fire, but it was panicked and ineffectual, as if they were more concerned with taking cover, than fighting back. Bullets pounded the dirt around them, zipped past, or ricocheted noisily off the roadway and bridgework.

Tom looked at Nathan and was dismayed he was now a whole horse length ahead of the rest of them. With no guns to fire he'd focused on the gallop, and Millie, being a competitive spirit, was determined to win the race. Tom cursed and spurred Jerry to greater speed. The last thing he wanted was the Captain out alone by himself, making an easy target.

And his fear seemed to play itself out, as a man stepped out onto the roadway between Nathan's galloping horse, and the bridge deck. He held up his hand in a sign that meant halt and leveled a pistol at Nathan. But whether by luck or by design, at that moment Nathan slumped forward in the saddle. His head rested against the back of Millie's neck, covered by her flowing black mane.

The man standing in the road looked surprised. No longer able to see the rider he'd been attempting to waylay, he realized the horse wasn't going to stop.

Before he could react, Millie was on him. A man threatened her master; she caught him in the chest with a steel shod hoof, knocking him to the ground. She'd meant to kill him, if she could. He lay motionless as she galloped past.

They thundered onto the bridge deck, and across, looking back and firing at anyone who raised a head. Back on solid ground they moved quickly away.

All the traffic on the bridge deck had moved aside to let them pass, and those on the road ahead had cleared a way. It wasn't every day people in Richmond heard heavy gunfire, and it caused panic among those on the roadway—but also great excitement. Tom saw people turn toward them as they rode past, as if wondering, *Who are these men?*

⁆⁂⁆⁂⁆⁂⁆⁂⁆⁂

Evelyn finally arrived home just after sundown. She felt a strange combination of worry, fear, anxiety, anger, and frustration. It was a jumble of emotions she struggled to sort out, though fear seemed the most dominant.

She'd arrived at the Hughes house an hour earlier in a raw fury, determined to give Jonathan a piece of her mind. He had promised to keep Nathan safe! That obviously had *not* happened. Despite Jonathan's assurances, and his insistence Nathan should *not* be told of the danger, he'd been assaulted at gunpoint on the street, knocked unconscious—God knows how badly injured— and carried away by his enemies, according to what Mr. Stuart had said.

But when she began to vent her anger at Jonathan, he was so apologetic and remorseful she could not sustain the emotion. Clearly Jonathan was as worried as she was, and on top of that was feeling a heavy burden of guilt.

And … not only he'd had no news of Nathan, or Tom Clark and their men, but one of Jonathan's own men—one who'd been assigned to watch over Nathan—had also gone missing. In the end Evelyn had exchanged a tearful hug with Angeline, along with a promise that whoever heard something first would immediately contact the others.

When she entered her house, she was not surprised Harriet waited up for her. And the sour look she received was also entirely expected. She silently agreed she deserved it this time.

"Before you start on me, Momma, allow me to apologize. I had no intention of staying out so long, nor of worrying you. I am so sorry, but it couldn't be helped. You see ... while I was out, I heard ... a rumor ... that Mr. Chambers was in danger, because he had disagreed with the secessionists. Of course, I immediately tried to find him to warn him. But ... though I went all over town, and asked several people who might know, in the end I never could find him. Oh, Momma, I am so worried!"

She had not intended to say so much, nor to stir her own emotions in the process, but now she found tears welling up in her eyes once again.

"Oh, my goodness, Evelyn. That's horrible! And if you'd have just come straight home with me, you'd have seen him. He was *here* while you were out!"

"*What?!*"

"Yes ... about a half hour after I got home from church, he knocked on the door, looking for you."

Evelyn stepped into the main room and sat heavily in a chair.

"*No ...*" she whispered, eyes wide, tears welling up.

"Yes ... he seemed very eager to talk to you."

It was such a terrible shock she could hardly speak. If she'd come home after church instead of going out looking for him ... Nathan might be safe and sound now, instead of ... *what?*

"What ... what did he say, Momma?" she managed in a half-whisper.

"Not much, really ... just that he was planning to leave town today, and he wished to speak with you before he left. He was very disappointed you weren't here, but he did say he would not leave town until he spoke with you. He left me the address of his residence in town, a boarding house over toward the capitol."

"Oh, Momma! The last news I heard was ... armed men challenged him on the street. They fought, and Nathan was carried away, either unconscious or ..." she trailed off, voice choked with emotion, unable to even speak the unthinkable alternative.

Harriet was quiet for several moments as if in thought. "Well ... clearly he has refused to go along with the secession. And ... unless I'm sorely mistaken about him, probably told them he would fight for the *other* side if it came to it."

Evelyn nodded her agreement, finding her voice choked up.

But after another long silence, Harriet surprised her by saying, "Well ... maybe it's for the best."

"*What?!*"

"Oh ... not that Mr. Chambers might have been hurt! No, I didn't mean that. I pray he is well and safe. No, rather I meant, maybe it is best you weren't here, and he didn't ask you ... well, what he *might* have asked you. He is, after all, proving himself disloyal to Virginia, and we might be better off not associating with him."

Evelyn was nearly speechless and felt anger rising. "*Disloyal?!* How can you say that, Momma? He has spent the last four months here in Richmond trying to *save* Virginia! Just because he disagrees with the secessionists, doesn't mean he is a disloyal Virginian. In my opinion it means quite the opposite. He's served in the United States Army, in time of war even. He knows what will happen if *that* Army is used against Virginia ... she will be devastated Momma, and likely us with her!"

"No, no ... you misunderstand me again, Evelyn. I don't mean he was disloyal for fighting against the secession while it was being argued. Though I must confess I don't understand all those political issues one way or the other. No, what I meant was, now that it's been decided, if he chooses to fight *against* Virginia, he is not being loyal. That's all I meant."

"Well ... maybe it means he is loyal to something more important ... something more meaningful. Like the country as a whole ..."

"Yes, yes, I'm sure there are all kinds of arguments on both sides. And like I said, I don't really understand the politics, anyway. All I know is ... people are saying it's time for all

Virginians to come together, along with the rest of the Southern states, to protect the way things are ..."

"Momma ... I don't want to argue this with you right now. I'm worried sick about Nathan, and now you tell me he was here, which makes me feel even sicker. If I'd been here to warn him of the ... *rumors*, he wouldn't be ... *whatever he is* ..."

"But ... you told me you only heard these rumors after you left church today. If that was the case, you wouldn't have been able to warn him anyway, even if you'd seen him. Unless ... you already knew he was in danger. Did you?"

Evelyn realized in her fear and anxiety for Nathan she had slipped up and told Harriet more than she should have. Now she would have to backtrack.

"Oh ... yes, you're right, Momma. I was so worried I wasn't thinking clearly. If I'd not yet heard the rumors, I couldn't have warned Nathan even if I had seen him here earlier."

She'd spoken in a hypothetical form, so it wasn't a lie, strictly speaking, though she still felt a little guilt about it. It seemed to satisfy Harriet, however, and she didn't pursue it further. But Evelyn knew she'd have to be more careful in the future. If Harriet began to suspect she was involved in ... *certain activities* ... it could become a very serious problem.

Later that evening Harriet passed by Evelyn's door and again heard sobbing. But she had decided Mr. Chambers was *not* good for Evelyn given the current state of affairs in Richmond. In her mind, she had already written him out of her plans for Evelyn. Maybe that handsome young Peter Stevens might still be interested? She would have to make inquiries ...

Chapter 13. A Hailstorm of Lead

"War is the remedy our enemies have chosen,
and I say let's give them all they want."
– Major General William Tecumseh Sherman,
U.S. Army

Sunday Apr. 21, 1861 - Manchester, Virginia:

Once they were well clear of the bridge and several blocks away, they slowed to a trot so as not to exhaust the horses. They rode quickly through the small town of Manchester, a matter of only a dozen or so blocks—an expansion of Richmond onto the south side of the James. They continued to check back over their shoulders but saw no sign of pursuit. When they were about halfway through town, Joseph led them a block over to their right, before turning west again. This put them on the street that became Old River Road and headed west, generally following the river.

They crossed the railroad tracks of the Richmond and Petersburg Railroad, and continued west. The town began to give way to a more rural, agricultural area before fading away altogether, leaving only fields, forests, and the occasional farmhouse. Without the city lights it was quickly becoming too dark to see where they were going. The sky was overcast, so there was no moonlight to help guide them.

Tom turned to Joseph, who was riding next to him, "Well, what now? We can't continue riding into the darkness, or we're likely to stray off the road and suffer an injury to ourselves or the horses."

"You're right about that, Mr. Clark. And I'm sure Mr. Chambers must have rest as soon as it can be had. I know a place … not much farther … where we can get off the road and be hidden from sight."

"Lead on, then Joseph. You've steered us well so far. I've no reason to misbelieve you now."

Joseph just smiled by way of answer, though it was getting so dark Tom could barely make it out.

They continued on for several more minutes when Joseph called out, "Slow now. I must find the trail. It's hard to spot even in daylight. We must walk a ways, so I don't miss it in the dark."

So now the horses walked. Joseph moved to the left edge of the roadway, and rode bent low in the saddle, examining the terrain as they passed. They continued on in this manner for ten or fifteen minutes, now moving through a heavily wooded area. Tom continued to gaze back anxiously the way they'd come, fearing to see riders coming along the road. When he wasn't doing that, he was worrying over Nathan who seemed to alternate between having his head up looking around and slumping forward with his head resting against the back of Millie's neck. William now rode next to him, and Tom saw him speaking quietly with the Captain from time to time, especially when he was slumped over, though Tom couldn't catch any of the words.

Finally, when Tom's anxiety was about to get the better of his judgment, Joseph called out, "Ah! Here it is. Come, gentlemen, down into the borrow pit just here, then up the other side where the ground levels out. Follow me … single file, if you please. It'll leave fewer marks for someone to notice."

Joseph led them down into the borrow pit, which had a gentle slope on the side next to the road but rose more steeply on the other. When he reached the top, he turned to the side and said, "Mr. Clark, gather your men over in that small clearing and wait. I will see what I can do to hide our trail."

So after they were all across and up into the woods on the far side, they paused, and Joseph got down off his horse, handing the reins to Tom. He looked around on the ground for a few minutes, as if searching for something, then stooped and came up with a fallen branch. It was not too large or heavy on the broken end, and the other end still held some leaves, as if it had only recently fallen. He turned and walked back into the borrow pit. They heard a scraping sound that continued for several minutes. Then Joseph appeared again, tossed the branch into the woods, and climbed back into the saddle.

"Now even I wouldn't know I've been here," he said with a smile. He turned his horse and led them off into the woods. With trees looming all around it was nearly pitch black, forcing them to proceed slowly and cautiously. Tom realized Joseph was not just leading them off randomly into the woods; there was a trail here, though old and overgrown. Fortunately, after only a mile or so the trees gave way to a clearing—an agricultural section where the land had been cleared, though the field appeared untended at the present. They rode through waist-high weeds. Ahead they could just make out the shape of a large building in the darkness.

They paused in front of the building—a good-sized barn. All dismounted, except for Nathan, who was still tied to the saddle.

"Do you have a candle in your gear, Mr. Clark?"

"*I* do," Georgie answered for him. He went back to the mule, and started rummaging around, coming back a few moments later, handing Joseph the candle.

Joseph pulled out a match and lit the candle. He pulled his small pistol from his pocket. "Mr. Clark, would you care to join me? I've stayed here before on my travels. It's been abandoned for a while but is not so old as to be excessively leaky in the rain, nor in danger of imminent collapse. But ... I must assume I'm not the only traveler familiar with it. Let's make sure no one is home, especially anyone ... *unsavory* ... before we lead your Captain inside, shall we?"

Tom pulled the pistol from his waistband by way of answer. Joseph led him to the barn door, unlatched the handle, pulled it open and walked inside. "Hello? Is anyone in here? We mean you no harm, only wanting to get in out of the night. Hello?" The only answer was a sudden fluttering of wings up in the rafters—a barn owl they'd disturbed with their light and their human voices.

Joseph stuck his pistol back in his pocket, "Well, old Mr. Owl wouldn't be in here hunting if there were any men about. Come, let us get Mr. Chambers off that horse and bedded down."

ಬಿಎಸ್ಡಿಎಸ್ಡಿಬಿಎಸ್ಡಿಸಿಬಿಎಸ್ಡಿಸಿಬಿ

Tom woke and looked up. He saw the faint outline of an open window high up in the barn, which meant dawn was not far off.

He glanced around at the other bedrolls and noticed two were empty—William's, who currently had the watch, and Joseph's. He had a momentary twitch of suspicion; had the man snuck off and abandoned them, or gone off to tell their enemies their whereabouts? But as the sleep cleared from his head, he realized how foolish those thoughts were. The man could have betrayed them many times yesterday and hadn't. In fact, he'd done the opposite, steering them away from trouble on several occasions. Besides which, he'd risked getting shot when they'd stormed across the bridge, hadn't he?

Then he thought of the Captain and turned his attention to the man lying next to him. Nathan was lying on his side with his face turned toward Tom. His mouth was slightly open, and a stream of drool ran out the side. In all the times they'd slept out in the wilds he'd never seen Nathan look like that. Tom felt an icy chill of fear. Even in sleep the Captain had always been in control.

That he was still sound asleep at this hour was even more frightening. Tom had a running challenge with himself to wake up and be out of bed before the Captain, but it rarely happened. Nathan was a man of such strict habits it was almost automatic he'd be up and dressed as the sun first broke into the sky. But not Tom. He'd never liked getting up early when he was a younger man, and even now he had to work at it. He leaned over and placed his hand on the Captain's forehead. His skin felt cool and Tom's touch elicited no response.

Tom jumped out of bed and rubbed the sleep from his eyes while looking around for his hat and boots. He soon had them on and headed for the door, determined to talk with William about the Captain. But on his way, he gave Georgie a kick, "Up and at 'em, Private," for which he received a groan, and a grumbling, "Yessir."

He went out, closing the door behind him. He stepped out into the weedy field surrounding the farm and gazed around in every direction. The field to the south spread out for what appeared to be several hundred acres to a tree line on the far side. In the east the sun was just breaking over the horizon into a cloudless sky, and a great stretch of low rolling fields extended as far as the eye could see.

Back to the north, the direction from which they'd come last night, the tree line was less than a hundred yards away. That would be William's current station, though Tom couldn't spot him. *Good man*, Tom thought. He'd have been very unhappy if William had been visible. But William had surprised everyone in the Army by applying his superior brainpower to becoming a good soldier, such that he had become one of their most reliable men. It was the main reason Tom had invited him to come back east with them. It was a decision that had paid dividends many times over, especially in a situation like they had now, where one of their men was injured.

Tom made a loud bird whistle. After a moment a nearly identical whistle came from the woods, so Tom headed in that direction.

A few more bird-whistle exchanges and Tom found William's location. He noted with satisfaction it was a good one. Up in the crook of an oak tree where several branches came together, it was set back a few yards from the trail they'd come in on. It afforded the watcher a good view back down the trail with very little possibility of being seen. Anyone coming along that trail would be at the mercy of his guns before they ever knew what hit them.

Tom clambered up next to him, so they might talk without shouting.

"Good morning, William."

"Good morning, Mr. Clark. How's the Captain doing?"

"That's what I came to talk with you about. I stayed awake long into the night watching him. All night he lay there not moving. More like a man unconscious than a man sleeping. When he suffered that bad cut back in Texas he moaned, thrashed, and twitched all night, which worried me a great deal. But this seems worse … somehow."

"Yes … it *is* concerning. It is … *not* a good sign, I'm afraid."

"But … you examined his wound … you said it only cut the flesh and hadn't broken any bones."

"Yes … and probably the Captain's own hat, though badly stove-in no doubt, kept the metal of the pistol from dirtying the wound. So it's much cleaner than the wound he suffered in the cantina."

"Well … he should recover quickly then, shouldn't he?"

William was quiet for a moment, removing his glasses and wiping them down, as if considering his answer.

"With any other part of the body, I'd say yes, but the head … it is … *different*. With a hard blow to the head such as this …"

"What?"

"I have heard some theorize it is best if the bones of the skull *are* broken during such an injury, so long as jagged bone shards aren't pushed into the brain."

"William, once again you utterly baffle me. How could broken bones possibly be a good thing?"

William sighed, and again was silent for a moment, as if struggling for an explanation that would make sense to Tom.

"Sir … you know when you get kicked in the shin, or … or … *no*—better yet—when you step in a hole and twist your ankle?"

"Yes … hurts like the devil, and you can't walk on it for days. Why?"

"Well, aside from being painful, and turning various odd colors, what else do you notice around the ankle when you suffer such an injury?"

"It stiffens and … it swells up. If you don't get your boot off quickly, you'll have to cut it off, or it'll feel like you're being squeezed in a vise."

"Exactly! Now … imagine the ankle is your brain, and it has been injured by a hard blow, and the skull is the boot …"

Tom thought for a moment, then his eyes widened, "Oh my God! Is that what's happening inside the Captain's head?"

"I fear so."

"Then … he must be in a tremendous amount of pain. He must feel like his head is being hammered on an anvil."

"Yes … I believe so, though he complains but little. And I …"

William didn't complete the sentence and went silent. Tom looked him in the eye and saw … worry? Fear?

"What is it, William?"

"Tom … sometimes men who suffer these injuries seem fine for days, but then suddenly …"

Tom stared at him, mouth agape. He felt a knot forming in his stomach, and tears filling in his eyes.

"But … what can we do?" Tom asked.

"Nothing good, I'm afraid. Ideally, he'd be kept quiet and still for several days, maybe a week even."

Tom shook his head, "I'm afraid it's going to be the opposite: likely bouncing along in the saddle instead. Though this place is safe for the moment, Joseph isn't the only one who knows about it. When they can't find us out on the road, how long before they come looking here?"

William didn't answer, just looked away.

"If you will take my watch for the moment, sir, I'll go back and examine him. If he's not yet awake, we must rouse him. I've also heard a man in his condition should *not* be allowed to sleep too long, lest he …

"Anyway, I'll go wake him, and send Georgie out to relieve you shortly."

"Thank you, William."

Tom sat in the perch gazing down the trail, mulling over the disturbing things William had said, when he spotted movement. He slowly drew his revolver from its holster, pulled back the hammer, and aimed it at the approaching figure, following it until a man appeared over his sights. Tom quickly lowered the hammer and put away the gun. It was Joseph, walking back down the trail in his direction. When Joseph was nearly even with where he sat in the tree, Tom whistled.

Joseph stopped and looked in Tom's direction but didn't see him. Tom whistled again, and Joseph looked up, finally spotting him. He walked up under the tree, "Good morning, Mr. Clark. Up visiting with the birds this morning?"

Tom laughed, "Good morning, Joseph. What news?"

"I was out watching the road well before dawn, and a good thing too. Just before sunrise a group of twelve men rode by, coming from Richmond in a great hurry. They carried pistols and rifles and led two spare horses loaded with equipment. It *may* be just a coincidence and may have nothing to do with us, but ..."

Tom snorted, "Not likely. At least I'd not wager any money on it ... nor my life ..."

"Yes, my thoughts exactly. Ah, I see your relief has arrived."

Georgie came up at that moment, wished them both a good morning, waited for Tom to climb down, then scrambled up in his place.

"Come, Mr. Clark, let's go check on Mr. Chambers. And see if we can devise a plan that will keep us alive for another day, shall we?"

When they entered the barn Nathan was sitting up, with William's help, and having a drink of water from a canteen.

"Good morning, sir."

Nathan looked up, and for a moment stared in Tom's direction without speaking. Finally, he said, "Good morning, Tom," in a weak, raspy sounding voice.

Joseph came over and sat cross-legged on the ground in front of him, and Tom did the same.

"Good morning, Mr. Chambers. We hadn't time for proper introductions yesterday. I am called Joseph. I am ... in league with certain individuals in Richmond who have been ... hmm. Let's just say, secretly opposing the Slave Power for a number of years. Mostly helping to relieve them of some of their more valuable ... *property,* if you understand me."

Nathan gazed at him a moment, then said, "The Underground Railroad?"

"I have heard it called that, yes."

"You don't appear especially reputable, Joseph."

Joseph laughed, "They told me you tended toward brutal honesty, and I can see now it's no exaggeration, sir."

"Sorry ... not meaning disrespect ... I only meant—"

"No apology necessary, sir. As you have surmised, it is something of a disguise. Or rather a *character* I have assumed to escape notice as I move about."

"Captain, Joseph and his people have been watching over you, apparently for some time now, for fear the slavers might make a

330

move against you. It was he who came to fetch us at the boarding house, that we might affect your rescue."

"Then … I thank you, Joseph, and I owe you my life …"

"Nonsense, Mr. Chambers. If I hadn't failed so badly in my original duty, there'd have been no *need* of a rescue."

"Well, be that as it may, I am still much obliged, sir."

"Captain … I'm afraid we're not out of danger yet. Joseph spied a group of heavily armed men with extra horses and traveling gear this morning, riding down the road, heading west."

"A hunting party?"

"Yes, I believe so … and we're the likely prey."

"Hmm … Joseph, where are we exactly?"

"We're roughly seven miles southwest from Manchester. We are currently about a mile and a quarter off the main road in an abandoned barn."

"The Old River Road that turns west somewhere around here, then runs along the south side of the river toward the small town of Scottsville?"

"Yes, that's the one. I wasn't aware you were familiar with the regions surrounding Richmond, Mr. Chambers."

"I'm not. But I was considering riding home from Richmond on horseback, so I'd studied a map for a potential route. I intended to speak with someone familiar with the roads before departing, but … anyway, I'd planned on passing through Lynchburg on the way …"

"Yes, likely you will need to pass close to Lynchburg before heading into the mountains, if you don't want to cross the James again."

"So, Joseph, what route did you have in mind from here?"

"To be honest, Mr. Chambers, I hadn't decided on anything yet. With things being what they were yesterday, I was just looking for a place to hide out for the night. Then I remembered this place and made for it. I had a vague idea of following the river road for a little further before cutting across to another road that runs more in a southwesterly direction."

"You mean the one that runs through Cumberland Church and there forks—the more northerly heading on westward toward Maysville, and the southern branch heading southwest toward Farmville?"

"Yes ... that's right. But ... you said you didn't know this area. You can't possibly be remembering all that from gazing at a map?"

"Oh, yes he can!" Tom said and laughed, "the Captain can remember anything he has looked at only once, to the smallest detail."

"You exaggerate, Tom. But ... yes, I have a good recall of maps and ... other things, once I've looked at them."

Joseph stared at him opened mouthed for a moment, "Well ... I've heard of such things before, but have never seen it for myself ..."

Tom noticed the longer he talked, the more the Captain seemed like his old self, no longer listless and befuddled. It warmed his heart, and he exchanged a look with William, who returned a slight smile and a shrug.

"Since the road to Cumberland Church is the most direct westerly road, isn't it likely to be the first place they'll search?"

"Yes ... it's a reasonable point, Mr. Chambers."

"What if we travel cross country, in a southwesterly direction, hooking up with the road that runs from Manchester to Amelia then goes on to connect with the branch coming down from Cumberland at Farmville? It's a little farther out of our way, so might throw searchers off our trail."

"Yes ... could be ... and it's mostly just farmland, interspersed with some wooded areas between here and the road, so should be fairly easy going. A few streams to ford, but nothing that requires finding a bridge, now that the rains have let off, and the flooding earlier in the month has passed. Yes, why not?"

They broke out some hardtack from their packs and passed it around. It was tasteless and dry—a hard biscuit baked to a dense crunchiness intended to survive being bounced about on the road in a saddlebag or pack without turning to crumbs. There was no pleasure in eating it, but it took the edge off their hunger. Tom again cursed the enemy for keeping them from retrieving their supplies from the boarding house, including the plentiful food he had packed for their journey. Fortunately, they'd stored their canteens and water skins with the other traveling gear at the stables. And they'd filled them all before departing, so water wouldn't be an issue.

Nathan took only a few nibbles, and then would eat no more. Tom noticed a grimace of pain on his face as he tried to swallow.

"How're you feeling, sir?"

"I ... I've felt better, Tom."

"Can't eat any more, sir? You should try ... you need to keep up your energy for the journey."

"I find my stomach ... is unhappy with my head. And I can't say I blame it."

"Head still hurts, sir?"

Nathan looked at him and gave a slight nod.

"Tom ... tie me on the saddle again today and let's get moving. We dare not stay in one place too long. Avoid any houses, people, or roads if you can. The fewer people who see us the better."

"Yes, sir."

"And, Tom ..."

"Sir?"

"Thanks for getting me out yesterday. I was in a bad spot ..."

Tom thought of all the things he might say in answer to that; how truly frightening it had been when he feared the worst; how he'd rather die himself than have something like that happen to Nathan; how he'd do it again a hundred times without hesitation; how there was no need to thank him for it, and on and on. But finally, he just settled on, "You're welcome, sir," and moved off to pack up for the journey.

෨෨෬෬෨෨෬෬෨෨෬෬

As the evening shadows began to grow long, Joseph led them into a small wooded section a short distance off the road. He told them they were now only a mile or so outside the small town of Amelia. And since they didn't want anyone to see them, it would be best to stop here for the night. They'd work their way around the town in the morning.

It had been a long, but uneventful day. They'd started out across the farm fields, which alternated with wooded areas, for a couple of hours before striking the southwesterly road.

They'd debated moving off the road and following it from a distance. But the land was so flat here, mostly open farm fields, someone riding along the road could spot them a long way off. And it would not only be more difficult and time-consuming, but would look more suspicious as well. In the end they decided to ride along the road whenever the surrounding countryside was flat and open. And to move off the road in the more wild and wooded areas.

The sky had cleared from the overcast of the previous day, making it a pleasant sunny day. Riding across an idyllic countryside, under normal circumstances one might have called it a very pleasant outing. But Nathan seemed to pass in and out of consciousness, adding to Tom's growing anxiety, and there was the ever-present fear of pursuit. They'd had several tense moments throughout the day when other travelers appeared on the road, but none had turned out to be threatening, or even suspicious.

And now that they had stopped to make camp, they remembered their empty stomachs. Tom wouldn't let them eat any more of the hardtack, except the Captain, if he would. Not knowing how or when they might find more food, he meant to make it last as long as possible. Not for the last time Tom wished Billy were with them; he'd likely be able to trap or snare some wild game, or bring something down with his bow. He sighed, *no good wishing for things to be different than they are*, he decided.

They made a simple camp, laying out bedrolls on the ground, forgoing setting up tents, with the weather fair and dry.

Joseph announced he would walk into town to find out what he might learn from the locals. He wanted to know if any heavily armed strangers had passed through town, or if anyone was keeping a watch out for Mr. Chambers and company. His plan was to return before dark. But if for some reason he didn't, he told them to continue on without him at first light.

He returned a few hours later, as the sun was setting. He was in a good humor and told them all was well. There had been no talk of strangers in town, and no sign of anyone looking for them. And best of all, he brought with him a loaf of bread and a block of cheese. The bread was slightly stale—he'd managed to beg it off the baker who planned to feed it to the hogs. But the cheese was good—he'd had a few coins with him and had paid for that. To the men, after a long hungry day of riding, this humble fare seemed like a feast.

ഇൗഞരുആ ഇൗഞരുആ ഇൗഞരുആ

In the morning they started out in better spirits, finishing the bread and cheese for breakfast—a great improvement over hardtack—along with coffee Georgie had brewed over a small cookfire.

However, the Captain's lack of improvement continued to put a damper on the mood. Once again, he was over-long waking up, and took an even longer time to hold a coherent conversation. Tom exchanged concerned looks with William, but there was nothing they could do.

They started the day by skirting Amelia, circling around it a few miles to the south before rejoining the main road. Joseph figured given the news from the previous evening it was safe to ride on the road until they neared Farmville, about twenty-five miles away. At that point things would get chancy again. It was there the more northerly route's southern branch connected back into the southerly road they'd been following. That made it much more likely someone seeking them would pass that way. Once again, they'd be back on the most likely route.

They reached the outskirts of Farmville at midday. They again stopped short of town and hid in the woods so Joseph could go reconnoiter. This time he returned in about an hour, but to Georgie's disappointment, did not bring any food with him. But that was not the worst news.

"Riders have passed through this morning, a couple of hours past dawn. Of course, rumors aren't very reliable, and even eyewitnesses tell conflicting stories. But it is clear these men were

335

armed, and there were between six and eight of them, with extra horses. They were asking if anyone had seen another group of armed men. After stopping long enough to query the locals, they rode out west along the main road toward Lynchburg. No way to know if these are the same men I saw outside Manchester."

"Damn!" Tom said, "Whether they're the same or others, it makes little difference. We must assume they're looking for us."

"Yes ... I agree."

They both turned and looked over at Nathan intending to ask his thoughts on what to do next. But his eyes were half closed, and he had a glazed and faraway expression. He sat on a stump with a supporting hand from William, but his head hung, and he did not look up at them.

"Well, I guess it's up to you, Mr. Clark," Joseph said, "what now?"

"We must go on. Every hour we're in the saddle is ... *hard* on him. We must get him home where he can safely rest as soon as may be. But if we meet these men on the open road, outnumbered, with their rifles against our pistols ... I fear it will go badly for us."

Tom walked over to Nathan and knelt in front of him, "Captain ... can you hear me, sir?"

Nathan seemed to stir himself and looked up at Tom. "I hear you, Tom."

"Captain, can you recall anything of the map between Farmville and Lynchburg?"

"Yes ... the road from Farmville loops south in an arc to the town of Pamplin, then back north to Clover Hill. It's about ... twenty-seven miles, give or take, from Farmville to Clover Hill. After that it's pretty much due west to Lynchburg, another ... twenty miles or so."

Tom stared at him and shook his head. Nathan had recited the information from memory with no expression or emotion, in a monotone voice, as if unaware he was even doing it.

"Yes ... that's sounds right, now that I think on it," Joseph said.

"In that case, what if we cut across country, due west from Farmville to Clover Hill, cutting off the southward arc? The straighter route might save us travel time and keep us out of sight."

"It's a good idea, Mr. Clark, but … *no*. As I recall, the road winds south to avoid some rough country, heavily wooded and steep, with lots of small streams and gullies. Though it'd doubtless throw the enemy off our trail, it might cost us several extra days of travel."

"Then, what? Farther to the south than where the road takes us? How much time will that cost?"

Joseph didn't immediately answer, but sat crossed legged on the ground, his head resting on his hand.

After a few moments he looked up, "I have an idea … and it might just work perfectly!"

"What is it?" Tom asked.

"Well, as I recall, the Southside Railroad tracks run parallel to the roadway all the way along from Farmville to Clover Hill and beyond."

"So … are you suggesting we get on the train at Farmville? After those men spread the word this morning, we'd surely be noticed. And likely when we got to the next stop we'd have a very unfriendly reception waiting for us, courtesy of the telegraph lines."

"It's a thought, but no. I wasn't considering *riding* the train, but rather riding our horses on the train *tracks*."

"But … if the tracks parallel the road, wouldn't anyone riding along the road spot us?"

"Maybe … but from what I recall, even though the tracks parallel the road on the south side, there is a separation — anywhere from a few hundred feet to a few hundred yards — all the way along. And … the area between, being unusable for agriculture, has become almost completely overgrown with trees and underbrush …"

"Ah … so, from the road, the trees block the view of the train tracks?"

"Yes, except for along a few short clearings, as I recall. When I rode that stretch of road before, I heard the train, and saw its smoke, but I almost never *saw* the train itself. Gentlemen, if we ride on the railroad tracks our enemy could be within spitting distance, and we might ride right past him without being seen!"

"I like it! It's brilliant, Joseph! Let's saddle up and get going, men. We have a train to catch … or rather its tracks!"

An hour later, having skirted Farmville, they rode their horses at a steady walk in the gravel along the edge of the tracks leading west. And to Tom's joy, and Joseph's great satisfaction, they couldn't see the roadway only a few dozen yards to the north.

Tom told the men to maintain strict silence. And they kept their horses to a fast walk to minimize the noise of their footfalls.

They kept a constant lookout for any breaks in the trees to the north. Whenever they encountered these they paused, and the men took turns dismounting, trotting over to spy out the road, and signaling when it was safe to cross.

Of course, they also had to keep an eye out for approaching trains. But that proved not too challenging—they heard the noise a long way off, and the smoke and steam rising above was visible for miles.

By mid-afternoon they made it to Pamplin, and skirted the town without delay, rejoining the tracks on the other side. Up to that point, they'd had to get out of the way of two trains, one in each direction. And they'd reconnoitered a half-dozen or so gaps in the trees, during which they had seen only a few innocent travelers, but no sign of the enemy. Joseph's plan was working beautifully, and Tom was hopeful they'd soon make camp outside Clover Hill for the night without incident.

They were about five miles from Clover Hill when they met the first serious flaw in Joseph's plan. When they came around a bend in the tracks, they saw a gap in the trees in front of them. This one they could *not* spy out and sneak across. This gap extended approximately a quarter mile. And to make matters worse, the road was fewer than thirty yards distant at the narrowest point along the gap.

The good news, however, was the cause of the gap in the trees. In this section, in the narrow strip between the roadway and the train tracks, a pond had formed that entirely filled the land between the two. It was impossible to tell how deep it was, but they had to assume it was too deep to walk across, so that was some help; if they encountered the enemy here, at least they could not come at them from the road without taking the time to swim their horses.

It was little consolation, however, as the land to the south side of the train tracks also appeared to be deep water. It extended far out into a swampy looking region that was likely impassible for a man on horseback. There'd be no escape in that direction, if worse came to worst.

"*Shit!* I have no memory of this pond area … maybe it was dry the last time I was through here and the heavy spring rains have filled it. I'm sorry, Tom."

"Never mind, Joseph. No plan is perfect, but this one's worked out about as well as any I've seen … up to now."

They sat their horses just back from the gap and its pond, taking it all in. In front of them to the west the roadway appeared to take a sharp bend to the north, which added to the danger. They'd not be able to see anyone coming along the road until whoever it was came out the far side of the gap. And, of course, they would not be able to spot anyone coming from behind them from the east until Tom and company were midway along the gap. Then they'd be able to spy back along the road, but at that point it'd be too late to retreat.

Once again Tom looked toward the Captain for advice. But he lay with his head against Millie's neck, once again asleep. Tom was loath to wake him, and … in the end, what would he say? There was no going back … only forward!

Tom stood in his saddle and slowly surveyed the gap from end to end then sat back down. "All right men … we'll just have to take it at a fast trot. Georgie … add Millie and the Captain to the front of the lead line with the pack horses and the mule. Then hand the lead to Joseph."

"I'll take point. Joseph you come next with the Captain and the pack animals. William and Georgie, take rear guard and watch our back trail."

Georgie hopped down from the saddle, bringing the pack animals forward. In an efficient, workmanlike manner he quickly attached Millie to the lead before handing it to Joseph. "Be sure and give 'em a little slack, sir, so's they don't get tangled with your own horse … 'specially if it turns into a race. Even without the lead they'll follow you, so if you drop it, just keep on riding!"

Joseph nodded, appreciating the advice from the experienced soldier, as he was not accustomed to the task. But he understood if it came to a gunfight, it was better to have the soldiers free to fight. He'd worry about the Captain and the spare horses.

This gave him a thought. He looped the lead around his saddle horn, hopped down, and walked over next to the Captain.

Tom raised an eyebrow, wondering what he might be up to, but said nothing. Joseph reached up and pulled Nathan's revolver from its holster, then reached over into his jacket pocket and removed the small Colt he always kept there. Next, Joseph pulled his own small pistol out and walked over to Tom, handing him the Captain's large revolver. "You may as well have this. If there's trouble, you may need all the firepower you can get, and it's not doing him much good at the moment."

Tom looked over at Nathan still slumped against Millie's neck and nodded. Joseph turned, walked back and handed the two small pistols to William and Georgie, "I assume you gentlemen will know what to do with these?"

They smiled and nodded, with Georgie adding, "Much obliged, sir."

Once Joseph was back in his saddle Tom said, "Let's move," and kicked Jerry into motion, heading out toward the gap.

They moved out across the open space at a quick trot, and all seemed well. No one appeared on the road ahead of them, and the distance to the far side was quickly shrinking.

But just as they neared the midway point Georgie called out, "Riders come up the road behind!"

The words had barely come out of his mouth when they heard a loud noise, like someone hitting a drum with a hammer. Tom heard something scream past over his head. A second later they heard another loud pounding noise—this time dirt kicked up just past them on the tracks.

Tom stopped his horse and turned toward Joseph. "Get the Captain across and on to safety, whatever it takes. We will hold them back!"

Joseph knew what Tom was suggesting was likely suicidal—they were vastly outnumbered, and without rifles, at a huge disadvantage in firepower.

He started to argue, "But—" Then he saw the determined look in Tom's eyes, and knew it was a waste of breath. "Yes, sir! I salute you … and … Godspeed!"

He spurred his horse forward, giving the lead line a hard tug to start the other animals moving, including Millie with Nathan again passed out in the saddle.

Tom rode back to where William and Georgie sat on their horses, turned back to face the threat. He was proud to see there was no panic in them. Even as another three incoming rounds kicked up dust around them, neither had even drawn a pistol, knowing at roughly two hundred yards it would be a useless waste of ammunition.

"Damn our lack of rifles!" Georgie groused. "If we had those Springfields we'd drive them from the road screaming like schoolgirls chased by a bumblebee!"

William nodded, "Those we didn't kill outright."

"Well, men, seems we're fresh out of that *particular* remedy," Tom answered with a wry grin. "But fortunately, they've fired off the rounds they had loaded, and seem none too efficient at reloading. Let's shorten the distance and give them a dose of the medicine we *do* have! We'll ride up to within about sixty yards then give 'em both barrels. Empty your first two guns, then turn and ride like hell out. Captain should be safely away by then. Save your third Colt for the return trip! William, follow me on the left side of the tracks; Georgie, you take the right."

They nodded their understanding, and Tom crossed over into the gravel on the left side of the wooden railroad ties. William followed him and Georgie moved over to the right side as ordered. Tom immediately kicked Jerry into a gallop with a shout. Georgie and William did likewise.

Their sudden change of direction took the enemy by surprise. They'd expected their prey to run and had fired hoping to slow them down, thinking to pursue after. But they'd shot from horseback, which was never good for aim — in their case far worse than it would've been for the soldiers. Their horses were not military-trained and flinched nervously, unused to the noise and the smell of gun smoke.

Tom noted with satisfaction a growing panic among their foes as they watched their prey turn to attack. One rider lost his nerve altogether, turning and spurring in the opposite direction. Two others had the sense to dismount, so they might reload faster, and aim steadier. The rest frantically tried to reload while still in the saddle, although one wisely dropped his rifle and pulled out a pistol.

In seconds Tom and company were within seventy-five yards. So Tom gave another shout, and pulled back on the reins, bringing Jerry to a bouncing stop at the sixty-yard mark he'd called for. William and Georgie followed suit, and before their horses had come to a stop, they had each pulled out two revolvers.

While an experienced and efficient rifleman might fire and reload at a rate of three shots a minute, a single-action Colt revolver could fire a round every second. And with two pistols alternating, that meant *two* large .44 caliber slugs per second, flying at 750 feet per second. With three men each firing two pistols, in just over six seconds the enemy had to endure thirty-six incoming rounds.

Though wildly inaccurate, it was a hailstorm of lead they simply could not ignore, and it sent them scrambling for cover. Two horses were hit. One went down with its rider, the other screamed, reared, and threw its rider, bolting back down the road to the east.

As he turned Jerry around, Tom looked back and saw that at least one man now lay face down in the road, not moving. And the others had either jumped off their horses and lay prone on the ground or tried to stay in the saddle — the latter now battling to

342

gain control of panicky mounts down in the borrow pit off the far side of the road.

Tom and company holstered their now-empty weapons, and each pulled out his third gun from his belt, as they spurred their horses back the other direction. They turned and fired off a shot or two as they rode away, just to give the enemy something more to worry about. Ahead they no longer saw Joseph or the other horses, so Tom said a quick silent prayer of thanks—their tactic had worked.

Then even as he was feeling things had gone splendidly, he heard another rifle shot from behind. Apparently, someone had *not* panicked, and had reloaded and fired his rifle. To his left he heard Georgie give a shout, "Ahhh! *Damn it!* I'm hit ..."

Tom looked over and saw Georgie wobble in the saddle and close his eyes as if in pain. He eased Jerry across the tracks and over next to Georgie's horse. Reaching over he gripped Georgie's right sleeve with his left hand to steady him. But Georgie opened his eyes and looked over, shaking off the help, "I can ride, Sergeant. No need of that ..."

"All right, Georgie ... but we'll stop shortly, soon as we're out of danger. Then we'll have a look at you."

In moments they were across the gap and back into the trees. And though the train tracks didn't turn as sharply as the road, still they made a broad curve to the north just past the gap.

They kept moving and were soon past the point where the opening was visible behind them. And now they saw horses stopped ahead of them on the tracks.

As they came up, they saw the Captain was now awake and gazing back at them.

Tom stopped short and snapped a salute.

"Report, Sergeant ..." Nathan said, in a rasping voice, not even bothering to return the salute. He looked pale, and his eyes were red and puffy.

"We have engaged the enemy and driven him back in disarray. I counted twelve enemy riders and two spare horses. They suffered at least one, and possibly two casualties, and likely two horses out of commission as well."

"Well done, Sergeant. Men. But we have *also* suffered casualties ..."

Georgie still sat in the saddle, holding his left shoulder with his right hand, his face looking pale and pained. A pool of blood soaked the shirtsleeve, oozing out from under his hand. "Took a hit from behind on the way out, sir. I ... I'll be all right. Though ... might need ... a little *rest* is all."

Joseph said, "Gentlemen, it looks like the ground is drier here. I was already thinking it was time to get down off these tracks and slip into the woods to make camp for the night. Now with Georgie needing some tending, this seems as good a time as any to do it."

Nathan turned to him and nodded.

"Single file down off the tracks, if you please. Then I'll see about covering our trail again, once we're safely out among the trees," Joseph continued.

A half-hour later they stopped to set up camp. The spot was nothing special, only a slight rise in the woods. But it was enough to afford them a small advantage against anyone coming at them. And with the sun quickly sinking behind the trees, the likelihood of an attack this day was almost nil, anyway. Still, they'd not light a fire. There was nothing to cook anyway, and the weather was mild.

Tom and William helped Georgie from the saddle, while Joseph did the same for the Captain. They laid Georgie down on a blanket, rolling him onto his right side so his left shoulder was in the air. William unbuttoned Georgie's shirt and carefully stripped it off him. Tom brought out a candle and lit it, so William would have some light.

William saw the bullet had come at an angle from Georgie's right moving toward his left. It made sense; that was the direction of the enemy when they were riding away. It had entered at the left edge of his shoulder blade then passed through the upper part of Georgie's left arm. There it'd left a nasty exit wound halfway between the top of the shoulder and the start of the bicep. William poked around the wound, starting around the shoulder blade, checking if the bone was broken. He saw the bullet had hit the bone and apparently glanced off it. But it did not appear to have fractured it, surprisingly. At least when he pressed on it, it seemed solid, and Georgie only groaned quietly. A broken bone would likely have been much more painful.

Next, he examined where the bullet had torn through the flesh of his shoulder. Again, it appeared the slug may have grazed the humerus, but hadn't broken it. And though the wound was ragged, nasty looking, and bloody, no major blood vessels had been severed. All in all, a *very* lucky wound, and William told him so. But Georgie groaned, and said he wasn't feeling so very lucky, at that moment.

Then when William got out his medical kit, and poured whiskey into the wound, Georgie squawked, "Ow! Damn it, William, that burns!"

But William was tired, and hungry, and had just been through a frightening, adrenaline-pumping experience, which he had not had time to fully digest. He was in no mood to coddle Georgie.

"Come on, Georgie, show a little courage, will you? I've stitched the Captain up half a dozen times, on wounds much worse than this. And he's never once complained, nor even flinched."

"Well, I *ain't* the Captain, I reckon."

But William ignored him and started in to stitching the wound.

"Ow! *Goddamn*, William! Now you're making it hurt o' purpose!"

"Oh, shut up and be a man, Georgie. I bet your baby sister's got more courage in her little finger than you're showing right now."

"Well ... it ain't about *courage* ... it's about *pain!* Damn thing *hurts!* And besides, my little sister never had a bullet shot through that courageous little finger o' hers!"

William had to agree he had a point there, but he continued to sew, nonetheless. And Georgie, to his credit and despite his protests, never flinched nor tried to pull away. William finally decided Georgie was plenty brave; the cursing and complaining was his way of dealing with the pain, the same as rigid stoicism was the Captain's way. But William decided from the surgeon's perspective the stoicism was preferable.

By the time William had finished with Georgie, the Captain was already asleep in his bedroll, and Joseph was busily reloading the pistols. He had collected all nine weapons and laid them out on a blanket, along with three piles of lead balls: the .44 caliber, the .36 caliber, and the .31 caliber for the pocket pistols. He also had a pile of percussion caps. He decided they had plenty of powder and caps but were short on lead, as much of what they had was in the form of .50 caliber Minni balls for the rifles they'd left behind at the boarding house. It would be possible to melt them down into the right size balls over a hot fire, but they had no molds.

Joseph looked over at Tom and said, "The guns are all reloaded now. But we've got no more lead balls for the pistols. One more gunfight and we'll be down to throwing rocks and sticks!"

"Well, then that's just what we'll do, I reckon. But I'm hoping to avoid any more such encounters, or we'll also be out of men," Tom answered.

Joseph nodded his agreement.

"Think I'll wander on over to town and see if I can find out anything about our *friends* from back on the road. Likely they'll go into town to lick their wounds."

"Hmm … too bad we're so shorthanded or we might ride in there and put an end to their mischief once and for all!" Tom suggested.

"Yes … it's a temptation all right, but I'm afraid the odds are against us, even with a surprise attack. No, I think you were right before; our best hope is to avoid them from here on. Maybe I'll overhear something that'll tell us what they're planning. I should be back shortly, then we can discuss where to go from here."

ಶಲುಚ್ರಿಚೆ⹁ಲುಚ್ರಿಚೆ⹁ಲುಚ್ರಿ

Evelyn once again sat in the library at the Hughes' house, sipping tea. This time only Jonathan was present, Angeline having a previous commitment elsewhere.

"Thank you for coming, Evelyn. I wanted to tell you everything I've learned concerning Mr. Chambers."

"Oh! You have news?" Evelyn had been hoping it was the reason for the sudden summons. She'd been in an almost constant state of worry and anxiety ever since the day Nathan had disappeared.

"Well … *no* … not what I'd call 'news' exactly … but I do know more now than I knew last time we spoke. I have additional … *information* … and I would like you to help me puzzle out what it means."

"Oh … all right," she said, suppressing a feeling of disappointment. "What information?"

"My people have been to the scene of various incidents, have spoken with eyewitnesses, including Mrs. Wilkerson, and some pieces of the puzzle are now coming together. But, before I tell you all I've learned, I wanted to give you something."

He stood and walked over to the desk, returning with a large, round tin box, which he handed to Evelyn.

"A hat box?" she raised an eyebrow at him, but he said nothing, nodding his head toward the box.

When she opened the lid, she gasped in surprise, "It's … Nathan's hat!"

She lifted it carefully from the box and examined it: thick black felt with a broad brim and a thin, stylishly engraved hatband of silver. It was the elegant hat of a gentleman, but more in the Western style—not typical in Richmond. There could be no mistake whose hat it was. She had seen him wear it many times, including most recently at the ill-fated ball where they'd had their brief encounter.

As she turned it and examined the top and the insides she said, "I assume your men found this at … at the place where the *confrontation* occurred? But, Jonathan, it appears unharmed. If they'd hit Nathan on the head with a pistol, wouldn't the hat show signs of the blow? Perhaps he was not so badly struck after all!"

But Jonathan frowned and did not immediately respond. He stood and paced back to the window, gazing out.

"Evelyn … as much as I wish to protect your feelings, I am compelled to tell you the whole truth, no matter how painful."

347

"Yes, of course, Jonathan … you must always tell me the truth, no matter the cost, else our … *business* … will never succeed," even as she said this, she felt a hollow knot of dread in the pit of her stomach.

"When I first obtained this hat, it was … *not* as you see it now. I'm afraid it was … *damaged.*"

"Damaged?" she whispered.

"Yes … the top was caved in, the felt dented and parted in the center of the top. And … inside … I'm afraid it was darkly stained …"

"Blood?"

He nodded. "I've had it cleaned and repaired with the hopes of returning it to him one day …"

Evelyn's eyes filled with tears, and she fought down a surge of emotion threatening to choke her.

"I was thinking … perhaps you can keep it until …"

"Thank you."

"Anyway … now let me share with you everything I have learned …"

For the next hour Jonathan described everything his various employees had been able to learn from their investigations. That Nathan had apparently been taken unconscious to an abandoned warehouse where his assailants intended to torture and murder him. That Tom and Nathan's other men had apparently arrived in time to rescue him and kill his attackers.

Evelyn scowled, and embarrassed herself by cursing out loud when Jonathan informed her one of the dead men was Peter Stevens, the man who had escorted her to the ball the night she'd met Nathan there.

They continued to discuss all the unusual events of the evening and what they might mean; the odd happenings at Mrs. Wilkerson's boarding house, the apparent shootout at the bridge, and Tom's odd abandonment of many of their supplies, including food, rifles, and ammunition!

Other than Nathan's apparent rescue, the only good news, to Evelyn's mind, was learning one of Jonathan's best men, who went by the name of Joseph and dressed as a street vagabond, was likely leading Nathan's men in their attempt to escape the city.

Finally, they discussed what might be done to help. Evelyn suggested sending out more of Jonathan's men with weapons and supplies. But Jonathan disabused her of the idea, saying he had already considered and rejected it—any men he sent out would likely not be able to find them, and if they did, would likely be shot as enemies.

They were quiet and thoughtful for a long moment, then Jonathan said, "I just might have an idea … Evelyn, does Mr. Chambers have any more of his ex-soldiers back at the farm in western Virginia? The ones he brought with him to Richmond have proven highly capable. And it just occurred to me if he has more of those at home, they might launch their own rescue mission from the 'other side' so to speak."

"Oh, yes! Yes, of course! He has more soldiers back at the farm. What an excellent idea, Jonathan! Yes, they would be the best ones to affect a rescue. We must send a message to Miss Abbey at once!"

"Oh, good. I was hoping you would say that. But as for a message … I fear the enemy intercepting a telegram, and a letter … well, there's no guarantee it would arrive timely. I considered sending one of my men, but Miss Abbey wouldn't know him from Adam, so might not trust he speaks the truth."

"No … that's perfect, Jonathan. Only … I'll write her a letter for your fellow to deliver. She knows me and knows I … *care for Nathan* … so she'll believe what your man tells her. And in case something happens along the way, I'll not say anything specific in the letter—just tell her to believe whatever the man says. Then … hmm … I'll tell your man something only *I* would know. When he repeats it to her, she'll know he is who he's supposed to be. Oh! And you can also send her Nathan's hat for proof."

"Ah, excellent! Yes, I believe that'll work. Your letter along with the hat and the personal message will prove the truth of my man's mission. And a lone traveler, such as the fellow I have in mind, will not attract any undue attention. If he goes by train, he can be there tomorrow evening. Let's get that letter written, shall we?"

Joseph returned to camp about a half-hour after sunset, giving the appropriate bird whistle to make sure they didn't greet him with a pistol bullet on his return.

He sat on the ground next to Tom and smiled broadly letting out a quick chuckle.

"Well, you seem pretty pleased with yourself ... for a man who's likely as hungry as me, and clearly didn't obtain any food."

"Yes, well, sorry about that ... I had no chance to acquire any food without serious risk of being caught. There's only one small general store in town, and it's currently filled with our friends from the road."

This got Tom's attention, and he sat up straighter.

"They're there? What condition are they in?"

"They looked pretty ragged and very unhappy. In fact, one of them kicked me and another spit on me while I was sitting up next to the outside wall of the store, pretending to beg. But I didn't care, being so pleased by their suffering.

"They brought in one dead man, wrapped in a blanket and tied to the back of a horse. And they carried another man into the building with what appeared to be a broken leg. And they had no extra horses—the fellow with the broken leg was forced to ride double with another man. Though I suppose once they deposit the dead man and Mr. Broken-leg, they'll have one spare mount again."

"Well, it's good we did them some damage, though by my count they are still ten against our five. But ... I'm guessing that's not why you're smiling, since it only confirms what we already assumed. Did you learn anything about what they plan to do next?"

"No ... they were a surly and grumpy group, and none too talkative. If they discussed any plans, they didn't do it in front of me. And I dared not go into the store with them all gathered inside. In the light of the lamps it's possible one of them might've recognized me from seeing me at a distance earlier today. So I stayed outside in my 'drunken stupor.'"

"So then, why the big grin?"

"Oh, that! Yes, well that's on account o' me doing a little mischief such as I haven't done since I was a schoolboy. You see, the general store has a couple of rooms out back, which I'm assuming they'll stay in tonight. There is also a small corral off to the side, where guests can leave off their horses, with a small tack house to store their gear.

"Once it'd got dark, and there was no sign any of them had intentions of coming back out for the night, an evil plot hatched in my mind. At first, I figured to go in the tack room and cut up all their gear to it'd be unusable until they made repairs or obtained replacements.

"But then I thought better of it; nothing would advertise our whereabouts quicker than that! So instead, I opened the corral door, and quietly shooed the horses out. By morning they'll be scattered over half the county which ought to slow our friends down for a while. And, they'll just assume some careless farm boy didn't properly latch the gate!"

Now Tom smiled, "Nicely done, Joseph, nicely done! I approve."

"Thanks, Tom. But sorry I couldn't procure any food this evening. Tomorrow we'll be in farm country, and I promise I'll come up with something better'n hardtack to fill our poor empty bellies."

"That'd be a relief, I'll admit. Thank you, and I'll happily hold you to that promise."

"Oh, by the way, I also found out the town is no longer called Clover Hill."

"Oh? What's it called now?"

"Well, it seems they've built a new county courthouse there, so they've renamed the place, apparently proud of their new status in the county. They now call the town 'Appomattox Courthouse.'"

ಬಲಬಲ

They stopped at midday, in a forest they guessed was about five miles south of Lynchburg. It was on a slight rise that might be considered a hill. The rise overlooked farmland, and they saw a barn and other buildings off through the trees to the north.

They got Nathan down off his horse for a rest, but Georgie climbed down on his own. And though stiff and sore, he was surprised how much better he felt already. He told William so, thanking him for his ministrations, and sheepishly apologizing for his earlier whining and complaining.

But William smiled at him, and said, "Think nothing of it, brother. I'm just gratified you are doing so well."

Georgie smiled, "Brother? Yes ... I like the sound o' that, William. *Brother* ..."

William answered, "In the old days, soldiers used to refer to each other as 'brothers in arms' or a 'band of brothers.' Seems to me those of us who came east with the Captain are like *that* now."

"Yep ... I reckon you have the right of it, William. Thanks again ... *brother.*"

Once they'd laid the Captain down for a rest, Tom turned to Joseph and said, "So ... how about your promise of yesterday? I've not forgotten, nor has my stomach."

"Exactly what I was thinking on as well, if one can *think* with one's stomach. Come, Tom ... let us, you and I, form up a foraging party, and see what we can find down at yonder farm."

"Agreed. William, you look after the wounded. We'll be back shortly."

"I don't need no looking after," Georgie protested. But then he added, "But I'll admit a little rest would be welcome." He grinned as he lay back with his head propped against a fallen log, pulling his hat down over his face and immediately closing his eyes. It was again a mild day, though only partially sunny, with a layer of high clouds blocking much of the sun's rays.

The country they'd ridden across today was a rolling farmland interspersed with woodlands, much like the first day out from Richmond. They'd stayed well away from the main road, so ended up several miles more southerly than they would have by following the road to Lynchburg.

Tom and Joseph crouched behind a bush at the edge of the clearing, looking out over the farm. This was a large, prosperous estate, and reminded Tom of Mountain Meadows. They saw numerous outbuildings and barns, with an elegant brick manor house on the far side, about a half mile from where they squatted. Out to the sides there were seemingly endless fields, filled with knee-high green plants. Cotton, Tom assumed. He saw several groups of slaves moving among the rows of plants.

Immediately in front of them were the outbuildings, starting about fifty yards away, all neatly painted a dull red color with white and black trim. They saw a couple of male slaves moving near a building that appeared to have hog pens attached to it. Tom guessed they were slopping the hogs. They also saw a tall, thin black woman walking along a path with a bucket. Other than that, they saw no one else around.

They'd discussed just walking up to the house and asking to purchase some food, but Tom had no money, and Joseph only enough to be insulting. They'd even discussed begging for it, but thought they'd likely just be shown the door. Tom decided he probably looked just as disreputable as Joseph normally did in his vagrant disguise; they'd been outdoors traveling with no change of clothes and no bath or shave for the better part of a week.

Besides all that, they were still reluctant to let anyone know where they were, in case their pursuers came calling.

So in the end they'd decided there was no choice but to conduct a little thievery. Tom felt guilty about it, but he felt worse about the Captain having nothing to eat in his condition. And the rest of them could also do with some sustenance. They decided the easiest and quickest thing to procure and carry would be a couple of chickens. And if they grabbed them in the henhouse, they might find a few eggs to stick in their pockets for good measure. Further, if a nice fat goose happened to wander across their path, they'd not be opposed to confiscating that as well.

So they waited until they saw no one looking their way, then dashed out from their hiding place. They raced across the open ground, a field apparently used for pasturing cattle, based on the large dark piles they had to avoid as they ran.

When they reached the back side of the first outbuilding, they crept around the side. They paused and scanned for the chicken house, while keeping a lookout for anyone moving among the buildings. Finally, they spotted it—a small cabin, slightly raised off the ground with a telltale miniature doorway in front, reached by a small wooden ramp. It had a human-sized door on the side, so they cautiously worked their way toward it. Tom figured this would have been much better done at night, but he didn't like the thought of spending the rest of the day with nothing to eat. And what if there were no farms near wherever they might end up tonight? Hunting would be extremely challenging without rifles, besides which they didn't want to make any noise that might attract the wrong kind of attention.

So a daylight raid was the only alternative. The good news was, apparently most of the farm workers were out in the fields this time of day. They made it to the door, and after a quick glance around, ducked inside. If they'd have been a pair of foxes, the chickens would've squawked and fluttered about in a panic, but they were well used to humans coming in to gather eggs. So several continued to roost on their wooden nesting boxes, stacked three high along two of the walls. It was not a duty Tom enjoyed, but he knew it was necessary; they quickly snatched hens and broke their necks before they could make a sound. In this way they each secured two hens, which was all they planned to take.

Next, they searched through the nest boxes, filling their pockets with a half-dozen or more eggs each. Several of the hens had become nervous at the unexpected activity, so had hopped up and headed out the small door into the yard. Tom and Joseph moved to the door, with a hen dangling from each hand. Tom opened the door a crack and peered out. He still saw no one about, so he stepped out, with Joseph right behind him.

They moved toward the corner of the hen house, Tom in the lead, intending to peek around the corner to make sure it was still clear. But just as he approached the end of wall a woman came around the corner, nearly running into him.

"Oh!" she said, dropping the wooden bucket of grain she'd been carrying. It hit the ground with a thud, spilling most of its contents.

In an instant Tom's pistol was in his hand and the chickens he'd been holding dropped to the ground. As he leveled the gun at her, he held his finger up to his mouth in a shushing sign. He recognized her as the tall, thin black woman he'd seen walking along with a bucket earlier. Likely she'd been going to fetch grain to feed the chickens. She'd probably seen several hens come hastily out of the hen house and had come to investigate.

Joseph leaned forward and whispered in Tom's ear, "Quickly ... put her in the hen house!"

Tom nodded, and motioned the woman forward, waving his pistol toward the hen house door. The woman's eyes were wide, and a hand covered her mouth, but she nodded her head in compliance, and moved toward the door.

Joseph stooped to recover the bucket, quickly scooping handfuls of the spilled grain back into it. He turned and followed Tom and the woman as they re-entered the hen house. Joseph stuck the bucket on the floor inside the door. Then he whispered to Tom, "Convince her to stay here and be quiet long enough for us to make our escape."

Tom nodded, as Joseph slipped back outside to keep a lookout, pulling the door closed behind him. Tom turned toward the woman, and said, "Sit!" motioning toward the floor with his pistol. She complied, never speaking a word.

Tom looked her in the eyes. She had a pretty face, though she was nearly old enough to be his mother. He saw a look of fear and realized he was nothing more than a common criminal to her — a thief come to rob the farm or ... *worse*. It occurred to him at this moment he had become what he had always despised, the kind of man he had often hunted out West. He felt a wave of shame and embarrassment wash over him, and suddenly it was important this woman know he was not ... *that!*

He lowered the hammer on his pistol and slipped it back into its holster. "I ... I apologize, miss. It ... it wasn't right of me to point my gun at you and ... I'm sorry if I frightened you."

The look of surprise she returned, encouraged him to continue.

"I'm not what I appear. I'm not a thief, it's just—"

But before he could finish his sentence, the words of the erstwhile train robber back in Texas came unbidden to his mind, *"I'm not a thief; me and the boys is just down on our luck is all."* If he gave her an excuse, even one that was true ... wouldn't he sound just as disingenuous as that boy?

Then a thought struck him: an entirely different line of reasoning. With all that'd been happening, he and this black slave woman were natural allies. He might use that to gain her cooperation without fear or the threat of force.

"You see, ma'am, me and my friends are hungry, and two have been wounded on account o' we're on Mr. Lincoln's side; the slavers are hunting us down, trying to kill us."

The fear left her face, "You ... you are Mr. Lincoln's men, master?" she said, in a voice filled with awe.

Tom paused a moment. He'd never thought of it that way before, but ... "Yes ... yes, miss, I reckon we are. But I'm *not* your master ... I'm only a soldier, like my friends back in the woods. We're some of Mr. Lincoln's soldiers. But now our enemies are trying to keep us from getting back to ... to the North so we can fight for Mr. Lincoln."

"Oh! God bless you, sir! God bless you. Is it *true* then? Is Mr. Lincoln gonna free us all?"

"I ... don't know, miss. But I believe it *could* be so ..."

"Wait'll I tell the others I done seen some o' Mr. Lincoln's soldiers ... come to free us!"

"Oh ... well, I wouldn't tell them *that* just yet, miss. Likely there'll have to be a big old war first before we can ... come back here and ... set y'all free ..."

"Yes ... yes, I see. Them slavers ain't fixin' to let us go without a fight, are they, sir?"

"No miss, I expect not."

"Well, God bless you, anyways, sir. And I'll just sit here quiet-like not makin' a sound 'til y'all can get clean away with them chickens."

"Thank you, miss. And also ... please tell the white men we were no more'n common thieves ... no sense telling them who we *really* are. They might want to come out and fight with us."

"Oh, *no* sir, I'll not tell them a word of it. And, sir ... when you see Mr. Lincoln, can you tell him ... tell him ... well, just tell him, *'God Bless you, sir!'*"

Tom smiled, "Yes miss, the next time I see Mr. Lincoln, I will surely tell him that ... from *you.*" Then he realized he didn't know her name and ... also ... that she reminded him of someone he knew, somehow, though he couldn't recall who.

"My name's Tom, miss. And you are ...?"

"Very nice to make your acquaintance, Mr. Tom. My name's Lilly."

But before the answer was all the way out of her mouth, the door opened. Joseph reached a hand in, grabbed the back of Tom's shirt, and yanked him out. "We have company, Tom. Gotta go!"

As the door swung closed again, the woman continued to sit, alone now but with a smile on her face, slowly shaking her head. Then she looked up toward the door where the polite young gentleman, one of Mr. Lincoln's own soldiers, had stood just moments ago. She laughed quietly, suddenly filled with a joy she couldn't quite understand. Tears filled her eyes and streamed down her cheeks.

ɛʊɛɔɔ𝕮ɔ𝕮ɔɛʊɛɔɔ𝕮ɔ𝕮ɔɛʊɛɔɔ𝕮ɔ𝕮ɔ

An hour and a half later they once again made a hasty camp. When they'd returned with the chickens, they'd immediately saddled up and moved on. They had no desire for another armed confrontation—this time with an angry farmer looking for chicken thieves!

Tom and Joseph once again helped Nathan from the saddle and laid him out on a bedroll. Georgie gathered dry sticks for a cook fire using his one good arm, while William cleaned and plucked two of the chickens.

They were soon enjoying the smell of chicken and eggs cooking in a large iron skillet. Though they had no rifles, and had brought along precious little food, they were well supplied with cooking gear; it had been stored with the other traveling equipment out in the stables.

The savory smells even roused the Captain. He managed to swallow a few pieces of chicken, and most of an egg, before he quit and waved off offers of any more. He turned to Tom and managed a slight smile, "That was a nice change. Where did you manage to buy those chickens?"

Tom again felt embarrassment at the question, and stared at his boots, "I'm afraid ... we were forced to resort to thievery, sir."

"Oh ... I see." Nathan was quiet for a while, gazing at the fire as if lost in thought. Tom figured he might nod off again, when he suddenly looked back up, "Tom, do me a favor, will you?"

"Yes, sir?"

"Remember the place where we ... *acquired* these chickens. Then ... later, when things are ... back as they should be, we'll return and pay for them."

This made Tom smile. Leave it to the Captain to worry about doing things properly, even in the midst of a crisis. "Yes, sir. I promise you I'll not soon forget the place, nor the role I played there."

But even as he said this, something in the back of his mind nagged at him ... something about the place ... having nothing to do with his thievery. But what? He tried to puzzle out what was bothering him ... but it just wouldn't come. Well, maybe later when things were more settled, he'd think of it.

After their meal, they gathered in a circle to discuss where to go next. Joseph informed them his knowledge from personal experience ended at Lynchburg. He'd never spent any time west of there and had never crossed the Alleghenies over to the west side of Virginia. Without a map, he had only a vague general idea of the possible routes from this point on.

And Tom, Georgie, and William were northerners who'd never lived in Virginia before coming east with the Captain.

So they turned to Nathan's memory of the map.

"After Lynchburg I saw two possible routes home but hadn't decided which to take. They are roughly the same number of miles.

"The first route heads northwest from Lynchburg, over a small mountain ridge to Lexington ... that's about forty-five miles. Just outside Lexington the route joins up with the main road from Richmond into the West. So likely it's a better maintained roadway, and I'd originally reckoned we'd get on the train there for most of the remainder of the journey. From there the road makes broad arcs to the north and south, generally following a westerly course. It winds through the mountains to the town of Clifton Forge, another thirty miles or so from Lexington. Then it's through the mountains to Covington, twelve miles, and on to White Sulphur Springs, twenty miles further. And finally, five miles more to Mountain Meadows."

"And the other route?" Tom prompted.

"The other route ..." Nathan paused for a long moment, and Tom feared something might be amiss. But he continued, "... the other route heads due west from here until it passes through the village of Liberty. After that it turns in a northwesterly direction to the town of ... of ..."

There was another long pause. Nathan stared straight ahead. Then he looked at Tom and said, "I don't remember."

"What? You mean you didn't study that part of the map, sir?"

"No ... I'm sure I did. It's just ... before ... when I thought about the map it was clear and sharp in my mind, as if it were spread out on a table in front of me. But now ... it's ... it's like someone spilled water on it and the ink has run ... all is unclear."

He looked over at William. "William, what's wrong with me? The pain ... it never seems to ease. I figured I'd feel better by now. But ... I believe it's gotten worse. And now *this* ..."

Tom had to fight back tears, and a cold chill ran down his back. This was more frightening even than when the enemy had captured the Captain. He'd known how to deal with *that* situation—knew the dangers, and the likely outcomes, good and bad. But this? How could one combat something like *this?*

William looked at Nathan a moment, removing and wiping off his glasses before answering. "Well, sir ... no one knows for sure what's going on with this kind of injury. But I believe it is something like ... well, like if you were kicked in the leg by a mule. Even were it not broken, you'd have a lame leg for a while. And no matter how hard you tried, you wouldn't be able to run as fast or walk as far as you could before the injury, until you'd given it time to heal. One might say the leg, while injured, does not function as well as when it is fully healthy.

"Likely it's the same with the brain; the blow to your head has injured it, so it stands to reason it will not work as well as when it's healthy. So naturally you can't remember things as clearly as before. As for the pain ... I don't know. It may *not* get better until we can find a place where you can rest and lay still for several days. I suspect bouncing along on the back of a horse is preventing the injury from healing properly."

Nathan nodded his head but said nothing in reply.

They all sat, each with his own thoughts, wondering what to do next.

Tom considered the one route they *did* know ... the main road, winding through the mountains. Rugged country allowing little opportunity to travel off the road and stay out of sight. It was the obvious path, and surely would be watched. But wouldn't the enemy by now suspect they'd take a less obvious way? They'd already proven themselves ready to do that, so it would no longer be unexpected. And ... without the Captain's memory of the map, they didn't even know the other route. They'd have to stop somewhere and either obtain a map or ask the locals until they found someone to tell them the way. That held its own risks.

We've made it as far as Lynchburg, but now what? he wondered.

At the thought of Lynchburg, the thing that'd been bothering him began nagging once again. *Lynchburg* ... what was it about Lynchburg?

"William ... I seem to recall discussing something about Lynchburg one day when we were back in Richmond, before all these troubles. But now ... I can't remember what it was."

"Lynchburg? I ... I've never been there before ... and don't know anyone from there, so I don't ...? Oh! *Wait!* Yes ... now, I remember. Lynchburg was where the farmer lived who'd bought the slave girl Rosa's mother off the bankrupt farm in Petersburg. The man's name was ... uh ... something from the old days ...

what was it the boy said ...? Oh yes, *Benedict* ... like the traitor, only this was his *last* name. And Rosa's mother's name was ... also some kind of flower ... *Lilly.* Yes, her name was Lilly."

Tom's mouth opened wide, and he slapped his forehead. "*Damn* ..." he said, in almost a whisper.

"What is it?"

"I may have just seen her."

"Seen who?"

"The mother ... Lilly. When we were stealing the chickens, I ran into a slave woman, and I talked with her for several minutes. She was tall, thin, and had a pretty face. A woman somewhere in her late thirties, maybe. She was pleasant and spoke kindly. And I thought at the time ... that she reminded me of someone I knew, but I couldn't think of who. But just now thinking on it ... she reminded me of Rosa!"

"Oh! Do you think it *could* be?"

Tom groaned. "The more I think back on it, the more I believe it *must* be so. The resemblance is ... remarkably strong and ... to beat all ... she told me her name was *Lilly!*"

"Oh, my God! Should we go back for her then, do you think?"

"No ... we dare not. By now they may be scouring the woods in search of the infamous chicken thieves. Besides which, the likelihood of encountering her again by herself is almost nil. No ... I'm afraid there's no going back now. *Damn it!* If it'd just occurred to me *then* we might have brought her out with us."

"*No!*"

They both turned and were surprised to see the Captain looking at them. They hadn't thought he was paying attention to their conversation.

"No, Tom. Even if you'd thought of it, *that* we could not do. Not now. Stealing chickens is one thing, but stealing slaves? We'd likely have half the county out looking for us if we'd done *that.* Bad enough those men we're already dealing with."

"Yes, I'm sure you're right, sir. Still, it seems a damned shame to have been so close, and yet ..."

"Never mind, Tom. It just gives us one more reason to return to that farm."

"Yes, sir, I reckon so."

"*Fincastle!*"

"I beg your pardon, sir. What's that you said?"

"I said *Fincastle* … it's the next town after Liberty, and sixty miles from Lynchburg. After that the road heads straight up into the mountains—zig-zags and becomes extremely windy. But it generally follows a westerly route to a small town called Paint Bank. There it turns due north to Sweet Springs. That's … forty-some miles from Fincastle. Then it's only fifteen more miles north to White Sulphur Springs and then we're home."

"Your memory! It's back, sir!"

"The map suddenly appeared in my mind … I don't know why. I may be damaged … but I'm not completely out of commission yet," he managed a thin smile. But Tom thought the look still betrayed a great deal of pain.

For the next hour or so, they discussed the relative merits and disadvantages of the two courses. In the end it came down to a tradeoff between potential speed, the more northerly main road, versus potential cover and safety, the southerly route.

They could not come to a consensus, but all knew in the end it wasn't a democracy, anyway. As long as the Captain was involved, they all understood *he* would make the final decision. Everyone else's opinions were only information for him to digest and use as he saw fit.

"Gentlemen … there are many good arguments for both options … and many valid arguments against. But in the end, we must choose one or the other. My head cannot decide … perhaps because it has been damaged … as William says."

He looked at William and smiled weakly. William returned the smile and nodded his head in acknowledgment.

"But … my *gut* seems to function still, and it tells me … we should take the path less traveled: the southerly route. On that road there is no train, and no telegraph, and only a few tiny towns.

"We are soldiers from the West, used to spending weeks at a time out in the wilds—living off the land, traveling across rugged terrain with no roads nor even animal trails to follow.

"Our enemies are city men. I believe ... this must be the deciding factor. It gives us the one advantage our enemies can't match. We are men who don't fear the wild places and can survive in them. Gentlemen ... if we're to win, we must go into the wild."

All were quiet for a moment, absorbing the Captain's words. The soldiers would never question their commander's decision, and Joseph was just happy a decision had finally been made.

"Mr. Chambers ... esteemed gentlemen ... this seems a wise decision to me, and it serves to underscore what I'm about to say. First, I want to tell y'all ... it has been one of the greatest honors in my life traveling with you. And to provide you whatever *small* help I've been able to provide."

"It has not been *small* help, Joseph. It has been indispensable!" Tom objected.

"Thank you, Mr. Clark. But, be that as it may, this has been a great adventure I will not soon forget. But ... perhaps because of the great respect and, dare I say, *affection* ... I have developed for y'all ... I have gone well beyond where I had originally intended to go. I'm sure my people back in Richmond are ... anxious for news of my whereabouts ... and yours, for that matter. I would be remiss if I continued to disregard their feelings and went further on this journey with you. As I've told you before, this is where my knowledge of the countryside ends. And I am *not* a soldier, trained for survival in the wilds as y'all are. In the end, I am a city man, even as those that pursue you. I fear I will be of little help from here on. Most likely I would be just another mouth to feed ..."

After all they'd been through together, the thought of losing Joseph at this point in the journey was a bitter pill for Nathan's men. It hit Tom especially hard. He'd leaned on Joseph's wisdom and advice on multiple occasions. "As far as 'mouths to feed' goes ... I'll gladly give up my meals if it will convince you to come with us," he said.

Joseph smiled, "Thank you, Tom. I am touched. I have come to ... to feel you are *true* friends now ... all of you. And I will *never* forget our comradeship.

"But it is time for me to go. I have duties back in Richmond, and people who will be worried about me. If it helps, I am confident you will succeed and finally reach your home safely. Let's make camp here tonight and allow everyone a good rest.

"Then, in the morning we must part ways."

ಬಿಕಾಗಿಬಿಕಾಗಿಬಿಕಾಗಿ

The next morning, they ate the remains of the chicken they'd cooked the day before. They still had the two remaining chickens; they'd need to cook and eat those in the evening lest they spoil and become inedible.

Once again, Nathan had a hard time waking up—if anything, worse than before. And it took a long time for him to even speak or to acknowledge the conversations of the men around him.

They packed up the camp in a somber mood. No one seemed anxious to acknowledge the parting of ways to come.

But finally, the time came. All was packed, and they climbed into their saddles. Joseph had offered to walk back to Richmond, as the horse he'd been riding belonged to Nathan. But Nathan had refused to allow it, gifting him the horse and saddle for all his invaluable help getting them safely out of Richmond. Joseph said it wasn't necessary, but thanked him kindly, and they shook hands on it. Joseph worried at the weak shakiness of Nathan's grip. He imagined it was a nothing like his normal, firm handshake.

As usual, Nathan was tied into his saddle, still unsteady, and not trusting himself to remain conscious throughout the long day's ride.

They prepared to depart, and Joseph moved his horse to the side, "Well, I guess this is goodbye, for now, gentlemen."

The men said their goodbyes and walked their horses up next to him one at a time to shake his hand. All but Tom.

He wouldn't meet Joseph's eye and sat his horse unmoving, staring at the ground. Joseph gazed at him for a moment, then shrugged his shoulders, and started to turn his horse. But suddenly Tom looked up and moved his horse closer to Joseph's.

He sat straight in the saddle and gave Joseph his most crisp Army sergeant's salute.

Joseph appeared surprised at first, but then smiled, and returned the salute, though in a slovenly, civilian-like manner. It made Tom chuckle, and Joseph as well.

Then Joseph moved his horse right next to Tom's and motioned to him to lean forward, to which Tom complied. The others watched with curiosity as Joseph leaned in close, put his arm on Tom's back, and whispered something in his ear. Tom sat up straight and they shared a smile and shook hands warmly. Joseph turned his horse and trotted away without a backward glance.

But as Tom turned his horse in the other direction, he felt a hard lump in his jacket pocket. He reached in and pulled out a small leather pouch, that jingled when shaken. He laughed; when they'd embraced, Joseph had slipped the coins into his pocket as a little going away gift. It wasn't much, but it was all Joseph had. It might buy a loaf of bread, or a block of cheese if there were any to be bought.

Nathan's men turned to the west and headed out themselves. Georgie was burning with curiosity, so he trotted his horse up next to Tom. "What'd he say to you, Mr. Clark, there at the last?"

Tom looked at Georgie and grinned, "He told me his *real* name."

Chapter 14. Fear in the Wild

"Yea, though I walk through the
valley of the shadow of death,
I will fear no evil: for thou art with me …"
– Psalms 23:4

Thursday Apr. 25, 1861 - Greenbrier County, Virginia:

Jim came in the front door headed for the library. The summons hadn't surprised him after hearing that a strange gentleman had come calling on Miss Abbey. The Watch had intercepted the man coming up the road, and Jamie had ridden out to ask his business. The nicely dressed, mild-mannered gentleman from Richmond was clearly *not* one of Walters' men. Though polite, he said he would only state his business to Miss Abbey. So after a thorough search for weapons came up empty, Jamie let him pass. Then he rode straight to Jim to report the news.

"Mr. Smith, I'd like you to meet Mr. Wiggins. Mr. Wiggins is one of our most trusted men and oversees the farm in Mr. Chambers' absence," Miss Abbey said, not bothering to rise from her seat as Jim entered the library. "Jim, Mr. Smith has just come from Richmond with … urgent news for us …" Smith rose to shake Jim's hand, and then the two men took their seats.

Jim noticed Miss Abbey had a worried look, as did Megs. He had a bad feeling about this.

"Mr. Smith … kindly show Mr. Wiggins the things you have brought with you … and tell him what you just told me. I apologize for making you repeat yourself, but … I want Jim to hear it all for himself …" Miss Abbey continued.

"It's no bother, ma'am. I have traveled all the way here to give this message, so I am not opposed to making the trip worth my while by saying it twice."

He smiled good naturedly, but Jim could tell he too was *not* in a jovial mood. He had dark hair, neatly trimmed beard, and wore spectacles. And as Jamie had described, he dressed as a proper gentleman. Jim noted a bowler hat sitting on the side table.

The man leaned to the side and picked up a large, round-shaped, blue tin box of the type hats were kept in. He handed the box to Jim, who gave Miss Abbey a questioning look. She nodded, so he opened the lid and lifted out the contents.

Jim stared at the black hat a moment, took a deep breath, then set it back in the tin box. He closed the lid and set it on the floor. He stared straight ahead for a moment, took another deep breath and said, "Then ... is ... he ...?"

"Oh ... *No*, Jim! Not *that*! At least ... not as far as we know ..." Miss Abbey responded, tears now filling her eyes.

"Oh! *Thank God*. Well then ... perhaps you'd best explain what this is all about, Mr. Smith."

"Yes, certainly, Mr. Wiggins. But before I do, there is one other thing you should see. Miss Abbey, if you please ..."

Miss Abbey picked up a piece of paper sitting next to her and handed it across to Jim. He unfolded it, and slowly read the contents:

> *Richmond*
> *April 24, 1861*
>
> *My Dear Miss Abbey,*
>
> *The man who bears this letter brings you tidings best not written down. You will know you can trust him when he tells you something only I, and the people at Mountain Meadows would know.*
>
> *I have missed you all terribly, and I hope someday we may be reunited in happier times. Please give my love to Megs, and of course to Mr. Chambers when next you see him.*
>
> *Affectionately yours,*
>
> *E.H.*

Jim looked up at Miss Abbey, "E.H.?"
"Evelyn Hanson."

"Ah … yes, of course. All right, Mr. Smith, what is it then, that only Miss Evelyn would know?"

"She told me I was to say this: 'The wedding couples danced beautifully to Mr. Chopin's waltz.' It is … some sort of code … I assume, as I have no idea what significance it has otherwise."

But Jim smiled. "Yep, that's her all right. Okay … tell us your tale then, Mr. Smith."

Jim sat still, stoically taking it in, as Smith laid out the story, even as Jonathan Hughes and Evelyn had laid it out for him. All the known facts, along with their guesses and suppositions, explained as such. They wanted Miss Abbey and company to form their own ideas and opinions based on what was known versus what was only guessed at.

Smith never mentioned Jonathan Hughes' name, of course, only referring to him as "The Employer," the same term used by Joseph while escorting Tom and company.

When Mr. Smith had finished his narrative, he added one more thing, "Miss Abbey, I have been instructed by The Employer to tell you one other thing. He says to tell you; regardless of whatever personal relationship Miss Evelyn may have with Mr. Chambers, they are also now natural allies in the larger conflict. But Miss Evelyn's part in this conflict must remain a secret. Further, please assume any written communication is likely to be read by the common enemy. Therefore, any such should be kept to the minimum necessary, such as informing her of Mr. Chambers' safe arrival, and should be as impersonal as possible. Anything more than that might put Miss Evelyn in grave danger. He asks you to pass these instructions on to Mr. Chambers whenever he arrives."

"Oh my! Whatever has that girl got herself caught up in?" Miss Abbey asked.

Smith looked at her and smiled, "I expect the same thing we will *all* be caught up in soon enough, Miss Abbey."

Miss Abbey shook her head, and met eyes with Megs, who returned the look with a shrug. Then she turned to Jim and said, "Now you know the story, Jim. Please get the men ready to mount a rescue, such as Miss Evelyn has proposed."

But Jim did not immediately respond. He continued to sit and stare straight ahead as if in deep thought. A wateriness in Jim's eyes surprised Miss Abbey. She'd never seen him that way before. He'd always seemed as tough as nails, and completely unflappable.

"*Damn* ... if only I'd been there ..." he finally said in a near whisper.

But then he sat up straight, wiped his eyes, and said, "No! No, that's *not* right ... just selfish talk. It sounds to me Tom and the other men have done right by the Captain—have done as well as any men could. Have given even *heroic* service at the risk of their own lives. No one could ask more, and nothing good comes from wishing for things that can't never be.

"So ... what's to be done? Get together the men and go out looking, you say? Well first, where, Miss Abbey? There's likely a half dozen different routes they *might* take over them mountains. Which one shall we search? And if they are trying not to be found, as we are supposing, how will *we* find them?"

"But we have Billy ... I am told he is excellent at following trails in the woods, and such ..."

"Yes, ma'am, Billy is a good man to have, it's true. As good as any I've ever seen at reading sign on the ground. But ... he's only a man, not a magician. He can't follow a trail unless we find it first."

"But—"

"And don't forget about Walters, Miss Abbey. If he should get wind of this—that all us soldiers was out scourin' the hills for the Captain, leaving Mountain Meadows unguarded—what do you suppose he'd do?"

"Yes, I know you're right about that but ... I'm surprised at you, Jim. I would've thought you'd be the first to jump on your horse and ride out after them."

"Oh, believe me ma'am, that's exactly what I'm just itchin' to do. It'd be the most satisfying thing I can think of, and it takes all my willpower to resist the desire to do it.

"But a man's also got to do what's smart, and what's his duty, regardless of his own wants. And my duty is to protect *you*, and the rest of the people on this farm. Riding around in the woods looking for men who don't want to be found, ain't gonna benefit anyone, Miss Abbey."

"Then *what*? How can we help them? We can't just sit here doing nothing, leaving them somewhere out there in the wild mountains—Nathan hurt, and all of them likely starving. With no rifles to hunt for meat, nor to defend themselves from those men chasing them, trying to *kill* them! We *must* do something!"

"I know what the Captain would say we should do."

"What's that?"

"I reckon he'd say we should *pray*, ma'am."

They were quiet for a moment.

Finally, Jim said, "It's not as hopeless as it sounds, Miss Abbey. I've been in these same situations many times with these same men out in Texas. We'd be lost, cold, and hungry, running low on ammunition, caring for wounded men, and surrounded by enemies bent on red murder. But a man can go a long time without food if he has to. And even if the Captain is too hurt to help, Tom Clark is one of the best men in a pinch I know. If anyone can get them out, *he* can.

"Have faith, Miss Abbey ... you too, Megs ... I believe they *will* make it out and return safely to us. And if it'll make you feel better, I'll make sure the men are packed and ready to ride out for a rescue on a moment's notice—should we hear any news of their possible whereabouts."

"Thank you, Jim," Miss Abbey put a handkerchief to her eyes and could no longer hold back the flow of tears. Megs came over and wrapped her arms around her.

ഐജ૦ය૦ఐജ૦ය૦ఐජ૦ය૦ఐජ૦ය

The next two days were uneventful as they made their way to a camp just west of Fincastle. The first day, from Lynchburg to Liberty was more rolling farmlands and woodlands, the same as they'd encountered east of Lynchburg. So they'd been able to make good time even while avoiding the road.

But between Liberty and Fincastle was a stretch of rough country. There the westerly road took a sharp turn south to avoid a tall ridge, before turning due north on the other side of it to run on to Fincastle. Along that section they'd been forced back onto the road, and Tom had been in constant fear of an ambush. If the enemy was to set a trap, he figured this would be a good place for it. In one narrow canyon, he'd been so anxious he'd had the men unholster their pistols and hold them at the ready as they rode along. They nervously peered up at the surrounding canyon walls, fearing at any moment to hear rifle fire and see the telltale puff of gun smoke.

But in the end, nothing happened, and they saw no sign of their pursuers.

And though things had gone well thus far, Tom's sense of dread and anxiety continued to build. For one, they had now finished the last of the chicken, and farms had become smaller and further between, making it difficult to conduct another chicken raid.

Yet another worry, the weather, which had started out mild and sunny when they'd left Richmond, had gradually changed to a dark overcast. And with a cool breeze coming out of the mountains, the temperature had dropped dramatically. The lowering clouds were threatening rain just as they were preparing to head up into the mountains. At the higher elevations, the cold could become a serious problem. They had their oiled overcoats, but they'd left their other warm garments behind at the boarding house.

But worst of all was the Captain's condition. With each passing day his condition seemed to grow worse rather than better. Every morning it was more difficult to rouse him, and now it felt like he spent more time asleep during the day than awake. And even when he was awake, he said but little, and often gazed about in a confused manner, as if he did not know where he was. And he regularly rubbed the sides of his head with his hands, as if trying to dull the pain.

The next morning, they ate the last of the hardtack, but Nathan refused any. From Fincastle the road west climbed up a north-south running ridge in a series of steady switchbacks. It was a long, slow climb, and Nathan spent most of it leaning against Millie's neck, asleep.

The wind picked up and blew in fitful gusts that passed right through their clothing. After a few miles, Tom's teeth began to chatter. And no matter how tightly he pulled the oiled overcoat up under his neck the cool breeze found a way in, sending a cold shiver down his back.

At first, he'd been worried about meeting their pursuers on the narrow, winding track. But soon the biting cold became a bigger concern. At some point he thought he'd almost welcome a gunfight if only to get warm for a few minutes. And all the while he smelled the threat of moisture in the wind. He shuddered at the thought of adding rain to the frigid mix.

At the top of the ridge the road immediately plunged down again. But before he started back down the other side, Tom paused and gazed out to the west at the vista the height presented. But rather than enjoying the beautiful, awe-inspiring scene, Tom grimaced at the sight: more and more ridges as far as the eye could see, with clouds now so heavy and low they nearly touched the ridgetops. They'd have to climb up each one of those heights, and down again, one after the other in seemingly endless succession.

According to the Captain's earlier report, it was supposed to be only eighteen miles from Fincastle to Newcastle. But they'd learned in this country distances on a map were not the same as distances winding back and forth, up and down ridges. Tom figured they had to travel two or three times farther than a map would indicate. In the end, what should have taken them half a day according to the map took the entire day on the ground, from sunrise to sunset.

It was so cold and dark that Tom ordered them to set up the two tents they'd brought with them from Richmond but had never yet used. The night was so black they could barely make out each other a few feet away. So he had no fear of the white canvas tents giving away their position in the woods. They'd dismantle them before first light to prevent that becoming an issue.

He also chanced not setting out a guard. The night was just too miserably cold to subject themselves to it. And he couldn't imagine any circumstances under which the men from the city would venture out into the dark woods in this weather.

Tom slept in one tent with Nathan, William and Georgie in the other. A few minutes after settling into his bedroll, Tom felt a little warmth for the first time that day. He quickly fell into the deep sleep of the utterly exhausted.

The next morning presented Tom with the first serious crisis since Joseph's departure. They could not awaken the Captain no matter what they tried. He would briefly open his eyes if they lifted him into a sitting position. And they could get him to take a few swallows of water. But he wouldn't speak and seemed entirely unaware of their presence. If unsupported he would immediately lie back down and fall asleep.

Tom looked at William and saw fear in his eyes. He looked back at Nathan, lying on top of his blankets, face pale and lifeless, arms crossed over his chest. He was still wearing his best black suit—the same he'd worn to church in Richmond before being attacked—though it was now bloodstained, and travel worn. It was a funereal vision that sent a shiver down Tom's spine. *No! That must NOT happen!* The fright of it filled him with renewed determination, and he fought down the tears trying to build in his eyes, and the hopelessness threatening to paralyze him.

"What'll we do, Sergeant?" Georgie asked, wide-eyed.

Tom did not immediately respond, becoming quiet and thoughtful.

"We must build a horse stretcher, such as we used out in the wilderness in Texas. Do you remember how they looked?"

William nodded, "I saw one used once … pretty much the same as a hand-carried stretcher, isn't it? Only everything's bigger and longer so as to carry a man between two horses."

"Yes, that's right. Let's get to work on it. Georgie, get that small ax and cut us two poles—about as big around as your upper arm and … hmm … about sixteen feet long ought to do it."

"Yes, sir! If'n there's one thing we got plenty of here in these hills it's trees." He waved his hand in the general direction of the woods that hemmed them in on all sides.

"We'll have to use the canvas from one of the tents. If necessary, we'll share a tent from here on. Might be a bit tight, but the upside is it'll be warmer. Cut yourself a section of the cloth and then we'll all pitch in and stitch it around the poles Georgie brings us."

"Yes, sir. How big a piece of canvas, do you think?"

"Well, let's see … needs to be a little taller than the Captain, so just make it seven feet long. And then … needs to be as wide as a horse, so we can tie the poles to the saddle on each side. So that'd be about three … maybe three and a half feet …"

"Plus, enough to wrap around the poles leaving a good width for stitching a seam," William added.

"Yes, true … *oh*, also we need to allow some slack for the sagging the weight of a man's body will cause. Wouldn't do if it were too stiff. So … hmm … go ahead and cut it seven feet wide as well. We can always trim some off later if we need to."

As it was cold, and they had no food to break the night's fast, Georgie and William felt highly motivated to complete their tasks—they set to with a vigor. Tom helped William stretch out the tent canvas and hold it tight as he measured and cut with a sharp knife he used for working on wounds. A few minutes after they'd completed their task, they'd folded up and repacked the remains of the tent just as Georgie returned with the poles.

They laid out the canvas and the poles and broke out their sewing kits. They always carried heavy-duty needles and thread strong enough to repair canvas on tents, wagon covers, etc.—an old habit from their Army days. Fortunately, they'd stored that equipment with the other traveling gear at the horse stables, rather than at the boarding house.

Georgie and Tom started out on opposite ends of one side, and William, being the most proficient among them with needle and thread, started out on the other. Shortly after Tom and Georgie came together in the middle of their side, William finished his side. Georgie leaned over and examined William's handiwork.

Not only had he done it in half the time, it was much more even and neat looking than the side finished by the other two men.

"William, you should've been a seamstress! That's as pretty o' needlework as I've ever seen."

But William smiled at him and said, "You should be grateful I'm *not* a seamstress, else who would've been around to stitch up *your* sorry hide?"

Georgie laughed as they lifted the stretcher and carried it over to where they'd tied the horses. They briefly debated whether they ought to attach the stretcher between ridden horses so they could more carefully control them, or between baggage animals. In the end they decided on the pack animals. They feared what might happen if there were a gunfight, and two men had to coordinate two connected horses. Better to have the pack horses on a lead and keep the riding horses free to maneuver as needed.

So they tied the front poles to the extra pack horse with the stretcher leading back behind it, then attached the other end to the mule, with the stretcher to her front. They also shifted some baggage from the two pack animals onto Millie's back. She would no longer bear the Captain, and that would lighten the load on the other two who now carried an extra two hundred pounds or so between them.

Next, they padded the stretcher with extra blankets and lifted Nathan in, covering him up tightly.

"All right. Well done, men. Let's keep a close watch on these animals for a spell. They're not used to being hitched together, nor this kind of burden, so may be skittish at first."

Georgie and William nodded their understanding.

"Let's move."

They made their way through the woods skirting the edges of the small town of Newcastle, rejoining the road a mile or so west of the last house.

Wind continued to blow, only now it came in fitful gusts that threatened to rip their hats off their heads. And they hadn't traveled more than a few miles from town before they started feeling raindrops mixed in with the wind gusts.

If the previous day had been a slow, cold, miserable slog, this day was worse. Wind-driven rain lashed their faces in sudden bursts, then stopped entirely, only to return a few minutes later just as they were starting to hope it had ended. Tom thought a steady rain might almost be better so one could get used to it and become numbed to its effects. But the inconstant on and off, gusting winds, and pounding rain was almost torturous.

But the worst for Tom was his unceasing fear for Nathan's deteriorating health. On top of the anxiety he also bore a crushing weight of guilt—that by trying to save him they were slowly killing him. The constant movement, day after day, had clearly made the injury to his brain worse. But what could they do? To stand still was to starve, and likely freeze to death. And eventually their enemies would find them and surely kill them.

So they did the only thing they could do: continue winding back and forth and up and down, ridge after ridge, heads down in a vain attempt to keep off the pounding rain.

𒉿𒊏𒀹𒄿𒉿𒊏𒀹𒄿𒉿𒊏𒀹𒄿

The Captain had said the next town over was named Paint Bank. *Odd name*, Tom thought. And he recalled it was only sixteen or so miles away. But he no longer believed what the map indicated, assuming it would once again take all day to make the trek. He also recalled the Captain saying Paint Bank was the furthest point west they would travel until they were just outside White Sulphur Springs, at which point they would be almost home. It was the furthest west because the road headed due north after Paint Bank all the way to the main east-west road—the same road they would have traveled had they taken the more northerly route to begin with.

For Tom, if this wasn't the longest day of his life, he couldn't think of the one that was. By late afternoon they shivered from the bitter cold, soaking wet anywhere their oiled overcoats didn't cover them. Their stomachs knotted in hunger. Tom had called a stop every hour or two to check on Nathan and force him to drink some water. Each time he'd prayed to see the Captain's eyes open with a look of recognition, but each time he came away disappointed and more fearful.

At the top of each ridge they hoped to see ahead the town they'd set as their target for the day. But each cresting only brought a view of more wilderness, if they saw anything at all through the lowering clouds streaked with rain.

As they trudged down another ridge, the dark gloomy day had become suddenly much darker, their only sign the sun was setting. Tom began looking around for a likely campsite, but that was proving a challenge on the steep wooded hillside.

Then Georgie called out, "Look, sir … just up ahead where the road levels out …"

Tom wiped water from his eyes and squinted ahead into the gathering gloom. He now saw the road did level off a short distance ahead into what appeared to be a wide valley. But at first, he couldn't tell what had excited Georgie. His first thought was enemy riders, but he realized the tone of Georgie's voice would've been more alarmed and concerned. This had sounded more excited and hopeful. Then he saw it … a light in the darkness. And when he focused on it for a few moments, he noticed it was coming from the window of a building. *Paint Bank* at last!

༄༅༄༅༄༅༄༅༄༅༄༅༄༅

They paused on the edge of town and briefly discussed what to do next. But Tom had already made up his mind; Nathan must have warmth and rest, or he would surely die. And the rest of them were not much better off. He was determined to find some kind of warm, dry shelter this night.

"You men stay here with the Captain. I'm going to ride into town and reconnoiter. If our enemies are *not* there, I mean to find us warm accommodations for the night, and something to eat.

"If I don't return in a half hour, you must assume the enemy has taken me. Head into the woods, pitch the tent, and try to stay warm tonight. Then in the morning skirt the town and continue north. According to the Captain, it's another seven miles to Sweet Springs. And seventeen more to White Sulphur Springs. But with

377

all these hills I wouldn't put much faith in those numbers unless you're a bird."

There was nothing more to say, so Tom kicked his horse forward. He walked his horse through town and saw several houses set well back from the road, with a number of outbuildings in between. Lights came from the houses, but he saw no one outside. No surprise there, as it was now almost completely dark, and the nasty weather would have long since driven anyone inside.

His biggest concern was the enemy riders. If they were searching these hills, this town would be a likely stop. Up ahead he saw a building close to the road on the left side with lights on inside shining out from several windows. They'd built a small corral and barn next to it on the side closest to him. He rode up next to the corral and looked for telltale signs of a group of horses being stabled there but couldn't see any. Of course, they'd likely be back in the barn anyway, in this weather. He debated getting down and going for a look in the barn but decided against it. He was cold, tired, and hungry, and wanted to get this over with, come what may.

So he unbuttoned his pistol holster on the right side, loosened the pistol he held tucked into his belt on the left, and went on. As he drew even with the front of the building, he saw it was a neat-looking two-story red brick structure. It had a sign outside he could barely read in the fading light, "Paint Bank General Store." That sounded hopeful, so he dismounted, and looped Jerry's reins around the hitching post.

He walked two steps up to a small outer landing, opened the door and stepped inside. A gust of wind snatched the door from his hand, and swung it all the way inward, where it hit the wall with a loud bang. After the darkness outside, the light of the lamps in the store almost dazzled his eyes. And the warmth of the room flowed over him in a wave of hot air that nearly took his breath away.

A quick glance told him the enemy was *not* here, but his sudden, noisy appearance had clearly startled the occupants; a man and woman, somewhere around the Captain's age, and a young boy, about ten. They sat at a small table on the far side of the room, next to a woodstove.

They stared at him a moment without speaking, and he suddenly felt self-conscious, realizing he must look a frightful sight—dirty and unshaven, soaking wet, and armed with two pistols.

"Sorry ... didn't mean to frighten you folks ... wind caught the door."

He turned and grabbed the door, pushing it shut with an effort; the wind tried to blow it back again until he had it properly latched.

"Oh, not to worry, sir. It happens all the time when the wind blows this way," the man said, standing up from the table. He smiled, in an obvious attempt at welcoming, but Tom still detected a look of concern. And though his instinct was to put the man and his family at ease, it occurred to him he might need to use their fear to his advantage. For one, he had no money to pay them, and he meant to obtain food and shelter through whatever means necessary. It was now a matter of life and death for the Captain at least, and maybe for the rest of them. It was also possible these people would sympathize with their enemies and refuse to help once they figured out which side they were on.

He looked at the man for a moment, then turned his gaze to the woman and the child. The woman looked fearful, but the young boy had a different look ... excitement maybe? Tom supposed to a young boy an unknown, armed man bursting in the door in the night was nothing more than a grand adventure. The young boy's expression helped Tom determine the right course of action; he'd tell the truth and come what may.

"Hello, my name's Tom Clark. I live just north of here ... on a farm between White Sulphur Springs and Lewisburg. Me and my men are returning home from Richmond and have got caught out in the storm. We are cold and hungry, and two of my men are wounded."

"Wounded?" the woman said, rising from her seat and taking a couple of steps forward. "Whatever happened, sir?"

Tom looked her in the eye and saw her fear had turned to sincere concern.

"We have been attacked, ma'am, by men who mean us harm."

"Oh!" she said, covering her mouth with her hand, her eyes now wide in shock and alarm.

"What kind of men would do such a thing, Mr. Clark?" the man asked, "We've never had any such trouble in these hills before."

"It didn't happen here in your hills, sir. One of my men, my Capt—I mean … my *boss*, was injured all the way back in Richmond, and the other man just outside Lynchburg. These men have been pursuing us all that way, though we haven't seen them since Lynchburg, so I'm hopeful they have given up the chase."

"But I don't understand … why would these men do this?"

Tom paused a moment, then said, "I assume you've heard about the secession …"

"Well yes, of course. Even up here in the hills the talk of it has spread like wildfire …"

"Yes, I'd imagine so. Well, my boss was one of those men who tried to stop it. He worked against it and has remained loyal to the Union of the United States even now it's been decided. The men who attacked him, and who've been following us want to murder him because of it."

"That's horrible! What *wicked* men!" the woman said.

But the man immediately stepped up to Tom and held out his hand, "I am Charles Hampton, Mr. Clark—happy to make your acquaintance! I am also a loyal Union man! Even voted for Mr. Lincoln, as did most of the other folks here 'bouts."

Tom shook his hand and smiled for the first time in days. It almost felt odd, like his face had become unused to the gesture. "Well then, I can honestly say it is a *very* great pleasure to meet you, Mr. Hampton."

"And this is my wife, Annabel, and my son Eddie."

"Pleased to meet you, ma'am … Eddie."

"But sir … what of your men? Are they not outside in the cold night? You must bring them inside that they might be warmed

380

and fed without further delay! And we will do what we can for your wounded men, though we have no doctor in town."

"Thank you, ma'am, but we have no need of a doctor. Fortunately, one of our men is the best doctor I know. But I will take you up on the warmth of your store, and your offer of food. We've not eaten in two days of hard travel. But ... first I must tell you we have only a few coins with which to pay you. We were forced to leave Richmond without most of our belongings, and with no money but the few coins we happened to have about us."

"Never you mind about that, Mr. Clark. We're more than happy to help as we can," Charles said.

"But if you feel inclined to repay us, I'm sure once you're safely back home you can return and settle up whenever it's convenient. Come, sir, let us fetch your friends. Here ... take this lantern so you can see where you're going in the dark."

A few minutes later William and Georgie were warming their hands by the woodstove, chatting amiably with Mrs. Hampton and Eddie, as the latter busily laid out plates, flatware, food and drink for the men on the small table.

Tom knelt on the floor next to Nathan, where they'd laid him out after carrying him inside.

Mr. Hampton was still outside, having volunteered to take care of the horses—watering them, feeding them, and unburdening them of all their tack and baggage before finally setting them up in warm dry stalls back in the barn. Tom had offered to help, but Charles wouldn't hear of it, insisting Tom go inside with the others and get warm. Tom had not argued too vigorously; he felt himself starting to wilt.

Mrs. Hampton stepped up beside Tom, "How is your boss ... Mr. ...?"

"Chambers, ma'am. Nathaniel Chambers."

"How is Mr. Chambers, doing, sir?"

"Not well, I'm afraid. He has been ... unconscious, even as you see him now ... all this day, though previously on our journey it has not been so. I believe he needs bed rest for a time if he's to get better."

"Oh … well, we will happily provide him with that. But what of your other wounded man? You said *two* of your men had been injured … but I see only Mr. Chambers."

"That would be *me*, Miss Annabel," Georgie answered. "Took a bullet clean through my left shoulder. Went in back there," he pointed over his left shoulder with his right hand. "Then came out just here," he finished, pointing to where the bullet had exited the front of his arm just below the shoulder. "But William here is a fine doctor and has patched me up near as good as new. Still a little sore and stiff, but generally I can use it already for most things, long as I don't have to raise my hand high or lift anything heavy."

Annabel smiled at him and at William, but Eddie came up to Georgie, mouth agape and said, "Was you really shot clean through with a bullet, mister? And you're still alive?"

"Yep, went straight through, just like I said. And I'm still alive on account o' my brother here, Mr. Jenkins, done sewed me back together so's I'd stop bleeding all over the place. Well, you can't hardly tell now, what with all the dirt and grime, but if you look close, you can see there's a hole in my shirt, both sides, where the bullet passed through. And them dark stains are from all the blood that done come out."

Georgie leaned down so Eddie could have a look. The boy reached out and carefully poked the end of his finger through the hole in the sleeve of Georgie's shirt.

"There really is a bullet hole, Momma! How about *that!* Wait'll the other boys hear about this!"

"All right now, Eddie, stop pestering these nice men and finish setting the table so they can eat."

"Yes, ma'am."

ଔଈଓଓଔଈଓଓଔଈଓଓ

The Hamptons kept several rooms in the back of the General Store for travelers, which Tom had gladly accepted when offered.

After dinner Mrs. Hampton brought out a small two-man stretcher they kept in the storeroom for general community usage. They had clearly not needed it in a while — a plume of dust came

382

from it when she gave it a shake. Tom took it from her gratefully and set it down next to Nathan. He and William carefully lifted the Captain onto it, after which they carried him back to the guest rooms. Mrs. Hampton offered them a room with three sets of double-bunk beds, and they laid the Captain in the middle one on the bottom bunk. Tom decided he wanted the lower bunk closest to the door leading to the store … just in case. Georgie took the third lower bunk, so he'd not have to climb with his sore arm. William took the bunk above Georgie.

That night they slept in real beds for the first time since leaving Richmond, and they were warm and dry for the first time in several days. After what they'd been through, it seemed a great luxury.

And though Nathan still did not awaken in the morning, he was no longer shivering, and seemed to be resting more peacefully. Tom thought he had more color in his face than in past days, though he wasn't sure if that was just wishful thinking.

They spent that day resting and recuperating from their recent ordeal, enjoying the simple pleasures of walking around all day on their own two feet, warm and dry, while eating regular meals. They made the acquaintance of many of the townspeople who either came in to purchase supplies or purposely came to meet and chat with the strangers.

Tom spent most of his time either gazing out the window watching the rain pouring down or sitting next to Nathan on his bed watching him sleep.

William also came to check on him every few hours, but there was nothing else he could do. He learned Mrs. Hampton had a few books available for lend to the townsfolk—a small public library of sorts, comprising a half dozen very used books. William happily accepted her invitation to borrow one. He picked out one he hadn't read before and spent most of the day reading it, up on his bunk, listening to the sound of rain on the roof or pelting the windows whenever the wind blew.

Georgie found himself the subject of near hero-worship by the boy Eddie, who followed him everywhere, asking a seemingly endless series of questions about his adventures. Georgie enjoyed talking with the boy, bragging on his days out West, and even the recent adventures closer to home.

But at one point Georgie turned the tables on Eddie and asked *him* a question that had been on his mind ever since their arrival. "Say, Eddie, tell me about the name of this-here town. *Paint Bank* is a very odd name. Can't say I've ever heard the like before. How *ever* did the town come by that name? If you know …"

"Oh, yes, Mr. Thompson. I know the story well … none better! Would you like me to tell it to you?"

"Yes, I would, Eddie, if you please."

"Well, according to what my Pa has told me, all this land hereabouts was once Indian country—Cherokee Indians, they was. And it just so happens the banks of the creek that runs through town is full o' something called iron ochre—it's of a rusty red color, and it makes the clay soil red. The creek's called Potts Creek now, though Pa says it wasn't called that back then. Likely the Indians had their own name for it, though nobody now remembers what that was. Anyway, they say the Indians used to come down to the creek when they was making ready for a big fight amongst themselves. Or against the white men, I guess. They'd use the iron ochre for war paint on their faces. And the Indian women would come and use the red clay for making pots.

"Later, when the Indians left, the white men came, of course. Like the Indians, they used the red earth for making paint, but also for making red bricks, including the ones used to build this store. So they called the place Paint Bank, on account o' the red paint that comes from the bank of the creek!"

"Well, I'll *be!* That's a right fine tale, Eddie. I thank you kindly for satisfying my curiosity on it."

"You're welcome, Mr. Thompson."

"Oh, Eddie … you can just call me Georgie, like everyone else does. *Mr. Thompson* sounds much too stuffy, like someone who thinks he's more important than he is."

"All right, Georgie, I'll do it if it pleases you, though Momma says it ain't polite to call older men by their given name."

384

"Well, I expect your Momma's done told you rightly, Eddie. Only I ain't an 'older man.' I reckon I ain't all *that* much older than you!"

"Really? How old *are* you, Georgie?"

"Well, last month I turned twenty years old. How old're you?

"I'm eleven, but I'll be twelve right after Christmas."

"See there? I'm only about eight years older'n you. So it stands to reason you don't have to call me 'mister' but can go ahead and call me by my name."

"All right, Georgie, thanks. I like that better. Anyway, did you really like my Indian story? I love stories about Indians, especially the ones you've been telling from out West. I can't believe you've seen them for real."

"Of course, I've seen them for real! In fact, one o' my best friends is a *real* Indian."

"Honest? But I thought they were bad, and you was fightin' against them out in Texas. How is it you made friends with one?"

"Oh no, Eddie, Indians ain't all bad. Some are, and some ain't. Same as white folks."

"You mean like those bad men that done shot a hole in you?"

"Yep, exactly. Those men are much worse'n most Indians I've known. Anyway, to answer your question about my Indian friend, in Texas there's a tribe of Indians called Comanche."

"I've heard of them! They say they're the fiercest of all the Indians."

"Yep, I've heard that said too, and from what I've seen, I can't disagree. But that don't mean they're all bad. They're fierce fighters, that's true, but you could say the same for me and my soldier friends, though we're not *bad* men. Like I said, some're bad and some ain't.

"But this friend o' mine is from another tribe of Indians called Tonkawa. You ever heard of them? No? Well, most people outside Texas ain't. They're a much smaller tribe, both in numbers and in the size of the men. But they're mighty tough fighters all the same. Anyway, Billy—that's the name of my Indian friend ... *Billy Creek*—he says the Tonkawa and Comanche have hated each other since they had a big war way back during the time called 'The Breaking.'"

"The Breaking? What's that?"

"It was a bad time ... a long time ago before the white men came out to the West. Times were desperate, and some men decided to solve their problems by having a war ... and everything in their world got broken."

"Oh, you mean like how they say there's gonna be a war *now*? Between the United States Union and the South on account o' Mr. Lincoln being elected president? And the secession—whatever that is—and that fort that got bombed, and ... whatnot?"

"Yep, I reckon so, though I still hope there ain't gonna be a big old war. Anyway, my friend Billy's one o' them Tonkawa Indians. His people have joined with us soldiers to fight the Comanche that needs fightin'. Billy's a real smart fellow too, on top of being a tough fighter. He's the best tracker I ever seen. He can follow a track all day long the rest of us can't even see."

"No foolin'? Georgie, I ain't never met a man who's had as many adventures as you!"

"Well, Eddie, one day you'll be old enough to have your own adventures."

"Yep ... and when I do, I reckon I want to be a soldier out in the West, just like you, Georgie!"

ഇരുന്നു

"So I figure the enemy chose to guard the main road instead of this one, which's why we haven't seen them," Tom said, as the three men sat together at lunch.

"It's a hopeful thing, though there's no guarantee they might not still show up on this road at some point. But I've been thinking on our situation all morning, and I've decided we shouldn't move the Captain again until he's doing better. At least not by horseback."

"But Tom, that could take a while. There's no knowing how long an injury like this might take to heal properly," William said.

"Yes, I know, though it seems sleeping in a warm bed last night and this morning has made a noticeable improvement."

"I agree with that. And I agree the longer he can stay here without being moved the better. But it seems to me the longer we stay here the greater the risk of those riders showing up."

"Yes, I'm aware of that. Which is why I'm sending Georgie home for help."

At this Georgie stopped shoveling food into his mouth, swallowed what he'd been chewing, and looked at Tom, "Send me home? Without you guys?"

"Yes. I've been discussing the road between here and White Sulphur Springs with Mr. Hampton. According to my calculations, if you start out tomorrow by first light, you should be able to hit the main east-west road between Richmond and Lewisburg before sundown. That puts you about three miles east of White Sulphur Springs. From there, if you're careful, you can ride the rest of the way along the road even in the dark. You should arrive at Mountain Meadows a couple of hours past sunset. In the morning you can bring back the rescue party with a well-padded and covered wagon to take the Captain home in. If you begin your ride a few hours before dawn, you should hit the cutoff to here just as the sun rises. You'll be back here before sunset.

"So if all goes well, you'll be back here day after tomorrow. Then we can take the Captain back slowly and comfortably the next day, even staying in White Sulphur Springs at that nice new hotel, if it gets too late."

"But why not just borrow a wagon from Mr. Hampton and take the Captain home ourselves?" William asked.

"I considered that. But under-manned as we are, if we were to run into the enemy on the road—with a wagon in tow—we'd be in a very desperate situation.

"With the additional Mountain Meadows men, and plenty of rifles and ammo, our *'friends'* who've been following us won't dare come near. And if they do, we'll finally have our reckoning with them," he said this last part with a gleam in his eye. William knew Tom would enjoy paying off *that* particular bill!

"All right, I'll do it, and gladly, but ... it don't feel right leaving you two and the Captain here. If something were to happen ..."

387

"Look, Georgie, sending *you* makes the most sense. William needs to stay here to do any doctoring that needs doing for the Captain. And I'll not leave the Captain under any circumstances, short of being dead. Besides, if we need to carry him on the stretcher for any reason, you'll not be able to help do it with your injured arm. But you shouldn't have any trouble riding a horse."

"Mule."

"What?"

"I should ride the mule. In case those fellows are out there somewhere on the road, they won't suspect a fellow riding a mule. Besides, the mule can carry me all day long without tiring or needing to take on fodder. So I won't have to stop near as often, and I'll make better time."

"All right, that makes sense."

"And no guns."

"No guns?"

"Yep ... I'll leave my guns with y'all. And I'll borrow a straw hat from the store. That way, riding the mule, I'll look like a farmer out for a visit to one of his kin folks. No farmer'd be carrying soldier pistols. Besides, if they *are* out there, I ain't gonna shoot my way past 'em. And, if worse comes to worst, and they do show up here, it'll give you a little more firepower."

"It does makes sense, Tom, you have to admit," William said. "And ... trade shirts with me, Georgie. We're about the same size, and mine doesn't have bullet holes and blood stains on it. A farmer wearing a shirt like that would also look pretty suspicious."

"Ah. Good thought, William, and thank you kindly. I could do with a new shirt by now, anyway, though I suspect neither one's smelling much like a rose at this point."

"I'll vouch for that," Tom answered with a grin.

ಚಿಞಿ೧ಞಲ೮ಚಿಞಿ೧ಞಲ೮ಚಿಞಿ೧ಞಲ೮

The next morning, they were up hours before sunrise, preparing for Georgie's departure. William changed Georgie's bandage one more time, to ensure he had a fresh one for the long ride home. He pronounced the wound well on the mend and said

388

he'd remove the stitches upon Georgie's return. Then, taking advantage of Georgie already having his shirt off, they performed the planned shirt exchange, followed by good-natured ribbing about whose smelled worse.

Meanwhile, Tom was out in the barn getting the mule ready to go. Keeping with the theme of making Georgie out to be a common farmer, he went with the pack saddle, even though it'd be less comfortable for riding. The riding saddles they had were military style—a farmer using one might raise the enemy's suspicion.

They shared a hearty breakfast, courtesy of Mrs. Hampton, and went outside to say their goodbyes. Georgie was up in the saddle, his oiled overcoat wrapped tightly around him. A steady rain came pelting down, running off his new straw hat in a steady stream. Thankfully the wind had stopped, at least for the moment, but still it promised to be a long soggy ride. The sky was barely light enough to see the ground around them. But it was impossible to tell if the sun had yet peaked over the horizon because of the thick dark clouds that continued to cover the sky.

Georgie was about to start out when a bleary-eyed Eddie came out the front door to say goodbye, not wanting to miss seeing off his new hero.

After that, Tom and William settled in for their long wait. At best they'd not see anything of the Mountain Meadows men until late the next day. In the meantime, there was little to do other than gaze out the window at the dreary weather and be thankful they weren't out in it.

☙ℰℬℭℬ☙ℰℬℭℬℭ☙ℰℬℭℬ

Georgie had a long sodden day of it. But other than a few tense moments when he saw riders approaching a few miles north of town, coming in the southerly direction, the day was uneventful. In the end his disguise had proven entirely unnecessary.

The riders turned out to be a local farmer and his two teenage sons, heading back to Paint Bank from a visit to the man's brother farther north. They exchanged pleasantries—as much as the dripping cold weather would allow, anyway—and went on their way.

About an hour after that, he passed through the town of Sweet Springs, in a blinding downpour that made it seem as if he rode through a fog. He could barely make out the houses as he passed in front of them.

Then out of the swirling mists he saw a thing so strange it was as if he were dreaming with his eyes open. Ever since leaving Lynchburg the houses, barns, and buildings in the towns had steadily become simpler, and more country-like. Survival in these hills did not tend to promote extravagance, nor did it engender a culture of excess. Rugged, self-reliant people lived here, and the structures they built reflected that personality. Except ... here.

The thing that now loomed up in his view made Georgie's jaw drop open, and he stopped Molly in her tracks. He stared at it and rubbed the rain from his eyes to make sure he was really seeing what he thought he was seeing. It was a huge, elegant building, in a style reminiscent of the capitol building in Richmond, only this was, if anything, even more grand. They'd built it of red brick a full three stories high, and it extended down the street as far as he could see into the fog. It had four separate peaked and columned porticos, all in a row, their white paneled and carved woodwork and columns, contrasting sharply with the red brick. He saw two grand, wide staircases leading up to the two outer porticos on the second story. A veranda with a white-painted railing connected the entire front of the building. The first floor consisted entirely of a row of large arches in the brickwork. It was dark inside those arches such that Georgie had no idea what might be inside.

He saw no people about, but that wasn't surprising, considering the weather. No sensible person would be out in it, he reminded himself, and smiled. Nothing he'd done lately could be considered sensible, that was for sure.

In fact, he realized, this dreamlike building seemed to fit right in with the whole odd, surreal adventure he found himself in the middle of. Ever since the day when a strange vagabond came knocking on Mrs. Wilkerson's door, telling them their Captain was in danger, nothing had been as it once was.

Richmond itself had changed in a moment from the most civilized place he'd ever been to a place of fear and danger, where enemies, intent on murder, lurked around every corner. And then there was the Captain himself. Georgie had never seen him anything less than in complete control of any situation, much less a helpless invalid. Even out in Texas after Gold-tooth had cut him, and he was clearly in great pain, there was still a fire in his eyes. There was never a doubt he'd take care of himself if the need arose. But now ... they had to carry him like a baby.

And then the thrilling gallop down the train tracks, unloading their pistols at the enemy, and making a clean get away — suddenly turned nightmare when he took a bullet to the shoulder. He had never felt such intense, burning pain in his life. He'd seen men shot, of course, but had never suffered it himself. And William's less-than-gentle ministrations, though effective, drove the pain to a level he could have scarcely imagined possible.

And an almost miraculous healing followed. Within two days he was barely noticing the injury, unless he moved the arm quickly, or tried to lift something.

And, to beat all, just when things were looking darkest, the folks in Paint Bank took them in and turned out to be pro-Union, with a young boy who thought Georgie a hero.

Georgie kicked Molly back into motion, and as he moved along the street, he noticed a sign made of stone, set in front of the building in the center. Carved on the stone was "Sweet Springs Resort." He looked up at it again, and shook his head in wonder, then rode off into the mist.

What he didn't know was ... the resort, originally built for the very upper crust of Virginian society, looked very much like the Richmond capitol building for good reason. The same man had designed both in a very similar Roman style: Thomas Jefferson.

𝕭𝖀𝕾𝕺𝕮𝕾𝕭𝖀𝕾𝕺𝕮𝕾𝕭𝖀𝕾𝕺𝕮𝕾

Georgie finally arrived at Mountain Meadows about two hours past sundown. He was not especially surprised the first

391

person to greet him was Billy. He stepped out onto the roadway about halfway between the turn off from the main road, and the farm proper. Georgie didn't know why Billy was out here on this dark wet night, but that was just the way he was.

"Hello, Georgie. You're back."

"Billy? Is that you? I can hardly see a thing in this darkness and gloom. Lucky I didn't run over you."

"You are going too slow for that. Is the mule tired, or just you?"

"Both, I reckon. And … it sure is good to see you, Billy! By golly, it sure is!"

"It is good to see you too, Georgie, though you look like a half-drowned rat."

"Yes … I 'spect I'm a sight only a mother could love, after what I've been through. Let's get back to the farm, and I'll tell you all about it."

If Billy's reception had been nonchalant, the reception Georgie received back at the bunkhouse was the polar opposite. Big Stan scooped him up so his feet dangled off the floor, gave him a great hug, and kissed him on both cheeks. The others gathered around and patted him firmly on the back, until he begged for mercy, explaining about his wounded arm. After that they treated him more gently, but with no less enthusiasm. The whole troop of men marched him straight over to the Big House, to give Miss Abbey and Sergeant Jim the news. Sergeant Jim had taken to staying there during the Captain and Tom's absence, to better guard Miss Abbey. So he hadn't been at the bunkhouse when Georgie had arrived.

They all gathered in the great room, around Miss Abbey's grand piano, listening quietly to Georgie's narrative. He told the whole story, from the moment he'd arrived in Richmond, to the present, with only a few interruptions for questions. His heart felt heavy when he had to tell Miss Abbey about the Captain's present condition—unconscious, and bed-ridden. The tears freely streamed down her face as he told the tale, though she never interrupted. Megs stood next to her chair and held her hand during the whole recitation. Megs also looked teary eyed, though she seemed determined not to break down.

"Thank you, Georgie," Miss Abbey said, once he'd finished. "For ... for everything you did to save my Nathan. You are ... a very fine and brave man, and I shall be ever grateful to you, whatever happens ..."

She became choked up and could say no more.

All eyes then turned to Jim. They knew he'd be the one to decide the next course of action.

"I know y'all want to start out this moment and fetch back the Captain. But we can't all go, and we can't ride off unprepared in the middle of the night.

"Some of us've gotta stay here and guard the farm. Walters is still out there, just itchin' to get his revenge on us. Georgie ... I hate to ask it—you bein' wounded, and having spent all day in the saddle and all—but ... I'd surely like you to lead the rescue seein's how you know the lay of the land."

"Oh! Of course, Sergeant Jim. It never even occurred to me to do anything other. I'll happily go back, soon's everyone's ready to go, and ... after I've changed my shirt!"

"Good! Let's go make sure the wagon's ready, and there's plenty of food, warm clothing, blankets and whatnot. And rifles, of course! The rescue party's gotta leave well before daybreak to be sure and get to this 'Paint Bank' place before dark."

The men headed for the door, and in a few moments the house was quiet. Miss Abbey was once again alone in the library, still holding hands with Megs.

"Oh, Megs ... I'm *so* afraid. If anything happens to Nathan ... I ... I don't think I can survive it."

"Me neither, Miss Abbey. Me neither."

ಬಎಂಡಡಬಎಂಡಬಎಂಡ

In the end Jim sent just Georgie, Jamie, Zeke and Billy, with extra rifles and pistols. He figured between them, with Tom and William on the other end, they could deal with the city-bred amateurs who'd been chasing them—if they even made another appearance. He was still worried about what Walters might try, especially now the secession had happened, and Captain Chambers was presumably out of favor in Richmond. He kept Stan home—if there was another serious fight, Stan was the man you wanted with you. He considered the farmhands good lads, but he had little faith in their fighting skills, except for maybe Zeke. That Tony, on the other hand … now *he* showed some promise—if they could trust him not to run off again.

The rescue party departed Mountain Meadows during a steady drizzle, two hours before dawn. Georgie drove the wagon, to give his arm a rest. It was a flatbed filled with blankets and other supplies, with a canvas tarp stretched over it to keep everything dry, including the Captain on the ride home. The others rode horses.

After they'd passed out of sight into the darkness and gloom, Stan looked over at Jim.

"Sergeant Jim … I am feeling like caged bear with no meat. I do *not* like the waiting …"

"Yes, I know. But it don't do no good to fetch the Captain and bring him home if there's no home to come back to! Somebody's gotta stay here and make sure Walters don't try nothing again. And if it's going to be down to only two of us, I figure it ought to be you and me, Stan."

Stan gazed down the road where the others had gone, then made a sound something like a bear growling, "I know is right medicine. But is bitter pill for the swallowing, Sergeant Jim."

"Yep, reckon I can't argue with that. But at least we'll be suffering it together," Jim smiled, and reached over to give Stan a pat on the back.

"*Hmph!* I am never liking the suffering, together or otherwise. Much better making the *other* fellow do suffering. 'Specially these *bezobraznik* fuckers trying to kill our Captain. I am wanting squeeze scrawny necks!"

"You and me both, Stanny Boy! You and me both."

ಬಿಡಿಂಡಿಶಿ ಬಿಡಿಂಡಿಶಿ ಬಿಡಿಂಡಿಶಿ

About an hour after lunchtime, Tom had tired of staring out the window and went back to the rooms to check on the Captain

394

again. There was no real point to it; William had been back there most of the day, watching him and reading a book. But it was something to do, and it reassured him to know the Captain was still breathing. And he did seem to *look* better, though he still hadn't awakened.

He'd been sitting with the Captain for only a few minutes when the door to the room opened, and Eddie slipped inside, closing the door quietly behind him. His eyes were wide with excitement.

"Mr. Clark, Pa sent me here to tell you some strange men just arrived in town, such as the bad men you told us of. They've been over to the stables, so have seen your horses and gear there. They'll be here in moments. You must take the Captain and flee out the back door. Wade the creek and then head off into the woods. Pa will try and stall them, but they're armed, and there's not much he can do. Please hurry!"

Before he'd finished talking William was down from his bunk, and was strapping on his holster, and stuffing two other guns in his belt.

Tom immediately did the same, while asking, "How many, do you know?"

"He said nine or ten."

"Should we try to shoot it out with them, do you think?" William asked.

But Tom shook his head, "No ... we'll not catch them by surprise this time, and they have us way outgunned. Besides, the boy and his family might get caught in the crossfire. Quick William, put on your overcoat, and grab the Captain's."

William jumped to comply and tossed Tom his as well.

Tom grabbed the stretcher from where they'd propped it up against the wall. "I'll owe your folks for this as well, Eddie."

"It's okay, Mr. Clark. I'm sure they won't mind."

Tom gave the boy a quick smile, as he pulled on the coat. He folded a blanket and laid it on top of the stretcher. He laid another one halfway on and the other half off, so he could wrap the Captain in it. "Come, William, let's move him to the stretcher."

But William did not immediately comply this time.

"Tom ... we'll be out in the cold, wet mountains with no tent, no horses, and no gear. At the risk of sounding like a coward, doesn't there come a time when a soldier must admit defeat and surrender to the enemy?"

"William, if we surrender, they'll surely kill the two of us for all the trouble we've caused them. They'll either do it right here, or later, off in the woods where there's no witnesses. They might try to take the Captain back to Richmond, but you and I both know with the state he's in, that ride would surely kill him."

He gave William a hard look, "William ... there's no amount of suffering I'm not willing to endure for *his* sake. What say *you*?"

William thought a moment, nodded, and said, "I'm with you there, Sergeant."

"All right then, *let's move!*"

They quickly lifted the Captain onto the stretcher, folded the blanket over him, and tucked it in the other side. His oiled overcoat they laid over him, pulling it up over his face so the rain wouldn't pelt him. They put on their hats, bent down and lifted the stretcher, then headed for the door, Tom in front.

Eddie cracked the door open and peered down the hallway leading back toward the store. In the other direction was the back door. "Clear so far. Let's go, sirs."

They opened the door and hurried down the hall. The Captain was a big man, weighing over two hundred pounds, which meant each man had to carry more than a hundred pounds extra weight. William felt the strain on his shoulders almost instantly but was determined to keep up his end. Eddie opened the outside door at the end of the hall and looked out, then waved them forward, opening it wide. As they moved out the door, they were hit in the face by pounding rain. The wind had picked up again, and now seemed to be worse than before, if that was possible.

"Over yonder through those trees is Potts Creek. You'll have to wade across but it's not too deep this time of year—I do it all the time. Then across the pasture ... about a hundred yards I'd say, and you'll be safely into the woods."

"Thank you, Eddie, you've been very brave and helpful. Your friend Georgie would be proud of you. Now you've had an adventure, like him. Goodbye."

"Goodbye, Mr. Clark, and you too Mr. Jenkins. And good luck!"

They moved with as much speed as they could muster across the yard, and into the trees beyond. Just as the boy had said, it led down a shallow slope to the creek, which was only a few dozen feet wide and less than knee deep. Still, with the weight of the stretcher it was a difficult challenge to keep from losing their footing. But they were soon across and moving up the far bank, through another set of trees, then into the pasture Eddie had described. The rain continued to lash their faces, but at least they didn't feel cold; they were already sweating heavily from their exertions.

They moved at a steady pace across the pasture. Tom resisted the urge to run—he could almost feel someone aiming a rifle right at the center of his back. But they needed to save their strength for the long haul.

The dreaded gunshot never happened, and soon they found themselves at the edge of the woods—the woods that would stretch from here all the way to White Sulphur Springs if they didn't return to the road anywhere in between. They moved a dozen or so yards into the trees and then Tom stopped to rest and let them catch their breath. They gently laid the Captain on the ground and sat down heavily next to him, breathing hard, their breath coming in great, steamy gasps. William's shoulders ached from the effort, and the muscles in his legs burned as if they were on fire. He assumed Tom felt the same, though he said nothing.

They kept a watch out toward the field through the gaps between the trees. After a few minutes they heard men shouting and whistling in the distance but saw no one.

Then a horseman appeared out on the pasture. He rode at a slow trot, moving from right to left in their view, a few yards out from the tree line on the other side of the pasture. He gazed steadily at the ground as he went. When he was almost directly opposite them, he stopped, staring at something on the ground.

He suddenly sat up straight in the saddle, and turned around, facing the direction from which he'd come. He gave a loud whistle and waved his arms in a beckoning motion. A minute later two other riders came up at a gallop and stopped beside him. William saw the first rider animatedly talking with the newcomers, pointing at the ground where he'd been gazing. He turned and pointed his finger in a line along the ground, ending up pointing almost directly at where they sat, hidden from view behind the trees.

"Looks like they've seen our trail, Sergeant."

"Well, carrying the Captain's weight across the field after all this rain, I'm sure we left a trail a child could follow. The good news is the ground is much harder here in the woods."

"Ought we go?" William asked, as they watched the riders approach.

"Not yet. They can't bring their horses into these woods, so we have a little time yet. I want to see what they plan on doing. If just those three follow us into the forest, I mean to kill them *now*, right here. That's three less to deal with later."

William nodded his understanding and unconsciously felt the handle of the pistol in the holster at his waist.

They continued to watch as the riders approached the woods. The day was so dark they had no fear of being seen where they crouched under the trees, though it was only thirty feet or so from the pasture.

The riders paused where the field met the forest, pointing and talking among themselves. After a few minutes one of them pulled on his reins, and peeled off, heading back toward the General Store.

"*Uh oh,*" Tom whispered.

William agreed, but said nothing, understanding it likely meant the rider went to fetch the others.

"Let's still wait … I want to see how many come after us, if they do. And how prepared they are for a long hike."

They didn't have long to wait. In a few minutes they saw more riders coming across the pasture.

Tom made a quick count, "There's all ten. Let's watch what they do."

The newcomers pulled up next to the two who'd been waiting. A large man with a full beard rode up in front of the others. He was talking and gesturing at them like he was in charge. After a few minutes of discussion, several men dismounted, while the others stayed in the saddle. The men on foot handed their reins to the ones still mounted in exchange for extra pistols. Tom counted five now on foot. They seemed to be gathering packs from their saddles, and each held a rifle.

"*Damn!* Five ... well-armed and provisioned. Time to go, William!"

They lifted the Captain and headed off again at a steady pace. Tom had to remind himself once again not to run. Though the enemy had seen their tracks in the pasture, it'd be a lot more difficult to follow them here among the trees.

After they'd gone but a few dozen more yards, Tom turned at a sharp angle to the left. He continued on that route for nearly an hour, before changing course again. No sense giving them a nice straight line to follow. They carried on in this manner for several more hours, scrambling over logs, up over rises, and down into gullies, pushing their way through the undergrowth where they could, going around where they couldn't. All the while the rain continued to pour down, and the wind blew fitfully, though here in the thick woods they didn't feel it as strongly. But it made strange howling noises in the treetops.

After several hours, Tom called a halt, and they set the Captain down as gently as their exhausted limbs would allow. They collapsed on the ground where they were, no longer caring about the rain pounding down on them and soaking them through every possible opening in their overcoats.

William covered his face with his hat and closed his eyes, thinking to rest for a moment. He was instantly awakened by someone shaking him, and calling his name, "William! Wake up, time to go."

He groaned, "But sir, we've only sat down a minute ago ..."

"No, William, we've been lying here more than an hour. Longer than I'd planned, but I also nodded off. Our pursuers have nothing to carry so won't tire as easily. We must keep moving."

But instead of answering, William reached up and grabbed Tom by the front of his coat and pulled him down, raising his finger to his mouth in a "shushing" sign. He pointed back the way they'd come. Tom turned and saw two men carrying rifles, moving through the woods toward them, only fifty feet away.

"*Damn it!*" Tom said in a whisper. "Stay here with the Captain. I'll lead them off. Once I've got them off our trail, I'll circle back. Don't worry if you hear gunshots, that's just me getting their attention."

William nodded.

Tom turned around, still in a crouch, looking at the approaching men. He turned his head back toward William, "If I'm not back in two hours, I'm dead."

He moved off through the bushes on his hands and knees. William laid next to the Captain and stayed still, straining his ears to hear anything other than the pelting rain and howling wind.

After a few minutes he began to wonder if the enemy had passed him by. But he nearly jumped out of his skin when a man, close enough to spit on, suddenly shouted, "Hey! I just seen one. Over here!"

At first William feared they'd discovered him, but a voice answered from a little further off, "Where?"

"Over there ... through them trees next to that holler—just now, moving off that a way!"

He heard a pistol shot from the distance. *Tom*, William thought.

The pistol shot was answered by several rifle shots. William lay still, praying none had hit Tom.

He continued to hear intermittent shots for several more minutes. But they steadily faded into the distance until he could hear only the rain and wind. Then he remembered to check his pocket watch, so he'd know when two hours were up. He figured it'd been less than a half hour so far. But then he thought, *And what exactly am I going to do if two hours does go by?*

He had no answer, so finally decided he'd cross that bridge if he came to it.

William was shaken awake, "No sleeping on duty, soldier," a voice said.

"Huh? Oh, sorry, sir ... I was just ... *Oh, Tom!* You're still alive!"

"Yes, but so are *they,* I'm sorry to say — though I never expected to hit anything through the trees in this drippy gloom. At least I've led them astray for the moment. Let's move."

They lifted the Captain again and trudged on for several more hours. William had long since lost any sense of direction with all the twistings and turnings — some intentional on Tom's part, and others necessary to avoid impassible obstacles. William hoped Tom still knew their direction. With no sun in the murky sky, they could just as easily be heading south, rather than north, as far as William was concerned.

And it seemed to him the day was now getting darker. Likely the sun was setting, though it was hard to tell through the heavy overcast.

His arms and legs no longer ached — they were so tired they'd become numb to the pain, or maybe it was from the cold. Or he'd just gotten used to it; he wasn't sure which and didn't care.

But finally, he got to the point he knew his body could go no further, "Tom ... I ... can't—"

But before finishing the sentence he was cut off by a tremendous noise like an explosion. The Earth shook followed by a blinding flash of light. His first instinctive reaction was a gunshot. But he realized no gun made by man could produce such a noise, not even a cannon. It came again, *BOOM* ... this time the flash happened in the same instant.

"The lightning ... it's right on top of us," Tom shouted. "Come, quickly ..." he led them to a spot in a small clearing, as far from any trees as possible, then stopped. "Lay the Captain down here and lie down next to him. Pull your coat up over your head—"

Another tremendous, *BOOM* and flash of light interrupted him. William did as he was bid, and they huddled together on the ground. The thunder and lightning pounded the forest all around them. William glanced up in time to see a great tree suddenly light up, spraying sparks in every direction. He ducked his head under the overcoat.

And as he laid there, shaking with fear, he imagined strange sounds coming from the whistling wind: bizarre, demonic voices screaming in terror. And the rolling thunder seemed to echo like the sound of multiple gunshots off through the woods, mixed with more shrieking from the wind.

A few minutes after the first lightning strike, a pounding sheet of rain hit them. It was so intense they could no longer see the outline of the trees at the edge of the small clearing. Then the rain became painful, like someone was pelting them with small rocks, and William realized it had turned to hailstones, as big around as his thumb.

The wind howled with such ferocity it shook and bent the trees, sending several crashing to the ground near where they lay. William closed his eyes and prayed a tree wouldn't fall on them and they'd not be struck by lightning. It was a nightmarish end to a hellish day, and he thought this must be what the mythical, apocalyptic "end of the world" would be like. Or perhaps this *was* the end of the world … at least for the three of them.

ಬಿಞಞಣಣಬಿಞಞಣಣಬಿಞಞಣಣ

It was a long but uneventful day, and Georgie was feeling a tiredness deep down in his bones. He'd been traveling nonstop, under stressful, fearful conditions for the better part of a week. Not to mention being wounded along the way. A nice long relaxing break from traveling, he decided, would be just the thing once they made it home again.

But he perked up briefly when they passed through Sweet Springs. The shocked expression on the faces of his companions as they passed by the hot springs resort was most satisfying. He'd told them about it, of course. But he knew they hadn't really believed him, figuring he'd either made the whole thing up or greatly exaggerated to make his ride sound more interesting. It was gratifying to smile at them and shrug his shoulders as they gawked at the enormous, incongruous building. No words were necessary.

They were now nearly to Paint Bank—another mile or so more, Georgie figured—when Billy suddenly raised up his hand to signal a stop. They halted.

"What is it, Billy?" Jamie whispered.

"Someone watches ... over there in the bushes."

They pulled their pistols, and Georgie called out, "Come on outta there now, and you'll not get hurt!"

They saw movement in the bushes, and then a small figure stepped out, and walked over to stand in the road in front of them.

"Eddie? Eddie ... is that you?"

"Georgie? Oh! I'm so happy to see you!" the boy said as he trotted over toward the men. They lowered and holstered their guns.

"Eddie, what in God's name are you doing out here in this awful weather?"

"Georgie ... Pa sent me out here to meet you and warn you ... on account o' those bad men that's been following y'all, arrived in town earlier today."

"What?! What about *our* men?"

"Slipped away into the woods, carrying your Captain on a stretcher just before the bad men could catch them. They're somewhere out in the deep woods by now."

"Well, that's a relief anyhow. But what about these *bad* men. How many are they, and what're they up to?"

"There's ten altogether. A right mean looking bunch, arrived all on horseback, with lots of guns. They rode around the pasture out back looking for your men. Five dismounted and went off into the woods, after your Captain. The rest rode up and down the road all day, but never found nothing. Right now, the five riders are all gathered back at the General Store, eating Momma and Pa out of house and home, I expect. Ain't seen nor heard from those that headed out into the trees."

403

The others looked over at Georgie, as if expecting him to decide what to do next. It was an odd feeling for him; he'd always felt himself the lowliest of their company, and now he had men looking up to him, expecting him to take the lead. Something had changed for the better, he decided. And ... to his own surprise, he found he *did* have an idea—one that just might work.

"I've got a plan, but we'll need your help, Eddie."

"Sure, Georgie, anything you say!"

"It's a very important, *man* kind of job, but I think you can handle it. I need you to stay here and take care of our horses until we come back. Do you think you can do that for us, Eddie?"

"Well, golly ... yes, sir! I reckon I can. I've been helping Pa take care of horses up at the stables for ... well, almost two years now."

"Good man ... much obliged!"

But instead of responding, Eddie stood still with a shocked expression on his face. Georgie realized he was staring up at Billy, whom he seemed to have noticed for the first time.

"Are you ... are you the *Indian*, named Billy? The one Georgie told me about?"

"I guess it must be so," Billy answered, with a puzzled look.

"Golly! Wait'll I tell the other boys I met a *real live* Indian!"

Billy looked confused at first, then smiled and said, "Yes ... reckon I'm still *alive* ... so far."

‘’ ∞ ‘ ’ ∞ ‘ ’ ∞ ‘ ’

Jeremy Washburn sat alone at the small table in the Paint Bank General Store, scratching his full, black beard. He was feeling extremely frustrated, to the point of outright anger—which was probably why none of his men sat with him. He knew he'd been unfairly harsh with them, but he didn't care. Henry Wise had trusted him to kill or capture Chambers. But so far, all he had to show for it was one man dead, another crippled, and an aching backside from spending long days in the saddle.

And after all that, they'd finally tracked down their quarry only to have them slip out right from under their noses, into the endless western Virginia hills. Now they'd had no word at all from the men he'd sent in after them.

It was maddening! They'd missed capturing Chambers by mere minutes, after nearly a week of searching! It really wasn't fair. The man led a charmed life, apparently. He scowled, reached out for the glass of whiskey in front of him, and downed it in a quick swallow.

"Hey! What the hell ...?" Sammy Timmons said, looking out the window. "Some fella just pulled up in a wagon, and now he's ... he's ... *singing*, I think."

"What?!" the others rushed over to gaze out the window, but Jeremy continued to sit at the table.

"Yep ... he's singing all right ... or chanting ... or something. And ... I'll be damned if he ain't ... *an Indian!*"

"An Indian?" Jeremy asked, "You seeing things Sammy?"

"No, boss," another answered, "he looks like an Indian, all right."

Jeremy turned toward Hampton, the store owner who'd been doing his best to act busy back behind the counter all afternoon. "You know anything about this Indian?"

But he saw Hampton was just as surprised as the rest of them, "No, sir. I've never seen nor heard of the like in these parts before."

The others continued to stare out the window and gawk. But Jeremy had grown tired of their chatter and whining—it was at least a good excuse to get them outside for a while, so he'd have a little quiet.

"You men go outside and see what it's about."

Sammy looked at him, "But boss ... it's pouring down rain, and blowing like a gale out there."

"Do I look like a man who gives a *good Goddamn* about a little bad weather?" he scowled.

The men moved to the door and opened it, with its requisite gust of wind and spray blowing into the room. They filed outside and pulled the door closed behind them.

The sight they encountered was strange beyond their reckoning. As Sammy had said, a smallish-looking man stood in the driver's seat of a wagon pulled by a single horse. He'd stopped the wagon in front of the store next to the hitching post. The man's eyes were closed, and he held his hands palms up, at face level, rainwater streaming from them. He wore a long, gray-colored overcoat, and a wide-brimmed hat, with a large eagle feather sticking up from the hat band. And sure enough, up close he appeared to be an Indian, though most of the men had only seen them in picture books. But oddest of all, the man sang a strange song in a foreign tongue. He had a strong, clear tenor voice, though he sang softly, as one might do when performing for a small, intimate gathering.

The men gathered around the wagon stared at him in disbelief and exchanged puzzled looks and shrugs. Finally, Sammy said, "Hey, *you!* Mister! What're you doing there? Why you standing out here in the rain like that … and *singing?*"

The song suddenly stopped. The strange man lowered his hands and opened his eyes, looking at them for the first time.

He smiled, and answered, "Why am I doing this? Well … I'm an Indian, of the Tonkawa tribe. And sometimes we like to do *odd* things, like singing in the rain. But mostly … I did it to get y'all to come outside …"

Even as he said this, he reached behind his back and pulled out two pistols, cocking the hammers and aiming them at the men standing in front of him in one smooth motion. At the same instant the tarp covering the back of the wagon lifted, and three men stood up. They were dressed like the driver, less the feather in the hat, and each held two pistols.

"Hands up, gentlemen," Georgie said, "unless you're fixin' to die right now out here in this nasty weather."

They'd caught the men from the store completely by surprise, and their look of shock was most satisfying to the men in the wagon. The captives raised their hands in compliance.

Nobody spoke until Billy said, "There's only four here … the boy said five. You think he can count, Georgie?"

"Oh, yeah, he can count all right. That-there's a right smart boy! Hey, you there … where's the other'n of your bunch? Speak up, I got plenty o' others here to ask and I reckon if I put a bullet in you these others'll talk all the faster."

The man's eyes widened, and he nodded his head toward the store, "He's still inside. Sent us out in the rain to check on your Indian, whiles he stays warm and dry."

Billy jumped down from the wagon, intending to move into the store. But at that moment the door swung open and a big man with a dark beard stepped out.

"What the devil's going on out here?" he asked. His curiosity had finally gotten the better of him and in his ill temper he'd made the fatal mistake of not looking out the window first, before stepping out the door. He stopped, noticing the newcomers for the first time. He instinctively reached for the pistol holstered on his right hip.

Jamie pointed his right-hand pistol at the man, "Don't do it boyo ... *don't* do it ..."

For a moment, the man seemed to relax and began to move his hand deliberately away from the holster. But in a flash, he reached for the gun. There was a loud concussion, and gun smoke curled up around the wagon for an instant before being swept away by the wind. Nobody moved and there was an odd silence filled only by the sound of wind and rain.

The man with the beard stood where he was, pistol still gripped in his hand, but pointed at the ground. His face twisted in pain, and he clapped his left hand onto his stomach. They saw a red liquid oozing out between the fingers. Then suddenly the pained look turned to anger, and he raised his pistol toward Jamie.

Another gunshot rang out.

The man fell face down on the wooden landing with a loud thud, a bullet hole in his forehead. A gaping exit wound in the back of his head splattered blood across the boards where he'd fallen.

Jamie turned his attention back to the others and glared, "Any o' you other lads wanting some o' what this fellow just bought?"

They held their hands up higher and emphatically shook their heads *no*.

ᏋᎯᏋᎧᏣᎧᏨᏋᎯᏋᎧᏣᎧᏨᏋᎯᏋᎧᏣᎧᏨ

Caleb Ward was weary, footsore, cold, and wet. And he suspected they were lost, or at least had lost the trail of the men they were pursuing. On top of all that, he now had the uneasy feeling they were being followed, though that made no sense.

The search had started out promising enough. The leader of their group, a man named Wilkins was an experienced hunter and woodsman who'd been able to pick up the tracks in the woods. But it was slow going as Wilkins feared missing any sudden changes in direction.

And then, a little over an hour in, they seemed to have caught up with their quarry; someone saw a man running away through the woods. There was a brief exchange of gunfire, but Caleb had never even fired a shot, being unable to see a thing from his position at the back of the group.

After that there was silence for a long time as they searched the woods for the men they were following. But they had no further glimpses of them, and after several more minutes Wilkins stopped and admitted he'd lost the trail. They'd need to backtrack to where they'd been when they'd first seen the man running.

Since then it had been a long fruitless march through the dark, tangled woods, with the wind howling and rain lashing their faces. He wondered how long they would continue before giving it up and heading back to town. He couldn't imagine spending the night out here in this strange, spooky forest in this foul weather. But it grew darker with every mile. Soon there could be no doubt; night was falling in a sky so gloomy it blotted out the sun.

And the last few miles he'd had a twitchy feeling between his shoulder blades. Like someone was following behind and aiming a gun at his back. At first, he imagined it must be the man they'd seen, who'd fired at them from out in the woods. Maybe he'd circled around them and now the hunters were being hunted. He kept glancing behind, every few yards, but saw nothing.

Then one time he thought he saw movement back in the woods, so he stopped and stared. But there was nothing, so he turned and trotted ahead to catch up with the others. A little further on he saw it again, only this time he got a better glimpse:

a large, low body covered in fur, moving quickly through the woods. And he glimpsed eyes, glowing in the gloom, staring straight at him.

He gave a shout, "Hey!"

The others stopped and turned around. Wilkins came back and stood by him, "What is it? Did you see someone?"

"No. It was ... an *animal* of some kind. A big one. And I ... I think it's been following us."

Wilkins scowled at him, "I'm not interested in any *animal*, unless it's the two-legged kind. We're well armed; no *animal* will bother us. Come on." He turned and headed back down the trail. The others gave Caleb withering looks, then turned and followed.

Caleb again looked back, but now he saw nothing. So he shrugged, turned and followed the others. But he wasn't as confident as Wilkins, and a fear of something deadly, even supernatural, continued to grow.

With every mile he felt more wretched and frightened. He'd decided to speak up and insist on turning back, when their leader suddenly stopped and looked back at them.

Wilkins had a satisfied grin, "I've found them again! And *very* fresh; they've just passed here. Come boys, we almost have them!"

They picked up the pace even as the light seemed to plummet, threatening to cover them in complete darkness at any moment.

Caleb continued to glance back along their trail, but now it was so gloomy he could see only a few feet. He saw nothing, but that was not especially reassuring.

They climbed a long, relatively open slope and crested a rise overlooking a small clearing in the trees. Wilkins paused, and Caleb turned back to look down the slope.

In the gathering darkness a large shape with glowing eyes appeared at the bottom of the slope. It began moving toward him at great speed.

He gasped. As he hurried to raise the rifle, there was a sudden, blinding flash of light. The Earth shook with a deafening *BOOM!* He lost his grip on the rifle. It fell to the ground, tumbling away into the darkness.

Immediately another great flash and deafening concussion shook the ground. In the flash Caleb glimpsed a horrifying beast, huge mouth agape, dripping saliva. It was coming fast, now mere yards away.

He screamed and pulled his revolver, firing blindly back down the slope. In the gun's flash he saw the terrible animal leap. A crushing pain in his right arm drove him to the ground. He hit his head hard against a rock.

As consciousness faded, the lightning flashed again, and he screamed — a monstrous animal shook his own arm in its mouth. Blood sprayed about, pistol still gripped in a hand he no longer felt.

☙❧☙❧☙❧☙❧☙❧☙❧

William awoke during the night with a sudden realization he was cold. Very, very cold, and his body shivered uncontrollably. He peeked out from under his coat and saw the ground was covered in white from accumulated hailstones. He quickly tucked his head back in. The breezy air had a frigid bite to it. But he noticed the sky was no longer completely black. Moonlight was streaming down into the forest. Perhaps the storm had passed.

But at the moment, it seemed but little consolation. He feared they'd be frozen to death by morning. But he felt too exhausted and chilled to care. He felt the Captain's body up next to his, but only as a hard lump. He felt no heat coming from it. He tried to stay awake … to wiggle his toes and fingers to keep them from going numb, but at some point, he passed out again.

Someone shook him. He opened his eyes a crack and a bright light shone into them, almost dazzling after the previous day of gloom. Tom knelt over him, prodding him to awaken.

"Come on, William … you still alive, or are you dead?"

"Not sure, Sergeant … *dead* … I think … maybe."

"Up and at 'em, Private. The sun is shining, or at least it's trying to. There's a much thinner layer of clouds this morning. No rain and no wind, thank God. But you'd best get up and move around a bit, so you don't freeze solid."

"I believe I am already frozen solid. But ... I've never disobeyed your orders before, so I guess I'll not start now."

"That's the spirit. Good man! Here, I'll give you a hand."

With Tom's help, he was up on his feet, though sore and wobbly from the prior day's exertions and the night's chill. He saw Tom was right about the change in the weather, though it was still so cold his breath came out in steamy puffs. And white hailstones covered the ground, looking like midwinter, though it was nearly May.

Tom saw William's gaze and smiled, "Those hailstones and all the blown-down trees will cover our tracks better'n anything I can imagine. And we wandered around enough yesterday we couldn't find our own selves ... not even with a map! But we'd best wait a bit and let this stuff melt off. As good as it was for covering our tracks from yesterday, if we walk on it now, we'll leave a trail a blind fool could follow."

"Staying in one place for even a few hours sounds wonderful, sir. But what about the Captain?"

Tom's face turned serious at the question. "Still breathing, and thanks to being wedged between the two of us all night, he may have fared better than we did from the cold. But he still won't respond to my attempts at waking him."

William leaned down and pulled the overcoat off the Captain's face. He looked reasonably well for a man who'd spent the night outside in a thunderstorm, but it continued to worry William he wouldn't awaken.

Tom asked, "Is there anything ... you know ... any kind of *medical* thing ... to be done for him? What if he never wakes up again? I can get him to swallow water in his sleep, but he won't chew food. A man can't last forever like that."

"I have heard of ... well, you remember I said it might have been better if the skull had been cracked? I have heard of physicians cutting away a small piece of the skull to ease the pressure inside; kind of like cutting away part of a boot after twisting an ankle. I ... have only read about it—have never seen it done. I don't know how well it has actually worked in practice."

411

"That makes some sense, now you've explained the whole brain swelling thing to me."

They stood quietly, staring at the Captain's inert form, each lost in his own thoughts.

"William ... do you think you could do such a thing?"

"Oh no! Certainly not! Tom ... the men who've done this have practiced it on cadavers dozens of times before ever trying it on a live man. And even then, I think it's likely they killed the first several patients they attempted to save. No ... I would *not* do this thing to the Captain ..."

"Not even if it was the *only* way to save his life?"

William was quiet for a moment. "It's a moot point at the moment. I have no proper tools to attempt such a surgery, and no means to manufacture them. If we reach Mountain Meadows, and it becomes ... *necessary* ... then we may discuss it again."

"There is no *if* to reaching Mountain Meadows, William! I swear by God we *will* make it home ... or die trying, even if I have to carry him the whole way on my back."

"That will only be necessary when I'm dead, sir. And now that I'm on my feet and have regained some feeling in my limbs, I believe I may yet live, after all."

In a little more than an hour the sun came out, and the hailstones quickly melted away, except in the deepest shade of the trees. They were soon back on their way, heading generally northward.

They discussed whether they should try to connect up with the rescue party. It should be somewhere close by now, assuming Georgie had made it back home. But they couldn't figure any safe way to do it. They might try to make their way back to the road, if they could even find it at this point. But not knowing where anyone might be, they were just as likely to meet the enemy. So they steeled themselves for the long, tiresome, and hungry hike home through the woods.

They trudged on for several hours. William was about to ask Tom if they might take a rest, when the Captain suddenly started twitching, moaning and thrashing his head from side to side.

"Uh ... Sergeant ... Sergeant ... *Tom!*"

412

Tom looked back at William, who nodded toward the Captain. When Tom saw what was happening, he stopped. They looked around and found a grassy spot in a small opening in the trees and carefully laid the stretcher down.

Nathan continued to roll his head back and forth, and at times his whole body became rigid, like he was cramping up all over.

Tom leaned down, and touched his forehead, "Captain ... *Captain!* Can you hear me, sir?"

He got no response, other than an occasional moaning sound, like a man in pain.

Tom and William's eyes met, "What's happening, William?"

"I ... I don't know ... but I fear ... I fear he may be taking a turn for the worse."

They watched in helpless silence for several minutes, before Tom spoke again. But he surprised William with what he said, tears streaming down his face, "It makes me think of ... of that Psalm—you know the one, about walking through a terrible bad place of fear?"

"I think you mean Psalm twenty-three. *'Yea, though I walk through the valley of the shadow of death, I will fear no evil ...'*"

"Yes, that's the one. Seems to me the Captain is walking in that deadly valley even now, and there's nothing we can do to help him find his way out."

"Maybe so, but don't forget the last part of it ... *'I will fear no evil ... for thou art with me.'* If ever a man could count on God walking with him, it's the Captain. Now we can only wait, and ... *pray*, I suppose."

They settled themselves on the ground by Nathan's stretcher, watching as he continued to twitch and thrash about. After a half hour or so, he stopped moving. William reached over and felt at his neck. "Still alive ..."

Tom let out a deep sigh, then jumped up and looked back in the direction they'd come. "Someone comes through the woods!"

They unholstered their pistols and positioned themselves on either side of the Captain. Tom knelt behind a stump, and William crouched next to a fallen log.

William held his breath and listened. At first, he heard nothing and looked over at Tom with a questioning glance. But Tom nodded his head back out toward the woods. A moment later William heard it himself, a rustling back in the woods. Someone was coming up their trail.

ഇൽൽൽൽൽൽൽൽൽൽൽൽ

Billy, Jamie, and Zeke had been wandering around in the forest now for half the day, ever since first light. But despite their efforts, they seemed no closer to finding Tom and the others than when they'd first started.

It'd been a painful, difficult decision to wait until dawn to start their search. And they'd held a heated debate over it, with Georgie and Jamie nearly coming to blows. Georgie wanted to start right away, but Jamie argued it'd be dark in minutes, and they'd be many miles behind the other men at that point.

Billy finally decided the debate, though he'd said nothing up to that point. "We will wait until first light. I am not a bat nor an owl, only a man. I cannot follow a trail in the dark."

The search had started first thing in the morning with the boy Eddie showing them the back door and pointing them in the direction he'd instructed Tom to take. The three men went in search of the Captain and his pursuers while Georgie stayed behind to rest and guard the captives.

Despite the frightful storm of the night before, the tracks the men had made crossing the field, carrying the Captain, were still clear to see even for Jamie and Zeke. As were the tracks of the riders who'd followed them.

But once they were into the forest, the trail quickly grew cold, and Billy declared the rain and hailstorm had destroyed all trace of it. Their only hope was if one of the men had left a track close enough to a tree trunk that it hadn't been beaten down by the hailstones.

But to complicate things, the storm had also blown down many branches, leaves, pine needles, and even entire trees. So Billy started a search pattern back and forth through the trees,

414

moving to the west, and then crossing back to the east, generally moving in a northerly direction.

And worse than the frustration and fatigue of the search, Jamie felt a growing anxiety. Not only were their men hounded by enemies bent on murder, they'd been caught out in a storm the likes of which he'd rarely seen. Its fury had shaken the General Store and rattled its windows, making for a very sleepless night. The men out in the woods may have been struck by lightning or hit by falling trees. And even if none of those things had happened, they were surely soaked to the bone, cold, hungry and exhausted. And as for the Captain ... how could a man in his condition possibly survive such an ordeal?

Jamie had to fight to keep the fear and anxiety from turning to hopelessness and despair. And for the hundredth time since they'd started, he resisted the urge to offer any advice or suggestion to Billy. Billy knew this business better than anyone— if Billy couldn't find them, then they couldn't be found. Nothing Jamie did or said would change it.

But he'd served with Billy long enough to know when even *he* was starting to lose hope. Though Billy said nothing, his body language betrayed his feelings. Jamie watched Billy as he moved through the trees, gazing constantly at the ground, side to side, over and over and over. But in the last several miles Jamie noticed the gaze had lost a little intensity, and the searching seemed more desperate and uncertain.

Well, even Billy can use a break once in a while, he thought, *perhaps if we stop and have a little lunch, things will look brighter.*

He looked over at Billy and opened his mouth to suggest it but closed it again without a word. Billy had stopped and was staring in front of him, a startled expression on his face.

Jamie trotted over to see what Billy was gazing at. At first, he only saw a small clearing half-covered in melting hailstones. Then he saw *it* and gasped, *"Oh my God!"*

Zeke came up next to him and looked over his shoulder, "What?" But when Zeke saw what they were looking at, he turned around and bent over, as if he would be sick.

415

In front of them was a man's severed arm, drenched in blood, roughly torn off just above the elbow. The lifeless fist still loosely gripped a Colt pistol.

"One of ours?" Jamie managed, in a near whisper.

Billy stooped to examine it. "No. Not one of our men. And look; there's the rest of him," he pointed to a bush not far away, toward the edge of the clearing. They saw booted legs sticking out.

But when they got there, they discovered this was *not* the missing body. This man had both arms, though his throat had been torn out, and his head lay at an odd angle to his body. His rifle lay a few feet away, and they saw it *had* been fired.

A quick search around the clearing turned up another body. Like the first, this one still had both arms, but was missing his throat. Here, blood splatter was everywhere, as if the body had been violently shaken while still bleeding.

Billy returned to where they'd found the arm and began a systematic search. "A man can't walk far missing an arm," he answered to Jamie's inquisitive look.

That made sense to Jamie, and Billy soon found what he was looking for—another body, not ten feet from the arm, face down in a shallow gully. This one *was* missing his right arm. He'd apparently bled out from the injury or died from the shock; he still had his throat, unlike the others.

For Billy and Jamie, who'd served in the Army out in Texas, the sight of dead men, killed violently, was nothing new. But these bodies had been torn apart in a way that sent chills even through them.

For Zeke, who'd never even seen a dead man before Walters' failed attack on Mountain Meadows, it was a horror beyond imagining. He looked pale and shaken. "What did it, d'you suppose?" he managed in a voice choked with emotion, "A bear?"

"Yep; had to've been a bear, I reckon, lad," Jamie answered. "Nothing else has the size and strength to do *that* to a man."

But Billy surprised them, "No. These tracks are *not* a bear. These are wolf tracks, though a wolf like no other. The grandfather of all wolves by his size. And not of a right mind attacking armed men."

He asked Jamie and Zeke to stay still while he examined tracks around the site. He wanted to learn exactly what had happened: how many men had been here, if any had escaped, and if so, where they'd gone. And finally, what had become of the wolf that'd attacked them. It now presented another lurking danger they must be prepared for.

Fortunately, they had come armed for battle; they each had two pistols, and both Jamie and Zeke carried rifles. Billy had left his rifle behind. He needed to keep his hands free so he could crawl around looking at sign on the ground when necessary.

For the next quarter-hour, he carefully examined the signs around the site, sometimes slowly walking upright gazing at the ground in front of him, sometimes pausing and stooping low for a closer look. Still other times crawling on all fours.

Jamie watched intently for a while before his mind began to wander. But then he saw Billy stop and get down on all fours. After a moment he bounced up as if he'd seen something that excited him. This piqued Jamie's curiosity, and he elbowed Zeke, who was gazing off in the other direction, trying to avoid looking at the mutilated bodies.

"Hey, Zeke ... Billy's found something."

Billy was already trotting back over to where they stood, and they saw he was excited.

"What is it, Billy? Did you find something interesting?"

"Well ... no more dead men, though two lived—dropped their rifles and ran from this place. Oddly, the animal did *not* pursue them. It left in a different direction. Each of the dead men fired one round. But the beast was *not* hit—it trails no blood."

"Oh. That means there are still two enemy men out here somewhere, plus the mad wolf, of course. We must be on our guard. But, tell me lad; just now you looked excited. Like you'd found something surprising?"

"Yes ... there is a track here I recognize."

"Oh! That *is* good news, then. Is it William's or Tom's?"

"No ... it is *neither* ..."

417

Billy looked up and met eyes with Jamie. He had an odd expression, like a man who'd seen a thing that greatly surprised him.

"It is … a most *unexpected* thing … but now I know how to find the Captain!"

Chapter 15. A Thousand Purple Stars

"God writes the Gospel not in the Bible alone,
but also on trees, and in the flowers
and clouds and stars."
– Martin Luther

Thursday May. 2, 1861 – outside Paint Bank, Virginia:

The rustling sound was coming nearer, and Tom knew they would see whoever it was in an instant. But then he heard another sound—a very odd sound, like nothing a man would make. He realized it had to be some sort of large animal coming through the trees—not a man at all.

And then the beast came out through the bushes into the clearing. It stopped, staring in their direction and sniffing, as if it smelled them, but couldn't yet see them where they crouched behind cover. It was a wolf ... its mouth open and panting, showing a row of huge teeth dripping saliva. The wolf had a lean, hungry look. Evil-seeming, beady yellow eyes stared out from beneath mangy-looking fur hanging down in great, dark clumps. But it was the biggest, mangiest wolf Tom had ever seen, with a huge, thick head and broad chest. He carefully aimed his pistol, waiting for the beast to move enough to allow him a clean shot at its midsection.

The wolf raised its head and sniffed the air. But as Tom was about to pull the trigger the animal made an odd, whining, whimpering sound that made Tom pause. The sound seemed to stir something deep inside him—a sound of deep sorrow as of the worst broken heart imaginable, but also somehow hopeful and excited. For reasons he didn't entirely understand he stood up and faced the beast. "Hold your fire, William."

William stood also, but still held his gun out in front of him. "What's wrong with it, do you think?" he asked, "Does it have the Hydrophobia, maybe?"

"I … don't know … there's something *odd* about it … but it's not *sick* I think …"

The wolf now glanced at them, but did not seem to fear them, in fact it paid them little mind, despite the pistols they held leveled at its body. It sniffed again and gazed directly toward where the Captain lay on the ground. It made the strange whining noise again, though not as loudly as before, and it took a step forward.

"Don't let it come near the Captain!" William said, and they both prepared to open fire. Tom took careful aim, not wanting to miss and risk having a violent, wounded animal anywhere near Nathan.

"*Peace!* Hold your fire! This creature will not harm me!" a voice said. It was raspy and weak, but the tone of command was clear. Tom and William both turned around and their eyes widened as they saw the Captain sitting up on his stretcher.

The wolf cautiously stepped forward, right up to the Captain. Nathan gazed evenly at the approaching beast and showed no fear as it leaned forward and sniffed at the wound on the top of his head. To the men's shock and disbelief, the animal licked the Captain on the face. Then it lay down next to him, belly up, again making the strange whining sound, only more softly this time.

Tom stood with mouth agape, "Why … I can't *believe it!* It's … it's …"

"Yes, it's Harry," Nathan answered, reaching out to scratch the dog's scruffy, filthy coat. He was obviously shedding his winter coat, and the fur came out in large clumps when Nathan pulled at it.

"And … you're finally awake, sir! How do you feel?"

"Tired … like I'm just back from the dead."

Tom and William holstered their pistols and sat next to him. Tom noticed he now had color in his face, and there was a light in his eyes.

Nathan continued to stroke the fur on Harry's broad chest. But the dog suddenly jumped to his feet and moved back toward where they'd first seen him come out of the woods. He stood for a moment sniffing the air and twisting his head as if listening. The fur on his back bristled up, and he emitted a low growl.

"Men come," Tom said, "the dog smells them."

"He hears them, but he can't possibly smell them," William said, "the breeze comes from the other direction."

"All right, he hears them then … in any case, we must be ready again."

They ducked behind cover as they'd been before Harry's arrival. Nathan laid back on the stretcher, still too weak to move.

They heard nothing for several minutes, listening for anything moving in the distance. Harry tilted his head and listened as well.

The only sound to break the silence of the woods was a bird singing in the distance. But to William's surprise, Tom stood up and holstered his pistol, "I recognize that bird!"

William looked at him as if he'd lost his mind, but asked, "What kind is it, I wonder?"

But instead of answering, Tom put his fingers to his mouth, and made a loud whistle. Then he looked over at William and smiled, "This bird wears feathers, but it never can fly!"

William looked puzzled for a moment, then smiled, *"Billy!"*

And then Billy, Jamie, and Zeke stepped out of the bushes, and came forward smiling happily, shaking hands with Tom and William, and patting them on the back.

They were overjoyed to see the Captain sitting up and talking, after what Georgie had told them of his condition.

Tom turned to Billy and asked, "But … however did you find us? I figured that terrible hail and windstorm had buried our trail and pounded it flat, such that even *you* would never find it."

"The trail *was* lost in the storm … and I am ashamed for my part in that."

"Whatever do you mean, Billy?" Jamie asked. "Surely, you're not responsible for the weather, boyo?"

But Billy didn't immediately answer. He had a sheepish expression and shrugged his shoulders. "You remember when Georgie said I should sing a Tonkawa song to distract the enemy?"

"Aye ... and you sang it beautifully too, lad—as sweet as any Irish lullaby, though I never understood the words."

"Yes ... well, when he asked for a Tonkawa song, my mind went blank. I have not thought of any such for many long years, spending all my days among you white men. And then ... maybe the stormy weather made me think of a song ..."

"So ...?"

"It is a song to invoke the wrath of the thunder gods. The People used to sing it in the summertime to bring on lightning storms. They believed the lightning from the gods would kill the pests plaguing them and eating their food stocks. And some believed lightning striking the water sweetened it and gave it a power to heal the sick."

He smiled and shrugged, "I'm sorry ... it was the only song of my People I could think of in the moment."

"Well, it surely worked, I reckon!" Jamie said, shaking his head in wide-eyed amazement.

"Anyway ... yes, the storm erased your trail," Billy continued. "We searched many miles with no sign of it. But finally, I found the tracks of the Captain's great hound. I know them well—none better. I have followed his tracks for days through the woods and across the snow when Stan and I searched for him. When I found those same tracks today, I knew he would lead us to the Captain, so we followed ... and here we are."

Nathan smiled up at Billy, "Yes, he somehow knew how to find me ... and ... not only in *this* world, I think."

The others looked puzzled, though Billy had a more knowing expression.

Nathan explained, "I had the strangest dream ... or maybe it was *real* ... I don't know. I wandered for a long time in a dark place and couldn't find my way home. Everything was black, and strange frightful beasts and evil-looking men stared silently at me from the darkness. I dared not stray from the path. But every way I went the trail twisted in around on itself. I walked and walked for what seemed like days, but I always returned to the same place.

"And the evil men beside the path began taunting me, calling me traitor and coward. And it seemed to me they had faces of my Slave Power enemies, though deathly pale. I defied them and called them out as faithless oath-breakers and turncoats. That apparently enraged them, and they came howling after me. They were many and they had strange sharp knives while I carried no weapons.

"So I ran into the darkness. And though it seemed my feet would move but slowly, they did not immediately catch me. Each time I looked back they were ever closer, and I saw blood dripping from their knives. And though they had never touched me, I began to bleed from many painful wounds, even as I ran.

"But then familiar voices began echoing all around me ... yours Tom, and yours too, William, and others, though I can't recall whose. So I called out to you for help."

He looked up at Tom and chuckled quietly. "It seems ludicrous now, but I begged you'd just toss me my cavalry saber that I might turn on my tormentors and smite them."

He smiled and slowly shook his head, then continued in a more serious vein, "It seemed you were far away and couldn't hear me, nor did I ever see you in the darkness. My enemies were nearly on me. In desperation I had decided to turn and fight with nothing but bare fists, when I heard another familiar voice. It was the howl of this dog. He was crying out to me in a voice filled with great need and desperation—ever searching, but never finding. So I called for him, shouting and whistling as I ran. But unlike you men, it seemed the dog *could* hear me. He answered, barking with great excitement.

"I heard him searching, sniffing the ground, howling and whining, running and running like to burst his heart—but coming ever closer.

"Suddenly the noise of him was all around me, deafeningly loud, echoing through the darkness. I looked back and saw my enemies hesitating, gazing about in bewilderment, fearful of this new, terrifying sound.

"Then Harry was among them, growling, snarling, and snapping. In my dream he had grown larger than in life: a

423

monstrous wolf bigger than a bear. He tore into them, rending their flesh, tearing off their limbs and tossing his huge head from side to side in a great splattering of blood. They scattered, screaming off into the darkness.

"Then I saw a bright light, and … I opened my eyes. And the dog was here."

Tom and William shared a look. Tom said, "It seems God *was* with you as you walked through the 'valley of the shadow of death,' just like in the Psalm. And perhaps he sent this dog to fetch you home."

"Yes … I think you may have the right of it, Tom."

But Billy and Jamie shared a wide-eyed look that Tom noticed. Zeke also seemed shocked, slowly shaking his head.

"What is it? You fellows look as if you've just seen one of the Captain's demons from his dream," Tom said.

Billy answered, "I don't believe it was only a dream, Captain. My people call that place the 'spirit world,' though maybe your white man's name 'valley of the shadow of death' is better. We believe this place is on the very edge of life, where one can gaze across and see the spirits of the dead. They say if one strays from the path, or allows the spirits to touch him, he will cross over into death and never return. His body will die truly in the real world."

Nathan looked at him, nodding his head, but Tom shuddered at the thought of how close they may have come to losing him.

Billy continued, "And we have not yet told our full tale. You may find it … *interesting*. As we searched for your trail after the storm we came upon the site of a battle. Blood was splattered everywhere, though it had been partially covered by hailstones. We found three dead, and they had been—"

"Torn to bits!" Jamie interrupted. "It was a might gruesome sight, aye. Throats torn out, and an arm that weren't no longer attached to a body!" he shuddered as he recalled the image. "The dead were our enemies—those as was after the Captain. Their rifles lay on the ground where they'd been dropped. They had pistols too, though only one had managed to unholster his before—" he grimaced and made the sign of the cross on his chest.

"Anyway, *I* figured it for a bear, but Billy says, 'No, it's a wolf, but the biggest one ever.'"

Then Billy continued, "I had only glanced at the animal tracks, being more concerned with the human ones. I found two sets of these running off into the woods, heading back toward the town. The wolf did not pursue, leaving in a different direction. Finally, I knelt and looked carefully at the wolf's tracks. I was amazed when I realized it was *not* a wolf, but rather the Captain's great dog!"

Tom was incredulous, "You mean ... the hound attacked the Captain's enemies in the real world ... *and* in this ... 'spirit world' ... at the same time? How can that be?"

"I have heard of such things among my people," Billy answered, "though I have never seen it myself. It is some kind of ... *spiritual joining* between man and beast. They say such a joining is a gift only a god may grant. There is an old story of a shaman who befriended a hawk, and they had such a joining. They say he could see through the hawk's eyes as it flew, high above the Earth. In this way his enemies never snuck up on him, and he ever watched over the People and kept them safe."

Nathan said, "Well, I know a God who's capable of such miracles—it seems I've been the beneficiary of one."

He turned to the dog, "And as for you, Harry ... I owe you my thanks ... and my *life*, very likely. And, also ... my sincere apologies for leaving you behind at the farm when I went off to Richmond, knowing how hurtful it would be for you. I'll *not* do it again ... this I swear—never again in life!"

They sat on the ground around the Captain and Jamie broke out the food and water he'd brought along in his pack. They were finally able to relax and enjoy a much-needed meal, including a portion they shared out to the dog who wolfed it down ravenously.

Even Nathan ate a few bites, though he said he was still queasy.

When they'd finished their meal, he looked up at them and said, "Gentlemen ... I find I'm feeling a bit ... *done in* by all this traveling. I would like to go *home* now, if you would be so kind ..."

425

Tom met eyes with William and shook his head. They shared a smile, and both now had tears streaming unashamedly down their faces. Tom wiped his eyes, looked back at Nathan and answered, "Yes, *sir!*"

ℬ𝒰ℰ𝒪𝒞ℛℰ𝒪ℬ𝒰ℰ𝒪𝒞ℛℰ𝒪ℬ𝒰ℰ𝒪𝒞ℛℰ𝒪

Thursday May 9, 1861 - Greenbrier County, Virginia:

Megs walked across the lawn toward where Nathan stood, under the magnificent magnolia tree, staring up into its branches. It was full to bursting with pale lavender and white blossoms that appeared to cover every square inch of the tree, save the massive trunk.

The huge dog sat next to him, only feet away, gazing intently up at him. The animal had fattened up a bit since he'd come back, no longer looking like an emaciated wolf. And the Captain had pulled out the loose clumps of fur he'd been shedding and brushed him down, so he looked more respectable.

She noticed he stayed much closer to his master now than he ever did before. And the man also paid more attention to the animal, speaking with him, and stroking his fur regularly. Something had definitely changed between them, but she didn't entirely understand what or why, unless it had been the long, forced separation.

She'd seen Nathan out the window and became concerned for him; he'd not been out walking alone since his return. As she got closer, she saw he was leaning on a cane. She hadn't seen it before and wondered where he'd come by it.

"Hello, Captain. How's you feeling?"

"Oh, hello, Megs. A little better. My head still pounds mercilessly and I'm still a little weak and wobbly. It's a strange thing for me, never having experienced the like before."

"Yes, I can imagine. Even as a young boy you was always strong and vigorous. You sure you ought to be out here by yourself?"

"Likely not, but I was feeling the need for some fresh air, and was growing tired of being waited upon and pampered. And, as you can see, I do have my guardian," he grinned and nodded toward the dog, but Megs noted a wince of pain in it.

She scowled, "Well at least you've got yourself a cane to lean on. Where'd you get it, anyway? I don't recall anyone ever using one around here before, less it was your granddaddy. But that would've been before my time."

"No, you're right ... it's actually new. Stan carved it for me. Apparently, he needed something to do while waiting for the others to bring me back from the hills. So he carved it to help with my recovery. At first, I was reluctant, not wanting to appear an invalid. But I find it's useful and helps me walk about a little without a supporting arm or an escort. Other than good old Harry here, of course."

The dog tilted his head and looked up at the sound of his own name.

Megs came and stood next to Nathan—on the opposite side from Harry, not wanting to risk coming between them—and she looked up into the tree. "Like a thousand purple stars, you used to say when you was a boy."

He looked over at her and smiled, "Yes, I remember. It *is* one of God's great miracles, isn't it? Such a *beautiful* thing ..."

"Yes, it surely is. Though I've seen the thing bloom for more'n forty years now, it never ceases to amaze me, year after year."

He reached over with his left arm and put it around her shoulders and pulled her close. She leaned into him happily.

"I remember you used to hold and comfort me like this if I'd fallen and hurt myself, when I was a young child. Or if I was lonesome, you'd come and sit with me and talk, or read me a story. I thanked you once before for teaching me my lessons and helping to raise me. But I don't reckon I ever thanked you for any of the comforting or warmth that you showed me. Nor told you how much it meant to me. So ... *thank you*, Megs."

She looked up at him and smiled. She felt tears welling and feared if she tried to speak, she'd choke up. So she just leaned into him more, and wrapped her arms around his broad chest, enjoying the feel of his strong arm around her shoulders.

\<End of Book 3\>

If you enjoyed *Sedition*,
please post a review.

BREAKOUT
ROAD TO THE BREAKING – BOOK 4

Tony was the "anchor man" on the right side, standing a few feet behind and to the right of Sergeant Jim. To his left, Cobb anchored the left side, behind Mr. Georgie. And to Tony's immediate right was Johnny, then Big George, then Ned, and then … a whole row of others, looking wide-eyed and anxious.

Tony had unslung his rifle as soon as he'd stopped, and the others had done likewise even as they were moving into position. He now stood up straight and still, his rifle butt planted on the ground, barrel up at his side.

Once again, he experienced the odd sensation of not wanting to be still; his skin crawling and his heart pounding in his ears.

Looking out across the field he saw a row of white men likewise standing with rifles. There appeared to be a lot more of them than there were on his side. But he remembered the Bible quote from the Captain and felt better. If ever there was a time God ought to help good men outnumbered in a righteous fight, surely this was it! He waited anxiously for the orders he knew were coming … the orders to fight and kill—and maybe to die.

As the infantry deployed, Nathan looked out across the field and was gratified by the shocked surprise on the faces of the enemy. He looked over at Tom and they met eyes, exchanging a warm smile, knowing it might be their last, but never once thinking it would be so.

Nathan pulled his two pistols and spurred Millie forward. His other horsemen did likewise. But this time it was only a feint, meant to distract the enemy from the real danger forming up behind the horsemen. After only a few yards Nathan fired a single shot from both pistols, as did the rest of the riders. He grabbed Millie's reins, peeling her off to the right. Tom did likewise, peeling off to the left, the others following one or the other. They galloped to the sides, so they'd no longer be in front of their own line of men. Even as they spurred across the front of their line, Jim called out "Present ... arms!"

Tony lifted the rifle up to his chest. He was only vaguely aware of the others on either side of him doing the same, along with the two officers.

And as the Captain reached the end of the row, and began to turn Millie back behind, Sergeant Jim called, "Aim!"

Tony lifted the rifle to his shoulder, pulled back the hammer, and looked down the sights. He pointed the rifle directly at a man standing across the field in front of him. He aimed at the man's head, as he'd been taught, knowing the bullet would drop to chest level from this distance. He didn't know the man he targeted, nor did he hate him especially, but he was the enemy—among those who would take away his new freedom. The man had to die.

And as the last of the horses cleared the row of Mountain Meadows men, "Fire!"

Tony squeezed the trigger. There followed a thunderous noise and thick smoke all around him.

Acknowledgments

I'd like to thank the following individuals for assisting in the writing and editing of *Breakout*, including reading the beta version and providing invaluable feedback: Bruce Wright, Craig Bennett, Debbie Palmer, Gay Petersen, Leslie Johns, Marilyn Bennett, Mike Bennett, Patricia Bennett, and Rachel Bennett.

And special thanks to my editor, Ericka McIntyre, who keeps me honest and on track, and my proofreader Travis Tynan, who makes sure everything is done correctly!

And, last but not least (at all!), the experts at New Shelves Books; my trusted advisor on all things "bookish," Keri-Rae Barnum, and the guru Amy Collins!

Recommended Reading

If you'd like to read more about pro-Union Virginians' efforts to prevent secession, I recommend **Lawrence M. Denton's** fascinating and informative (non-fiction) book, *Unionists in Virginia: Politics, Secession and Their Plan to Prevent Civil War.*

For first-hand accounts of what it was like to be a slave in the Civil War era, please read *To be a Slave* by **Julius Lester**.

And for a thoroughly enjoyable and painless way to learn about the Civil War and all its major players, I highly recommend **Michael Shaara's** *Killer Angels* (about the battle of Gettysburg) and his prolific son **Jeff Shaara's** long list of Civil War novels, as well as a prequel about the major Civil War personalities in his book on the Mexican-American War. Although the Shaaras' books are technically historical *fiction* (because they are written in novel form, "filling in the blanks" of what people might have said to each other, what they may have been thinking at the time, etc.) their accounts of the actual historical events are excellent and compelling, and from what I can tell, extremely accurate.

Get Exclusive Free Content

The most enjoyable part of writing books is talking about them with readers like you. In my case that means all things related to *Road to the Breaking*—the story and characters, themes, and concepts. And of course, Civil War history in general, and West Virginia history in particular.

If you sign up for my mailing list, you'll receive some free bonus material I think you'll enjoy:

- A fully illustrated *Road to the Breaking* **Fact vs. Fiction Quiz.** Test your knowledge of history with this short quiz on the people, places, and things in the book (did they really exist in 1860, or are they purely fictional?)

- **Cut scenes from *Road to the Breaking*.** One of the hazards of writing a novel is word and page count. At some point you realize you need to trim it back to give the reader a faster-paced, more engaging experience. However, now you've finished reading the book, wouldn't you like to know a little more detail about some of your favorite characters? Here's your chance to take a peek behind the curtain!

- I'll occasionally put out a **newsletter with information about the Road to the Breaking Series**—new book releases, news and information about the author, etc. I promise not to inundate you with spam (it's one of my personal pet peeves, so why would I propagate it?)

To sign up, visit my website:
http://www.ChrisABennett.com

Road to the Breaking Series: